TIME MACHINES

TIME MACHINES

The Greatest Time Travel Stories Ever Written

Edited by Bill Adler, Jr.

Carroll & Graf Publishers, Inc.
New York

Introduction and headnotes copyright © 1998 by Bill Adler, Jr.

All rights reserved

First Carroll & Graf edition 1998

Carroll & Graf Publishers, Inc.
19 W. 21st Street
New York, NY 10010

Library of Congress Cataloging-in-Publication Data

Time machines : the anthology of the best time travel stories ever
written / edited by Bill Adler, Jr.—1st Carroll & Graf ed.
    p.   cm.
  ISBN 0-7867-0493-4
  1. Time travel—Fiction.   2. Science fiction, American.
3. Science fiction, English.   I. Adler, Bill, 1956–   .
PS648.T55T55   1997
813'.087620838—dc21   97-29705
                                                              CIP

Manufactured in the United States of America

To Karen and Claire, who will get to
explore a wondrous future.

CONTENTS

■ ■ ■

Introduction

MY WIFE, PEGGY, LIKES TO READ JANE AUSTEN AND WATCH French subtitled films. I like to read Stephen King and go to see the latest *Die Hard* movie. But we both enjoy time travel stories. Many people who hold science fiction in disdain love a good tale about somebody traveling back in time—either to repair the future, to observe the past, or to become a part of the past.

Why are time travel stories so universally loved? The answer isn't all that complicated: It's a human trait to dream of what ifs. What if you were in Dallas in 1963? What if you knew the outcome of each Kentucky Derby for the next ten years? What if you could revisit an old flame and this time do things right? And what if you could see what actually happened when Rome fell? What would it be like to live one hundred years from now? Oh the things we could do.

From *A Connecticut Yankee in King Arthur's Court* to *Back to the Future* to *Time and Again* and *The Alienist* to *Star Trek: The Journey Home* to *Twelve Monkeys*—time travel stories have fascinated us ever since the notion was conceived. Time travel is one of the most popular genres in fiction It is one of the few science fiction themes that have crossed over to mainstream fiction.

How to travel back in time—that is, of course, the most important question. Authors have solved the problem of time travel through various inventive means: sheer intellect, a rift in space, a long-lost tunnel, tapping into neutrinos, or a fantastically complicated machine are some of the mechanisms that time travelers use. For some readers, the how of moving backward and forward through time is the enthralling part of the story; for others it is what the characters do with their fortune—or misfortune that is interesting. For others still, time travel stories are interesting for what they reveal about notions of the future at the time the stories were written.

In compiling *Time Machines* it would have been easy to stick with stories written in the past five years, for there is a plethora of time travel stories. The more recent the story, the more sophisticated the use of contemporary physics. Black holes and superstring theory, are two of the more contemporary cosmological discoveries that have made time travel easier. But older stories are equally inventive, because imagination knows no bounds.

Like you, I've been a fan of time travel stories since I was a kid. I started reading them when I was about 10, and some, including Mark Clifton's *Star, Bright,* Rod Serling's *The Odyssey of Flight 33,* Jack Lewis' *Who's Cribbing?,* and Isaac Asimov's *What If,* were so wonderful that I remember them vividly thirty years later. But it's one thing to remember a story written three decades ago—it's another to actually find a short story three decades old. I'm pleased to say that I was able to find all these time travel stories—and more.

When you consider the science of it all, is time travel actually possible? I think so—but only in one direction. Forward. It's a well-known physical law that time slows down as you move faster. Not Corvette faster, but much, much faster than that. There are numerous practical problems associated with achieving these speeds, including the vast amount of energy needed, and the fact that accelerating to those speeds would smoosh the ship's occupants along the way. But the theory of time says, "Fine, you *can* travel into the future."

Nobody knows what the future will look like. Will there be another world-wide war? Will we cure cancer? Will nations live in harmony? Will any of us be able to solve age-old mysteries by actually witnessing them? Will we ever be able to travel backward or forward in time? Perhaps. But does it really matter? After all, even if we can't ever travel in time, we have these stories. And they are good enough.

Bill Adler, Jr.

Washington, DC
www.adlerbooks.com

TIME
MACHINES

Anthony Boucher

A Shape in Time

From *Microcosmic Tales,* 1970

*Agent L-3H works for the Marriage Prevention Bureau, which sends opera-
tives back in time to thwart unions that once had a deleterious effect on
history. Controlling time is a powerful and effective tool. Marriage Prevention
Bureau agents work by seducing their targets away from their true loves. But
for the first time, Agent L-3H fails her mission. Why? How could she fail?
No man before has been able to resist her seductions, especially when she
removes her clothes. Still, on this trip Agent L-3H does prevent the marriage,
through fright rather than seduction—and prevents two singular genes from
combining. Down the time stream evolution unfolds differently, and humans
in L-3H's time were no longer like the time she was visiting.*
   Seduction is as much a matter of genetics as it is technique, after all.
B. A.

TEMPORAL AGENT L-3H IS ALWAYS DELECTABLE IN ANY SHAPE;
that's why the bureau employs her on marriage-prevention assignments.

But this time, as she reported to my desk, she was also dejected.
"I'm a failure, Chief," she said. "He ran away—from *me.* The first
man in twenty-five centuries . . ."

"Don't take it so seriously," I said. She was more than just
another agent to me; I was the man who'd discovered her talents.
"We may be able to figure out what went wrong and approach it
on another time line."

"But I'm no good." Her body went scrawny and sagging. Sometimes I wonder how people expressed their emotions before mu-
tation gave us somatic control.

"Now, there," I said, expanding my flesh to radiate confidence,
"just tell me what happened. We know from the dial readings
that the Machine got you to London in 1880—"

"To prevent the marriage of Edwin Sullivan to Angelina Gil-
bert," she grimaced. "Time knows why."

I sighed. I was always patient with her. "Because that marriage joined two sets of genes which, in the course of three generations, would produce—"

Suddenly she gave me one of her old grins, with the left eyebrow up. "I've never understood the time results of an assignment yet, and don't try to teach me now. Marriage prevention's fun enough on its own. And I thought it was going to be extra good this time. Edwin's beard was red and this long, and I haven't had a beard in five trips. But something went—The worst of it is, it went wrong when I was naked."

I was incredulous and said so.

"I don't think *even* you really understand this, Chief. Because you are a man," her half smile complimented me by putting the italics of memory under "man," "and men never have understood it. But the fact is that what men want naked, in any century, in any country, is what they're used to seeing clothed, if you follow me. Oh, there are always some women who have to pad themselves out or pull themselves in, but the really popular ones are built to fit their clothes. Look at what they used to call 'feelthy peectures'; anytime, anyplace, the girls that are supposed to be exciting have the same silhouette naked as the fashion demands clothed. Improbable though it seems."

"L!" I gasped. She had suddenly changed so completely that there was hardly more than one clue that I was not looking at a boy.

"See?" she said. "That's the way I had to make myself when you sent me to the 1920s. And the assignment worked; this was what men wanted. And then, when you sent me to 1957 . . ."

I ducked out of the way as two monstrous mammae shot out at me. "I hadn't quite realized . . ." I began to confess.

". . . Or the time I had that job in sixteenth century Germany."

"Now you look pregnant!"

"They all did. Maybe they were. Or when I was in Greece, all waist and hips . . . But all of these worked. I prevented marriages and improved the genetic time flow. Only with Edwin . . ."

She was back in her own delectable shape, and I was able to give her a look of encouraging affection.

"I'll skip the buildup," she said. "I managed to meet Edwin, and I gave him this . . ." I nodded; how well I remembered this and its effects. "He began calling on me and taking me to theaters, and I knew it needed just one more step for him to forget all about that silly pink-and-white Angelina.''

"Go on," I urged.

"He took a step, all right. He invited me to dinner in a private room at a discreet restaurant—all red plush and mirrors and a screen in front of the couch. And he ordered oysters and truffles and all that superstitious ritual. The beard was even better than I'd hoped: crisp and teasing ticklish and . . ." She looked at me speculatively, and I regretted that we'd bred out facial follicles beyond even somatic control. "When he started to undress me— and how much trouble that was in 1880!—he was delighted with this."

She had changed from the waist up, and I had to admit that *this* was possibly more accurate than *these*. They were as large as the startling 1957 version, but molded together as almost one solid pectoral mass.

"Then he took off my skirts and . . ." L-3H was as near to tears as I had ever known her, "Then he . . . ran. Right out of the restaurant. I would've had to pay the check if I hadn't telekinned the Machine to bring me back now. And I'll bet he ran to that Angelina and made arrangements to start mixing genes and I've ruined everything for you."

I looked at her new form below the waist. It was indeed extraordinary and hardly to my taste, but it seemed correct. I checked the pictures again in the Sullivan dosier. Yes, absolutely.

I consoled her and absolved her. "My dear L, you are—Time help me!—perfectly and exactly a desirable woman of 1880. The failure must be due to some slip on the part of the chronopsychist who researched Edwin. You're still a credit to the bureau, agent L-3H!—and now let's celebrate. No, don't change back. Leave it that way. I'm curious as to the effects of—what was the word they used for it in 1880?—of a woman's bustle."

Jack Lewis

Who's Cribbing?

From *Better Publications*, 1953

A budding young science fiction writer has one problem: Everything he writes has already been written before. When he finally realizes what's happening— that somebody from the past is plagiarizing his work—and tries to get this idea published, it, too, has been cribbed.

B. A.

April 2, 1952

Mr. Jack Lewis
90-26 219 St.
Queens Village 28, NY

Dear Mr. Lewis:

We are returning your manuscript, "The Ninth Dimension." At first glance, I had figured it a story well worthy of publication. Why wouldn't I? So did the editors of *Cosmic Tale* back in 1934 when the story was first published.

As you no doubt know, it was the great Todd Thromberry who wrote the story you tried to pass off on us as an original.

Let me give you a word of caution concerning the penalties resulting from plagiarism:

It's not worth it. Believe me.

> Sincerely,
> Doyle P. Gates
> Science Fiction Editor
> *Deep Space Magazine*

■   ■   ■

> April 5, 1952

Mr. Doyle P. Gates, Editor
Deep Space Magazine
New York 3, NY

Dear Mr. Gates:

I do not know, nor am I aware of the existence of any Todd Thromberry. The story you rejected was submitted in good faith, and I resent the inference that I plagiarized it.

"The Ninth Dimension" was written by me not more than a month ago, and if there is any similarity between it and the story written by this Thromberry person, it is purely coincidental.

However, it has set me thinking. Some time ago, I submitted another story to *Stardust Scientifiction* and received a penciled notation on the rejection slip stating that the story was, "too Thromberrish."

Who the hell is Todd Thromberry? I don't remember reading anything written by him in the ten years I've been interested in science fiction.

> Sincerely,
> Jack Lewis

■   ■   ■

April 11, 1952

Mr. Jack Lewis
90-26 219 St.
Queens Village 28, NY

Dear Mr. Lewis:

Re: Your letter of April 5.

While the editors of this magazine are not in the habit of making open accusations and are well aware of the fact in the writing business there will always be some overlapping of plot ideas, it is very hard for us to believe that you are not familiar with the works of Todd Thromberry.

While Mr. Thromberry is no longer among us, his works, like so many other writers', only became widely recognized after his death in 1941. Perhaps it was his work in the field of electronics that supplied him with the bottomless pit of new ideas so apparent in all his works. Nevertheless, even at this stage of science fiction's development it is apparent that he had a style that many of our so-called contemporary writers might do well to copy. By "copy," I do not mean rewrite word for word one or more of his works, as you have done. For while you state this has been accidental, surely you must realize that the chance of this phenomenon actually occurring is about a million times as great as the occurrence of four royal flushes in one deal.

Sorry, but we're not that naive.

Sincerely yours,
Doyle P. Gates
Science Fiction Editor
Deep Space Magazine

■   ■   ■

April 13, 1952

Mr. Doyle P. Gates, Editor
Deep Space Magazine
New York 3, NY

Sir:

 Your accusations are typical of the rag you publish.
Please cancel my subscription immediately.

Sincerely,
Jack Lewis

■ ■ ■

April 14, 1952

Science Fiction Society
114 S. Front Ave
Chicago 28, IL

Gentlemen:

 I am interested in reading some of the works of the late
Todd Thromberry.
 I would like to get some of the publications that feature
his stories.

Respectfully,
Jack Lewis

■ ■ ■

April 22, 1952

Mr. Jack Lewis
90-26 219 St.
Queens Village 28, NY

Dear Mr. Lewis:

 So would we. All I can suggest is that you contact the publishers if any are still in business, or haunt your second-hand
bookstores.

If you succeed in getting any of these magazines, please let us know. We'll pay you a handsome premium on them.

Yours,
Ray Albert
President
Science Fiction Society

■   ■   ■

April 24, 1952

Mr. Sampson J. Gross, Editor
Strange Worlds Magazine
St. Louis 66, MO

Dear Mr. Gross:

I am enclosing the manuscript of a story I have just completed. As you see on the title page, I call it "Wreckers of Ten Million Galaxies." Because of the great amount of research that went into it, I must set the minimum price on this one at not less than two cents a word.

Hoping you will see fit to use it for publication in your magazine, I remain,

Respectfully,
Jack Lewis

■   ■   ■

May 19, 1952

Mr. Jack Lewis
90-26 219 St.
Queens Village 28, NY

Dear Mr. Lewis:

I'm sorry, but at the present time we won't be able to use "Wreckers of Ten Million Galaxies." It's a great yarn though, and if at some future date we decide to use it we will make out the reprint check directly to the estate of Todd Thromberry.

That boy sure could write.

> Cordially,
> Sampson J. Gross
> Editor
> *Strange Worlds Magazine*

. . .

May 23, 1952

Mr. Doyle P. Gates, Editor
Deep Space Magazine
New York 3, NY

Dear Mr. Gates:

While I said that I would never have any dealings with you or your magazine again, a situation has arisen which is most puzzling.

It seems that all my stories are being returned to me by reason of the fact that except for the byline, they are exact duplicates of the works of this Todd Thromberry person.

In your last letter you aptly described the odds of one accidental occurrence of this phenomenon in the case of one story. What would you consider the approximate odds on no less than half a dozen of my writings?

I agree with you—astronomical!

Yet in the interest of all mankind, how can I get the idea across to you that every word I have submitted was actually written by me! I have never copied any material from Todd Thromberry, nor have I ever seen any of his writings. In fact, as I told you in one of my letters, up until a short while ago I was totally unaware of his very existence.

An idea has occurred to me however. It's a truly weird theory, and one that I probably wouldn't even suggest to anyone but a science fiction editor. But suppose—just suppose—that this Thromberry person, what with his experiments in electronics and everything, had in some way managed to crack through this time-space barrier mentioned so often in your magazine. And suppose—egotistical as it sounds—he had singled out my work as being the type of material he had always wanted to write.

Do you begin to follow me? Or is the idea of a person from a different time cycle looking over my shoulder while I write too fantastic to accept?

Please write and tell me what you think of my theory?

Respectfully,
Jack Lewis

■   ■   ■

May 25, 1952

Mr. Jack Lewis
90-26 219 St.
Queens Village 28, NY

Dear Mr. Lewis:

We think you should consult a psychiatrist.

Sincerely,
Doyle P. Gates
Science Fiction Editor
Deep Space Magazine

■   ■   ■

June 3, 1952

Mr. Sam Mines
Science Fiction Editor
Standard Magazines Inc.
New York 12, NY

Dear Mr. Mines:

While the enclosed is not really a manuscript at all, I am submitting this series of letters, carbon copies, and corre- spondence, in the hope that you might give some credulity to this seemingly unbelievable happening.

The enclosed letters are all in proper order and should be

self-explanatory. Perhaps if you publish them, some of your readers might have some idea how this phenomena could be explained.

I call the entire piece, "Who's Cribbing?"

Respectfully,
Jack Lewis

. . .

June 10, 1952

Mr. Jack Lewis
90-26 219 St.
Queens Village 28, NY

Dear Mr. Lewis:

Your idea of a series of letters to put across a science-fiction idea is an intriguing one, but I'm afraid it doesn't quite come off.

It was in the August 1940 issue of *Macabre Adventures* that Mr. Thromberry first used this very idea. Ironically enough, the story title also was, "Who's Cribbing?"

Feel free to contact us again when you have something more original.

Yours,
Samual Mines
Science Fiction Editor
Standard Magazines Inc.

Mack Reynolds

The Business, As Usual

Fantasy House, 1952

In this story, souvenir hunters from the 20th Century visit the 30th Century in the hope of bringing back precious goods. They discover that time has its own way of taking care of tourists from other centuries.

B. A.

"LISTEN," THE TIME TRAVELER SAID TO THE FIRST PEDESTRIAN who came by, "I'm from the Twentieth Century. I've only got fifteen minutes and then I'll go back. I guess it's too much to expect you to understand me, eh?"

"Certainly, I understand you."

"Hey! You talk English fine. How come?"

"We call it Amer-English. I happen to be a student of dead languages."

"Swell! But listen, I only got a few minutes. Let's get going."

"Get going?"

"Yeah, yeah. Look, don't you get it? I'm a time traveler. They picked me to send to the future. I'm important."

"Ummm. But you must realize that we have time travelers turning up continuously these days."

"Listen, that rocks me, but I just don't have time to go into it, see? Let's get to the point."

"Very well, what have you got?"

"What d'ya mean, what've I got?"

12

The other sighed. "Don't you think you should attempt to acquire some evidence that you have been in the future? I can warn you now, the paradoxes involved in time travel prevent you from taking back any knowledge which might alter the past. On your return, your mind will be blank in regard to what happened here."

The time traveler blinked. "Oh?"

"Definitely. However, I shall be glad to make a trade with you."

"Listen, I get the feeling I came into this conversation half a dozen sentences too late. What d'ya mean, a trade?"

"I am willing to barter something of your century for something of mine, although, frankly, there is little in your period that is of other than historical interest to us." The pedestrian's eyes held a gleam now. He cleared his throat. "However, I have here an atomic pocket knife. I hesitate to even tell you of the advantages it has over the knives of your period."

"Okay. I got only ten minutes left, but I can see you're right. I've got to get something to prove that I was here."

"My knife would do it," the pedestrian nodded.

"Yeah, yeah. Listen, I'm a little confused, like. They picked me for this job last minute—didn't want to risk any of the professor guys, see? That's the screwiest knife I ever saw, let me have it for my evidence."

"Just a moment, friend. Why should I give you my knife? What can you offer in exchange?"

"But I'm from the Twentieth Century."

"Ummm. And I'm from the Thirtieth."

The time traveler looked at him for a long moment. Finally, "Listen, pal, I don't have a lot of time. Now, for instance, my watch—"

"Ummm. And what else?"

"Well, my money, here."

"Of interest only to a numismatist."

"Listen, I gotta have some evidence I been in the Thirtieth Century!"

"Of course. But business is business as the proverb goes."

"I wish the hell I had a gun."

"I have no use for a gun in this age," the other said primly.

"No, but I have," the time traveler muttered. "Look, fella, my time is running out by the second. What d'ya want? You see what I got, clothes, my wallet, a little money, a key ring, a pair of shoes."

"I'm willing to trade, but your possessions are of small value. Now some art object—an original Al Capp or something."

The time traveler was plaintive. "Do I look like I'd be carrying around art objects? Listen, I'll give you everything I got but my pants for that screwy knife."

"Oh, you want to keep your pants, eh? What're you trying to do, Anglo me down?—or does your period antedate the term?"

"Anglo . . . what? I don't get it."

"Well, I'm quite an etymologist—"

"That's too bad, but—"

"Not at all, a fascinating hobby," the pedestrian said. "Now as to the phrase, 'Anglo me down,' the term 'Anglo' first came into popular use during the 1850-1950 period. It designated persons from the eastern United States, English descent principally, who came into New Mexico and Arizona shortly after the area was liberated—I believe that was the term used at the time—from Mexico. The Spanish and the Indians came to know the Easterners as Anglos."

The time traveler said desperately, "Listen, pal, we get further and further from—"

"Tracing back the derivation of the phrase takes us along two more side trails. It goes back to the fact that these Anglos became the wealthiest businessmen of the Twentieth Century—so much so that they soon dominated the world with their dollars."

"Okay, okay. I know all about that. Personally I never had enough dollars to dominate anybody, but—"

"Very well, the point is that the Anglos became the financial wizards of the world, the most clever dealers, the sharpest bargainers, the most competent businessmen."

The time traveler shot a quick despairing look at his watch. "Only three—"

"The third factor is one taken from still further in the past. At one time there was a racial minority, which many of the Anglos held in disregard, called the *Joos*. For many years the term had been used, to *Joo* you down—meaning to make the price lower. As the Anglos assumed their monetary dominance, the term evolved from *Joo* you down to Anglo you down; and this it has come down to our own day, although neither Anglo nor *Joo* still exists as a separate people."

The time traveler stared at him. "And I won't be able to take the memory of this story back with me, eh? And me a guy named

Levy." He darted another look at his watch and groaned. "Quick!" he said, "Let's make this trade; everything I got for that atomic knife!"

The deal was consummated. The citizen of the Thirtieth Century stood back, his loot in his arms, and watched as the citizen of the Twentieth, nude but with the knife grasped tightly and happily in hand, faded slowly from view.

The knife poised momentarily in empty air, then dropped to the ground as the time traveler completely disappeared.

The other stooped, retrieved it, and stuck it back in his pocket. "Even more naive than usual," he muttered. "Must have been one of the very first. I suppose they'll never reconcile themselves to paradoxes. Obviously, you can carry things forward in time, since that's the natural flow of the dimension; but you just can't carry anything, not even memory, backward against the current."

He resumed his journey homeward.

Marget, hands on hips, met him at the door. "Where in Kert have you been?" she snapped.

"You mustn't swear, darling," he said. "I met another time traveler on the way home."

"You didn't—"

"Certainly, why not? If I didn't somebody else would."

"But you've already got the closet overflowing with—"

"Now Marget, don't look at it that way. One of these days some museum or collector—"

She grunted skeptically and turned back into the house.

Jack Finney

The Third Level

From *The Third Level*, Rinehart & Company, 1957

Everyone thinks that there are only two levels of Grand Central Station. But Charley knows that there's a third level. And if you can find it, by taking the right twists and turns down corridors and stairs, you will discover that the third level transports you to 1894.

B. A.

THE PRESIDENTS OF THE NEW YORK CENTRAL AND THE NEW YORK New Haven and Hartford railroads will swear on a stack of time-tables that there are only two. But I say there are three, because I've *been* on the third level of Grand Central Station. Yes, I've taken the obvious step: I talked to a psychiatrist friend of mine, among others. I told him about the third level at Grand Central Station, and he said it was a waking-dream wish fulfillment. He said I was unhappy. That made my wife kind of mad, but he explained that he meant the modern world is full of insecurity, fear, war, worry and all the rest of it, and that I just want to escape. Well, who doesn't? Everybody I know wants to escape, but they don't wander down into any third level at Grand Central Station.

But that's the reason, he said, and my friends all agreed. Everything points to it, they claimed. My stamp collecting, for example; that's a "temporary refuge from reality." Well, maybe, but my grandfather didn't need any refuge from reality; things were pretty nice and peaceful in his day, from all I hear, and he started my collection. It's a nice collection, too, blocks of four practically

16

every U.S. issue, first-day covers, and so on. President Roosevelt collected stamps, too, you know.

Anyway, here's what happened at Grand Central. One night last summer I worked late at the office. I was in a hurry to get uptown to my apartment so I decided to take the subway from Grand Central because it's faster than the bus.

Now, I don't know why this should have happened to me. I'm just an ordinary guy named Charley, thirty-one years old, and I was wearing a tan gabardine suit and a straw hat with a fancy band; I passed a dozen men who looked just like me. And I wasn't trying to escape from anything; I just wanted to get home to Louisa, my wife.

I turned into Grand Central from Vanderbilt Avenue, and went down the steps to the first level, where you take trains like the Twentieth Century. Then I walked down another flight to the second level, where the suburban trains leave from, ducked into an arched doorway heading for the subway—and got lost. That's easy to do. I've been in and out of Grand Central hundreds of times, but I'm always bumping into new doorways and stairs and corridors. Once I got into a tunnel about a mile long and came out in the lobby of the Roosevelt Hotel. Another time I came up in an office building on Forty-sixth Street, three blocks away.

Sometimes I think Grand Central is growing like a tree, pushing out new corridors and staircases like roots. There's probably a long tunnel that nobody knows about feeling its way under the city right now, on its way to Times Square, and maybe another to Central Park. And maybe—because for so many people through the years Grand Central has been an exit, a way of escape—maybe that's how the tunnel I got into . . . But I never told my psychiatrist friend about that idea.

The corridor I was in began angling left and slanting downward and I thought that was wrong, but I kept on walking. All I could hear was the empty sound of my own footsteps and I didn't pass a soul. Then I heard that sort of hollow roar ahead that means open space and people talking. The tunnel turned sharp left; it went down a short flight of stairs and came out on the third level at Grand Central Station. For just a moment I thought I was back on the second level, but I saw the room was smaller, there were fewer ticket windows and train gates, and the information booth in the center was wood and old-looking. And the man in the booth wore a green eyeshade and long black sleeve protectors.

The lights were dim and sort of flickering. Then I saw why; they were open-flame gaslights.

There were brass spittoons on the floor, and across the station a glint of light caught my eye; a man was pulling a gold watch from his vest pocket. He snapped open the cover, glanced at his watch, and frowned. He wore a derby hat, a black four-button suit with tiny lapels, and he had a big, black, handle-bar mustache. Then I looked around and saw that everyone in the station was dressed like eighteen-ninety-something; I never saw so many beards, sideburns and fancy mustaches in my life. A woman walked in through the train gate; she wore a dress with leg-of-mutton sleeves and skirts to the top of her high-buttoned shoes. Back of her, out on the tracks, I caught a glimpse of a locomotive, a very small Currier & Ives locomotive with a funnel-shaped stack. And then I knew.

To make sure, I walked over to a newsboy and glanced at the stack of papers at his feet. It was *The World*; and *The World* hasn't been published for years. The lead story said something about President Cleveland. I've found that page since, in the Public Library files, and it was printed June 11, 1894.

I turned toward the ticket windows knowing that here—on the third level at Grand Central—I could buy tickets that would take Louisa and me anywhere in the United States we wanted to go. In the year 1894. And I wanted two tickets to Galesburg, Illinois.

Have you ever been there? It's a wonderful old town still, with big old frame houses, huge lawns and tremendous trees whose branches meet overhead and roof the streets. And in 1894, summer evenings were twice as long, and people sat out on their lawns, the men smoking cigars, and talking quietly, the women waving palm-leaf fans, with the fireflies all around, in a peaceful world. To be back there with the First World War still twenty years off, and World War II, over forty years in the future . . . I wanted two tickets for that.

The clerk figured the fare—he glanced at my fancy hat band, but he figured the fare—and I had enough for two coach tickets, one way. But when I counted out the money and looked up, the clerk was staring at me. He nodded at the bills. "That ain't money, mister," he said, "and if you're trying to skin me you won't get very far," and he glanced at the cash drawer beside him. Of course the money in his drawer was old-style bills, half again as big as the money we use nowadays, and different-looking. I turned away and got out fast. There's nothing nice about jail, even in 1894.

And that was that. I left the same way I came, I suppose. Next day, during lunch hour, I drew three hundred dollars out of the bank, nearly all we had, and bought old-style currency (that really worried my psychiatrist friend). You can buy old money at almost any coin dealer's, but you have to pay a premium. My three hundred dollars bought less than two hundred in old-style bills, but I didn't care; eggs were thirteen cents a dozen in 1894.

But I never again found the corridor that leads to the third level at Grand Central Station, although I've tried often enough.

Louisa was pretty worried when I told her all this, and she didn't want me to look for the third level anymore, and after a while I stopped. I went back to my stamps. But now we're both looking, every weekend, because now we have proof that the third level is still there. My friend Sam Weiner disappeared! Nobody knew where, but I sort of suspected because Sam's a city boy, and I used to tell him about Galesburg—I went to school there—and he always said he liked the sound of the place. And that's where he is, all right. In 1894.

Because one night, fussing with my stamp collection, I found— well, do you know what a first-day cover is? When a new stamp is issued, stamp collectors buy some and use them to mail envelopes to themselves on the first day of sale; and the postmark proves the date. The envelope is called a first-day cover. They're never opened; you just put blank paper in the envelope.

That night, among my oldest first-day covers, I found one that shouldn't have been there. But there it was. It was there because someone had mailed it to my grandfather at his home in Galesburg; that's what the address on the envelope said. And it had been there since July 18, 1894—the postmark showed that—yet I didn't remember it at all. The stamp was a six-cent, dull brown, with a picture of President Garfield. Naturally, when the envelope came to Granddad in the mail, it went right into his collection and stayed there—till I took it out and opened it.

The paper inside wasn't blank. It read:

94 Willard Street
Galesburg, Illinois
July 18, 1894

Charley:

   I got to wishing that you were right. Then I got to believing
you were right. And Charley, it's true; I found the third level!
I've been here two weeks, and right now, down the street at
Daly's, someone is playing a piano, and they're all out on the
front porch singing, "Seeing Nellie Home." And I'm invited
over for lemonade. Come on back, Charley and Louisa. Keep
looking till you find the third level! It's worth it, believe me!

   The note is signed Sam.
   At the stamp and coin store where I go, I found out that Sam
bought eight hundred dollars worth of old-style currency. That
ought to set him up in a nice little hay, feed and grain business;
he always said that's what he really wished he could do, and he
certainly can't go back to his old business. Not in Galesburg, Illinois, in 1894. His old business? Why, Sam was my psychiatrist.

Ray Bradbury

A Touch of Petulance

From *The Toynbee Convertor*, 1988

You will murder your wife. You will murder her because she has become nagging, annoying, unpleasant, and just generally impossible to live with. Although you love her dearly now and you have only been married a year, in twenty years you will feel just the opposite, difficult as that is to believe. You know this because the man on the train tells you: He is from the future. He is you.

And what do you do about it? To help prevent the awful future, do you tell your wife every day that you love her? Do you leave her this moment— just walk out the door? Ignore your future self and let fate take its course? Or do you kill her now and save yourself from years of misery? But perhaps the real question is: While you trust your present-day self, can you trust your future-self to have the same interests as you do now?

B. A.

ON AN OTHERWISE ORDINARY EVENING IN MAY, A WEEK BEFORE his twenty-ninth birthday, Jonathan Hughes met his fate, commuting from another time, another year, another life.

His fate was unrecognizable at first, of course, and boarded the train at the same hour, in Pennsylvania Station, and sat with Hughes for the dinnertime journey across Long Island. It was the newspaper held by this fate disguised as an older man that caused Jonathan Hughes to stare and finally say:

"Sir, pardon me, your *New York Times* seems different from mine. The typeface on your front page seems more modern. Is that a later edition?"

"No!" the older man stopped, swallowed hard, and at last managed to say, "Yes. A very late edition."

Hughes glanced around. "Excuse me, but—all the other editions look the same. Is yours a trial copy for a future change?"

"Future?" The older man's mouth barely moved. His entire body seemed to wither in his clothes, as if he had lost weight with a single exhalation. "Indeed," he whispered. "Future change. God, what a joke."

Jonathan Hughes blinked at the newspaper's dateline:

May 2, 1999.

"Now, see here—" he protested, and then his eyes moved down to find a small story, minus picture, in the upper-left-hand corner of the front page:

WOMAN MURDERED
POLICE SEEK HUSBAND
Body of Mrs. Alice Hughes found shot to death—

The train thundered over a bridge. Outside the window, a billion trees rose up, flourished their green branches in convulsions of wind, then fell as if chopped to earth.

The train rolled into a station as if nothing at all in the world had happened.

In the silence, the young man's eyes returned to the text:

Jonathan Hughes, certified public accountant,
of 112 Plandome Avenue, Plandome—

"My God!" he cried. "Get away!"

But he himself rose and ran a few steps back before the older man could move. The train jolted and threw him into an empty seat where he stared wildly out at a river of green light that rushed past the windows.

Christ, he thought, who would do such a thing? Who'd try to hurt us—us? What kind of joke? To mock a new marriage with a fine wife? Damn! And again, trembling, Damn, oh, damn!

The train rounded a curve and all but threw him to his feet. Like a man drunk with traveling, gravity, and simple rage, he swung about and lurched back to confront the old man, bent now into his newspaper, gone to earth, hiding in print. Hughes brushed the paper out of the way, and clutched the old man's shoulder. The old man, startled, glanced up, tears running from his eyes. They were both held in a long moment of thunderous traveling. Hughes felt his soul rise to leave his body.

"Who are you?"

Someone must have shouted that.

The train rocked as if it might derail.

The old man stood up as if shot in the heart, blindly crammed something into Jonathan Hughes's hand, and blundered away down the aisle and into the next car.

The younger man opened his fist and turned a card over and read a few words that moved him heavily down to sit and read the words again:

JONATHAN HUGHES, CPA
679–4990. Plandome.

"No!" someone shouted.

Me, thought the young man. Why, that old man is . . . me.

       ■ ■ ■

There was a conspiracy, no, several conspiracies. Someone had contrived a joke about murder and played it on him. The train roared on with five hundred commuters who all rode, swaying like a team of drunken intellectuals behind masking books and papers, while the old man, as if pursued by demons, fled off away from car to car. By the time Jonathan Hughes had rampaged his blood and completely thrown his sanity off balance, the old man had plunged, as if falling, to the farthest end of the commuter's special.

The two men met again in the last car, which was almost empty. Jonathan Hughes came and stood over the old man, who refused to look up. He was crying so hard now that conversation would have been impossible.

Who, thought the young man, who is he crying for? Stop, please, stop.

The old man, as if commanded, sat up, wiped his eyes, blew his nose, and began to speak in a frail voice that drew Jonathan Hughes near and finally caused him to sit and listen to the whispers:

"We were born—"

"We?" cried the young man.

"We," whispered the old man, looking out at the gathering dusk that traveled like smokes and burnings past the window, "we, yes, we, the two of us, we were born in Quincy in nineteen fifty. August twenty-second—"

Yes, thought Hughes.

"—and lived at Forty-nine Washington Street and went to Central School and walked to that school all through first grade with Isabel Perry—"

Isabel, thought the young man.

"We . . ." murmured the old man. "Our" whispered the old man. "Us." And went on and on with it.

"Our woodshop teacher, Mr. Bisbee. History teacher, Miss Monks. We broke our right ankle, age ten, iceskating. Almost drowned, age eleven; Father saved us. Fell in love, age twelve, Impi Johnson—"

Seventh grade, lovely lady, long since dead, Jesus God, thought the young man, growing old.

And that's what happened. In the next minute, two minutes, three, the old man talked and talked and gradually became younger with talking so that his cheeks glowed and his eyes brightened, while the young man, weighted with old knowledge given, sank lower in his seat and grew pale so that both almost met in mid-talking, mid-listening and became twins in passing. There was a moment when Jonathan Hughes knew for an absolute insane certainty that if he dared to glance up he would see identical twins in the mirrored window of a night-rushing world.

He did not look up.

The old man finished, his frame erect now, his head somehow driven high by talking out, the long lost revelations.

"That's the past," he said.

I should hit him, thought Hughes. Accuse him. Shout at him. Why aren't I hitting, accusing, shouting?

Because . . .

The old man sensed the question and said, "You know I'm who I say I am. I know everything there is to know about us. Now— the future?"

"Mine?"

"Ours," said the old man.

Jonathan Hughes nodded, staring at the newspaper clutched in the old man's right hand. The old man folded it and put it away.

"Your business will slowly become less than good. For what reasons, who can say? A child will be born and die. A mistress will be taken and lost. A wife will become less than good. And at last, oh believe it, yes, do, very slowly, you will come to—how shall I say it—hate her living presence. There, I see I've upset you. I'll shut up."

They rode in silence for a long while, and the old man grew old again, and the young man along with him. When he had aged

just the proper amount, the young man nodded the talk to continue, not looking at the other who now said:

"Impossible, yes, you've been married only a year, a great year,
the best. Hard to think that a single drop of ink could color a
white pitcher of clear fresh water. But color it could and color it
did. And at last the entire world changed, not just our wife, not
just the beautiful woman, the fine dream."

"You—" Jonathan Hughes started and stopped. "You—killed
her?"

"We did. Both of us. But if I have my way, if I can convince
you, neither of us will, she will live, and you will grow old to
become a happier, finer me. I pray for that. I weep for that.
There's still time. Across the years, I intend to shake you up,
change your blood, shape your mind. God, if people knew what
murder is. So silly. So stupid, so ugly. But there is hope, for I have
somehow got here, touched you, and begun to change. That will
save our souls. Now, listen. You do admit, do you not, that we are
one and the same, that the twins of time ride this train this hour
this night?"

The train whistled ahead of them, clearing the track for an
encumbrance of years.

The young man nodded the most infinitely microscopic of
nods. The old man needed no more.

"I ran away. I ran to you. That's all I can say. She's been dead
only a day, and I ran. Where to go? Nowhere to die, save Time.
No one to plead with, no judge, no jury, no proper witnesses
save—you. Only you can wash the blood away, do you see? You
drew me, then. Your youngness, your innocence, your good hours,
your fine life still untouched, was the machine that seized me
down the track. All of my sanity lies in you. If you turn away, great
God, I'm lost, no, we are lost. We'll share a grave and never rise
and be buried forever in misery. Shall I tell you what you must
do?"

The young man rose.

"Plandome," a voice cried. "Plandome."

And they went out on the platform with the old man running
after, the young man blundering into walls, into people, feeling
as if his limbs might fly apart.

"Wait!" cried the old man. "Oh, please!"

The young man kept moving.

"Don't you see, we're in this together, we must think of it together, solve it together, so you won't become me and I won't have to come impossibly in search of you, oh, it's all mad, insane, I know, I know, but listen!''

The young man stopped at the edge of the platform where cars were pulling in, with joyful cries or muted greeting, brief honkings, gunnings of motors, lights vanishing away. The old man grasped the young man's elbow.

''Good God, your wife, mine, will be here in a moment, there's so much to tell, you can't know what I know, there's twenty years of unfound information lost between which we must trade and understand. Are you listening? God, you don't believe!''

Jonathan Hughes was watching the street. A long way off a final car was approaching. He said: ''What happened in the attic at my grandmother's house in the summer of nineteen-fifty-eight? No one knows but me. Well?''

The old man's shoulders slumped. He breathed more easily, and as if reciting from a prompt-board said, ''We hid ourselves there for two days, alone. No one ever knew where we hid. Everyone thought we had run away to drown in the lake or fall in the river. But all the time, crying, not feeling wanted, we hid above and . . . listened to the wind and wanted to die.''

The young man turned at last to stare fixedly at his older self, tears in his eyes. ''You love me, then?''

''I had better,'' said the old man. ''I'm all you have.''

The car was pulling up at the station. A young woman smiled and waved behind the glass.

''Quick,'' said the old man, quietly. ''Let me come home, watch, show you, teach you, find where things went wrong, correct them now, maybe hand you a fine life forever, let me—''

The car horn sounded, the car stopped, the young woman leaned out.

''Hello, lovely man!'' she cried.

Jonathan Hughes exploded a laugh and burst into a manic run. ''Lovely lady, hi—''

''Wait.''

He stopped and turned to look at the old man with the newspaper, trembling there on the station platform. The old man raised one hand, questionably.

''Haven't you forgotten something?''

Silence. At last: ''You,'' said Jonathan Hughes. ''You.''

■   ■   ■

The car rounded a turn in the night. The woman, the old man, the young swayed with the motion.

"What did you say your name was?" the young woman said, above the rush and run of the country and road.

"He didn't say," said Jonathan Hughes, quickly.

"Weldon," said the old man, blinking.

"Why," said Alice Hughes, "That's my maiden name."

The old man gasped inaudibly, but recovered. "Well, is it? How curious!"

"I wonder if we're related? You—"

"He was my teacher at Central High," said Jonathan Hughes, quickly.

"And still am," said the old man. "And still am."

And they were home.

He could not stop staring. All through dinner, the old man simply sat with his hands empty half the time and stared at the lovely woman across the table from him. Jonathan Hughes fidgeted, talked much too loudly to cover the silences, and ate sparsely. The old man continued to stare as if a miracle was happening every ten seconds. He watched Alice's mouth as if it were giving forth fountains of diamonds. He watched her eyes as if all the hidden wisdoms of the world were there and now found for the first time. By the look of his face, the old man, stunned, had forgotten why he was there.

"Have I a crumb on my chin?" cried Alice Hughes, suddenly. "Why is everyone watching me?"

Whereupon the old man burst into tears that shocked everyone. He could not seem to stop, until at last Alice came around the table to touch his shoulder.

"Forgive me," he said. "It's just that you're so lovely. Please sit down. Forgive."

They finished off dessert and with a great display of tossing down his fork and wiping his mouth with his napkin, Jonathan Hughes cried, "That was fabulous. Dear wife, I love you!" He kissed her on the cheek, thought better of it, and rekissed her, on the mouth. "You see?" He glanced at the old man. "I very much love my wife."

The old man nodded quietly and said, "Yes, yes, I remember."

"You remember?" said Alice, staring.

"A toast!" said Jonathan Hughes, quickly. "To a fine wife, a grand future!"

His wife laughed. She raised her glass.

"Mr. Weldon," she said, after a moment. "You're not drinking? . . ."

■   ■   ■

It was strange seeing the old man at the door to the living room.

"Watch this," he said, and closed his eyes. He began to move certainly and surely about the room, eyes shut. "Over here is the pipestand, over here the books. On the fourth shelf down a copy of Eisley's *The Star Thrower*. One shelf up H. G. Wells's *Time Machine*, most appropriate, and over here the special chair, and me in it."

He sat. He opened his eyes.

Watching from the door, Jonathan Hughes said, "You're not going to cry again, are you?"

"No. No more crying."

There were sounds of washing up from the kitchen. The lovely woman out there hummed under her breath. Both men turned to look out of the room toward that humming.

"Someday," said Jonathan Hughes, "I will hate her? Someday, I will kill her?"

"It doesn't seem possible, does it? I've watched her for an hour and found nothing, no hint, no clue, not the merest period, semicolon or exclamation point of blemish, bump or hair out of place with her. I've watched you, too, to see if you were at fault, we were at fault, in all this."

"And?" The young man poured sherry for both of them, and handed over a glass.

"You drink too much is about the sum. Watch it."

Hughes put his drink down without sipping it. "What else?"

"I suppose I should give you a list, make you keep it, look at it every day. Advice from the old crazy to the young fool."

"Whatever you say, I'll remember."

"Will you? For how long? A month, a year, then, like everything else, it'll go. You'll be busy living. You'll be slowly turning into . . . me. She will slowly be turning into someone worth putting out of the world. Tell her you love her."

"Every day."

"Promise! It's that important! Maybe that's where I failed myself, failed us. Every day, without fail!" The old man leaned forward, his face taking fire with his words. "Every day! Every day!"

Alice stood in the doorway, faintly alarmed.

"Anything wrong?"

"No, no," Jonathan Hughes smiled. "We were trying to decide which of us likes you best."

She laughed, shrugged, and went away.

"I think," said Jonathan Hughes, and stopped and closed his eyes, forcing himself to say it, "it's time for you to go."

"Yes, time." But the old man did not move. His voice was very tired, exhausted, sad. "I've been sitting here feeling defeated. I can't find anything wrong. I can't find the flaw. I can't advise you, my God, it's so stupid, I shouldn't have come to upset you, worry you, disturb your life, when I have nothing to offer but vague suggestions, inane cryings of doom. I sat here a moment ago and thought: I'll kill her now, get rid of her now, take the blame now, as an old man, so the young man there, you, can go into the future and be free of her. Isn't that silly? I wonder if it will work? It's that old time-travel paradox, isn't it? Would I foul up the time flow, the world, the universe, what? Don't worry, no, no, don't look that way. No murder now. The old man having done nothing whatever, having been no help, will now open the door and run away to his madness."

He arose and shut his eyes again.

"Let me see if I can find my way out of my own house, in the dark."

He moved, the young man moved with him to find the closet by the front door and open it and take out the old man's overcoat and slowly shrug him into it.

"You have helped," said Jonathan Hughes. "You have told me to tell her I love her."

"Yes, I did do that, didn't I?"

They turned to the door.

"Is there hope for us?" the old man asked, suddenly, fiercely.

"Yes. I'll make sure of it," said Jonathan Hughes.

"Good, oh, good. I almost believe!"

The old man put one hand out and blindly opened the front door.

"I won't say goodbye to her. I couldn't stand looking at that lovely face. Tell her the old fool's gone. Where? Up the road to wait for you. You'll arrive someday."

"To become you? Not a chance," said the young man.

"Keep saying that. And—my God—here—" The old man fumbled in his pocket and drew forth a small object wrapped in crumpled newspaper. "You'd better keep this. I can't be trusted, even now. I might do something wild. Here. Here."

He thrust the object into the young man's hands. "Goodbye. Doesn't that mean: God be with you? Yes. Goodbye."

The old man hurried down the walk into the night. A wind shook the trees. A long way off, a train moved in darkness, arriving or departing, no one could tell.

Jonathan Hughes stood in the doorway for a long while, trying to see if there really was someone out there vanishing in the dark.

"Darling," his wife called.

He began to unwrap the small object.

She was in the parlor door behind him now, but her voice sounded as remote as the fading footsteps along the dark street.

"Don't stand there letting the draft in," she said.

He stiffened as he finished unwrapping the object. It lay in his hand, a small revolver.

Far away, the train sounded a final cry, which failed in the wind.

"Shut the door," said his wife.

His face was cold. He closed his eyes.

Her voice. Wasn't there just the tiniest touch of petulance there?

He turned slowly, off balance. His shoulder brushed the door. It drifted. Then:

The wind, all by itself, slammed the door with a bang.

Wayne Freeze

The History of Temporal Express

From *Dark Forces*, 1997

Time travel is not always about the glamorous exploration of places past. What about the mundane, day to day activities? What can you do if your boss is breathing down your neck on Wednesday about a report that was supposed to be on his desk Monday morning? A time machine can also get you out of a tight spot when it "Absolutely, positively has to be there yesterday."

B. A.

The History of Temporal Express
by Wayne S. Freeze
Miss Goemmer's 12th Grade History Class
Senior Research Report, 2015

THIS YEAR'S SENIOR RESEARCH REPORT WAS TO RESEARCH A MODern business or government organization and write a paper that discussed the key events in its history. The report must be at least 2,000 words long and must include a minimum of four different sources of information. I selected Temporal Express for my report since many of its key events occurred during my lifetime.

It is all but impossible to discuss modern business without talking about Temporal Express. Its motto, "When it absolutely, positively must be there yesterday" has changed the face of today's world. Although formed in the early twenty-first century, its origins actually date back to the late 1990s. Formed by a group of researchers at Maryland State University who were pushing the then known limits of high energy physics, TempEx (as it is more commonly known) has brought with it a whole new era of prosperity.

The Discovery

Temporal Express was founded in 2001 by Dr. Christopher Jameson, Dr. Samantha Ashburn, and Dr. Terry Katz. These same individuals are credited with building the first practical time transporter. The fundamental breakthrough that allowed them to build the time transporter occurred in 1998 while they were trying to build a device that would transport objects instantly from one location to another.

Their initial experiments were wholly unsuccessful. Objects placed on the transport platform disappeared as expected, but did not reappear on the receiving platform. This led to a vigorous debate as to where the objects actually went. On 1 April 1998, Dr. Jameson found one of the test objects on the receiving platform— a child's wooden block with the letter T on the side. Thinking that either Dr. Ashburn or Dr. Katz was playing an April Fool's joke on him, Jameson placed the block back on the shelf and forgot about it. He didn't notice that there was an identical block sitting right next to it.

Later in the week, the researchers decided to try transporting an object from the receiving platform back to the original transporter pad. While this was supposed to work according to their theories, they hadn't tried it before. When Dr. Katz went to get a test block, he found two blocks with the letter T on the shelf. Wondering why there were two blocks with the same letter, he grabbed the original one and placed it on the receiver pad.

When this block disappeared, Dr. Katz laughed and said that they were in luck and got the second block from the shelf. Dr. Jameson looked at it closely and instantly recognized the paint smudge that was identical to the block he had found on the receiver platform earlier in the week. Dr. Ashburn shook his head and said "Wouldn't it be funny if the blocks were actually going backward in time?"

The more they thought about it, the more Dr. Ashburn's explanation seemed to make sense. Further experiments proved that Dr. Ashburn was correct—the blocks actually did go back in time. They had actually built a time transporter!

The Evolution

To say that the researchers made a unique discovery was an understatement. However when Dr. Jameson, Dr. Ashburn, and Dr. Katz released their initial findings to their peers, no one believed them. They were treated as objects of ridicule. Eventually they took their case to the general public.

On the now famous episode of "Sixty Minutes," they were able to convince Dan Rather that their machine actually worked. They were able to send Dan's watch back in time sixty minutes while he and five different cameras recorded the event. Dan Rather actually picked up his future watch and compared it to the one on his wrist. It was identical. He then held on to the future watch and placed the one on his wrist on the time transporter's pad, and exactly sixty minutes after the first watch was sent, he pressed the button to send his watch back into the past.

The subsequent publicity overwhelmed the researchers with requests for time travel projects. The most common requests were for pictures and artifacts from ancient history. An original copy of *King Lear* by Shakespeare, a scroll from Moses, and a piece of the cross from the Crucifixion of Christ were among the most popular.

Unfortunately these requests were impossible to fulfill. Early in their time transporter research, the doctors quickly identified three main limitations to their new device. The first limitation is that the time transporter can transport objects only to another version of itself. The second is the more massive the object, the more power it requires to transport it. Thus sending one two pound object requires significantly more power than sending two one pound objects. The third limitation is that sending an object back in time two days requires more than twice the power required to send an object back one day.

In addition to these three limitations, the researchers found another problem. It appeared to be possible to change the future. Dr. Ashburn received a message from herself in the future that suggested that she buy a lottery ticket with a particular set of numbers which would win a large sum of money. But on that evening's drawing, Dr. Ashburn didn't win anything. Subsequent experiments showed that sending the winning number back into the past worked only when someone didn't act on that information. The Theory of Useless Information was coined by Dr. Katz to describe this phenomenon.

Once the three limitations plus the Theory of Useless Information became known to the general public, interest in the time transport device waned. It looked like the time transporter was destined to become a research oddity that would never become practical.

The Idea

The researchers continued working on the time transporter, but with little hope of success. Then one day Dr. Ashburn wanted to join her fellow scientists for lunch, but didn't have enough money. Payday was only a day away, and as with most absent minded professors, Dr. Ashburn was always forgetting her money. Just before she was going to tell the others to go without her, she noticed an envelope on the time transporter. In the envelope was a twenty dollar bill and a note in her own handwriting that said "pay me back later."

While at lunch, the three professors discussed a minor technical problem with the machine. Dr. Jameson said that one of the displays on his computer had stopped working. If he had the parts, he could fix it in five minutes, but it would take two days to get the parts from the vendor.

Dr. Katz said that what he needed was a time machine that could send the part back to when the display died, and then he uttered the now famous line, "When it absolutely, positively must be there yesterday." Everyone laughed for a moment and then Dr. Ashburn thought about it for a minute and shared her tale from earlier in the day. From this lunch sprouted the seeds of the most famous company in the world today.

The Beginning

Today, Temporal Express is a world-wide organization with its home offices in the City of Time also known as Columbia, Maryland. Columbia is located halfway between Washington, D.C. and

Baltimore, Maryland. This location was close to Maryland State University where the trio worked as professors. The location also proved important in later years since it provided easy access to the legislators who created the laws that made it possible for TempEx to be very profitable.

But Temporal Express did not start out as an immediate success. Its early years were extremely rough. While Dr. Katz and Dr. Ashburn remained with the University, Dr. Jameson tried to raise money to build a second machine. Failing to do that, Dr. Jameson was at least able to raise sufficient money to buy the rights to the existing time transporter from the University. The University had begun to find the entire project an embarrassment and wished to distance itself from all the negative publicity. After getting sole possession of the temporal transporter and its related technology, the threesome then relocated the machine to Dr. Ashburn's garage. From there they began to offer their services..

At first most potential customers were skeptical of the service. The service was both expensive, (costing over ten thousand dollars for a one pound package delivered the previous day) and extremely restrictive due to the time transporter limitations and the Theory of Useless Information. However when a multi-million dollar machine was destroyed at a local manufacturing plant because a small, relatively inexpensive part failed, TempEx was able to save the day. They delivered the part just before the machine broke down, and the manufacturer's staff was able to replace the part before disaster struck.

Their second customer was a major airline who managed to avoid a huge aircraft disaster by replacing a small circuit board in the control system of their new Boeing 787 aircraft. If the board hadn't been replaced before the aircraft took off, it was almost certain that all twelve hundred passengers would have died.

These stories are simply the first in a series of disasters prevented by the timely delivery of a package by TempEx. Over the next twelve months, TempEx was able to move out of the garage into a large office complex. Two years later, TempEx completed a hostile takeover of Federal Express, followed shortly by DHL and Airborne Express. Thus the corporate motto, "Any time, any place." Other companies acquired over the years that followed include: Chrysler Corporation, General Electric, and Hewlett Packard. Temporal Express had reached the big time!

After all of the skepticism surrounding the initial announce-

ment, Dr. Jameson, Dr. Ashburn, and Dr. Katz deliberately sup-
pressed their theories about time travel which left their
competitors without sufficient information to build their own time
transporters. As TempEx grew, there were many attempts by their
competitors to build their own temporal transporters. The most
aggressive of their competitors was the United Parcel Service
(UPS). In the early twenty-first century, UPS had achieved a near
monopoly on the package delivery service in the United States.
Having bought the U.S. Postal Service from the federal government in 2003, it had very little competition left and it had sufficient funds to try to duplicate the temporal transporter.

When UPS was unable to develop the temporal transporter on
their own, they decided to sue TempEx for the information on
the grounds that the time transporter technology was developed
with public funds and thus should be open to everyone. TempEx
was successful in proving that their device was built using grant
money from several different corporations such as Hewlett Packard, Chrysler Corporation, and General Electric.

Following this decision, TempEx turned their attention to
Washington and Congress. They were able to convince Congress
that transporting objects though time was a risky business and
should only be attempted by organizations with sufficient experience. Since TempEx was the only organization with an opera-
tional time transporter, they were immediately granted a license
by Congress. A review board was established to determine if an
organization has sufficient expertise to experiment with time
transportation. Since the members of the review board were required by law to have temporal experience, no other organizations were permitted to develop that technology. For all practical
purposes, TempEx now had a monopoly on time transportation.

The Service

Temporal Express has positioned itself for growth well into the
twenty-second century. Currently it is the second largest corporation in America, only ten trillion dollars behind Microsoft. It is
larger than the rest of the Fortune 100 combined. Its research
and development budget is larger then the gross national product
of many countries.

Today, Temporal Express is an international organization that
can deliver and pick up packages anywhere on Earth as well as

the moon and Mars. According to a recent *Wall Street Journal* (www.WSJ.com) article, TempEx is planning to expand their services into the asteroid belt in the next 12 to 18 months.

Originally TempEx was organized as a star network, with a central hub in which all of the packages flowed through and where the temporal transporters were located. This is the same organization that proved successful for Federal Express. However, demand for TempEx's services overloaded the central facility. Now TempEx has several smaller hubs located at key points around the globe and one on the moon.

For normal previous day delivery in the United States, TempEx will pickup and deliver a one pound package for only $10,000. Two day delivery costs $35,000, and one week delivery is available by special quote. While not very popular, one week delivery is believed to have been used several times in the past at a cost of over $1 million dollars per delivery.

The largest package ever handled by TempEx was a twenty-six pound oxygen recycling module that was needed by the Lunar Authority to replace a similar unit that was damaged by a meteorite. With the primary unit already offline for major repairs, over half the colony's population would have died due to lack of oxygen before a replacement unit could make the 12 hour flight from Earth.

The Future

While the original founders of Temporal Express do not participate in the day to day operations of the company, they are active professors at Future University (the new name for Maryland State University after it was purchased by TempEx). They teach doctoral seminars in temporal theory at Future University and advise the University president, Dr. Therese Jillion, on policy and direction.

Through Future University, TempEx is actively pursuing technologies that will improve the range and efficiency of their current time transporter. Also TempEx is investing a large part of their research budget in an attempt to combine their time transporter technology with conventional spaceship technology to build the first practical starship. It is expected that this starship will be ready to launch within the next five years.

It is clear that from the beginning, Dr. Christopher Jameson,

Dr. Samantha Ashburn, and Dr. Terry Katz, believed that Temporal Express would be successful. Even though the early years were rough, all three professors stuck with their idea and nursed it into the corporation it is today.

Sources

"Future University: A Status Report to the Shareholders." Jaybird, J. B., Temporal Express Press, 2013.

"Temporal Express Annual Report." Temporal Express Press, 2013.

"The Official History of Temporal Express." Ashburn, S., Adler & Robin Books, 2012.

"The Rise and Fall of UPS." Brighamton, L., Chrissam Press, 2010.

"The Unauthorized Life of Christopher Jameson." Jillion, T., Chrissam Press, 2011.

Grade: A−

Your facts were very good and so was the presentation. While you used five references, you should have included references for the *Wall Street Journal* article and the "60 Minutes" television episode since you referred to them in your report. Overall a very good job.

—Miss Bonnie J. Goemmer

Mark Clifton

Star, Bright

From *The Mathematical Magpie,* Simon & Schuster, 1962

"At three years of age a little girl shouldn't have enough functioning intelligence to cut out and paste together a Moebius strip." So begins "Star, Bright," in which a little girl, Star, who is abnormally bright, learns how to bend space in her mind and use those thoughts to transport herself through time. Raising any child is hard enough—but when that little girl can travel through time at will, the task becomes even more challenging—not to mention fascinating and frightening.

B. A.

Friday, June 11th

AT THREE YEARS OF AGE A LITTLE GIRL SHOULDN'T HAVE enough functioning intelligence to cut out and paste together a Moebius strip.

Or, if she did it by accident, she surely shouldn't have enough reasoning ability to pick up one of her crayons and carefully trace the continuous line to prove it has only one surface.

And if by some strange coincidence she did, and it was still just an accident, how can I account for this generally active daughter of mine—and I do mean *active*—sitting for a solid half hour with her chin cupped in her hand, staring off into space, thinking with such concentration that it was almost painful to watch?

I was in my reading chair, going over some work. Star was sitting on the floor, in the circle of my light, with her blunt-nosed scissors and her scraps of paper.

Her long silence made me glance down at her as she was taping the two ends of the paper together. At that point I thought it was an accident that she had given a half twist to the paper strip before joining the circle. I smiled to myself as she picked it up in her chubby fingers.

"A little child forms the enigma of the ages," I mused.

But instead of throwing the strip aside, or tearing it apart as any other child would do, she carefully turned it over and around—studying it from all sides.

Then she picked up one of her crayons and began tracing the line. She did it as though she were substantiating a conclusion already reached!

It was a bitter confirmation for me. I had been refusing to face it for a long time, but I could ignore it no longer.

Star was a High I.Q.

For half an hour I watched her while she sat on the floor, one knee bent under her, her chin in her hand, unmoving. Her eyes were wide with wonderment, looking into the potentialities of the phenomenon she had found.

It had been a tough struggle, taking care of her since my wife's death. Now this added problem. If only she could have been normally dull, like other children!

I had made up my mind while I watched her. If a child is afflicted, then let's face it, she's afflicted. A parent must teach her to compensate. At least she could be prepared for the bitterness I'd known. She could learn early to take it in stride.

I could use the measurements available, get the degree of intelligence, and in that way grasp the extent of my problem. A twenty-point jump in I.Q. creates an entirely different set of problems. The 140 child lives in a world nothing at all like that of the 100 child and a world which the 120 child can but vaguely sense. The problems which vex and challenge the 160 pass over the 140 as a bird flies over a field mouse. I must not make the mistake of posing the problems of one if she is the other. I must know. In the meantime I must treat it casually.

"That's called the Moebius strip, Star," I interrupted her thoughts.

She came out of her reveries with a start. I didn't like the quick way her eyes sought mine—almost furtively, as though she had been caught doing something bad.

"Somebody already make it?" she disappointedly asked.

She knew what she had discovered! Something inside me

spilled over with grief, and something else caught at me with dread.

I kept my voice casual. "A man by the name of Moebius. A long time ago. I'll tell you about him sometime when you're older."

"Now. While I'm little," she commanded with a frown. "And don't tell. Read me."

What did she mean by that? Oh, she must be simply paraphrasing me at those times in the past when I've wanted the facts and not garbled generalizations. It could only be that!

"Okay, young lady." I lifted an eyebrow and glared at her in mock ferociousness, which usually sent her into gales of laughter. "I'll slow you down!"

She remained completely sober.

I turned to the subject in a physics book. It's not in simple language, by any means, and I read it as I could speak. My thought was to make her admit she didn't understand it, so I could translate it into basic language.

Her reaction?

"You read too slow, Daddy," she complained. She was childishly irritable about it. "You say a word. Then I think a long time. Then you say another word."

I knew what she meant. I remember, when I was a child, my thoughts used to dart in and out among the slowly droning words of any adult. Whole patterns and universes would appear and disappear in those brief moments.

"So?" I asked.

"So," she mocked me impishly. "You teach me to read. Then I can think quick as I want."

"Quickly," I corrected in a weak voice. "The word is 'quickly,' an adverb."

She looked at me impatiently, as if she saw through this allegedly adult device to show up a younger's ignorance. I felt like the dope!

September 1st

A great deal has happened in the past few months. I have tried a number of times to bring the conversation around to discuss Star's affliction with her. But she is amazingly adroit at heading me off, as though she already knows what I am trying to say and isn't concerned. Perhaps, in spite of her brilliance, she's too young to realize the hostility of the world toward intelligence.

Some of the visiting neighbors have been amused to see her sit on the floor with an encyclopedia as big as she is, rapidly turning the pages. Only Star and I know she is reading the pages as rapidly as she can turn them. I've brushed away the neighbors' comments with, "She likes to look at the pictures."

They talk to her in baby talk—and she answers in baby talk! How does she know enough to do that?

I have spent the months making an exhaustive record of her I.Q. measurements, aptitude speeds, reactions, tables, all the recommended paraphernalia for measuring something we know nothing about.

The tables are screwy, or Star is beyond all measurement.

All right, Pete Holmes, how are you going to pose those problems and combat them for her, when you have no conception of what they might be? But I must have a conception. I've got to be able to comprehend at least a little of what she may face. I simply couldn't stand by and do nothing.

Easy, though. Nobody knows better than you the futility of trying to compete out of your class. How many students, workers, and employers have tried to compete with you? You've watched them and pitied them, comparing them to a donkey trying to run the Kentucky Derby.

How does it feel to be in the place of the donkey for a change? You've always blamed them for not realizing they shouldn't try to compete.

But this is *your* own daughter! *I must* understand!

October 1st

Star is now four years old, and according to state law her mind has now developed enough so that she may attend nursery school. Again, I have tried to prepare her for what she might face. She listed through about two sentences and changed the subject. I can't tell about Star. Does she already know the answers? Or does she not even realize there is a problem?

I was in a sweat of worry when I took her to her first day at school yesterday morning. Last night I was sitting in my chair, reading. After she had put her dolls away, she went to the bookshelves and brought down a book of fairy tales.

This is another peculiarity of hers. She has an unmeasurably quick perception, yet she has all of the normal reactions of a little girl. She likes her dolls, fairy stories, playing grown up. No, she's not a monster.

She brought the book of fairy tales over to me.

"Daddy, read me a story," she asked quite seriously.

I looked at her in amazement. "Since when? Go read your own story."

She lifted an eyebrow in imitation of my own characteristic gesture.

"Children of my age do not read," she instructed pedantically. "I can't learn to read until I am in the first grade. It is very hard to do and I am much too little."

She had found the answer to her affliction—conformity! She had already learned to conceal her intelligence. So many of us break our hearts before we learn that.

But you don't have to conceal it from me Star! Not from me!

Oh well, I could go along with the gag, if that was what she wanted.

"Did you like nursery school?" I asked the standard question.

"Oh yes," she exclaimed enthusiastically. "It was fun."

"And what did you learn today, little girl?"

She played it straight back to me. "Not much. I tried to cut out paper dolls, but the scissors kept slipping." Was there an elfin deviltry back of her sober expression?

"Now look," I cautioned, "don't overdo it. That's as bad as being too quick. The idea is that everybody has to be just about standard average. That's the only thing we will tolerate. It is expected that a little girl of four should know how to cut out paper dolls properly."

"Oh?" she questioned, and looked thoughtful. "I guess that's the hard part, isn't it, Daddy—to know how much you ought to know?"

"Yes, that's the hard part," I agreed fervently.

"But it's all right," she reassured me. "One of the Stupids showed me how to cut them out, so now that little girl likes me. She just took charge of me then and told the other kids they should like me too, so of course they did because she's a leader. I think I did right, after all."

"Oh, no!" I breathed to myself. She knew how to manipulate other people already. Then my thoughts whirled around another concept. It was the first time she had verbally classified normal people as "Stupids," but it had slipped out so easily that I knew she'd been thinking to herself for a long time. Then my whirling thoughts hit a third implication.

"Yes, maybe it was the right thing," I conceded. "Where the little girl was concerned, that is. But don't forget you were being observed by a grown-up teacher in the room. And she's smarter."

"You mean she's older, Daddy," Star corrected me.

"Smarter, too, maybe. You can't tell."

"I can." She sighed. "She's just older."

I think it was growing fear which made me defensive.

"That's good," I said emphatically. "That's very good. You can learn a lot from her then. It takes an awful lot of study to learn how to be stupid."

My own troublesome business life came to mind and I thought to myself, "I sometimes think I'll never learn it."

I swear I didn't say it aloud. But Star patted me consolingly and answered as though I'd spoken.

"That's because you're only fairly bright, Daddy. You're a Tween, and that's harder than being really bright."

"A Tween? What's a Tween?" I was bumbling to hide my confusion.

"That's what I mean, Daddy," she answered in exasperation. "You don't grasp quickly. An In Between, of course. The other people are Stupids, I'm a Bright, and you're a Tween. I made those names up when I was little."

Good God! Besides being unmeasurably bright, she's a telepath!

All right Pete, there you are. On reasoning processes you might stand a chance—but not in telepathy!

"Star," I said on impulse, "can you read people's minds?"

"Of course, Daddy," she answered, as if I'd asked a foolishly obvious question.

"Can you teach me?"

She looked at me impishly. "You're already learning it a little. But you're so slow! You see, you didn't even know you were learning."

Her voice took on a wistful note, a tone of loneliness.

"I wish—" she said and paused.

"What do you wish?"

"You see what I mean, Daddy? You try, but you're so slow."

All the same, I knew. I knew she was already longing for a companion whose mind could match her own.

A father is prepared to lose his daughter eventually, Star, but not so soon.

Not so soon . . .

June again

Some new people have moved in next door. Star says their name is Howell—Bill and Ruth Howell. They have a son, Robert, who looks maybe a year older than Star, who will soon be five.

Star seems to have taken up with Robert right away. He is a well-mannered boy and good company for Star.

I'm worried, though. Star had something to do with their moving in next door. I'm convinced of that. I'm also convinced, even from the little I've seen of him, that Robert is a Bright and a telepath.

Could it be that, failing to find quick accord with my mind, Star has reached out and out until she made contact with a telepath companion?

No, that's too fantastic. Even if it were so, how could she shape circumstances so she could bring Robert to live next door to her? The Howells came from another city. It just happened that the people who lived next door moved out and the house was put up for sale.

Just happened? How frequently do we find such abnormal Brights? What are the chances of one *just happening* to move in next door to another?

I know he is a telepath because, as I write this, I sense him reading it.

I even catch his thought. "Oh, pardon me, Mr. Holmes. I didn't intend to peek. Really, I didn't."

Did I imagine that? Or is Star building a skill in my mind?

"It isn't nice to look into another person's mind unless you're asked, Robert," I thought back, rather severely. It was purely an experiment.

"I know it, Mr. Holmes. I apologize." He is in bed in his house, across the driveway.

"No, Daddy, he really didn't mean to." And Star is in her bed in this house.

It is impossible to write how I feel. There comes a time when words are empty husks. But mixed with my expectant dread is a thread of gratitude for having been taught to be even stumblingly telepathic.

Saturday, August 11th

I've thought of a gag. I haven't seen Jim Pietre in a month of Sundays, not since he was awarded a research fellowship with the museum. It will be good to pull him out of his hole, and this little piece of advertising junk Star dropped should be just the thing.

Strange about the gadget. The Awful Secret Talisman of the Mystic Junior G-Men, no doubt. Still, it doesn't have anything about crackles and pops printed on it. Merely an odd-looking coin, not even true round, bronze by the look of it. Crude. They must stamp them out by the million without ever changing a die.

But it is just the thing to send to Jim to get a rise out of him. He always could appreciate a good practical joke. Wonder how he'd feel to know he was only a Tween.

Monday, August 13th

Sitting here at my study desk, I've been staring into space for an hour. I don't know what to think.

It was about noon today when Jim Pietre called the office on the phone.

"Now, look, Pete," he started out. "What kind of gag are you pulling?"

I chortled to myself and pulled the dead pan on him.

"What do you mean, boy?" I asked back into the phone. "Gag? What kind of gag? What are you talking about?"

"A coin. A coin." He was impatient. "You remember you sent me a coin in the mail?"

"Oh yeah, that." I pretended to remember. "Look, you're an important research analyst on metals—too damned important to keep in touch with your old friends—so I thought I'd make a bid for your attention thataway."

"All right, give," he said in a low voice. "Where did you get it?" He was serious.

"Come off it, Jim. Are you practicing to be a stuffed shirt? I admit it's a rib. Something Star dropped the other day. A man-ufacturer's idea of kid advertising, no doubt."

"I'm in dead earnest, Peter," he answered. "It's no advertising gadget."

"It means something?"

In college Jim could take a practical joke and make six out of it.

"I don't know what it means. Where did Star get it?" He was being pretty crisp about it.

"Oh, I don't know," I said. I was getting a little fed up; the joke wasn't going according to plan. "Never asked her. You know how kids clutter up the place with their things. No father even tries to keep track of all the junk that can be bought with three box tops and a dime."

"This was not bought with three box tops and a dime." He spaced his words evenly. "This was not bought anywhere, for any price. In fact, if you want to be logical about it, this coin doesn't exist at all."

I laughed out loud. This was more like the old Jim.

"Okay, so you've turned the gag back on me. Let's call it quits. How about coming over to supper some night soon?"

"I'm coming over, my friend." He remained grim as he said it. "And I'm coming over tonight. As soon as you will be home. It's no gag I'm pulling. Can you get that through your stubborn head? You say you got it from Star, and of course I believe you. But it's no toy. It's the real thing." Then, as if in profound puzzlement, "Only it isn't."

A feeling of dread was settling upon me. Once you cried "Uncle" to Jim, he always let up.

"Suppose you tell me what you mean," I answered soberly.

"That's more like it, Pete. Here's what we know about the coin so far. It is apparently pre-Egyptian. It's hand-cast. It's made out of one of the lost bronzes. We fix it at around four thousand years old."

"That ought to be easy to solve," I argued. "Probably some coin collector is screaming all over the place for it. No doubt lost it and Star found it. Must be lots of old coins like that in museums and in private collections."

I was rationalizing more for my own benefit than for Jim. He would know all those things without mentioning them. He waited until I had finished.

"Step two," he went on. "We've got one of the top coin men in the world here at the museum. As soon as I saw what the metal was, I took it to him. Now hold on to your chair, Pete. He says there is no coin like it in the world, either in a museum or private collection.

"You museum boys get beside yourselves at times. Come down to earth. Sometime, somewhere, some collector picked it up in some exotic place and kept it quiet. I don't have to tell you how some collectors are—sitting in a dark room, gloating over some worthless bauble, not telling a soul about it—"

"All right, wise guy," he interrupted. "Step three. That coin is at least four thousand years old, *and it's also brand-new!* Let's hear you explain that away."

"New?" I asked weakly. "I don't get it."

"Old coins show wear. The edges get rounded with handling. The surface oxidizes. The molecular structure changes, crystallizes. This coin shows no wear, no oxidation, no molecular change. This coin might have been struck yesterday. *Where did Star get it?*"

"Hold it a minute," I pleaded.

I began to think back. Saturday morning. Star and Robert had been playing a game. Come to think of it, that was a peculiar game. Mighty peculiar.

Star would run into the house and stand in front of the encyclopedia shelf. I could hear Robert counting loudly at the base tree outside in the backyard. She would stare at the encyclopedia for a moment.

Once I heard her mumble, "That's a good place."

Or maybe she merely thought it and I caught the thought. I'm doing quite a bit of that of late.

Then she would run outside again. A moment later Robert would run in and stand in front of the same shelf. Then he also would run outside again. There would be silence for several minutes. The silence would rupture with a burst of laughing and shouting. Soon Star would come in again.

"How does he find me?" I heard her think once. "I can't reason it, and I can't ESP it out of him."

It was during one of their silences when Ruth called over to me.

"Hey, Pete! Do you know where the kids are? Time for their milk and cookies."

The Howells are awfully good to Star, bless 'em. I got up and went over to the window.

"I don't know, Ruth," I called back. "They were in and out only a few minutes ago."

"Well, I'm worried," she said. She came through the kitchen door and stood on the back steps. "They know better than to cross the street by themselves. They're too young for that. So I guess they're over at Marily's. When they come back, tell 'em to come and get it.''

"Okay, Ruth," I answered.

She opened the screen door again and went back into her kitchen. I left the window and returned to my work.

A little later both the kids came running into the house. I managed to capture them long enough to tell them about the cookies and milk.

"Beat you there!" Robert shouted to Star.

There was a scuffle and they ran out the front door. I noticed then that Star had dropped the coin and I picked it up and sent it to Jim Pietre.

■　■　■

"Hello, Jim," I said into the phone. "Are you still there?"

"Yep, still waiting for an answer," he said.

"Jim, I think you'd better come over to the house right away. I'll leave my office now and meet you there. Can you get away?"

"Can I get away?" he exclaimed. "Boss says to trace this coin down and do nothing else. See you in fifteen minutes."

He hung up. Thoughtfully I replaced the receiver and went out to my car. I was pulling into my block from one arterial when I saw Jim's car pulling in from a block away. I stopped at the curb and waited for him. I didn't see the kids anywhere out front.

Jim climbed out of his car, and I never saw such an eager look of anticipation on a man's face before. I didn't realize I was showing my dread, but when he saw my face he became serious.

"What is it, Pete? What on earth is it?" he almost whispered.

"I don't know. At least I'm not sure. Come on inside the house."

We let ourselves in the front, and I took Jim into the study. It has a large window opening on the back garden, and the scene was very clear.

At first it was an innocent scene—so innocent and peaceful. Just three children in the backyard playing hide-and-seek. Marily, a neighbor's child, was stepping up to the base tree.

"Now look, you kids," she was saying. "You hide where I can find you or I won't play."

"But where can we go, Marily?" Robert was arguing loudly. Like all little boys, he seems to carry on his conversations at the top of his lungs. "There's no garage, and there's those trees and bushes. You have to look everywhere, Marily."

"And there's going to be other buildings and trees and bushes there afterward," Star called out with glee. "You gotta look behind them too."

"Yeah!" Robert took up the teasing refrain. "And there's been lots and lots of buildings and trees there before—especially trees. You gotta look behind them too."

Marily tossed her head petulantly. "I don't know what you're talking about, and I don't care. Just hide where I can find you, that's all."

She hid her face at the tree and started counting. If I had been alone, I would have been sure my eyesight had failed me or that I was the victim of hallucinations. But Jim was standing there and saw it too.

Marily started counting, yet the other two didn't run away. Star reached out and took Robert's hand and they merely stood there. For an instant they seemed to shimmer and—*they disappeared without moving a step!*

Marily finished her counting and ran around to the few possible hiding places in the yard. When she couldn't find them, she started to blubber and pushed through the hedge to Ruth's back door.

"They runned away from me again," she whined through the screen at Ruth.

Jim and I stood staring out the window. I glanced at him. His face was set and pale, but probably no worse than my own.

We saw the instant shimmer again. Star, and then immediately Robert, materialized from the air and ran up to the tree, shouting, "Safe! Safe!"

Marily let out a bawl and ran home to her mother.

I called Star and Robert into the house. They came, still holding hands, and little shamefaced but defiant.

How to begin? What in hell could I say?

"It's not exactly fair," I told them. "Marily can't follow you there." I was shooting in the dark, but I had at least a glimmering to go by.

Star turned pale enough for the freckles on her little nose to stand out under her tan. Robert blushed and turned to her fiercely.

"I told you so, Star. I *told* you so! I said it wasn't sporting," he accused. He turned to me. "Marily can't play a good hide-and-seek anyway. She's only a Stupid."

"Let's forget that for a minute, Robert," I turned to her. "Star, just where do you go?"

"Oh, it's nothing, Daddy." She spoke defensively, belittling the whole thing. "We just go a little ways when we play with her. She ought to be able to find us a little ways."

"That's evading the issue. *Where* do you go—and *how* do you go?"

Jim stepped forward and showed her the bronze coin I'd sent him.

"You see, Star," he said quietly. "We've found this."

"I shouldn't have to tell you my game." She was almost in tears. "You're both just Tweens. You couldn't understand." Then, struck by contrition, she turned to me. "Daddy, I've tried and tried to ESP you. Truly I did. But you don't ESP worth anything." She slipped her hand through Robert's arm. "Robert does it very nicely," she said primly, as though she were complimenting him on using his fork the right way. "He must be better than I am, because I don't know how he finds me."

"I'll tell you how I do it, Star," Robert exclaimed eagerly. It was as if he were trying to make amends now that grownups had caught on. "You don't use any imagination. I never saw anybody with so little imagination!"

"I do, too, have imagination," she countered loudly. "I thought up the game, didn't I? I told you how to do it, didn't I?"

"Yeah, yeah!" he shouted back. "But you always have to look at a book to ESP what's in it, so you leave an ESP smudge. I just go to the encyclopedia and ESP where you did—and I go to that place—and there you are. It's simple."

Star's mouth dropped open in consternation.

"I never thought of that," she said.

Jim and I stood there, letting the meaning of what they were saying penetrate slowly into our incredulous minds.

"Anyway," Robert was saying, "you haven't any imagination." He sank down cross-legged on the floor. "You can't teleport yourself to any place that's never been."

She went over to squat down beside him. "I can too! What about the moon people? They haven't been yet."

He looked at her with childish disgust.

"Oh, Star, they have so been. You know that." He spread his hands out as though he were a baseball referee. "That time hasn't been yet for your daddy here, for instance, but it's already been for somebody like—well, say, like those from Arcturus."

"Well, neither have you teleported yourself to some place that never was." Star was arguing back. "So there."

Waving Jim to one chair, I sank down shakily into another. At least the arms of the chair felt solid beneath my hands.

"Now, look, kids," I interrupted their evasive tactics. "Let's start at the beginning. I gather you've figured out a way to travel to places in the past or future."

"Well, of course, Daddy." Star shrugged the statement aside nonchalantly. "We just TP ourselves by ESP anywhere we want to go. It doesn't do any harm."

And these were the children who were too little to cross the street!

I have been through times of shock before. This was the same—somehow the mind becomes too stunned to react beyond a point. One simply plows through the rest the best he can, almost normally.

"Okay, okay," I said, and was surprised to hear the same tone I would have used over an argument about the biggest piece of cake. "I don't know whether it's harmful or not. I'll have to think it over. Right now just tell me how you do it."

"It would be much easier if I could ESP it to you," Star said doubtfully.

"Well, pretend I'm a Stupid and tell me in words."

"You remember the Moebius strip?" she asked very slowly and carefully, starting with the first and most basic point in almost the way one explains to an ordinary child.

Yes, I remembered it. And I remembered how long ago it was that she had discovered it. Over a year, and her busy, brilliant mind had been exploring its possibilities ever since. And I thought she had forgotten it!

"That's where you join the ends of a strip of paper together with a half twist to make one surface," she went on, as though jogging my undependable, slow memory.

"Yes," I answered. "We all know the Moebius strip."

Jim looked startled. I had never told him about the incident.

"Next you take a sheet and you give it a half twist and join the edge to itself all over to make a funny kind of holder."

"Klein's bottle," Jim supplied.

She looked at him in relief.

"Oh, you know about that," she said. "That makes it easier. Well, then, the next step—you take a cube." Her face clouded with doubt again, as she explained, "You can't do this with your hands. You've gotta ESP it done, because it's an imaginary cube anyway."

She looked at us questioningly. I nodded for her to continue.

"And you ESP the twisted cube all together the same way you did Klein's bottle. Now if you do that big enough, all around you, so you're sort of half-twisted in the middle, then you can TP yourself anywhere you want to go. And that's all there is to it," she finished hurriedly.

"Where have you gone?" I asked her quietly.

The technique of doing it would take some thinking. I knew enough about physics to know that was the way the dimensions were built up. The line, the plane, the cube—Euclidian physics. The Moebius strip, the Klein bottle, the unnamed twisted cube—Einsteinian physics. Yes, it was possible.

"Oh, we've gone all over," Star answered vaguely. "The Romans and the Egyptians—places like that."

"You picked up a coin in one of those places?" Jim asked.

He was doing a good job of keeping his voice casual. I knew the excitement he must be feeling, the vision of the wealth of knowledge which must be opening before his eyes.

"I found it, Daddy," Star answered Jim's question. She was about to cry. "I found it in the dirt, and Robert was about to catch me. I forgot I had it when I went away from there so fast." She looked at me pleadingly. "I didn't mean to steal it, Daddy. I never stole anything, anywhere. And I was going to take it back and put it right where I found it. Truly I was. But I dropped it again, and then I ESP'd that you had it. I guess I was awful naughty."

I brushed my hand across my forehead.

"Let's skip the question of good and bad for a minute," I said, my head throbbing. "What about this business of going into the future?"

Robert spoke up, his eyes shining. "There isn't any future, Mr. Holmes. That's what I keep telling Star, but she can't reason—she's just a girl. It'll all pass. Everything is always past."

Jim stared at him, as though thunderstruck, and opened his mouth in protest. I shook my head warningly.

"Suppose you tell me about that, Robert," I said.

"Well," he began on a rising note, frowning, "it's kinda hard to explain at that. Star's a Bright and even she doesn't understand

it exactly. But, you see, I'm older.'' He looked at her with supe-
riority. Then, with a change of mood, he defended her. ''But
when she gets as old as I am, she'll understand it okay.''

He patted her shoulder consolingly. He was all of six years old.

''You go back into the past. Back past Egypt and Atlantis. That's
recent,'' he said with scorn. ''And on back, and on back, and all
of a sudden it's future.''

''That isn't the way *I* did it.'' Star tossed her head contrarily.
''I *reasoned* the future. I reasoned what would come next, and I
went there, and then I reasoned again. And on and on. I can,
too, reason.''

''It's the same future,'' Robert told us dogmatically. ''It has to
be, because that's all that ever happened.'' He turned to Star.
''The reason you could never find any Garden of Eden is because
there wasn't any Adam and Eve.'' Then to me, ''And man didn't
come from the apes, either. Man started himself.''

Jim almost strangled as he leaned forward, his face red and his
eyes bulging.

''How?'' he choked out.

Robert sent his gaze into the far distance.

''Well,'' he said, ''a long time from now—you know what I
mean, as a Stupid would think of Time-From-Now—men got into
a mess. Quite a mess . . .

''There were some people in that time who figured out the
same kind of traveling that Star and I do. So when the world was
about to blow up and form a new star, a lot of them teleported
themselves back to when the earth was young, and they started
over again.''

Jim just stared at Robert, unable to speak.

''I don't get it,'' I said.

''Not everybody could do it,'' Robert explained patiently. ''Just
a few Brights. But they enclosed a lot of other people and took
them along.'' He became a little vague at this point. ''I guess later
on the Brights lost interest in the Stupids or something. Anyway,
the Stupids sank down lower and lower and became like animals.''
He held his nose briefly. ''They smelled worse. They worshipped
the Brights as gods.''

Robert looked at me and shrugged.

''I don't know all that happened. I've only been there a few
times. It's not very interesting. Anyway,'' he finished, ''the Brights
finally disappeared.''

"I'd sure like to know where they went," Star sighed. It was a lonely sigh. I helplessly took her hand and gave my attention back to Robert.

"I still don't quite understand," I said.

He grabbed up some scissors, a piece of cellophane tape, a sheet of paper. Quickly, he cut a strip, gave it a half twist and taped it together. Then rapidly, on the Moebius strip, he wrote: "Cave Men, This Men, That Men, Mu Men, Atlantis Men, Egyptians, History Men, Is Now Men, Atom Men, Moon Men, Planet Men, Star Men."

"There," he said. "That's all the room there is on the strip. I've written clear around it. Right after Star Men comes Cave Men. It's all one thing, joined together. It isn't future, and it isn't past, either. It just plain *is*. Don't you see?"

"I'd sure like to know how the Brights got off the strip," Star said wistfully.

I had all I could take.

"Look, kids," I pleaded. "I don't know whether this game's dangerous or not. Maybe you'll wind up in a lion's mouth or something."

"Oh no, Daddy!" Star shrilled in glee. "We'd just TP ourselves right out of there."

"But fast," Robert chortled in agreement.

"Anyway, I've got to think it over," I said stubbornly. "I'm only a Tween, but Star, I'm your daddy and you're just a little girl, so you have to mind me."

"I always mind you," she said virtuously.

"You do, eh?" I asked. "What about going off the block? Visiting the Greeks and Star Men isn't my idea of staying on the block."

"But you didn't say that, Daddy. You said not to cross the street. And I never did cross the street. Did we, Robert? Did we?"

"We didn't cross a single street, Mr. Holmes," he insisted.

"My God!" said Jim, and he went on trying to light a cigarette.

"All right, all *right!* No more leaving this time, then," I warned.

"Wait!" It was a cry of anguish from Jim. He broke the cigarette in sudden frustration and threw it in an ash tray. "The museum, Pete," he pleaded. "Think what it would mean. Pictures, specimens, voice recordings. And not only from historical places, but Star Men, Pete. *Star Men!* Wouldn't it be all right for them to go places they know are safe? I wouldn't ask them to take risks, but—"

"No, Jim," I said regretfully. "It's your museum, but this is my daughter."

"Sure," he breathed. "I guess I'd feel the same way."

I turned back to the youngsters.

"Star, Robert,"I said to them both, "I want you to promise that you will not leave this time until I let you. Now I couldn't punish you if you broke your promise, because I couldn't follow you. But I want your promise on your word of honor you won't leave this time."

"We promise." They each held up a hand, as if swearing in court. "No leaving this time."

I let the kids go back outside into the yard. Jim and I looked at one another for a long while, breathing hard enough to have been running.

"I'm sorry," I said at last.

"I know," he answered. "So am I. But I don't blame you. I simply forgot, for a moment, how much a daughter can mean to a man." He was silent and then added, with the humorous quirk back at the corner of his lips, "I can just see myself reporting this interview to the museum."

"You don't intend to, do you?" I asked, alarmed.

"And get myself canned or laughed at? I'm not that stupid."

September 10th

Am I actually getting it? I had a flash for an instant. I was concentrating on Caesar's triumphant march into Rome. For the briefest of instants *there it was!* I was standing on the roadway, watching. But most peculiar, it was still a picture; I was the only thing moving. And then, just as abruptly, I lost it.

Was it only a hallucination? Something brought about by intense concentration and wishful thinking?

Now let's see. You visualize a cube. Then you ESP it a half twist and seal the edges together. You seal that surface all around you . . .

Sometimes I think I have it. Sometimes I despair. If only I were a Bright instead of a Tween!

October 23rd

I don't see how I managed to make so much work of teleporting myself. It's the simplest thing in the world, no effort at all.

Why, a child could do it! That sounds like a gag, considering that it was two children who showed me how, but I mean the whole thing is easy enough for almost any kid to learn. The problem is understanding the steps . . . no, not understanding, because I can't say I do, but working out the steps in the process.

There's no danger, either. No wonder it felt like a still picture at first, for the speeding up is incredible. That bullet I got in the way of, for instance—I was able to go and meet it and walk along beside it while it traveled through the air. To the men who were dueling I must have been no more than an instantaneous streak of movement.

That's why the youngsters laughed at the suggestion of danger. Even if they materialized right in the middle of an atomic blast, it is so slow by comparison that they could TP right out again before they got hurt. The blast can't travel any faster than the speed of light, you see, while there is no limit to the speed of thought.

But I still haven't given them permission to teleport themselves out of this time yet. I want to go over the ages pretty carefully before I do; I'm not taking any chances, even though I don't see how they could wind up in any trouble. Still, Robert claimed the Brights went from the future back into the beginning, which means they could be going through time and overtake any of the three of us, and one of them might be hostile . . .

I feel like a louse, not taking Jim's cameras, specimen boxes, and recorders along. But there's time for that. Plenty of time, once I get the feel of history without being encumbered by all that stuff to carry.

Speaking of time and history—what a rotten job historians have done! For instance:

George III of England was neither crazy nor a moron. He wasn't a particularly nice guy, I'll admit—I don't see how anybody could be with the amount of flattery I saw—but he was the victim of empire expansion and the ferment of the Industrial Revolution. So were all the other European rulers at the time, though he certainly did better than Louis of France. At least George kept his job and his head.

On the other hand, John Wilkes Booth was definitely psychotic. He could have been cured if they'd had our methods of psychotherapy then, and Lincoln, of course, wouldn't have been assassinated. It was almost a compulsion to prevent the killing, but I didn't dare . . . God knows what effect it would have had on history. Strange thing, Lincoln looked less surprised than anybody else when he was shot—sad, yes, and hurt emotionally, at least as much as physically, yet you'd swear he was expecting it.

Cheops was *plenty* worried about the number of slaves who died while the pyramid was being built. They weren't easy to replace. He gave them four hours off in the hottest part of the day, and I don't think any slaves in the country were fed or housed better.

I never found any signs of Atlantis or Lemuria, just tales of lands far off—a few hundred miles was a big distance then, remember—that had sunk beneath the sea. With the Ancients exaggerated notion of geography a big island was the same as a continent. Some islands did disappear, naturally, drowning a few thousand villages and herdsmen. That must have been the source of the legends.

Columbus was a stubborn cuss. He was thinking of turning back when the sailors mutinied, which made him obstinate. I still can't see what was eating Genghis Khan and Alexander the Great—it would have been a big help to learn the languages, because their big campaigns started off more like vacation or exploration trips. Helen of Troy was attractive enough, considering, but she was just an excuse to fight.

There were several attempts to federate the Indian tribes before the white man and the Five Nations, but going after wives and slaves ruined the movement every time. I think they could have kept America if they had been united and, it goes without saying, knew the deal they were going to get. At any rate, they might have traded for weapons and tools and industrialized the country somewhat in the way the Japanese did. I admit that's only speculation, but this would certainly have been a different world if they'd succeeded!

One day I'll put it all in a comprehensive and *corrected* history of mankind, *complete with photographs*, and then let the "experts" argue themselves into nervous breakdowns over it.

I didn't get very far into the future. Nowhere near the Star Men or, for that matter, back to the beginning that Robert told us about. It's a matter of reasoning out the path and I'm not a Bright. I'll take Robert and Star along as guides, when and if.

What I did see of the future wasn't so good, but it wasn't so bad either. The real mess obviously doesn't happen until the Star Men show up very far ahead in history, if Robert is right, and I think he is. I can't guess what the trouble will be, but it must be something ghastly if they won't be able to get out of it even with the enormously advanced technology they'll have. Or maybe that's the answer. It's almost true of us now.

Friday, November 14th

The Howells have gone for a weekend trip and left Robert in my care. He's a good kid and no trouble. He and Star have kept their promise, but they're up to something else. I can sense it, and that feeling of expectant dread is back with me.

They've been secretive of late. I catch them concentrating intensely, sighing with vexation, and then breaking out into unexplained giggles.

"Remember your promise," I warned Star while Robert was in the room.

"We're not going to break it, Daddy," she answered seriously.

They both chorused, "No more leaving this time."

But they both broke into giggles!

I'll have to watch them. What good it would do, I don't know. They're up to something, yet how can I stop them? Shut them in their rooms? Tan their hides?

I wonder what someone else would recommend.

Sunday night

The kids are gone!

I've been waiting an hour for them. I know they wouldn't stay away so long if they could get back. There must be something they've run into. Bright as they are, they're still only children.

I have some clues. They promised me they wouldn't go out of this present time. With all her mischievousness, Star has never broken a promise to me—as her typically feminine mind interprets it, that is. So I know they are in our own time.

On several occasions Star has brought it up, wondering where the Old Ones, the Bright Ones, have gone—how they got off the Moebius strip.

That's a clue. How can I get off the Moebius strip and remain in the present?

A cube won't do it. There we have a mere journey along the single surface. We have a line; we have a plane; we have a cube.

And then we have a supercube—a tesseract. That is the logical progression of mathematics. The Bright Ones must have pursued that line of reasoning.

Now I've got to do the same, but without the advantage of being a Bright. Still, it's not the same as expecting a normally intelligent person to produce a work of genius. (Genius by our standards, of course, which I suppose Robert and Star would classify as Tween.) Anyone with a pretty fair I.Q. and proper education and training can follow a genius' logic, provided the steps are there and especially if it has a practical application. What he can't do is initiate and complete that structure of logic. I don't have to—that was done for me by a pair of Brights, and I "simply" have to apply their findings.

Now let's see if I can.

Be reducing the present-past-future of a man to a Moebius strip, we have sheared away a dimension. It is a two-dimensional strip, because it has no depth. (Naturally it would be impossible for a Moebius strip to have depth; it only has one surface.)

Reducing it to two dimensions makes it possible to travel anywhere you want to go on it via the third dimension. And you're in the third dimension when you enfold yourself in the twisted cube.

Let's go a step higher, into one more dimension. In short, the tesseract. To get the equivalent of a Moebius strip with depth you have to go into the fourth dimension, which, it seems to me, is the only way the Bright Ones could get off this closed cycle of past-present-future-past. They must have reasoned that one more notch up the dimensions was all they needed. It is equally obvious that Star and Robert have followed the same line of reasoning; they wouldn't break their promise not to leave the present—and getting off the Moebius strip into *another* present world, is a sort of devious way, to keep that promise.

I'm putting all this speculation down for you, Jim Pietre, knowing first that you're a Tween like myself and, second, that you're sure to have been doing a lot of thinking about what happened after I sent you the coin Star dropped. I'm hoping you can explain all this to Bill and Ruth Howell—or enough, in any case, to let them understand the truth about their son, Robert, and my daughter, Star, and where the children may have gone.

I'm leaving these notes where you will find them, when you and Bill and Ruth search the house and grounds for us. If you read this, it will be because I have failed in my search for the youngsters. There is also the possibility that I'll find them and that we won't be able to get back onto this Moebius strip. Perhaps time has different value there or doesn't exist at all. What it's like off the strip is anybody's guess.

Bill and Ruth: I wish I could give you hope that I will bring Robert back to you. But all I can do is wish. It may be no more than wishing upon a star—my Star.

I'm trying now to take six cubes and fold them in on one another so that every angle is a right angle.

It's not easy, but I can do it, using every bit of concentration I've learned from the kids. All right, I have six cubes and I have every angle a right angle.

Now if, in the folding, I ESP the tesseract a half twist around myself and—

Bill Adler, Jr.

The Last Two Days
of Larry Joseph's Life—
In This Time, Anyway
1988

Exactly what connects us to time? Why do we move through time in one direction only—forward? If time is like a river, what prevents different individuals from moving through time at different rates, just as several different twigs might move through the same river at different speeds? Sometimes twigs get caught in whirls of water, and even move backward, up the river, for a short distance. The answer, of course, is that time isn't really like a river at all. Or is it? In "The Last Two Days of Larry Joseph's Life—In This Time, Anyway," *we find all that may be needed to travel in time, is a lack of interest in the time in which you are currently existing—and that time's lack of interest in you.*

B. A.

First Day

"HEY LARRY, YOU COMING?"

"Coming? Coming where?"

Lucy put her hands on her hips. She cocked her head to the left, as if emptying an ear of water. Lucy pointed to the invitation, a rag-tag Xeroxed sheet attached to the refrigerator door with a fake sushi-styled magnet, walked over to the paper and tapped it three times with her finger. "The party, Larry. The party." Lucy opened the fridge and scanned its contents. With equal unawareness she closed it. "What do you say? It should be fun."

She scanned Larry's clothes for a second and wondered who gave Larry his basic lessons in laundry. Certainly not his mother. Great pants—or at least they were—curry-colored with crisp pleats, cotton cool enough to give legs some comfort during Washington, D.C.'s summertime sauna, even finely cut. But why did Larry put them in the dryer? Jeez, everyone knows what hap-

62

pens when you put cotton clothing in the dryer with no intention of ironing it. Oh well, it doesn't seem to bother Larry, so it shouldn't bother me. Lucy smiled. "You're coming, right?"

"I'm not sure. I don't know anybody there."

"What are you going to do instead?"

Larry's face retained the same expression it had held for the past few minutes. Lucy wondered if his face changed at all. Was the mold set? Would it break, crumble into dust if she tried to recast it, to change some of its essential features? There are ways to coax people to change, she admitted to herself. But the steps are difficult and dangerous, especially living in such close quarters, the three of us in this house; too risky for me and for Jim if my suggestions go awry. But what am I thinking? A person's not clay, not paper, not computer parts (though she had more than a couple of doubts about some of the people in college who had asked her out). A person's a person, and Larry has a debilitating shyness—a problem—and perhaps I can help him overcome it. Parties help.

"Maybe read," Larry responded.

"No, you have to come. I don't know anybody there, either. They're Jim's friends. But it doesn't matter whether you know anybody—I'm sure we'll meet some people." Standard reasoning, she knew. "Besides," Lucy said, as she let a smile leak out of the corner of her mouth, "who will I have to talk with if Jim doesn't arrive till late?" Lucy scanned her clothes in the hallway mirror as she talked with Larry. Her eyes went from her shoes to her waist, and all the way up. She lost her concentration for a moment as Larry seemed to fade momentarily—or was it a light bulb that needed replacing?

"Well . . ." Larry's spine arched a few more degrees forward in gravity's favor; gravity seemed to claim responsibility for his posture.

"You'll have a good time! You might even find a date." But Larry, you've got to try, you've got to try, Lucy said to herself.

"All right. All right."

"Great! We should take off in about an hour." Lucy tapped on the crystal of Larry's Seiko watch. She and her other housemate, Jim, had gotten it for Larry for his birthday, in the hope of coaxing Larry to learn how to be on time. "Mind if I shower first?"

"Go ahead. I don't need to shower."

Lucy stepped back and recalled one absolute truth: In Wash-

ington, in August, the location on earth most similar to the surface of the planet Venus, everyone needs to shower. Shower and
drink diet soda. Only cab drivers and Larry went for days without
showering, Lucy thought. Larry would be a whole lot better off if
he showered. "Okay, I'll try to be swift," Lucy said. "You'll be
ready in thirty minutes, okay?" As she turned to bolt up the stairs,
she caught a glimpse of the late afternoon sunlight streaming
through Larry. Or so it seemed. Must be hotter than I thought,
Lucy said to herself.

■ ■ ■

"Your car or cab?" Lucy asked as she emptied some cash and a
single credit card from her wallet, placing these potential essen-
tials in her back pocket. She anxiously tugged the door knob.
"On second thought, we'd better drive. I thought you were going
to be ready in half an hour. It took you nearly an hour. And you
didn't really have anything to do to get ready."

"Sorry, Lucy." Larry's cheeks stretched apart in an apology. "I
didn't mean to be late. My watch said that only half an hour had
passed. I swear it was 7pm on the dot when you asked me, and
now it's only 7:30pm." Larry pointed to his watch. "Engmaghrr,"
Larry said as he lifted his shoulders and swayed them side to side.

"What?"

Larry replied, "I said it's only 7:30pm."

"Larry, you grunted."

"I don't think so."

"Well, it's 8pm anyway." Lucy checked her watch, then, reflex-
ively, her clothes in the mirror. "But that's okay, I guess. The
party's not going to get rolling until after 9 o'clock. But maybe
you should take that watch to a jeweler. Your birthday was only
two months ago—it should be keeping perfect time."

Larry looked at his watch and shrugged. He wiped the sweat
on his forehead leaving fresh newsprint from his fingers. "I'll
drive," Larry said. "Grungga," he muttered to himself.

Did he just grunt again? Lucy thought. Is this going to be another habit we're going to have to put up with?

"Fine, I think Jim's taking the Metro over anyway. If you get
lucky at the party, Jim and I can always take a taxi back." She
grinned at the idea. Lucy glanced at her shirt, tracing a path along
the pants which hugged her waist. Yes, I look good—sexy—Lucy
thought. Too bad I have to wait until I'm at the party for somebody to appreciate the work I've put into making myself a splash.

"Damn. I left my keys upstairs."

"Hey Larry, tuck your shirt in!" she shouted. Buy a new shirt, she thought.

"Okay, thanks."

The drive over was uneventful, which, Lucy acknowledged, is usually the best outcome for any automobile ride. Just a little lethargic, like a tour bus meandering by the nation's monuments. Lucy usually didn't mind driving with Larry, but wished that she didn't always have to ask him to roll his window down. Larry seemed to enjoy not having air conditioning, but Lucy hated to arrive at a party all sweaty.

Lucy quickly surveyed the apartment before looking for Jim. She located him by the food table on the far side of somebody's living room. His iridescent fish shirt was unbuttoned two buttons. Jim's shoulders stood square, and his dark, black hair seemed to sway gently. Lucy could smell faint wisps of Kouros cologne as she approached. "Hi Jim. How's the party?"

"Party's not bad. Great stuff to eat and the drinks are plentiful. Here, try one of these," he said, the sentence's last few words captured by the cheese puff that Jim had stuffed into his mouth. "Here," he said again, his fingers carrying a puff directly into Lucy's mouth. "Ymmm. Here, Larry, try one."

Larry did. "Good. Enghmm. Ugaraha."

Lucy rubbed her ear, as if that would make what Larry said clearer. Lucy faced Jim. Larry stood a couple of feet to her right. "Jim, who are your friends, the ones giving this party?" Lucy wanted to know. She thought (imagined?) she might have seen Larry nod.

"Deirdre and Debbie. They share this apartment. Over there. I'll introduce you."

"Later. I don't need to meet women at the moment. I'll mingle for a bit and then scoot back and you can introduce me." Lucy waved her brown hair from side to side and pushed her chest forward slightly. Perhaps unconsciously, but Jim noticed. So did two guys on the other side of the room. "Do you mind?"

"Of course not," Jim said. "We inhabit the same house, but that doesn't mean we have to move like a chain gang." With that Lucy wiggled off in the direction of the prime party spot, the kitchen.

"Over here, Larry," Jim said. "I'll introduce you to Deirdre and Debbie."

"Okay," Larry said.

Jim looked at Larry and noticed no quirky eye movements, the kind he could never restrain when on his way to meet attractive opposites. Jim introduced Larry as his brilliant housemate, the star of the General Accounting Office's science division, witty individual, and a nice guy in his own right. Besides D&D, there were two other women and two men in this bunch, so Jim felt fine leaving Larry on his own. Jim noticed that Larry seemed a little pale, almost translucent. Maybe Larry's a little under the weather, and that's why he's not in the swing of things. No, Larry's always kind of drowsy, but never this visibly washed out. Well, I've done all I can; at least he'll have something to do.

He caught Lucy between flirts. "Having a good time?"

"Uh huh. And you?"

"So-so. I'm not in an overly prowling mood."

"Sure you're not."

"Well at least Larry seems to be enjoying himself." Pause. "I hope so."

"Yeah. What a shame. All he needs to do is clean up his act and he'd be attractive to women. Trim his beard, cut his hair, lose ten pounds and voila! A new man!"

"And new clothes," Jim added.

"And brush his teeth. Can you imagine—somebody who doesn't brush his teeth every day. It's like the toothbrush hasn't been invented for him."

"No. I wouldn't believe it if I didn't witness it with my own eyes. And nose. No wonder he has trouble getting dates. He pretends he's maintenance free."

"It would help if he were on time now and then. A girl doesn't want to be kept waiting, you know," Lucy said. "You think he'd get that watch fixed, if that's really the problem."

Jim added, "It was a nice gift, if I must say so for ourselves. Weird sales person, though. Kind of slow and very uninterested in the customer. He didn't care whether we bought the watch or not. And I remember, he did stink. Kind of like Larry."

Lucy thought for a second. She scooped her celery into the dip. "He could do it—he could shape himself up. Even being on time. It wouldn't take a whole lot of effort or imagination." The celery made a particularly loud crunch.

"Yeah, but will he? How's the dip?"

"It's good. I don't know. But if he doesn't change he's going to evaporate. I mean, nobody notices him, so he might as well not be here at all."

Jim looked in Larry's direction. "Kind of looks a little peaked now, don't you think? Maybe Larry's coming down with something. But perhaps he's enjoying himself, surrounded by those friendly women."

"Do you really think so?"

"No."

Jim looked into Lucy's eyes. "We have to do something. Living with Larry is like living with a phantom. It's as if he's not 100 percent here and it is driving me crazy."

"I know," Lucy said. "Me, too. Like when he performs his morning ritual—that loud grunt. Kind of like a yawn, but it sounds almost animal-like. Yeah, sort of like what you might hear at the zoo."

"Come on Lucy, that's cruel."

"Maybe. But you probably agree with me."

Jim nodded.

Lucy continued. "And the newspapers. Why can't he bring in *The Post* when he leaves. I know he doesn't read the paper, but just to toss it inside, would that be too difficult? And I've never known any guy not to be interested in the sports page." Jim thought for a moment. "I guess I shouldn't complain. Otherwise, Larry's a pretty good housemate. I mean we never have to worry about him keeping us up at night." Jim checked his chin to see if there were any dip remnants remaining on it. He took a nacho chip and skated the dip. "This is good dip."

"So we're agreed," Lucy continued.

"Agreed?"

"Yes. We do something about Larry before he turns our house into an insane asylum."

Jim concurred. "But I have one question."

"What?"

"That's the question. What do we do? You know we can't say to his face, 'Larry, you're a slob, your hygiene is abysmal, and you grunt. Do something or see a therapist.' If he doesn't take our words kindly, life will be miserable at 2280 Oakdon Street." Jim pressed his hand against his leg and added, "More miserable than it is now."

"Yes. I've thought about that. So what do we do?"

"We tell him anyway." But she knew they never would.

Larry drove home. Lucy and Jim joked about his car being a turtle. Larry didn't seem to mind.

Last Day

"Coffee?"

"Uh huh. Thanks. What time is it?"

"It's ten thirty."

"Oh," Jim replied.

"I told you that you shouldn't have had that scotch before going to sleep."

"You should have told me louder."

"Where's Larry?"

Lucy opened the refrigerator door, examined the shelf and turned to Jim, "What kind of coffee do you want? He's still sleeping."

"Larry knows we're heading off to Ikea to get furniture for the house. We'll give him another half hour, then wake him," Jim said. "That watch we gave him for his birthday isn't doing Larry any good. It's quartz, it's kinetic—never needs a new battery—and yet he's perpetually late."

"Fine. Pass me the *Style* section if you're not reading it, will you?" Lucy said.

■ ■ ■

Back home.

Larry parked himself on the living room couch. Jim noticed that the couch didn't creak when Larry sat down in it. Maybe we don't need to replace that couch after all, Jim thought.

"Nice ax," Jim said, pointing to the stone-shaped tool next to Larry. "Did you get that at the Smithsonian store?"

"I don't remember," Larry replied. "I thought it was yours or Lucy's. I guess I must have."

"Well, don't bonk anybody over the head with it. I'm heading upstairs for a nap—I'll see you later."

"Okay," Larry responded, his body limp across the couch.

Jim bolted up the stairs. He took a sharp left toward his room, hesitated and then knocked on Lucy's door. She responded to the knock immediately.

"Yes? No. Don't come in. Who's there?"

"Jim."

"Jim and who?"

"Just Jim."

Lucy softened her voice. "Okay, come in." Jim walked in. Lucy said, "Close the door."

"What's all the secre . . ." Jim eyed the canvas that sat on Lucy's easel in her cramped bedroom/art studio. Good painting of our living room, Jim thought, though it looked misty. Some of the geometry struck Jim as wrong. Everything was in proper proportion, except Larry and the television set. Lucy had drawn the TV larger than the one they owned (ahh, Jim thought, if only it were true) and Larry smaller and somewhat paler than a human could be. The drawing was good—Lucy's work always was—but it was unsettling. Only partly colored—the TV mostly, though Lucy touched almost everything else in her painting with hints of pastel: The couch, drapes, coffee table with its magazine collection, the carpet, Mickey Mouse clock, everything had at least a little color. Except Larry. Larry was light gray. This drawing was more surreal than most of Lucy's art. As he looked more closely at it, what struck Jim as most paradoxical—realistic to his eye, but unrealistic to his brain—what he liked most in Lucy's interpretation, was that the television set was drawn too precisely, too heavily, with details that Jim had never noticed in the two years he watched their tube. Thick and fine lines defined the TV, characters on the screen seemed clearer and more lifelike than they would be during regular viewing. But Larry was just basic shape: His stomach outlined by a tattered shirt that almost floated around him, his beard fuzzy—like the signals their TV received from distant Baltimore stations. (He was almost a ghost in Lucy's drawing, present only by the light from the television that mostly, but not entirely, shined around him.) There were no details visible, such as curved lips or dangling ear lobes, that would make one say, "Hey, that's Larry." But Jim noticed that details weren't necessary for him to recognize their housemate. Jim whistled. "Good."

"Thanks."

"I see why you didn't shout 'Come in!' when I knocked."

Lucy nodded. "Do you like it?"

"Yes, it's one of your best. I can't believe that you just whipped it together. It's eerie. Larry looks like he's fading in and out. But you'd better finish it and get it out of this house."

"Thanks, I was inspired. And I will keep it hidden. I will. Anyway, it's almost finished. Want to know what I call this?" Jim did.

"I call it, 'Disappearing Act.' "

From this more oblique angle, Jim's conclusion was the same: Terrific drawing, depressed subject. "Lucy, we have to say something to Larry." Lucy glanced toward Jim. Jim continued. "Not about your painting. I mean, he's drifting through the doldrums. Larry becomes more withdrawn all the time. His ego is practically gone. You can't get a single word out of him about what he's doing, what he's thinking—nothing about what interests or excites him. We have to unshell him, give him some confidence."

"Yeah, we've been saying we have to talk with Larry for months and we're just too chicken. You know he left the screen door open again—it's a bug habitat, this house." Perhaps it wasn't forgetfulness, Lucy thought, but rather he just likes all those bugs. "Somebody has to tell him either to fix himself up or see a therapist."

"Let's do it. Maybe he'll hate us, but just maybe he will seek professional help and his life and ours'll be hundreds of times better." She considered pausing for Jim's answer, but decided to continue. "Chen's sound good?"

"Chinese food is okay with me. I'll ask Larry if he wants to go."

Jim opened the door a crack and stuck his head out, testing whether he could stretch his neck far enough to reach the stair case landing. He could not. He took three steps in that direction. "HEY, LARRY," Jim shouted.

"WHAT?"

"WE'RE GOING TO CHEN'S FOR DINNER. WANT TO COME?"

"Okay."

"LEAVE IN HALF AN HOUR. OKAY?"

"Okay," Larry replied.

∎ ∎ ∎

"Come on, Larry," Lucy yelled. "It's nearly 6:30—your half hour expired fifteen minutes ago."

"I'm sorry," Larry said, in a breathless voice, having nearly tumbled down the last three steps. "My watch says 6:10. It isn't my fault."

"Tell you what. I'll take the watch in to get it fixed for you."

"Gee, thanks, Lucy."

"Maybe over the weekend. Now let's get moving."

Jim balanced the screen door as Lucy walked and Larry barreled down the front steps. "Nice shirt," Jim offered.

"Thanks, my mom gave it to me," Larry said.

At least it fits and . . . it's clean, his roommates thought, collectively. But such hairy arms Larry really should wear long sleeve shirts no matter what the weather.

During the fifteen minute journey to Chen's, Jim and Lucy argued about the relative merits of various Pepperidge Farm cookies. Larry stayed silent, except for an occasional—and loud—grunt. Guess he doesn't like cookies anymore, Lucy thought.

At the restaurant Jim decided first. "I'm up for kung pao chicken."

"Sounds good," Lucy said. "I'll order spicy beef with broccoli."

"Great," Jim added. "How about some steamed dumplings to start?"

"That's tasty to me," Lucy chimed. She turned to Larry on her right. "What are you going to get? We've got chicken and beef, which leaves shrimp, pork, veggies . . . But I think whole fish with the eye staring up is out."

Larry absorbed the menu for a few more seconds. He looked to the wall, perhaps expecting to find a suggestion there, and then back at the menu. With the back of his hand he rubbed his nose and then said, "Whatever."

"How about Szechuan prawns," Jim offered.

Larry said, "Well maybe. But now that you ask, the juicy beef surprise would be good. I feel in the mood for beef."

"But we've already got a beef dish," Lucy said. "Let's go with Jim's idea for prawns."

"All right," Larry said.

"So how's work?" Jim asked.

"It's okay," Larry said.

"Any exciting new projects?" Jim wanted to know.

"Nope."

Lucy joined the conversation. "What happened to that Norway trip you were expected to take?" She poured everyone some tea.

"It fell through. About two months ago. Budget problems."

Lucy puffed her cheeks. "I'm sorry to hear that. You must have been dismayed."

"No big deal, really. I had lots of work to do anyway," Larry said.

Lucy thought changing the subject would help. "Whatever became of that blind date you had?"

Larry looked puzzled. "Date?" he said. "Yes. Uhgha. About a

year ago. Last summer. We had fun I guess, but just never got together again."

"You should have called back," Lucy insisted.

Larry shrugged.

"Why not?" Lucy asked.

Larry shrugged again. "Dunno." He brought the tea cup to his mouth.

"Larry, that's still super hot," Jim said, attempting to parry the cup away from Larry's mouth. But Larry wasn't bothered and drank the whole cup.

"Lucy," Jim said abruptly, hiding behind his chopsticks. "You're going to kill me. Andy called this afternoon. I forgot to tell you." Jim cringed as Lucy's eyes bulged toward him. "Oops. He called. There. Now I told you."

"You're right, I am going to kill you." She hurled a shrimp toward Jim, hitting the middle of his shirt and bouncing into his water glass. "Gee, I feel better already. Maybe I won't have to kill you after all."

■　■　■

While Lucy sought to decipher the check, Jim looked at his watch and said, "The Marine Orchestra is playing on the Capitol steps, starting in twenty minutes. What do you say we grab a cab and see them."

"Great idea. Vamanos!" Lucy said.

A few minutes into the ride Lucy noticed that Larry's leg was invading her scarce space, his bushy arm hairs rubbing against her arm, so she slid slightly toward Jim. Better, Lucy thought.

Because they arrived at the concert as it was starting, a prime lawn location was not an option. Jim and Lucy offered a few words of complaint, but were resigned to suffer for their tardiness. They leaned back on the grass and enjoyed Stravinsky's "The Rite of Spring," which, Lucy commented, wasn't being played half badly. A distant lightning storm gave the Capitol building a spectacular backdrop. During the breaks between pieces, Jim and Lucy made friends with the four people occupying the blanket next to them, and who were generous with their wine. The shared wine put the six in an even more pleasant mood. As the Marine band began their finale, Lucy poured another glass of Bordeaux, perhaps burgundy—it's so hard to tell in the dark with screw tops, she thought—into a paper cup her new friends had provided. From time to time, thunder would add an accompanying drum sound to the orchestra. "Hope it doesn't rain," Jim whispered into Lucy's ear.

"Have faith, Jimbo."

"Wo! Did you see that lightning?!" At the same instant six thousand people exhaled. "That was close! I'd rather have the rain than another bolt of lightning so close by." In the next instant six thousand people resumed their silence as the band played on.

In the dim light that spilled over the top of the U.S. Capitol building she saw Larry begin to fade.

"Jim," Lucy said. She pushed Jim's shoulder to penetrate his wine-induced fog. "Jim, look, Larry's disappearing." Jim sat up and looked in Larry's direction.

"Jesus. You're right. Parts of him are becoming transparent. I can see the grass beneath his legs. And do you see that!? There's some kind of animal picture I can see through him. A painting in bleached pastels. There are some spears in the picture, too."

"Yes, I see it. It's like a buffalo. Now his arms and torso are going."

Jim sat up straighter. "Not a buffalo—an elephant. It's a drawing on a wall of some kind. And the cave. Do you see the cave? Jeez, he's really vanishing. Look, the cave is glowing now—there's a campfire inside."

Lucy put both hands over her mouth. "Jim! Larry's almost no longer here. We should do something. Quickly, think—how do we stop this? Oh my God, we have to do something!" She stared at the space that Larry was rapidly no longer occupying.

Jim watched the diffused light replace Larry's shape. "Do what, Lucy?" Jim bowed his head to the weak impression in the grass that marked Larry's spot. "He's gone. But look, that's odd."

"What's odd?" Lucy asked.

"Larry's watch is still here." He picked up Larry's watch. "It says . . . 8:40pm." Jim glanced at Larry's watch, then Lucy's. "Exactly on time. Larry's watch is exactly correct. Never was before."

One of their newly acquired friends on the adjacent blanket uttered a harsh, "Shh!"

"Oh, sorry," Lucy said.

"Sorry," Jim said, turning his head back to watch the band. "Could you pass the wine?" Jim whispered.

Edgar Allan Poe

Three Sundays in a Week

1850

*Time travel isn't always a matter of extremes—a journey from the present to worlds that existed hundreds, or even thousands, of years ago. Sometimes delight can be found in smaller discoveries. As Poe illustrates in "*THREE SUNDAYS IN A WEEK,*" the recognition of physics at work in the natural world can seem at times like a little miracle.*

B. A.

"YOU HARD-HEADED, DUNDER-HEADED, OBSTINATE, RUSTY, crusty, musty, fusty, old savage!" said I, in fancy, one afternoon, to my grand uncle Rumgudgeon—shaking my fist at him in imagination.

Only in imagination. The fact is, some trivial discrepancy did exist, just then, between what I said and what I had not the courage to say—between what I did and what I had half a mind to do.

The old porpoise, as I opened the drawing-room door, was sitting with his feet upon the mantel-piece, and a bumper of port in his paw, making strenuous efforts to accomplish the ditty.

Remplis ton verre vide!
Vide ton verre plein!

"My dear uncle," said I, closing the door gently, and approaching him with the blandest of smiles, "you are always so very kind and considerate, and have evinced your benevolence in so many— so very many—ways that—that I feel I have only to suggest this

little point to you once more to make sure of your full acquies-
cence."

"Hem!" said he, "good boy! go on!"

"I am sure, my dearest uncle, (you confounded old rascal!),
that you have no design really, seriously, to oppose my union with
Kate. This is merely a joke of yours, I know—ha! ha! ha!—how
very pleasant you are at times."

"Ha! ha! ha!" said he, "curse you! yes!"

"To be sure—of course! I knew you were jesting. Now, uncle,
all that Kate and myself wish at present, is that you would oblige
us with your advice as—as regards the time—you know, uncle—
in short, when will it be most convenient for yourself, that the
wedding shall—shall come off, you know?"

"Come off, you scoundrel!—what do you mean by that?—Better wait till it goes on."

"Ha! ha! ha!—he! he! he!—hi! hi! hi!—ho! ho! ho!—hu! hu!
hu!—that's good!—oh that's capital—such a wit! But all we want
just now, you know, uncle, is that you would indicate the time
precisely."

"Ah!—Precisely?"

"Yes, uncle—that is, if it would be quite agreeable to yourself."

"Wouldn't it answer, Bobby, if I were to leave it at random—
some time within a year or so, for example?—must I say precisely?"

"If you please, uncle—precisely."

"Well, then, Bobby, my boy—you're a fine fellow, aren't you?—
since you will have the exact time I'll—why I'll oblige you for
once."

"Dear uncle!"

"Hush, sir!" [drowning my voice]—"I'll oblige you for once.
You shall have my consent—and the plum, we mustn't forget the
plum—let me see! when shall it be? Today's Sunday isn't it? Well,
then, you shall be married precisely—precisely, now mind!—
when three Sundays come together in a week! Do you hear me,
sir! What are you gaping at? I say, you shall have Kate and her
plum when three Sundays come together in a week—but not till
then—you young scapegrace—not till then, if I die for it. You
know me—I'm a man of my word—now be off!" Here he swallowed his bumper of port, while I rushed from the room in despair.

A very "fine old English gentleman," was my grand-uncle Rumgudgeon, but unlike him of the song, he had his weak points. He was a little, pursy, pompous, passionate semicircular somebody, with a red nose, a thick skull, a long purse, and a strong sense of his own consequence. With the best heart in the world, he contrived, through a predominant whim of contradiction, to earn for himself, among those who only knew him superficially, the character of a curmudgeon. Like many excellent people, he seemed possessed with a spirit of tantalization, which might easily, at a casual glance, have been mistaken for malevolence. To every request, a positive "No!" was his immediate answer, but in the end—in the long, long end—there were exceedingly few requests which he refused. Against all attacks upon his purse he made the most sturdy defense; but the amount extorted from him, at last, was generally in direct ratio with the length of the siege and the stubbornness of the resistance. In charity no one gave more liberally or with a worse grace.

For the fine arts, and especially for the *belles-lettres*, he entertained a profound contempt. With this he had been inspired by Casimir Perier, whose pert little query *"A quoi un poete est il bon?"* he was in the habit of quoting, with a very droll pronunciation, as the *ne plus ultra* of logical wit. Thus my own inkling for the Muses had excited his entire displeasure. He assured me one day, when I asked him for a new copy of Horace, that the translation of *"Poeta nascitur non fit"* was "a nasty poet for nothing fit"—a remark which I took in high dudgeon. His repugnance to "the humanities" had, also, much increased of late, by an accidental bias in favor of what he supposed to be natural science. Somebody had accosted him in the street, mistaking him for no less a personage than Doctor Dubble L. Dee, the lecturer upon quack physics. This set him off at a tangent; and just at the epoch of this story—for story it is getting to be after all—my grand-uncle Rumgudgeon was accessible and pacific only upon points which happened to chime in with the caprioles of the hobby he was riding. For the rest, he laughed with his arms and legs, and his politics were stubborn and easily understood. He thought, with Horsley, that "the people have nothing to do with the laws but to obey them."

I had lived with the old gentleman all my life. My parents, in dying, had bequeathed me to him as a rich legacy. I believe the old villain loved me as his own child—nearly if not quite as well as he loved Kate—but it was a dog's existence that he led me, after all. From my first year until my fifth, he obliged me with very regular floggings. From five to fifteen, he threatened me, hourly, with the House of Correction. From fifteen to twenty, not a day passed in which he did not promise to cut me off with a shilling. I was a sad dog, it is true—but then it was a part of my nature—a point of my faith. In Kate, however, I had a firm friend, and I knew it. She was a good girl, and told me very sweetly that I might have her (plum and all) whenever I could badger my grand-uncle Rumgudgeon, into the necessary consent. Poor girl!— she was barely fifteen, and without this consent, her little amount in the funds was not come-at-able until five immeasurable sum- mers had "dragged their slow length along." What, then, to do? At fifteen, or even at twenty-one, (for I had now passed my fifth olympiad), five years in prospect are very much the same as five hundred. In vain we besieged the old gentleman with importu- nities. Here was a *piece de resistance,* (as Messieurs Ude and Careme would say), which suited his perverse fancy to a T. It would have stiffed the indignation of Job himself, to see how much like an old mouser he behaved to us two poor wretched little mice. In his heart he wished for nothing more ardently than our union. He had made up his mind to this all along. In fact, he would have given ten thousand pounds from his own pocket, (Kate's plum was her own), if he could have invented any thing like an excuse for complying with our very natural wishes. But then we had been so imprudent as to broach the subject ourselves. Not to oppose it under such circumstances, I sincerely believe, was not in his power.

I have said already that he had his weak points; but in speaking of these, I must not be understood as referring to his obstinacy: which was one of his strong points—"*assurement ce n' etait pas sa foible.*" When I mention his weakness I have allusion to a bizarre old-womanish superstition which beset him. He was great in dreams, portents, *et id genus omne* of rigmarole. He was excessively punctilious, too, upon small points of honor, and, after his own fashion, was a man of his word, beyond doubt. This was, in fact, one of his hobbies. The spirit of his vows he made no scruple of setting at naught, but the letter was a bond inviolable. Now it was this latter peculiarity in his disposition, of which Kate's ingenuity enabled us one fine day, not long after our interview in the din-ing-room, to take a very unexpected advantage, and, having thus, in the fashion of all modern bards and orators, exhausted in pro-legomena, all the time at my command, and nearly all the room at my disposal, I will sum up in a few words what constitutes the whole pith of the story.

It happened then—so the Fates ordered it—that among the naval acquaintances of my betrothed, were two gentlemen who had just set foot upon the shores of England, after a year's absence, each, in foreign travel. In company with these gentlemen, my cousin and I, preconcertedly paid uncle Rumgudgeon a visit on the afternoon of Sunday, October the tenth,—just three weeks after the memorable decision which had so cruelly defeated our hopes. For about half an hour the conversation ran upon ordinary topics, but at last, we contrived, quite naturally, to give it the following turn:

CAPT. PRATT. "Well I have been absent just one year.—Just one year today, as I live—let me see! Yes!—this is October the tenth. You remember, Mr. Rumgudgeon, I called, this day last year to bid you good-bye. And by the way, it does seem something like a coincidence, does it not—that our friend, Captain Smitherton, here, has been absent exactly a year also—a year today!"

SMITHERTON. "Yes! just one year to a fraction. You will remember, Mr. Rumgudgeon, that I called with Capt. Pratol on this very day, last year, to pay my parting respects."

UNCLE. "Yes, yes, yes—I remember it very well—very queer indeed! Both of you gone just one year. A very strange coincidence, indeed! Just what Doctor Dubble L. Dee would denominate an extraordinary concurrence of events. Doctor Dub—"

KATE. [Interrupting.] "To be sure, papa, it is something strange; but then Captain Pratt and Captain Smitherton didn't go altogether the same route, and that makes a difference, you know."

UNCLE. "I don't know any such thing, you huzzy! How should I? I think it only makes the matter more remarkable, Doctor Dubble L. Dee—"

KATE. "Why, papa, Captain Pratt went round Cape Horn, and Captain Smitherton doubled the Cape of Good Hope."

UNCLE. "Precisely!—the one went east and the other went west, you jade, and they both have gone quite round the world. By the by, Doctor Dubble L. Dee—"

MYSELF. [Hurriedly.] "Captain Pratt, you must come and

spend the evening with us tomorrow—you and Smitherton—you can tell us all about your voyage, and we'll have a game of whist and—"

PRATT. "Wist, my dear fellow—you forget. Tomorrow will be Sunday. Some other evening—"

KATE. "Oh, no. fie!—Robert's not quite so bad as that. Today's Sunday."

PRATT. "I beg both your pardons—but I can't be so much mistaken. I know tomorrow's Sunday, because—"

SMITHERTON. [Much surprised.] "What are you all thinking about? Wasn't yesterday, Sunday, I should like to know?"

ALL. "Yesterday indeed! you are out!"

UNCLE. "Today's Sunday, I say—don't I know?"

PRATT. "Oh no!—tomorrow's Sunday."

SMITHERTON. "You are all mad—every one of you. I am as positive that yesterday was Sunday as I am that I sit upon this chair."

KATE. [Jumping up eagerly.] "I see it—I see it all. Papa, this is a judgment upon you, about—about you know what. Let me alone, and I'll explain it all in a minute. It's a very simple thing, indeed. Captain Smitherton says that yesterday was Sunday: so it was; he is right. Cousin Bobby, and uncle and I say that today is Sunday: so it is; we are right. Captain Pratt maintains that tomorrow will be Sunday: so it will; he is right, too. The fact is, we are all right, and thus three Sundays have come together in a week."

SMITHERTON. [After a pause.] "By the by, Pratt, Kate has us completely. What fools we two are! Mr. Rumgudgeon, the matter stands thus: the earth, you know, is twenty-four thousand miles in circumference. Now this globe of the earth turns upon its own axis—revolves—spins round—these twenty-four thousand miles of extent, going from west to east, in precisely twenty-four hours. Do you understand Mr. Rumgudgeon?—"

UNCLE. "To be sure—to be sure—Doctor Dub—"

SMITHERTON. [Drowning his voice.] "Well, sir; that is at the rate of one thousand miles per hour. Now, suppose that I sail from this position a thousand miles east. Of course I anticipate the rising of the sun here at London by just one hour. I see the sun rise one hour before you do. Proceeding, in the same direction, yet another thousand miles, I anticipate the rising by two hours—another thousand, and I anticipate it by three hours, and so on, until I go entirely round the globe, and back to this spot, when, having gone twenty-four thousand miles east, I anticipate the rising of the London sun by no less than twenty-four hours; that is to say, I am a day in advance of your time. Understand, eh?"

UNCLE. "But Dubble L. Dee—"

SMITHERTON. [Speaking very loud.] "Captain Pratt, on the contrary, when he had sailed a thousand miles west of this position, was an hour, and when he had sailed twenty-four thousand miles west, was twenty-four hours, or one day, behind the time at London. Thus, with me, yesterday was Sunday—thus, with you, today is Sunday—and thus, with Pratt, tomorrow will be Sunday. And what is more, Mr. Rumgudgeon, it is positively clear that we are all right; for there can be no philosophical reason assigned why the idea of one of us should have preference over that of the other."

UNCLE. "My eyes!—well, Kate—well, Bobby!—this is a judgment upon me, as you say. But I am a man of my word—mark that! you shall have her, boy, (plum and all), when you please. Done up, by Jove! Three Sundays all in a row! I'll go, and take Dubble L. Dee's opinion upon that."

Molly Brown

Bad Timing

From *Interzone 54*, Issue 1, November 1, 1991

Your true love travels through space and time, and luckily for you he's tall, blond, handsome, if not a bit awkward in certain social skills, and temporal mechanics. But then not everyone's a natural at handling the intricacies of a time machine, as Alan Strong finds out as he dauntlessly seeks the woman he's destined to marry. He's got to get it right eventually—and soon. After waiting a lifetime, his love's patience is wearing thin with her soul mate's bad timing.

B. A.

"Time travel is an inexact science. And its study is fraught with paradoxes."
—Samuel Colson, b. 2301 d. 2197.

ALAN RUSHED THROUGH THE ARCHWAY WITHOUT EVEN GLANCING at the inscription across the top. It was Monday morning and he was late again. He often thought about the idea that time was a point in space, and he didn't like it. That meant that at this particular point in space it was always Monday morning and he was always late for a job he hated. And it always had been. And it always would be. Unless somebody tampered with it, which was strictly forbidden.

"Oh my Holy Matrix," Joe Twofingers exclaimed as Alan raced past him to register his palmprint before losing an extra thirty minutes pay. "You wouldn't believe what I found in the fiction section!"

Alan slapped down his hand. The recorder's metallic voice responded with, "Employee number 057, Archives Department, Alan Strong. Thirty minutes and seven point two seconds late. One hour's credit deducted."

Alan shrugged and turned back towards Joe. "Since I'm not

getting paid, I guess I'll put my feet up and have a cup of liquid caffeine. So tell me what you found."

"Well, I was tidying up the files—fiction section is a mess as you know—and I came across this magazine. And I thought, 'what's this doing here?' It's something from the twentieth century called Woman's Secrets, and it's all knitting patterns, recipes, and gooey little romance stories: 'He grabbed her roughly, bruising her soft pale skin, and pulled her to his rock hard chest' and so on. I figured it was in there by mistake and nearly threw it out. But then I saw this story called 'The Love That Conquered Time' and I realized that must be what they're keeping it for. So I had a look at it, and it was . . ." He made a face and stuck a finger down his throat. "But I really think you ought to read it."

"Why?"

"Because you're in it."

"You're a funny guy, Joe. You almost had me going for a minute."

"I'm serious! Have a look at the drebbing thing. It's by some woman called Cecily Walker, it's in that funny old vernacular they used to use, and it's positively dire. But the guy in the story is definitely you."

Alan didn't believe him for a minute. Joe was a joker, and always had been. Alan would never forget the time Joe laced his drink with a combination aphrodisiac-hallucinogen at a party and he'd made a total fool of himself with the section leader's overcoat. He closed his eyes and shuddered as Joe handed him the magazine.

Like all the early relics made of paper, the magazine had been dipped in preservative and the individual pages coated with a clear protective covering which gave them a horrible chemical smell and a tendency to stick together. After a little difficulty, Alan found the page he wanted. He rolled his eyes at the painted illustration of a couple locked in a passionate but chaste embrace, and dutifully began to read.

It was all about a beautiful but lonely and unfulfilled woman who still lives in the house where she was born. One day there is a knock at the door, and she opens it to a mysterious stranger: tall, handsome, and extremely charismatic.

Alan chuckled to himself.

A few paragraphs later, over a candlelit dinner, the man tells the woman that he comes from the future, where time travel has become a reality, and he works at the Colson Time Studies Institute in the Department of Archives.

Alan stopped laughing.

The man tells her that only certain people are allowed to time travel, and they are not allowed to interfere in any way, only observe. He confesses that he is not a qualified traveler—he broke into the lab one night and stole a machine. The woman asks him why and he tells her, "You're the only reason, Claudia. I did it for you. I read a story that you wrote and I knew it was about me and that it was about you. I searched in the Archives and I found your picture and then I knew that I loved you and that I had always loved you and that I always would."

"But I never wrote a story, Alan."

"You will, Claudia. You will."

The Alan in the story goes on to describe the Project, and the Archives, in detail. The woman asks him how people live in the twenty-fourth century, and he tells her about the gadgets in his apartment.

The hairs at the back of Alan's neck rose at the mention of his Neuro-Pleasatron. He'd never told anybody that he'd bought one, not even Joe.

After that, there's a lot of grabbing and pulling to his rock hard chest, melting sighs and kisses, and finally a wedding and a "happily ever after" existing at one point in space where it always has and always will.

Alan turned the magazine over and looked at the date on the cover. March 14, 1973.

He wiped the sweat off his forehead and shook himself. He looked up and saw that Joe was standing over him.

"You wouldn't really do that, would you," Joe said. "Because you know I'd have to stop you."

∎ ∎ ∎

Cecily Walker stood in front of her bedroom mirror and turned from right to left. She rolled the waistband over one more time, making sure both sides were even. Great; the skirt looked like a real mini. Now all she had to do was get out of the house without her mother seeing her.

She was in the record shop wondering if she really should spend her whole allowance on the new Monkees album, but she really liked Peter Tork, he was so cute, when Tommy Johnson walked in with Roger Hanley. "Hey, Cess-pit! Whaddya do, lose the bottom half of your dress?"

The boys at her school were just so creepy. She left the shop and turned down the main road, heading toward her friend Candy's house. She never noticed the tall blond man that stood across the street, or heard him call her name.

· · ·

When Joe went on his lunch break, Alan turned to the wall above his desk and said, "File required: Authors, fiction, twentieth century, initial 'W'."

"Checking," the wall said. "File located."

"Biography required: Walker, Cecily."

"Checking. Biography located. Display? Yes or no."

"Yes."

A section of wall the size of a small television screen lit up at eye-level, directly in front of Alan. He leaned forward and read: Walker, Cecily. b. Danville, Illinois, U.S.A. 1948 d. 2037. Published works: "The Love That Conquered Time," March, 1973. Accuracy rating: fair.

"Any other published works?"

"Checking. None found."

Alan looked down at the magazine in his lap.

· · ·

"I don't understand," Claudia said, looking pleadingly into his deep blue eyes. Eyes the color of the sea on a cloudless morning, and eyes that contained an ocean's depth of feeling for her, and her alone. "How is it possible to travel through time?"

"I'll try to make this simple," he told her, pulling her close. She took a deep breath, inhaling his manly aroma, and rested her head on his shoulder with a sigh. "Imagine that the universe is like a string. And every point on that string is a moment in space and time. But instead of stretching out in a straight line, it's all coiled and tangled and it overlaps in layers. Then all you have to do is move from point to point."

Alan wrinkled his forehead in consternation. "File?"

"Yes. Waiting."

"Information required: further data on Walker, Cecily. Education, family background."

"Checking. Found. Display? Yes or . . ."

"Yes!"

Walker, Cecily. Education: Graduate Lincoln High, Danville,

1967. Family background: Father Walker, Matthew. Mechanic, automobile. d. 1969. Mother no data.

Alan shook his head. Minimal education, no scientific background. How could she know so much? "Information required: photographic likeness of subject. If available, display."

He blinked and there she was, smiling at him across his desk. She was oddly dressed, in a multi-colored tee-shirt that ended above her waist and dark blue trousers that were cut so low they exposed her navel and seemed to balloon out below her knees into giant flaps of loose-hanging material. But she had long dark hair that fell across her shoulders and down to her waist, crimson lips and the most incredible eyes he had ever seen—huge and green. She was beautiful. He looked at the caption: Walker, Cecily. Author: Fiction related to time travel theory. Photographic likeness circa 1970.

"File," he said, "Further data required: personal details, ie. marriage. Display."

Walker, Cecily M. Strong, Alan.

"Date?"

No data.

"Biographical details of husband, Strong, Alan?"

None found.

"Redisplay photographic likeness. Enlarge." He stared at the wall for several minutes. "Print," he said.

■   ■   ■

Only half a block to go, the woman thought, struggling with two bags of groceries. The sun was high in the sky and the smell of Mrs. Henderson's roses, three doors down, filled the air with a lovely perfume. But she wasn't in the mood to appreciate it. All the sun made her feel was hot, and all the smell of flowers made her feel was ill. It had been a difficult pregnancy, but thank goodness it was nearly over now.

She wondered who the man was, standing on her front porch. He might be the new mechanic at her husband's garage, judging by his orange cover-alls. Nice-looking, she thought, wishing that she didn't look like there was a bowling ball underneath her dress.

"Excuse me," the man said, reaching out to help her with her bags. "I'm looking for Cecily Walker."

"My name's Walker," the woman told him. "But I don't know any Cecily."

"Cecily," she repeated when the man had gone. What a pretty name.

. . .

Alan decided to work late that night. Joe left at the usual time and told him he'd see him tomorrow.

"Yeah, tomorrow," Alan said.

He waited until Joe was gone, and then he took the printed photo of Cecily Walker out of his desk drawer and sat for a long time, staring at it. What did he know about this woman? Only that she'd written one published story, badly, and that she was the most gorgeous creature he had ever seen. Of course, what he was feeling was ridiculous. She'd been dead more than three hundred years.

But there were ways of getting around that.

Alan couldn't believe what he was actually considering. It was lunacy. He'd be caught, and he'd lose his job. But then he realized that he could never have read about it if he hadn't already done it and got away with it. He decided to have another look at the story.

It wasn't there. Under Fiction: Paper Relics: 20th Century, subsection Magazines, American, there was shelf after shelf full of *Amazing Stories, Astounding, Analog, Weird Tales* and *Isaac Asimov's Science Fiction Magazine,* but not one single copy of *Woman's Secrets.*

Well, he thought, if the magazine isn't there, I guess I never made it after all. Maybe it's better that way. Then he thought, but if I never made it, how can I be looking for the story? I shouldn't even know about it. And then he had another thought.

"File," he said. "Information required: magazines on loan."

"Display?"

"No, just tell me."

"*Woman's Secrets,* date 1973. *Astounding,* date . . ."

"Skip the rest. Who's got *Woman's Secrets?*"

"Checking. Signed out to Project Control through Joe Two-fingers."

Project Control was on to him! If he didn't act quickly, it would be too late.

It was amazingly easy to get into the lab. He just walked in. The machines were all lined up against one wall, and there was no one around to stop him. He walked up to the nearest machine and sat down on it. The earliest model developed by Samuel Colson had looked like an English telephone box (he'd been a big

Doctor Who fan), but it was hardly inconspicuous and extremely heavy, so refinements were made until the latest models were lightweight, collapsible, and made to look exactly like (and double up as) a folding bicycle. The control board was hidden from general view, inside a wicker basket.

None of the instruments were labeled. Alan tentatively pushed one button. Nothing happened. He pushed another. Still nothing.

He jumped off and looked for an instruction book. There had to be one somewhere. He was ransacking a desk when the door opened.

"I thought I'd find you here, Alan."

"Joe! I . . . uh . . . was just . . ."

"I know what you're doing, and I can't let you go through with it. It's against every rule of the Institute and you know it. If you interfere with the past, who knows what harm you might do?"

"But Joe, you know me. I wouldn't do any harm. I won't do anything to affect history, I swear it. I just want to see her, that's all. Besides, it's already happened, or you couldn't have read that magazine. And that's another thing! You're the one who showed it to me! I never would have known about her if it hadn't been for you. So if I'm going now, it's down to you."

"Alan, I'm sorry, but my job is on the line here, too, you know. So don't give me any trouble and come along quietly."

Joe moved towards him, holding a pair of handcuffs. Attempted theft of Institute property was a felony punishable by five years' imprisonment without pay. Alan picked up the nearest bike and brought it down over the top of Joe's head. The machine lay in pieces and Joe lay unconscious. Alan bent down and felt his pulse. He would be okay. "Sorry, Joe. I had to do it. File!"

"Yes."

"Information required: instruction manual for usage of . . ." he checked the number on the handlebars, "Colson Model 44B Time Traveler."

"Checking. Found. Display?"

"No. Just print. And fast."

The printer was only on page five when Alan heard running footsteps. Five pages would have to do.

■   ■   ■

Dear Cher, My name is Cecily Walker and all my friends tell me I look just like you. Well, a little bit. Anyway, the reason that I'm writing to you is this: I'm starting my senior year in high school, and I've never had a steady boyfriend. I've gone out with a couple of boys, but they only want one thing, and I guess you know what that is. I keep thinking there's gotta be somebody out there who's the right one for me, but I just haven't met him. Was it love at first sight for you and Sonny?

■   ■   ■

Alan sat on a London park bench with his printout and tried to figure out what he'd done wrong. Under Location: Setting, it just said "See page 29." Great, he thought. And he had no idea what year it was. Every time he tried to ask someone, they'd give him a funny look and walk away in a hurry. He folded up the bike and took a walk. It wasn't long before he found a newsstand and saw the date: July 19, 1998. At least he had the right century.

Back in the park, he sat astride the machine with the printout in one hand, frowning and wondering what might happen if he twisted a particular dial from right to left.

"Can't get your bike to start, mate?" someone shouted from nearby. "Just click your heels three times and think of home."

"Thanks, I'll try that," Alan shouted back. Then he vanished.

■   ■   ■

"I am a pirate from yonder ship," the man with the eye patch told her, "and well used to treasure. But I tell thee, lass, I've never seen the like of you."

Cecily groaned and ripped the page in half. She bit her lip and started again.

"I have traveled many galaxies, Madeleine," the alien bleeped. "But you are a life-form beyond compare."

"No, don't. Please don't," Madeleine pleaded as the alien reached out to pull her towards its rock-hard chest.

Her mother appeared in the doorway. "Whatcha doin' hon?"

She dropped the pen and flipped the writing pad face down. "My homework."

■   ■   ■

The next thing Alan knew he was in the middle of a cornfield. He hitched a lift with a truck driver who asked a lot of questions, ranging from "You work in a gas station, do you?" to "What are you, foreign or something?" and "What do you call that thing?" On being told "that thing" was a folding bicycle, the man muttered something about whatever would they think of next, and now his kid would be wanting one.

There were several Walker's listed in the Danville phone book. When he finally found the right house, Cecily was in the middle of her third birthday party.

He pedaled around a corner, checked his printout, and set the controls on "Fast Forward." He folded the machine and hid it behind a bush before walking back to the house. It was big and painted green, just like in the story. There was an apple tree in the garden, just like in the story. The porch swing moved ever so slightly, rocked by an early summer breeze. He could hear crickets chirping and birds singing. Everything was just the way it had been in the story, so he walked up the path, nervously clearing his throat and pushing back a stray lock of hair, just the way Cecily Walker had described him in *Woman's Secrets*, before finally taking a deep breath and knocking on the door. There was movement inside the house—the clack of high heeled shoes across a wooden floor, the rustle of a cotton dress.

"Yes?"

Alan stared at her, open-mouthed. "You've cut your hair," he told her.

"What?"

"Your hair. It used to hang down to your waist, now it's up to your shoulders."

"Do I know you?"

"You will," he told her. He'd said that in the story.

She was supposed to take one look at him and realize with a fluttering heart that this was the man she'd dreamed of all her life. Instead, she looked at his orange jumpsuit and slapped her hand to her forehead in enlightenment. "You're from the garage! Of course, Mack said he'd be sending the new guy." She looked past him into the street. "So where's your tow truck?"

"My what?" There was nothing in "The Love That Conquered Time" about a tow truck. The woman stared at him, looking confused. Alan stared back, equally confused. He started to wonder if he'd made a mistake. But then he saw those eyes, bigger and greener than he'd ever thought possible. "Matrix," he said out loud.

"What?"

"I'm sorry. It's just that meeting you is so bullasic."

"Mister, I don't understand one word you're saying." Cecily knew she should tell the man to go away. He was obviously deranged; she should call the police. But something held her back, a flicker of recognition, the dim stirrings of a memory. Where had she seen this man before?

"I'm sorry," Alan said again. "My American isn't very good. I come from English-speaking Europe, you see."

"English-speaking Europe?" Cecily repeated. "You mean England?"

"Not exactly. Can I come inside? I'll explain everything."

She let him come in after warning him that her neighbors would come running in with shotguns if they heard her scream, and that she had a black belt in Kung Fu. Alan nodded and followed her inside, wondering where Kung Fu was, and why she'd left her belt there.

He was ushered into the living room and told to have a seat. He sat down on the red velveteen-upholstered sofa and stared in awe at such historical artifacts as a black and white television with rabbit-ear antennae, floral-printed wallpaper, a phone you had to dial, and shelf after shelf of unpreserved books. She picked up a wooden chair and carried it to the far side of the room before sitting down. "Okay," she said. "Talk."

Alan felt it would have been better to talk over a candlelit dinner in a restaurant, like they did in the story, but he went ahead and told her everything, quoting parts of the story verbatim, such as the passage where she described him as the perfect lover she'd been longing for all her life.

When he was finished, she managed a frozen smile. "So you've come all the way from the future just to visit little ole me. Isn't that nice."

Oh Matrix, Alan thought. She's humoring me. She's convinced I'm insane and probably dangerous as well. "I know this must sound crazy to you," he said.

"Not at all," she told him, gripping the arms of her chair. He could see the blood draining out of her fingers.

"Please don't be afraid. I'd never harm you." He sighed and put a hand to his forehead. "It was all so different in the story."

"But I never wrote any story. Well, I started one once, but I never got beyond the second page."

"But you will. You see, it doesn't get published until 1973."

"You do know this is 1979, don't you?"

"WHAT?"

"Looks like your timing's off," she said. She watched him sink his head into his hands with an exaggerated groan. She rested her chin on one hand and regarded him silently. He didn't seem so frightening now. Crazy, yes, but not frightening. She might even find him quite attractive, if only things were different. He looked up at her and smiled. It was a crooked, little boy's smile that made his eyes sparkle. For a moment, she almost let herself imagine waking up to that smile . . . She pulled herself up in her chair, her back rigid.

"Look," he said. "So I'm a few years behind schedule. The main thing is I found you. And so what if the story comes out a bit later, it's nothing we can't handle. It's only a minor problem. A little case of bad timing."

"Excuse me," Cecily said. "But I think that in this case, timing is everything. If any of this made the least bit of sense, which it doesn't, you would've turned up before now. You said yourself the story was published in 1973—if it was based on fact, you'd need to arrive here much earlier."

"I did get here earlier, but I was too early."

Cecily's eyes widened involuntarily. "What do you mean?"

"I mean I was here before. I met you. I spoke to you."

"When?"

"You wouldn't remember. You were three years old, and your parents threw a party for you out in the garden. Of course I realized my mistake instantly, but I bluffed it out by telling your mother that I'd just dropped by to apologize because my kid was sick and couldn't come—it was a pretty safe bet that someone wouldn't have shown—and she said, 'Oh you must be little Sammy's father' and asked me in. I was going to leave immediately, but your father handed me a beer and started talking about something called baseball. Of course I didn't have a present for you . . ."

"But you gave me a rose and told my mother to press it into a book so that I'd have it forever."

"You remember."

"Wait there. Don't move." She leapt from her chair and ran upstairs. There was a lot of noise from above—paper rattling, doors opening and closing, things being thrown about. She returned clutching several books to her chest, her face flushed and streaked with dust. She flopped down on the floor and spread them out in front of her. When Alan got up to join her, she told him to stay where he was or she'd scream. He sat back down.

She opened the first book, and then Alan saw that they weren't books at all; they were photo albums. He watched in silence as she flipped through the pages and then tossed it aside. She tossed three of them away before she found what she was looking for. She stared open-mouthed at the brittle yellow page and then she looked up at Alan. "I don't understand this," she said, turning her eyes back to the album and a faded black and white photograph stuck to the paper with thick, flaking paste. Someone had written in ink across the top: Cecily's 3rd birthday, August 2nd, 1951. There was her father, who'd been dead for ten years, young and smiling, holding out a bottle to another young man, tall and blond and dressed like a gas station attendant. "I don't understand this at all." She pushed the album across the floor towards Alan. "You haven't changed one bit. You're even wearing the same clothes."

"Did you keep the rose?"

She walked over to a wooden cabinet and pulled out a slim hardback with the title, "My First Reader." She opened it and showed him the dried, flattened flower. "You're telling me the truth, aren't you?" she said. "This is all true. You risked everything to find me because we were meant to be together, and nothing, not even time itself, could keep us apart."

Alan nodded. There was a speech just like that in "The Love That Conquered Time."

"Bastard," she said.

Alan jumped. He didn't remember that part. "Pardon me?"

"Bastard," she said again. "You bastard!"

"I . . . I don't understand."

She got up and started to pace the room. "So you're the one, huh? You're 'Mister Right,' Mister Happily Ever After, caring, compassionate and great in bed. And you decide to turn up now. Well, isn't that just great."

"Is something the matter?" Alan asked her.

"Is something the matter?" she repeated. "He asks me if something's the matter! I'll tell you what's the matter. I got married four weeks ago, you son of a bitch!"

"You're married?"

"That's what I said, isn't it?"

"But you can't be married. We were supposed to find perfect happiness together at a particular point in space that has always existed and always will. This ruins everything."

"All those years . . . all those years. I went through hell in high school, you know. I was the only girl in my class who didn't have a date for the prom. So where were you then, huh? While I was sitting alone at home, crying my goddamn eyes out? How about all those Saturday nights I spent washing my hair? And even worse, those nights I worked at Hastings' Bar serving drinks to salesmen pretending they don't have wives. Why couldn't you have been around then, when I needed you?"

"Well, I've only got the first five pages of the manual . . ." He walked over to her and put his hands on her shoulders. She didn't move away. He gently pulled her closer to him. She didn't resist. "Look," he said, "I'm sorry. I'm a real zarkhead. I've made a mess of everything. You're happily married, you never wrote the story . . . I'll just go back where I came from, and none of this will have ever happened."

"Who said I was happy?"

"But you just got married."

She pushed him away. "I got married because I'm thirty years old and figured I'd never have another chance. People do that, you know. They reach a certain age and they figure it's now or never . . . Damn you! If only you'd come when you were supposed to!"

"You're thirty? Matrix, in half an hour you've gone from a toddler to someone older than me." He saw the expression on her face, and mumbled an apology.

"Look," she said. "You're gonna have to go. My husband'll be back any minute."

"I know I have to leave. But the trouble is, that drebbing story was true! I took one look at your photo, and I knew that I loved you and I always had. Always. That's the way time works, you see. And even if this whole thing vanishes as the result of some paradox, I swear to you I won't forget. Somewhere there's a point in space that belongs to us. I know it." He turned to go. "Good-bye Cecily."

"Alan, wait! That point in space—I want to go there. Isn't there anything we can do? I mean, you've got a time machine, after all."

What an idiot, he thought. The solution's been staring me in the face and I've been too blind to see it. "The machine!" He ran down the front porch steps and turned around to see her standing in the doorway. "I'll see you later," he told her. He knew it was a ridiculous thing to say the minute he'd said it. What he meant was, "I'll see you earlier."

■   ■   ■

Five men sat together inside a tent made of animal hide. The land of their fathers was under threat, and they met in council to discuss the problem. The one called Swiftly Running Stream advocated war, but Foot of the Crow was more cautious. "The paleface is too great in number, and his weapons give him an unfair advantage." Flying Bird suggested that they smoke before speaking further.

Black Elk took the pipe into his mouth. He closed his eyes for a moment and declared that the Great Spirit would give them a sign if they were meant to go to war. As soon as he said the word, "war," a paleface materialized among them. They all saw him. The white man's body was covered in a strange bright garment such as they had never seen, and he rode a fleshless horse with silver bones. The vision vanished as suddenly as it had appeared, leaving them with this message to ponder: Oops.

■   ■   ■

There was no one home, so he waited on the porch. It was a beautiful day, with a gentle breeze that carried the scent of roses: certainly better than that smoke-filled teepee.

A woman appeared in the distance. He wondered if that was her. But then he saw that it couldn't be, the woman's walk was strange and her body was misshapen. She's pregnant, he realized. It was a common thing in the days of over-population, but he couldn't remember the last time he'd seen a pregnant woman back home—it must have been years. She looked at him questioningly as she waddled up the steps balancing two paper bags. Alan thought the woman looked familiar; he knew that face. He reached out to help her.

"Excuse me," he said. "I'm looking for Cecily Walker."

"My name's Walker," the woman told him. "But I don't know any Cecily."

Matrix, what a moron, Alan thought, wanting to kick himself. Of course he knew the woman; it was Cecily's mother, and if she was pregnant, it had to be 1948. "My mistake," he told her. "It's been a long day."

■   ■   ■

The smell of roses had vanished, along with the leaves on the trees. There was snow on the ground and a strong northeasterly wind. Alan set the thermostat on his jumpsuit accordingly and jumped off the bike.

"So it's you again," Cecily said ironically. "Another case of perfect timing." She was twenty pounds heavier and there were lines around her mouth and her eyes. She wore a heavy wool cardigan sweater over an oversized tee-shirt, jeans, and a pair of fuzzy slippers. She looked him up and down. "You don't age at all, do you?"

"Please can I come in? It's freezing."

"Yeah, yeah. Come in. You like a cup of coffee?"

"You mean liquid caffeine? That'd be great."

He followed her into the living room and his mouth dropped open. The red sofa was gone, replaced by something that looked like a giant banana. The television was four times bigger and had lost the rabbit-ears. The floral wallpaper had been replaced by plain white walls not very different from those of his apartment. "Sit," she told him. She left the room for a moment and returned with two mugs, one of which she slammed down in front of him, causing a miniature brown tidal wave to splash across his legs.

"Cecily, are you upset about something?"

"That's a good one! He comes back after fifteen years and asks me if I'm upset."

"Fifteen years!" Alan sputtered.

"That's right. It's 1994, you bozo."

"Oh darling, and you've been waiting all this time . . ."

"Like hell I have," she interrupted. "When I met you, back in 1979, I realized that I couldn't stay in that sham of a marriage for another minute. So I must have set some kind of a record for quickie marriage and divorce, by Danville standards, anyway. So I was a thirty-year-old divorcee whose marriage had fallen apart in less than two months, and I was back to washing my hair alone on Saturday nights. And people talked. Lord, how they talked. But I didn't care, because I'd finally met my soul mate and everything was going to be all right. He told me he'd fix it. He'd be back. So I waited. I waited for a year. Then I waited two years. Then I waited three. After ten, I got tired of waiting. And if you think I'm going through another divorce, you're crazy."

"You mean you're married again?"

"What else was I supposed to do? A man wants you when you're forty, you jump at it. As far as I knew, you were gone forever."

"I've never been away, Cecily. I've been here all along, but never at the right time. It's that drebbing machine; I can't figure out the controls."

"Maybe Arnie can have a look at it when he gets in, he's pretty good at that sort of thing—what am I saying?"

"Tell me, did you ever write the story?"

"What's to write about? Anyway, what difference does it make? *Woman's Secrets* went bankrupt years ago."

"Matrix! If you never wrote the story, then I shouldn't even know about you. So how can I be here? Dammit, it's a paradox. And I wasn't supposed to cause any of those. Plus, I think I may have started an Indian war. Have you noticed any change in local history?"

"Huh?"

"Never mind. Look, I have an idea. When exactly did you get divorced?"

"I don't know, late '79. October, November, something like that."

"All right, that's what I'll aim for. November, 1979. Be waiting for me."

"How?"

"Good point. Okay, just take my word for it, you and me are going to be sitting in this room right here, right now, with one big difference: we'll have been married for fifteen years, okay?"

"But what about Arnie?"

"Arnie won't know the difference. You'll never have married him in the first place." He kissed her on the cheek. "I'll be back in a minute. Well, in 1979. You know what I mean." He headed for the door.

"Hold on," she said. "You're like the guy who goes out for a pack of cigarettes and doesn't come back for thirty years."

"What guy?"

"Never mind. I wanna make sure you don't turn up anywhere else. Bring the machine in here."

"Is that it?" she said one minute later.

"That's it."

"But it looks like a goddamn bicycle."

"Where do you want me to put it?"

She led him upstairs. "Here," she said. Alan unfolded the bike next to the bed. "I don't want you getting away from me next time," she told him.

"I don't have to get away from you now."

"You do. I'm married and I'm at least fifteen years older than you."

"Your age doesn't matter to me," Alan told her. "When I first fell in love with you, you'd been dead three hundred years."

"You really know how to flatter a girl, don't you? Anyway, don't aim for '79. I don't understand paradoxes, but I know I don't like them. If we're ever gonna get this thing straightened out, you must arrive before 1973, when the story is meant to be published. Try for '71 or '72. Now that I think about it, those were a strange couple of years for me. Nothing seemed real to me then. Nothing seemed worth bothering about, nothing mattered; I always felt like I was waiting for something. Day after day I waited, though I never knew what for."

She stepped back and watched him slowly turn a dial until he vanished. Then she remembered something.

How could she have ever forgotten such a thing? She was eleven and she was combing her hair in front of her bedroom mirror. She screamed. When both her parents burst into the room and demanded to know what was wrong, she told them she'd seen a man on a bicycle. They nearly sent her to a child psychiatrist.

Damn that Alan, she thought. He's screwed up again.

■ ■ ■

The same room, different decor, different time of day. Alan blinked several times; his eyes had difficulty adjusting to the darkness. He could barely make out the shape on the bed, but he could see all he needed to. The shape was alone, and it was adult size. He leaned close to her ear. "Cecily," he whispered. "It's me." He touched her shoulder and shook her slightly. He felt for a pulse.

He switched on the bedside lamp. He gazed down at a withered face framed by silver hair, and sighed. "Sorry, love," he said. He covered her head with a sheet, and sighed again.

He sat down on the bike and unfolded the printout. He'd get it right eventually.

John W. Campbell, Jr.

Night

From *Astounding Science Fiction*, October 1935

The pilot of a 1935 experimental aircraft flies to a safe altitude of 45,000 feet, where he starts testing the antigravity coils, designed to enable aircraft to leave the Earth's gravity. Instead, the coils function as anti-time devices, and hurl the pilot and his craft into the far distant future: A future where the Earth, the Sun, and most other stars have long since died, where energy in the universe is dwindling, and where it is only a matter of a few thousand billion years more before the universe itself collapses and dies. In this distant future, the pilot encounters the only life left in the universe: Thinking, self-replicating machines that help him return to his own era.

B. A.

CONDON WAS STARING THROUGH THE GLASSES WITH A FACE INtense and drawn, all his attention utterly concentrated on that one almost invisible speck infinitely far up in the blue sky, and saying over and over again in the most horribly absent-minded way, "My Lord—my Lord—"

Suddenly he shivered and looked down at me, sheer agony in his face. "He's never coming down. Don, he's never coming down—"

I knew it, too—knew it solidly as I knew the knowledge was impossible. But I smiled and said, "Oh, I wouldn't say that. If anything, I'd fear his coming down. What goes up comes down."

Major Condon trembled all over. His mouth worked horribly for a moment before he could speak. "Talbot—I'm scared—I'm horribly scared. You know—you're his assistant—you know he's trying to defeat gravity. Men aren't meant to—it's wrong—wrong—"

His eyes were glued on those binoculars again, with the same terrible tensity, and now he was saying over and over in that absent-minded way, "wrong—wrong—wrong—"

Simultaneously he stiffened, and stopped. The dozen or so other men standing on that lonely little emergency field stiffened; then the major crumpled to the ground. I've never before seen a man faint, let alone an army officer with a DS medal. I didn't stop to help him, because I knew something had happened. I grabbed the glasses.

Far, far up in the sky was that little orange speck—far, where there is almost no air, and he had been forced to wear a stratosphere suit with a little alcohol heater. The broad, orange wings were overlaid now with a faint-glowing, pearl-gray light. And it was falling. Slowly, at first, circling aimlessly downward. Then it dipped, rose, and somehow went into a tail spin.

It was horrible. I know I must have breathed, but it didn't seem so. It took minutes for it to fall those miles, despite the speed. Eventually it whipped out of that tail spin—through sheer speed, whipped out and into a power dive. It was a ghastly, flying coffin, hurtling at more than half a thousand miles an hour when it reached the Earth, some fifteen miles away.

The ground trembled, and the air shook with the crash of it. We were in the cars and roaring across the ground long before it hit. I was in Bob's car, with Jeff, his laboratory technician— Bob's little roadster he'd never need again. The engine picked up quickly, and we were going seventy before we left the field, jumped a shallow ditch and hit the road—the deserted, concrete road that led off towards where he must be. The engine roared as Jeff clamped down on the accelerator. Dimly, I heard the major's big car coming along behind us.

Jeff drove like a maniac, but I didn't notice. I knew the thing had done ninety-five but I think we must have done more. The wind whipped tears in my eyes so I couldn't be sure whether I saw mounting smoke and flame or not. With diesel fuel there shouldn't be—but that plane had been doing things it shouldn't. It had been trying out Carter's antigravity coil.

We shot up the flat, straight road across wide, level country, the wind moaning a requiem about the car. Far ahead I saw the side road that must lead off towards where Bob should be, and lurched to the braking of the car, the whine and sing of violently shrieking tyres, then to the skidding corner. It was a sand road; we slithered down it and for all the lightness and power, we slowed to sixty-five, clinging to the seat as the soft sand gripped and clung.

Violently Jeff twisted into a branching cow path, and somehow the springs took it. We braked to a stop a quarter of a mile from the plane.

. . .

It was in a fenced field of pasture and wood lot. We leaped the fence, and raced towards it: Jeff got there first, just as the major's car shrieked to a stop behind ours.

The major was cold and pale when he reached us. "Dead," he stated.

And I was very much colder and probably several times as pale. "I don't know!" I moaned. "He isn't there!"

"Not there!" The major almost screamed it. "He must be—he has to be. He has no parachute—wouldn't take one. They say he didn't jump—"

I pointed to the plane, and wiped a little cold sweat from my forehead. I felt clammy all over, and my spine prickled. The solid steel of the huge diesel engine was driven through the stump of a tree, down into the ground perhaps eight or nine feet, and the dirt and rock had splashed under that blow like wet mud.

The wings were on the other side of the field, flattened, twisted straws of dural alloy. The fuselage of the ship was a perfect silhouette—a longitudinal projection that had flattened in on itself, each separate section stopping only as it hit the ground.

The great torus coil with its strangely twined wrappings of hair-fine bismuth wire was intact! And bent over it, twisted, utterly wrecked by the impact, was the main-wing stringer—the great dural-alloy beam that supported most of the ship's weight in the air. It was battered, crushed on those hair-fine, fragile bismuth wires—and not one of them was twisted or displaced or so much as skinned. The back frame of the ponderous diesel engine—the heavy supercharger was the anvil of that combination—was cracked and splintered. And not one wire of the hellish bismuth coil was strained or skinned or displaced.

And the red pulp that should have been there—the red pulp that had been a man—wasn't. It simply wasn't there at all. He hadn't left the plane. In the clear, cloudless air, we could see that. He was gone.

We examined it, of course. A farmer came, and another, and

looked, and talked. Then several farmers came in old, dilapidated cars with their wives and families, and watched.

We set the owner of the property on watch and went away—went back to the city for workmen and a truck with a derrick. Dusk was falling. It would be morning before we could do anything, so we went away.

Five of us—the major of the army air force, Jeff Rodney, the two Douglass Co. men whose names I never remembered and I—sat in my—our—room. Bob's and Jeff's and mine. We'd been sitting there for hours trying to talk, trying to think, trying to remember every little detail, and trying to forget every ghastly detail. We couldn't remember the detail that explained it, nor forget the details that rode and harried us.

And the telephone rang. I started. Then slowly got up and answered. A strange voice, flat and rather unpleasant, said, "Mr. Talbot?"

"Yes."

It was Sam Gantry, the farmer we'd left on watch. "There's a man here."

"Yes? What does he want?"

"I dunno. I dunno where he came from. He's either dead or out cold. Gotta funny kind of aviator suit on, with a glass face on it. He looks all blue, so I guess he's dead."

"Lord! Bob! Did you take that helmet off?" I roared.

"No, sir, no—no, sir. We just left him the way he was."

"His tanks have run out. Listen. Take a hammer, a wrench, anything, and break that glass faceplate! Quick! We'll be there."

Jeff was moving. The major was, too, and the others. I made a grab for the half-empty bottle of Scotch, started out, and ducked back into the closet. With the oxygen bottle under my arm I jumped into the crowded little roadster just as Jeff started it moving. He turned on the horn, and left it that way.

We dodged, twisted, jumped, and stopped with jerks in traffic, then leaped into smooth, roaring speed out towards the farmer's field. The turns were familiar now; we scarcely slowed for them, slewing around them. This time Jeff charged through the wire fence. A headlight popped; there was a shrill scream of wire, the wicked *zing* of wire scratching across the bonnet and mudguards, and we were bouncing across the field.

.   .   .

There were two lanterns on the ground; three men carried others; more men squatted down beside a still figure garbed in a fantastic bulging, airproof stratosphere suit. They looked at us, open-mouthed as we skidded to a halt, moving aside as the major leaped out and dashed over with the Scotch. I followed close behind with the oxygen bottle.

Bob's faceplate was shattered, his face blue, his lips blue and flecked with froth. A long gash across his cheek from the shattered glass bled slowly. The major lifted his head without a word, and glass tinkled inside the helmet as he tried to force a little whisky down his throat.

"Wait!" I called. "Major, give him artificial respiration, and this will bring him around quicker—better." The major nodded, and rose, rubbing his arm with a peculiar expression.

"That's cold!" he said, as he flipped Bob over, and straddled his back. I held the oxygen bottle under Bob's nose as the major swung back in his arc, and let the raw, cold oxygen gas flow into his nostrils.

In ten seconds Bob coughed, gurgled, coughed violently, and took a deep shuddering breath. His face turned pink almost instantly under that lungful of oxygen, and I noticed with some surprise that he seemed to exhale almost nothing, his body absorbing the oxygen rapidly.

He coughed again; then, "I could breathe a heck of a sight better if you'd get off my back," he said. The major jumped up, and Bob turned over and sat up. He waved me aside, and spat. "I'm—all right," he said softly.

"Lord, man, what happened?" demanded the major.

Bob sat silent for a minute. His eyes had the strangest look—a hungry look—as he gazed about him. He looked at the trees beyond and at the silent, watching men in the light of the lanterns; then up, up to where a myriad of stars gleamed and danced and flickered in the clear sky.

"I'm back," he said softly. Then suddenly he shivered, and looked horribly afraid. "But—I'll have to be—then—too."

He looked at the major for a minute, and smiled faintly. And at the two Douglass Co. men. "Your plane was all right. I started up on the wings, as arranged, went way up, till I thought surely I was at a safe height, where the air wasn't too dense and the field surely wouldn't reach to Earth—Lord!—reach to the Earth! I didn't guess how far that field extended. It touched Earth—twice.

"I was at forty-five thousand when I decided it was safe, and cut the engine. It died, and the stillness shocked me. It was so quiet. So quiet.

"I turned on the coil circuit, and the dynamotor began to hum as the tubes warmed up. And then—the field hit me. It paralyzed me in an instant. I never had a chance to break the circuit, though I knew instantly something was wrong—terribly wrong. But the very first thing it did was to paralyze me, and I had to sit there and watch the instruments climb to positions and meanings they were never meant for.

"I realized I alone was being affected by that coil—I alone, sitting directly over it. I stared at the meters and they began to fade, began to seem transparent, unreal. And as they faded into blankness I saw the clear sky beyond them; then for a hundredth of a second, like some effect of persistence of vision, I thought I saw the plane falling, twisting down at incredible speed, and the light faded as the Sun seemed to rocket suddenly across the sky and vanish.

"I don't know how long I was in that paralyzed condition, where there was only blankness—neither dark nor light, nor time nor any form—but I breathed many times. Finally, form crawled and writhed into the blankness, and seemed to solidify beneath me as, abruptly, the blankness gave way to a dull red light. I was falling.

"I thought instantly of the forty-five thousand feet that lay between me and the solid Earth, and stiffened automatically in terror. And in the same instant I landed in a deep blanket of white snow, stained by the red light that lighted the world.

. . .

"Cold. Cold—it tore into me like the fang of a savage animal. What cold! The cold of ultimate death. It ripped through that thick, insulated suit and slashed at me viciously, as though there were no insulation there. I shivered so violently I could scarcely turn up the alcohol valves. You know I carried alcohol tanks and catalyst grids for heating, because the only electric fields I wanted were those of the apparatus. Even used a diesel instead of gas engine.

"I thank the Lord for that then. I realized that whatever had happened I was in a spot indescribably cold and desolate. And in the same instant, realized that the sky was black. Blacker than the blackest night, and yet before me the snow field stretched to infinity, tainted by the blood-red light, and my shadow crawled in darker red at my feet.

"I turned around. As far as the eye could see in three directions the land swept off in very low, very slightly rolling hills, almost plains—red plains of snow dyed with the dripping light of sunset, I thought.

"In the fourth direction, a wall—a wall that put the Great Wall of China to shame—loomed up half a mile—a blood-red wall that had the luster of metal. It stretched across the horizon, and looked a scant hundred yards away, for the air was utterly clear. I turned up my alcohol burners a bit more and felt a little better.

"Something jerked my head around like a giant hand—a sudden thought. I stared at the Sun and gulped. It was four times—six times—the size of the Sun I knew. And it wasn't setting. It was forty-five degrees from the horizon. It was red. Blood red. And there wasn't the slightest bit of radiant heat reaching my face from it. That Sun was cold.

"I'd just automatically assumed I was still on Earth, whatever else might have happened, but now I knew I couldn't be. It must be another planet of another sun—a frozen planet—for that snow was frozen air. I knew it absolutely. A frozen planet of a dead sun.

"And then I changed even that. I looked up at the black sky above me, and in all the vast black bowl of the heavens, not threescore stars were visible. Dim, red stars, with one single sun that stood out for its brilliance—a yellowish-red sun perhaps a tenth as bright as our sun, but a monster here. It was another—a dead—space. For if that snow was frozen air, the only atmosphere must have been neon and helium. There wasn't any hazy air to stop the light of the stars, and that dim, red sun didn't obscure them with its light. The stars were gone.

"In that glimpse, my mind began working by itself; I was scared.

"Scared? I was so scared I was afraid I was going to be sick. Because right then I knew I was never coming back. When I felt that cold, I'd wondered when my oxygen bottles would give out, if I'd get back before they did. Now it was not a worry. It was simply the limiting factor on an already-determined thing, the setting on the time bomb. I had just so much more time before I died right there.

"My mind was working out things, working them out all by itself, and giving answers I didn't want, didn't want to know about. For some reason it persisted in considering this was Earth, and the conviction became more and more fixed. It was right. That was Earth. And it was old Sol. Old—old Sol. It was the time axis that coil distorted—not gravity at all. My mind worked that out with a logic as cold as that planet.

"If it was time it had distorted, and this was Earth, then it had distorted time beyond imagining to an extent as meaningless to our minds as the distance a hundred million light years is. It was simply vast—incalculable. The Sun was dead. The Earth was dead. And Earth was already, in our time, two billion of years old, and in all that geological time, the Sun had not changed measurably. Then how long was it since my time? The Sun was dead. The very stars were dead. It must have been, I thought even then, billions on billions of years. And I grossly underestimated it.

"The world was old—old—old. The very rocks and ground radiated a crushing aura of incredible age. It was old, older than—but what is there? Older than the hills? Hills? Gosh, they'd been born and died and been born and worn away again, a million, a score of a million times! Old as the stars? No, that wouldn't do. The stars were dead—then.

"I looked up again at the metal wall, and set out for it, and the aura of age washed up at me, and dragged at me, and tried to stop this motion when all motion should have ceased. And the thin, unutterably cold wind whined in dead protest at me, and pulled at me with the ghost hands of the million million million that had been born and lived and died in the countless ages before I was born.

"I wondered as I went. I didn't think clearly, for the dead aura of the dead planet pulled at me. Age. The stars were dying, dead. They were huddled there in space, like decrepit old men, huddling for warmth. The galaxy was shrunk. So tiny, it wasn't a thousand light years across, the stars were separated by miles where there had been light years. The magnificent, proudly sprawling universe I had known, that flung itself across a million million light years, that flung radiant energy through space by the millions of millions of tons was—gone.

"It was dying—a dying miser that hoarded its last broken dregs of energy in a tiny cramped space. It was broken and shattered. A thousand billion years before the cosmic constant had been dropped from that broken universe. The cosmic constant that flung giant galaxies whirling apart with ever greater speed had no place here. It had hurled the universe in broken fragments, till each spattered bit felt the chill of loneliness, and wrapped space about itself, to become a universe in itself while the flaming galaxies vanished.

· · ·

"That had happened so long ago that the writing it had left in the fabric of space itself had worn away. Only the gravity constant remained, the hoarding constant, that drew things together, and slowly the galaxy collapsed, shrunken and old, a withered mummy.

"The very atoms were dead. The light was cold; even the red light made things look older, colder. There was no youth in the universe. I didn't belong, and the faint protesting rustle of the infinitely cold wind about me moved the snow in muted, futile protest, resenting my intrusion from a time when things were young. It whinnied at me feebly, and chilled the youth of me.

"I plodded on and on, and always the metal wall retreated, like one of those desert mirages. I was too stupefied by the age of the thing to wonder; I just walked on.

"I was getting nearer, though. The wall was real; it was fixed. As I drew slowly nearer, the polished sheen of the wall died and the last dregs of hope died. I'd thought there might be someone still living behind that wall. Beings who could build such a thing might be able to live even here. But I couldn't stop then; I just went on. The wall was broken and cracked. It wasn't a wall I'd seen; it was a series of broken walls, knitted by distance to a smooth front.

"There was no weather to age them, only the faintest stirring of faint, dead winds—winds of neon and helium, inert and uncorroding—as dead and inert as the universe. The city had been dead a score of billions of years. That city was dead for a time ten times longer than the age of our planet today. But nothing destroyed. Earth was dead—too dead to suffer the racking pains of life. The air was dead, too dead to scrape away metal.

"But the universe itself was dead. There was no cosmic radiation then to finally level the walls by atomic disintegration. There had been a wall—a single metal wall. Something—perhaps a last wandering meteor—had chanced on it in a time incalculably remote, and broken it. I entered through the great gap. Snow covered the city—soft, white snow. The great red sun stood still just where it was. Earth's restless rotation had long since been stilled—long, long since.

"There were dead gardens above, and I wandered up to them. That was really what convinced me it was a human city, on Earth. There were frozen, huddled heaps that might once have been men. Little fellows with fear forever frozen on their faces huddled helplessly over something that must once have been a heating device. Dead perhaps, since the last storm old Earth had known, tens of billions of years before.

"I went down. There were vastnesses in that city. It was huge. It stretched forever, it seemed, on and on, in its deadness. Machines, machines everywhere. And the machines were dead, too. I went down, down where I thought a bit of light and heat might linger. I didn't know then how long death had been there; those corpses looked so fresh, preserved by the eternal cold.

"It grew dark down below, and only through rents and breaks did that bloody light seep in. Down and down, till I was below the level of the dead surface. The white snow persisted, and then I came to the cause of that final, sudden death. I could understand then. More and more I had puzzled, for those machines I'd seen I knew were far and beyond anything we ever conceived—machines of perfection, self-repairing, and self-energizing, self-perpetuating. They could make duplicates of themselves, and duplicate other, needed machines; they were intended to be eternal, everlasting.

"But the designers couldn't cope with some things that were beyond even their majestic imaginations—the imaginations that conceived these cities that had lived beyond—a million times beyond—what they had dreamed. They must have conceived some vague future. But not a future when the Earth died, and the Sun died, and even the universe itself died.

"Cold had killed them. They had heating arrangements, devices intended to maintain forever the normal temperature despite the wildest variations of the weather. But in every electrical machine, resistances, balance resistances, and induction coils, balance condensers, and other inductances. And cold, stark, spatial cold, through ages, threw them off. Despite the heaters, cold crept in colder—cold that made their resistance balances and their induction coils superconductors! That destroyed the city, Superconduction—like the elimination of friction, on which all things must rest. It is a drag and a thing engineers fight forever. Resistance and friction must finally be the rest and the base of all things, the force that holds the great bed bolts firm and the brakes that stop the machines when needed.

"Electrical resistance died in the cold and wonderful machines stopped for the replacement of defective parts. And when they were replaced, they, too, were defective. For what months must that constant stop—replacement—start—stop—replacement have gone on before, at last defeated forever, those vast machines must bow in surrender to the inevitable? Cold has defeated them by defeating and removing the greatest obstacle of the engineers that built them resistance.

"They must have struggled forever—as we would say—through a hundred billion years against the encroaching harshness of nature, forever replacing worn, defective parts. At last, defeated forever, the great power plants, fed by dying atoms, had been forced into eternal idleness and cold. Cold conquered them at last.

"They didn't blow up. Nowhere did I see a wrecked machine; always they had stopped automatically when the defective resistances made it impossible to continue. The stored energy that was meant to re-start those machines after repairs had been made had long since leaked out. Never again could they move, I knew.

.   .   .

"I wondered how long they had been, how long they had gone on and on, long after the human need of them had vanished. For that vast city contained only a very few humans at the end. What untold ages of lonely functioning perfection had stretched behind those at-last-defeated mechanisms?

"I wandered out, to see perhaps more, before the necessary end came to me, too. Through the city of death. Everywhere little self-contained machines, cleaning machines that had kept that perfect city orderly and neat stood helpless and crushed by eternity and cold. They must have continued functioning for years after the great central power stations failed, for each contained its own store of energy, needing only occasional recharge from the central stations.

"I could see where breaks had occurred in the city, and, clustered about those breaks were motionless repair machines, their mechanisms in positions of work, the debris cleared away and carefully stacked on motionless trucks. The new beams and plates were partly attached, partly fixed and left, as the last dregs of their energy was fruitlessly expended in the last, dying attempts of that great body to repair itself. The death wounds lay unmended.

"I started back up. Up to the top of the city. It was a long climb, an infinite, weary climb, up half a mile of winding ramps, past deserted, dead homes; past, here and there, shops and restaurants; past motionless little automative passenger cars.

"Up and up, to the crowning gardens that lay stiff and brittle and frozen. The breaking of the roof must have caused a sudden chill, for their leaves lay green in sheaths of white, frozen air. Brittle glass, green and perfect to the touch. Flowers, blooming in wonderful perfection showed still; they didn't seem dead, but it didn't seem they could be otherwise under the blanket of cold.

"Did you ever sit up with a corpse?" Bob looked up at us— through us. "I had to once, in my little home town where they always did that. I sat with a few neighbors while the man died before my eyes. I knew he must die when I came there. He died— I sat there all night while the neighbors filed out, one by one, and the quiet settled. The quiet of the dead.

"I had to again. I was sitting with a corpse then. The corpse of a dead world in a dead universe, and the quiet didn't have to settle there; it had settled a billion years ago, and only my coming had stirred those feeble, protesting ghosts of eon-dead hopes of that planet to softly whining protest—protest the wind tried to sob to me, the dead wind of the dead gases. I'll never be able to call them inert gases again. I know. I know they are dead gases, the dead gases of dead world.

"And above, through the cracked crystal of the roof, the dying suns looked down on the dead city. I couldn't stay there. I went down. Down under layer after layer of buildings, buildings of gleaming metal that reflected the dim, blood light of the Sun outside in carmine stains. I went down and down, down to the machines again. But even there hopelessness seemed more intense. Again I saw that agonizing struggle of the eternally faithful machines trying to repair themselves once more to serve the masters who were dead a million million years. I could see it again in the frozen exhausted postures of the repair machines, stilled forever in their hopeless endeavors, the last poor dregs of energy spilled in fruitless conflict with time.

"It mattered little. Time itself was dying now, dying with the city and the planet and the universe he had killed.

"But those machines had tried so hard to serve again—and failed. Now they could never try again. Even they—the deathless machines—were dead.

"I went out again, away from those machines, out into the il-limitable corridors, on the edge of the city. I could not penetrate far before the darkness became as absolute as the cold. I passed the shops where goods, untouched by time in this cold still beck-oned those strange humans, but humans for all that; beckoned the masters of the machines that were no more. I vaguely entered one to see what manner of things they used in that time.

"I nearly screamed at the motion of the thing in there, heard dimly through my suit the strangely softened sounds it made in the thin air. I watched it stagger twice—and topple. I cannot guess what manner of storage cells they had—save they were marvelous beyond imagination. That stored energy that somehow I had re-leased by entering was some last dreg that had remained through a time as old as our planet now. Its voice was stilled forever. But it drove me out—on.

"It had died while I watched. But somehow it made me more curious. I wondered again, less oppressed by utter death. Still, some untapped energy remained in this place, stored unimagin-ably. I looked more keenly, watched more closely. And when I saw a screen in one office, I wondered. It was a screen. I could see readily it was a television of some type. Exploratively, I touched a stud. Sound! A humming, soft sound!

"To my mind leaped a picture of a system of these. There must be—interconnected—a vast central office somewhere with vaster accumulator cells, so huge, so tremendous in their power once, that even the little microfraction that remained was great. A stor-age system untouchable to the repair machines—the helpless, hopeless power machines.

∎ ∎ ∎

"In an instant I was alive again with hope. There was a strange series of studs and dials, unknown devices. I pulled back on the stud I had pressed, and stood trembling, wondering. Was there hope?

"Then the thought died. What hope? The city was dead. Not merely that. It had been dead, dead for untold time. Then the whole planet was dead. With whom might I connect? There were none on the whole planet, so what mattered it that there was a communication system.

"I looked at the thing more blankly. Had there been—how could I interpret its multitudinous devices? There was a thing on one side that made me think of a telephone dial for some reason.

A pointer over a metal sheet engraved with nine symbols in a circle under the arrow of the pointer. Now the pointer was over what was either the first or the last of these.

"Clumsily, in these gloves, I fingered one of the little symbol buttons inlaid in the metal. There was an unexpected click, a light glowed on the screen, a lighted image! It was a simple projection—but what a projection! A three-dimensional sphere floated, turned slowly before my eyes, turning majestically. And I nearly fell as understanding flooded me abruptly. The pointer was a selector! The studs beneath the pointer I understood! Nine of them. One after the other I pressed, and nine spheres—each different—swam before me.

"And right there I stopped and did some hard thinking. Nine spheres. Nine planets. Earth was shown first—a strange planet to me, but one I knew from the relative size and the position of the pointer must be Earth—then, in order, the other eight.

"Now—might there be life? Yes. In those nine worlds there might be, somewhere.

"Where? Mercury—nearest the Sun? No, the Sun was too dead, too cold, even for warmth there. And Mercury was too small. I knew, even as I thought, that I'd have one good chance because whatever means they had for communication wouldn't work without tremendous power. If those incredible storage cells had the power for even one shot, they had no more. Somehow I guessed that this apparatus might incorporate no resistance whatever. Here would be only very high frequency alternating current, and only condensers and inductances would be used in it. Supercooling didn't bother them any. It improved them. Not like the immense direct-current power machinery.

"But where to try? Jupiter? That was big. And then I saw what the solution must be. Cold had ruined these machines, thrown them off by making them too-perfect conductors. Because they weren't designed to defend themselves against spatial cold. But the machines—if there were any—on Pluto for instance, must originally have been designed for just such conditions! There it had always been cold. There it always would be cold.

"I looked at that thing with an intensity that should have driven my bare eyesight to Pluto. It was a hope. My only hope. But—how to signal Pluto? They could not understand! If there were any 'they.'

"So I had to guess—and hope. Somehow, I knew, there must

be some means of calling the intelligent attendant, that the user might get aid. There was a bank of little studs—twelve of them—with twelve symbols, each different, in the center of the panel, grouped in four rows of three. I guessed. Duodecimal system.

"Talk of the problems of interplanetary communication! Was there ever such a one? The problem of an anachronism in the city of the dead on a dead planet, seeking life somewhere, somehow.

"There were two studs, off by themselves, separate from the twelve—one green, one red. Again I guessed. Each of these had a complex series of symbols on it, so I turned the pointer on the right to Pluto, wavered, and turned it to Neptune. Pluto was further. Neptune had been cold enough; the machines would still be working there, and it would be, perhaps, less of a strain on the dregs of energy that might remain.

"I depressed the green symbol hoping I had guessed truly, that red still meant danger, trouble and wrongness to men when that was built—that it meant release and cancellation for a wrongly pressed key. That left green to be an operative call signal.

"Nothing happened. The green key alone was not enough. I looked again, pressed the green key and that stud I had first pressed.

"The thing hummed again. But it was a deeper note, now, an entirely different sound, and there was a frenzied clicking inside. Then the green stud kicked back at me. The Neptune key under the pointer glowed softly; the screen began to shimmer with a grayish light. And, abruptly, the humming groaned as though at a terrific overload; the screen turned dull; the little signal light under Neptune's key grew dim. The signal was being sent—hurled out.

"Minute after minute I stood there, staring. The screen grew very slowly, very gently, duller, duller. The energy was fading. The last stored driblet was being hurled away—away into space. 'Oh,' I groaned. 'It's hopeless—hopeless to—'

"I'd realized the thing would take hours to get to that distant planet, traveling at the speed of light, even if it had been correctly aligned. But the machinery that should have done that through the years probably had long since failed for lack of power.

"But I stood there till the groaning motors ceased altogether, and the screen was as dark as I'd found it, the signal light black. I released the stud then, and backed away, dazed by the utter collapse of an insane hope. Experimentally, I pressed the Neptune symbol again. So little power was left now, that only the faintest wash of murky light projected the Neptune image, little energy as that would have consumed.

"I went out. Bitter. Hopeless. Earth's last picture was long, long since painted—and mine had been the hand that spent Earth's last poor resource. To its utter exhaustion, the eternal city had strived to serve the race that created it, and I, from the dawn of time had, at the end of time, drained its last poor atom of life. The thing was a thing done.

■   ■   ■

"Slowly I went back to the roof and the dying suns. Up the miles of winding ramp that climbed a half mile straight up. I went slowly—only life knows haste—and I was of the dead.

"I found a bench up there—a carved bench of metal in the midst of a riot of colorful, frozen towers. I sat down, and looked out across the frozen city to the frozen world beyond, and the freezing red Sun.

"I do not know how long I sat there. And then something whispered in my mind: 'We sought you at the television machine.' I leaped from the bench and stared wildly about me.

■   ■   ■

"It was floating in the air—a shining dirigible of metal, ruby-red in that light, twenty feet long, perhaps ten in diameter, bright, warm orange light gleamed from its ports. I stared at it in amazement.

" 'It—it worked!' I gasped.

" 'The beam carried barely enough energy to energize the amplifiers when it reached Neptune, however,' replied the creature in the machine.

"I couldn't see him—I knew I wasn't hearing him, but somehow that didn't surprise me.

" 'Your oxygen has almost entirely given out, and I believe your mind is suffering from lack of oxygen. I would suggest you enter the lock; there is air in here.'

"I don't know how he knew, but the gauges confirmed his statement. The oxygen was pretty nearly gone. I had perhaps another hour's supply if I opened the valves wide—but it was a most uncomfortably near thing, even so.

"I got in. I was beaming, joyous. There was life. This universe was not so dead as I had supposed. Not on Earth, perhaps, but only because they did not choose! They had space ships! Eagerly I climbed in, a strange thrill running through my body as I crossed the threshold of the lock. The door closed behind me with a soft *shush* on its soft gaskets, locked, and a pump whined somewhere for a moment; then the inner door opened. I stepped in—and instantly turned off my alcohol burners. There was heat—heat and light and air!

"In a moment I had the outer lacings loose, and the inner zipper down. Thirty seconds later I stepped out of the suit, and took a deep breath. The air was clean and sweet and warm, invigorating, fresh-smelling, as though it had blown over miles of green, Sun-warmed fields. It smelled alive, and young.

■ ■ ■

"Then I looked for the man who had come for me. There was none. In the nose of the ship, by the controls, floated a four-foot globe of metal, softly glowing with a warm, golden light. The light pulsed slowly or swiftly with the rhythm of his thoughts, and I knew that this was the one who had spoken to me.

"'You had expected a human?' he thought to me. 'There are no more. There have been none for a time I cannot express in your mind. Ah, yes, you have a mathematical means of expression, but no understanding of that time, so it is useless. But the last of humanity was allowed to end before the Sun changed from the original G-O stage—a very, very long time ago.'

"I looked at him and wondered. Where was he from? Who—what—what manner of thing? Was it an armor encased living creature or another of the perfect machines?

"I felt him watching my mind operate, pulsing softly in his golden light. And suddenly I thought to look out of the ports. The dim red suns were wheeling across those ports at an unbelievable rate. Earth was long since gone. As I looked, a dim, incredibly dim, red disk suddenly appeared, expanded—and I looked in awe at Neptune.

"The planet was scarcely visible when we were already within a dozen millions of miles. It was a jeweled world. Cities—the great, perfect cities—still glowed. They glowed in soft, golden light above, and below, the harsher, brighter blue of mercury vapor lighted them.

"He was speaking again. 'We are machines—the ultimate development of man's machines. Man was almost gone when we came.'

" 'With what we have learned in the uncounted dusty mega-years since, we might have been able to save him. We could not then. It was better, wiser, that man end than that he sink down so low as he must, eventually. Evolution is the rise under pressure. Devolution is the gradual sinking that comes when there is no pressure—and there is no end to it. Life vanished from this system—a dusty infinity I cannot sort in my memory—my type memory, truly, for I have complete all the memories of those that went before me that I replace. But my memory cannot stretch back to that time you think of—a time when the constellations—

" 'It is useless to try. Those memories are buried under others, and those still buried under the weight of a billion centuries.

" 'We enter'—he named a city; I cannot reproduce that name—'now. You must return to Earth, though, in some seven and a quarter of your days, for the magnetic axis stretches back in collapsing field strains. I will be able to inject you into it, I believe.'

"So I entered that city, the living city of machines, that had been when time and the universe were young.

"I did not know then that, when all this universe had dissolved away, when the last sun was black and cold, scattered dust in a fragment of a scattered universe, this planet with its machine cities would go on—a last speck of warm light in a long-dead universe. I did not know then.

" 'You still wonder that we let man die out?' asked the machine. 'It was best. In another brief million years he would have lost his high estate. It was best.'

" 'Now we go on. We cannot end, as he did. It is automatic with us.'

"I felt it then, somehow. The blind, purposeless continuance of the machine cities I could understand. They had no intelligence, only functions. These machines—these living, thinking, reasoning investigators—had only one function, too. Their function was slightly different—they were designed to be eternally curious, eternally investigating. And their striving was the more purposeless of the two, for theirs could reach no end. The cities fought eternally only the blind destructiveness of nature; wear, decay, erosion.

"But their struggle had an opponent forever, so long as they existed. The intelligent—no, not quite intelligent, but something else—curious machines were without opponents. They had to be

curious. They had to go on investigating. And they had been going on in just this way for such incomprehensible ages that there
was no longer anything to be curious about. Whoever, whatever
designed them gave them function and forgot purpose. Their
only curiosity was the wonder if there might, somewhere, be one
more thing to learn.

"That—and the problem they did not want to solve, but must
try to solve, because of the blind functioning of their very structure.

"Those eternal cities were limited. The machines saw now that
limit, and saw the hope of final surcease in it. They worked on
the energy of the atom. But the masses of the suns were yet tremendous. They were dead for want of energy. The masses of the
planets were still enormous. But they, too, were dead for want of
energy.

· · ·

"The machines there on Neptune gave me food and drink—
strange, synthetic foods and drinks. There had been none on all
the planet. They, perforce, started a machine, unused in a billion
years and more, that I might eat. Perhaps they were glad to do
so. It brought the end appreciably nearer, that vast consumption
of mine.

"They used so very, very little, for they were so perfectly efficient. The only possible fuel in all the universe is one—hydrogen.
From hydrogen, the lightest of elements, the heaviest can be built
up, and energy released. They knew how to destroy matter utterly
to energy, and could do it.

"But while the energy release of hydrogen compounding to the
heavy elements is controllable, the destruction of matter to energy
is a self-regenerative process. Started once, it spreads while matter
lies within its direct, contiguous reach. It is wild, uncontrollable.
It is impossible to utilize the full energy of matter.

"The suns had found that. They had burned their hydrogen
until it was a remnant so small the action could not go on.

"On all Earth there was not an atom of hydrogen—nor was
there on any planet, save Neptune. And there the store was not
great. I used an appreciable fraction while I was there. That is
their last hope. They can see the end, now.

"I stayed those few days, and the machines came and went.
Always investigating, always curious. But there is in all that uni-

verse nothing to investigate save the one problem they are sure they cannot solve.

"The machine took me back to Earth, set up something near me that glowed with a peculiar, steady, gray light. It would fix the magnetic axis on me, on my location, within a few hours. He could not stay near when the axis touched again. He went back to Neptune, but a few millions of miles distant, in this shrunken mummy of the solar system.

"I stood alone on the roof of the city, in the frozen garden with its deceptive look of life.

"And I thought of that night I had spent, sitting up with the dead man. I had come and watched him die. And I sat up with him in the quiet. I had wanted someone, anyone to talk to.

"I did then. Overpoweringly it came to me I was sitting up in the night of the universe, in the night and quiet of the universe, with a dead planet's body, with the dead, ashen hopes of countless, nameless generations of men and women. The universe was dead, and I sat up alone—alone in the dead hush.

"Out beyond, a last flicker of life was dying on the planet Neptune—a last, false flicker of aimless life, but not life. Life was dead. The world was dead.

"I knew there would never be another sound here. For all the little remainder of time. For this was the dark and the night of time and the universe. It was inevitable, the inevitable end that had been simply more distant in my day—in the long, long-gone time when the stars were mighty lighthouses of a mighty space, not the dying, flickering candles at the head of a dead planet.

"It had been inevitable then; the candles must burn out for all their brave show. But now I could see them guttering low, the last, fruitless dregs of energy expiring as the machines below had spent their last dregs of energy in that hopeless, utterly faithful gesture—to attempt the repair of the city already dead.

"The universe had been dead a billion years. It had been. This, I saw, was the last radiation of the heat of life from an already-dead body—the feel of life and warmth, imitation of life by a corpse. Those suns had long and long since ceased to generate energy. They were dead, and their corpses were giving off the last, lingering life heat before they cooled.

"I ran. I think I ran—down away from the flickering, red suns in the sky. Down to the shrouding blackness of the dead city below, where neither light, nor heat, nor life, nor imitation of life bothered me.

"The utter blackness quieted me somewhat. So I turned off my oxygen valves, because I wanted to die sane, even here, and I knew I'd never come back.

"The impossible happened! I came to with that raw oxygen in my face. I don't know how I came—only that here is warmth and life.

"Somewhere, on the far side of that bismuth coil, inevitable still, is the dead planet and the flickering, guttering candles that light the death watch I must keep at the end of time."

Jack McDevitt

Time Travelers Never Die

From *Standard Candles*, Tachyon Publications, 1996

If you invented a time machine, you might be inclined to keep it secret, as Dr. Shelborne did. All the things you could do—talk with Socrates, have dinner with Leonardo da Vinci, observe Sparta's victories, and, of course, do very well in the stock market. But what if one of the things you did was to look up your own biography (who could resist) only to discover that you died in the present. Would you go back to the present to meet your fate? And what if your decision not to go back changed time forever in such a way that the future ceased to exist? Would you sacrifice your life (you're dead already) to preserve the universe? But the paradox can get even tighter: What if you decide to end your life in ancient times—then you'll have two graves. To make things right, you can be dead in only one time. Is it too late to fix things because history records you dying in 79 A.D. and 1996 A.D.?

B. A.

Thursday, November 24. Shortly before noon.

WE BURIED HIM ON A COLD, GRAY MORNING, THREATENING SNOW. The mourners were few, easily constraining their grief for a man who had traditionally kept his acquaintances at a distance. I watched the preacher, white-haired, feeble, himself near the end, and I wondered what he was thinking as the wind rattled the pages of his prayer book.

Ashes to ashes—

I stood with hands thrust into my coat pockets, near tears. Look: I'm not ashamed to admit it. Shel was odd, vindictive, unpredictable, selfish. He didn't have a lot of friends. Didn't deserve a lot of friends. But I *loved* him. I've never known anyone like him.

—In sure and certain hope—

I wasn't all that confident about the Resurrection, but I knew that Adrian Shelborne would indeed walk the earth again. Even

119

if only briefly. I knew, for example, that he and I would stand on an Arizona hilltop on a fresh spring morning late in the twenty-first century, and watch silver vehicles rise into the sky on the first leg of the voyage to Centaurus. And we would be present at the assassination of Elaine Culpepper, a name unknown now, but which would in time be inextricably linked with the collapse of the North American Republic. Time travelers never really die, he was fond of saying. We've been too far downstream. You and I will live for a very long time.

The preacher finished, closed his book, and raised his hand to bless the polished orchid-colored coffin. The wind blew, and the air was heavy with the approaching storm. The mourners, anxious to be away, bent their heads and walked past, laying lilies on the coffin. When it was done, they lingered briefly, murmuring to each other. Helen Suchenko stood off to one side, looking lost. Lover with no formal standing. Known to the family but not particularly liked, mostly because they disapproved of Shel himself. She dabbed jerkily at her eyes and kept her gaze riveted on the gray stone which carried his name and dates.

She was fair-haired, with eyes the color of sea water, and a quiet, introspective manner that might easily have misled those who did not know her well.

"I can't believe it," she said.

I had introduced him to Helen, fool that I am. She and I had been members of the Devil's Disciples, a group of George Bernard Shaw devotees. She was an MD, just out of medical school when she first showed up for a field trip to see *Arms and the Man*. It was love at first sight, but I was slow to show my feelings. And while I was debating how best to make my approach, Shel walked off with her. He even asked whether I was interested, and I, sensing I had already lost, salvaged my pride and told him of course not. After that it was over.

He never knew. He used to talk about her a lot when we were upstream. How he was going to share the great secret with her, and take her to Victorian London. Or St. Petersburg before the first war. But it never happened. It was always something he was going to do later.

She was trembling. He really *was* gone. And I now had a clear field with her. That indecent thought kept surfacing. I was reasonably sure she had always been drawn to me, too, just as she was to Shel, and I suspected that I might have carried the day with her had I pressed my case. But honor was mixed up in it somewhere, and I'd kept my distance.

Her cheeks were wet.

"I'll miss him too," I said.

"I loved him, Dave."

"I know."

He had died when his townhouse burned down almost two weeks before. He'd been asleep upstairs and had never got out of bed. The explanation seemed to be that the fire had sucked the oxygen out of the house and suffocated him before he ever realized what was happening. Okay, I didn't believe it either, but that was what we were hearing.

"It'll be all right," I said.

She tried to laugh, but the sound had an edge to it. "Our last conversation was so goofy. I wish I'd known—" Tears leaked out of her eyes. She stopped, tried to catch her breath. "I would have liked," she said, when she'd regained a degree of control, "to have been able to say goodbye."

"I know." I began to guide her toward my Porsche. "Why don't you let me take you home?"

"Thank you," she said, backing off. "I'll be okay." Her car was parked near a stone angel.

Edmond Halverson, head of the art department at the university, drew abreast of us, nodded to me, tipped his hat to her, and whispered his regrets. We mumbled something and he walked on.

She swallowed, and smiled. "When you get a chance, Dave, give me a call."

I watched her get into her car and drive away. She had known so much about Adrian Shelborne. And so little.

He had traveled in time, and of all persons now alive, only I knew. He had brought me in, he'd said, because he needed my language skills. But I believe it was more than that. He wanted someone to share the victory with, someone to help him celebrate. Over the years, he'd mastered classical Greek, and Castilian, and Renaissance Italian. And he'd gone on, acquiring enough Latin, Russian, French, and German to get by on his own. But we continued to travel together. And it became the hardest thing in my life to refrain from telling people I had once talked aerodynamics with Leonardo.

I watched his brother Jerry duck his head to get into his limo. Interested only in sports and women, Shel had said of him. And making money. *If I'd told him about the Watch,* he'd said, *and offered to take him along, he'd have asked to see a Super Bowl.*

Shel had discovered the principles of time travel while looking into quantum gravity. He'd explained any number of times how the Watches worked, but I never understood any of it. Not then, and not now. "But why all the secrecy?" I'd asked him. "Why not take credit? It's the discovery of the ages." We'd laughed at the new shade of meaning to the old phrase.

"Because it's dangerous," he'd said, peering over the top of his glasses, not at me, but at something in the distance. "Time travel should not be possible in a rational universe." He'd shaken his head, and his unruly black hair had fallen into his eyes. He was only thirty-eight at the time of his funeral. "I saw from the first *why* it was theoretically possible," he'd said. "But I thought I was missing something, some detail that would intervene to prevent the actual construction of a device. And yet there it is." And he'd glanced down at the watch strapped to his left wrist. He worried about Causality, the simple flow of cause and effect. "A time machine breaks it all down," he said. "It makes me wonder what kind of universe we live in."

I thought we should forget the philosophy and tell the world. Let other people worry about the details. When I pressed him, he'd talked about teams from the Mossad going back to drag Hitler out of 1935, or Middle Eastern terrorists hunting down Thomas Jefferson. "It leads to utter chaos," he'd said. "Either time travel should be prohibited, like exceeding the speed of light, or the intelligence to achieve it should be prohibited."

We used to retreat sometimes to a tower on a rocky reef somewhere downstream. No one lives there, and there is only ocean in all directions. I don't know how he found it, or who built it, or what that world is like. Nor do I believe *he* did. We enjoyed the mystery of the place. The moon is bigger, and the tides are loud. We'd hauled a generator out there, and a refrigerator, and a lot of furniture. We used to sit in front of a wall-length transparent panel, sipping beer, watching the ocean, and talking about God, history, and women.

They were good days.

Eventually, he had said, I will bring Helen here.

The wind blew, the mourners dwindled and were gone, and the coffin waited on broad straps for the workmen who would lower it into the ground.

Damn. I would miss him.

Gone now. He and his Watches. And temporal logic apparently none the worse.

Oh, I still had a working unit in my desk, but I knew I would not use it again. I did not have his passion for time travel. Leave well enough alone. That's always been my motto.

On the way home, I turned on the radio. It was an ordinary day. Peace talks were breaking down in Africa. Another congressman was accused of diverting campaign funds. Assaults against spouses were still rising. And in Los Angeles there was a curious conclusion to an expressway pileup: two people, a man and a woman, had broken into a wrecked vehicle and kidnapped the driver, who was believed to be either dead or seriously injured. They had apparently run off with him.

Only in California.

■   ■   ■

Shel had been compulsively secretive. Not only about time travel, but about everything. The mask was always up and you never really knew what he was feeling. He used to drive Helen crazy when we went out to dinner because she had to wait until the server arrived to find out what he was going to order. When he was at the university, his department could never get a detailed syllabus out of him. And I was present when his own accountant complained that he was holding back information.

He used to be fond of saying knowledge is power, and I think that was what made him feel successful, that he knew things other people didn't. Something must have happened to him when he was a kid to leave him so in need of artificial support. It was probably the same characteristic that had turned him into the all-time great camp follower. I don't know what the proper use for a time machine should be. We used it to make money. But mostly we used it to argue theology with Thomas Aquinas, to talk with Isaac Newton about gravity, to watch Thomas Huxley take on Bishop Wilberforce. For us, it had been almost an entertainment medium. It seemed to me that we should have done *more* with it.

Don't ask me what. Maybe track down Michelangelo's lost statue of *Hermes*. Shel had shown interest in the project, and we had even stopped by his workshop to admire the piece shortly before its completion. The artist was about twenty years old at the time. And the *Hermes* was magnificent. I would have killed to own it.

Actually, I had all kinds of souvenirs: coins that a young Julius Caesar had lost to Shel over draughts, a program from the opening night of *The Barber of Seville*, a quill once used by Benjamin Franklin. And photos: We had whole albums full of Alexander and Marcus Aurelius and the sails of the Santa Maria coming over the horizon. But they all looked like scenes from old movies. Except that the actors didn't look as good as you'd expect. When I pressed Shel for a point to all this activity, he said, what more could there be than an evening before the fire with Al Einstein? (We had got to a fairly intimate relationship with him, during the days when he was still working for the Swiss patent office.)

There were times when I knew he wanted to tell Helen what we were doing, and bring her along. But some tripwire always brought him up short, and he'd turn to me with that maddeningly innocuous smile as if to say, you and I have a secret and we had best keep it that way for now. Helen caught it, knew there was something going on. But she was too smart to try to break it open.

We went out fairly regularly, the three of us, and my true love of the month, whoever that might be. My date was seldom the same twice because she always figured out that Helen had me locked up. Helen knew that too, of course. But Shel didn't. I don't think it ever occurred to him that his old friend would have considered for a moment moving in on the woman he professed (although not too loudly) to love. There were moments when we'd be left alone at the table, Helen and I, usually while Shel was dancing with my date. And the air would grow thick with tension. Neither of us ever said anything directly, but sometimes our gaze touched, and her eyes grew very big and she'd get a kind of forlorn look.

Helen was a frustrated actress who still enjoyed the theater. After about a year, she abandoned the Devil's Disciples, explaining that she simply did not have time for it anymore. But Shel understood her passion and indulged it where he could. Whenever there was a revival, we all went. Inevitably, while we watched Shaw's trapped characters careen toward their destinies, Shel would find an opportunity to tell me he was going to take her back to meet the great playwright.

I used to promise myself to stop socializing with her, to find an excuse, because it hurt so much to sit in the awful glare of her passion for him. But if I had done that, I wouldn't have seen her at all. At night, when the evening was over and we were breaking up, she always kissed me, sometimes lightly on the cheek, sometimes a quick hit-and-run full on the lips. And once or twice, when she'd drunk a little too much and her control had slipped, she'd put some serious effort into it.

2

Thursday, November 24. Noon.

The storm picked up while I drove home reminiscing, feeling sorry for myself. I already missed his voice, his sardonic view of the world, his amused cynicism. Together, we had seen power misused and abused all through the centuries, up close, sometimes with calculation, more often out of ignorance. Our shared experiences certainly unique in the history of the planet, had forged a bond between us. The dissolution of that bond, I knew, was going to be a long painful process.

He'd done all the research in his basement laboratory, had built the first working model of his Temporal Occluding Transport System (which, in a flash back to his bureaucratic days with the National Science Foundation, he called TOTS) in a space between his furnace and a wall filled with filing cabinets. The prototype had been a big, near-room-sized chamber. But the bulk of the device had dwindled as its capabilities increased. Eventually, it had shrunk to the size of a watch. It was powered by a cell clipped to the belt or carried in a pocket. I still had one of the power packs at the house.

I would have to decide what to do with our wardrobe. It was located in a second floor bedroom that had served as an anteroom to the ages. A big walk-in closet overflowed with costumes, and shelves were jammed with books on culture and language for every period that we'd visited, or intended to visit.

But if my time-traveling days were over, I had made enough money from the enterprise that I would never have to work again—if I chose not to. The money had come from having access to next week's newspapers. We'd debated the morality of taking personal advantage of our capabilities, but I don't think the issue was ever in doubt. We won a small fortune at various race tracks, and continued to prosper until two gentlemen dropped by Shel's place one afternoon and told him that they were not sure what was behind his winning streak, but that if it continued, they would break his knees. They must have known enough about us to understand it wouldn't be necessary to repeat the message to me.

We considered switching into commodities. But neither of us understood much about them, so we took our next plunge in the stock market. "It's got to be illegal," said Shel. And I'd laughed. "How could it be?" I asked him. "There are no laws against time travel."

"Insider trading," he suggested.

Whatever. We justified our actions because gold was the commodity of choice upstream. It was research money, and we told each other it was for the good of mankind, although neither of us could quite explain how that was so. Gold was the one item that opened all doors, no matter what age you were in, no matter what road you traveled. If I learned anything during my years as Shel's interpreter and faithful Indian companion, it was that people will do anything for gold.

While I took a vaguely smug view of human greed, I put enough aside to buy a small estate in Exeter, and retired from the classroom to a life of books and contemplation. And travel through the dimensions.

Now that it was over, I expected to find it increasingly difficult to keep the secret. I had learned too much. I wanted to tell people what I'd done. Who I'd talked to. *So we were sitting over doughnuts and coffee on St. Helena, and I said to Napoleon—*

There was a thin layer of snow on the ground when I got home. Ray White, a retired tennis player who lives alone on the other side of Carmichael Drive, was out walking. He waved me down to tell me how sorry he was to hear about Shel's death. I thanked him and pulled into the driveway. A black car that I didn't recognize was parked in front of the house. Two people, a man and a woman, were sitting inside. They opened their doors and got out as I drifted to a stop. I turned off the engine without putting the car away.

The woman was taller, and more substantial, than the man. She held out a set of credentials. "Dr. Dryden?" she asked. "I'm Sgt. Lake, Carroll County Police." She smiled, an expressionless mechanical gesture lacking any warmth. "This is Sgt. Howard. Could we have a few minutes of your time?"

Her voice was low key. She would have been attractive had she been a trifle less official. She was in her late thirties, with cold dark eyes and a cynical expression that looked considerably older than she was.

"Sure," I said, wondering what it was about.

Sgt. Howard made no secret of the fact that he was bored. His eyes glided over me, and he dismissed me as a lowlife whose only conceivable interest to him might lie in my criminal past.

We stepped up onto the deck and went in through the sliding glass panels. Lake sat down on the sofa, while Howard undid a lumpy gray scarf, and took to wandering around the room, inspecting books, prints, stereo, whatever. I offered coffee.

"No, thanks," said Lake. Howard just looked as if I hadn't meant him. Lake crossed her legs. "I wanted first to offer my condolences on the death of Dr. Shelborne. I understand he was a close friend of yours?"

"That's correct," I said. "We've known each other for a long time."

She nodded, produced a leather-bound notebook, opened it, and wrote something down. "Did you have a professional relationship?" she asked.

"No," I said slowly. "We were just friends."

"I understand." She paused. "Dr. Dryden," she said, "I'm sorry to tell you this: Dr. Shelborne was murdered."

My first reaction was simply to disbelieve the statement. "You're not serious," I said.

"I never joke, Doctor. We believe someone attacked the victim in bed, struck him hard enough to fracture his skull, and set fire to the house."

Behind me, the floor creaked. Howard was moving around. "I don't believe it," I said.

Her eyes never left me. "The fire happened between 2:15 and 2:30 A.M., on the twelfth. Friday night, Saturday morning. I wonder if you'd mind telling me where you were at that time?"

"At home in bed," I said. There had been rumors that the fire was deliberately set, but I hadn't taken any of it seriously. "Asleep," I added unnecessarily. "I thought lightning hit the place?"

"No. There's really no question that it was arson."

"Hard to believe," I said.

"Why?"

"Nobody would want to kill Shel. He had no enemies. At least, none that I know of."

I was beginning to feel guilty. Authority figures always make me feel guilty. "You can't think of *anyone* who'd want him dead?"

"No," I said. But he had a lot of money. And there were relatives.

She looked down at her notebook. "Do you know if he kept any jewelry in the house?"

"No. He didn't wear jewelry. As far as I know, there was nothing like that around."

"How about cash?"

"I don't know." I started thinking about the gold coins that we always took with us when we went upstream. A stack of them had been locked in a desk drawer. (I had some of them upstairs in the wardrobe.) Could anyone have known about them? I considered mentioning them, but decided it would be prudent to keep quiet, since I couldn't explain how they were used. And it would make no sense that I knew about a lot of gold coins in his desk and had never asked about them. "Do you think it was burglars?" I said.

Her eyes wandered to one of the bookcases. It was filled with biographies and histories of the Renaissance. My favorite period. The eyes were black pools that seemed to be waiting for something to happen. "That's possible, I suppose." She canted her head to read a title. It was Ledesma's biography of Cervantes, in the original Spanish. "Although burglars don't usually burn the house down." Howard had got tired poking around, so he circled back and lowered himself into a chair. "Dr. Dryden," she continued, "is there anyone who can substantiate the fact that you were here asleep on the morning of the twelfth?"

"No," I said. "I was alone." The question surprised me. "You don't think *I* did it, do you?"

"We don't really think *anybody* did it, yet."

Howard caught her attention and directed it toward the wall. There was a photograph of the three of us, Shel and Helen and me, gathered around a table at the Beach Club. A mustard-colored umbrella shielded the table, and we were laughing and holding tall, cool drinks. She studied it, and turned back to me. "What exactly," she said, "is your relationship with Dr. Suchenko?"

I swallowed and felt the color draining out of my face. *I loved her. I've loved her from the moment I met her.* "We're friends," I said.

"Is that all?" I caught a hint of a smile. But nobody knew. I had kept my distance all this time. I'd told no one. Even Helen didn't know. Well, she knew, but neither of us had ever admitted to it.

"Yes," I said. "That's all."

She glanced around the room. "Nice house."

It was. I had treated myself pretty well, installing leather furniture and thick pile carpets and a stow-away bar and some original art. "Not bad for a teacher," she added.

"I don't teach anymore."

She closed her book. "So I understand."

I knew what was in her mind. "I did pretty well on the stock market," I said. I must have sounded defensive.

"As did Dr. Shelborne."

"Yes," I said. "That's so."

"Same investments?"

Yes, they were the same. With only slight variations, we'd parlayed the same companies into our respective fortunes. "By and large, yes," I said. "We did our research together. An investment club, you might say."

Her eyes lingered on me a moment too long. She began to button her jacket. "Well, I think that'll do, Dr. Dryden," she said.

I was still numb with the idea that someone might have murdered Shelborne. He had never flaunted his money, had never even moved out of that jerkwater townhouse over in River Park. But someone had found out. And they'd robbed him. Possibly he'd come home and they were already in the house. He might even have been upstream. Damn, what a jolt that would have been: return from an evening in Babylon and get attacked by burglars.

I opened the sliding door for them. "You will be in the area if we need you?" Lake asked. I assured her I would be, and that I would do whatever I could to help find Shel's killer. I watched them drive away and went back inside and locked the door. It had been painful enough believing that Shel had died through some arbitrary act of nature. But that a thug who had nothing whatever to contribute to the species would dare to take his life filled me with rage.

I poured a brandy and stared out the window. The snow was coming harder now. I couldn't believe anyone would think for a moment that *I* could be capable of such an act. It chilled me.

In back somewhere, something moved. It might have been a

branch scraping against the side of the house, but it sounded *inside.*

Snow fell steadily against the windows.

It came again. A floor board, maybe. Not much more than a whisper.

I took down a golf club, went out into the hallway, looked up the staircase and along the upper level. Glanced toward the kitchen.

Wood creaked.

Upstairs.

I started up, ascending as quietly as I could, and got about halfway when a movement at the door to the middle bedroom caught my attention. The wardrobe.

One of the curious phenomena associated with sudden and unexpected death is our inability to accept it when it strikes those close to us. We always imagine that the person we've lost is in the kitchen, or in the next room, and that it requires only that we call his name in the customary way to have him reappear in the customary place. I felt that way about Shel. We had lunched with Cervantes and ridden with Washington and lived a thousand other miracles. And when it was over, we always came back through the wardrobe and out onto the landing.

He came out now.

Shel stood up there, watching me.

I froze.

"Hello, Dave," he said.

I hung on to the banister, and the stairs felt slippery. "Shel," I said shakily, "is that *you?*"

He smiled. The old, crooked grin that I had thought not to see again. Some part of me that was too slow-witted to get flustered started flicking through explanations. Someone else had died in the fire. It was a dream. Shel had a twin.

"Yes," he said. "It's me. Are you okay?"

"Yeah."

"I'm sorry. I know this must be a shock." He moved toward me, along the top of the landing. I'm not sure what I was feeling. There was a rush of emotions, of joy, of anger, even of fear. He came down a few stairs, took my shoulders, and steadied me. His hands were solid, his smile very real, and my heart sank. Helen's image rose before me.

"I don't understand," I said.

Adrian Shelborne was tall and graceful, blessed with the clean-cut features of a romantic hero. His eyes were bright and sad. We slid down into sitting positions. "It's been a strange morning," he said.

"You're supposed to be dead."

He took a deep breath. "I know. I do believe I *am*, David."

Suddenly it was clear. "You're *downstream*."

"Yes," he said. "I'm downstream." He drew his legs up in a gesture that looked defensive. "You sure you're okay?"

"I've spent two weeks trying to get used to this. That you were gone—"

"It's true." He spaced the words, not able to accept it himself.

"When you go back—"

"—The house will burn, and I will be in it."

For a long time neither of us spoke. "Don't do it," I said at last. "Stay here."

"I can't *stay here*," he said. "What does that do to the time stream?"

Damn the time stream. I was thinking how candlelight filled Helen's eyes, how she and Shel had walked to the car together at the end of an evening, the press of her lips still vibrant against my cheek.

"Maybe you're right," I said.

"Of course I am. They just buried me, Dave. They found me in my bed. Did you know I didn't even get out of my bed?"

"Yes," I said. "I heard that."

"I don't believe it." He was pale, and I noticed his eyes were red.

My first ride with him had been to Gettysburg to listen to Lincoln. Afterward, when I was still trying to come to terms with the fact that I had really been there, he talked about having dinner with Caesar and drinking with Voltaire.

He must have felt my company to be of value, because he invited me to go a second time. I'd wondered where we were headed, expecting historic significance, but we went only to 1978 New Haven. We were riding a large misshapen brown chamber then, a thing that looked like a hot water tank. "I want you to meet someone," he said, as we emerged into streets filled with odd-looking cars. Her name was Martha, and she had been Shel's fiancée. Six hours after our arrival she would fall asleep at the wheel of her Ford. And Shel's life would change forever. "She and I had dinner last night at The Mug," he told me while we waited for her to come out of the telephone company building where she worked. "I never saw her again."

It was 5:00 P.M., and the first rush out the door was beginning.

"What are you going to do?" I'd asked.

He was in a state of extreme nervous agitation. "Talk to her."

I laughed. "Are you serious? What are you going to tell her?"

"I'll be careful," he said. Don't want to create a paradox. "I just want to see her again."

A light rain had begun. People started pouring out through the revolving doors. They looked up at the dark clouds, grimaced, and scattered to cars and buses, holding newspapers over their heads.

And then Martha came out.

I knew her immediately, because Shel stiffened and caught his breath. She paused to exchange a few words with another young woman. The rain intensified.

She was twenty years old and full of vitality and good humor. There was something of the tomboy about her, just giving way to a lush golden beauty. Her hair was shoulder-length and swung easily with every move. (I thought I saw much of Helen in her, in her eyes, in the set of her mouth, in her animation.) She was standing back under the building overhang, protected from the storm. She waved goodbye to the friend, and prepared to run for her car. But her gaze fell on us, on Shel. Her brow furrowed and she looked at us uncertainly.

Shel took a step forward.

I discovered I was holding his arm. Holding him back. A gust of wind blew loose dust and paper through the air. "Don't," I said.

"I know."

She shook her head as if she recognized a mistake, and hurried away. We watched her disappear around the corner out onto the parking lot.

We had talked about that incident many times, what might have happened had he intervened. We used to sit in the tower at the end of time, and he'd talk about feeling guilty because he had not prevented her death. "Maybe we can't change anything. But I feel as if I should have tried."

Now, starting carefully downstairs, he seemed frail. Disoriented. "They think you were murdered," I said.

"I know. I heard the conversation." In the living room he fell into an armchair.

My stomach was churning and I knew I wasn't thinking clearly. "What happened? How did you find out about the funeral?"

He didn't answer right away. "I was doing some research downstream," he said finally, "in the Trenton Library. In the reference section. I was looking at biographies, so I could plan future flights. You know how I work."

"Yes," I said.

"And I did something I knew was a mistake. Knew it while I was doing it. But I went ahead anyhow."

"You looked up your own biography."

"I couldn't help it." He massaged his jaw. "It's a terrible thing," he said, "to have the story of your entire life lying at your elbow. Unopened. Dave, I walked away from it twice and came back both times." He smiled weakly. "I will be remembered for my work in quantum transversals."

"This is what comes of traveling alone." I was irritated. "I told you we should never do that."

"It's done," he said. "Listen, if I hadn't looked, I'd be dead now."

I broke out a bottle of burgundy, filled two glasses and we drank it off and I filled them again. "What are you going to do?"

He shook his head. *"It's waiting for me back there.* I don't know *what* to do." His breathing was loud. Snow was piling up on the windows.

"The papers are predicting four inches," I said.

He nodded, as if it mattered. "The biography also says I was murdered. It didn't say by whom."

"It must have been burglars."

"At least," he said, "I'm warned. Maybe I should take a gun back with me."

"Maybe."

"What happens if I change it?"

"I don't know," I said.

"Well." He took a deep breath and tried to smile. "Anyway, I thought you'd want to know I'm okay." He snickered at that. His own joke.

I kept thinking about Helen. "Don't go back at all," I said. "With or without a gun."

"I'm not sure that's an option."

"It sure as hell is."

"At some point," he said, "for one reason or another, I went home." He was staring at the burgundy. He hadn't touched the second glass. "My God, Dave, I'm scared. I've never thought of myself as a coward, but I'm afraid to face this."

I just sat.

"It's knowing the way of it," he said. "That's what tears my heart out." I got up and looked at the storm.

"Stay here for now," I said. "There's no hurry."

He shook his head. "I just don't think the decision's in my hands." For a long time, neither of us spoke. Finally, he seemed to make up his mind. "I've got a few places to go. People to talk to. Then, when I've done what I need to do, I'll think about all this."

"Good."

He picked up the glass, drained it, wiped his lips, and drifted back against the sofa. "Let me ask you something: are they sure it's me?"

"I understand the body was burned beyond recognition," I said.

"There's something to think about. It could be anyone. And even if it *is* me, it might be a Schrödinger situation. As long as no one knows for certain, it might not matter."

"The police probably know. I assume they checked your dental records."

His brows drew together. "I suppose they do that sort of thing automatically. Do me a favor, though, and make sure they have a proper identification." He got up, wandered around the room, touching things, the books, the bust of Churchill, the P.C. He paused in front of the picture from the Beach Club. "I keep thinking how much it means to be alive. You know, Dave, I saw people out there today I haven't seen in years."

The room became very still.

He played with his glass. It was an expensive piece, chiseled, and he peered at its facets.

"I think you need to tell her," I said gently.

His expression clouded. "I know." He drew the words out. "I'll talk to her. When the time is right."

"Be careful," I said. "She isn't going to expect to see you."

3

Friday, November 25. Mid-morning.

The critical question was whether we had in fact buried Adrian Shelborne, or whether there was a possibility of mistaken identity. We talked through the night. But neither of us knew anything about police procedure in such matters, so I said I would look into it.

I started with Jerry Shelborne, who could hardly have been less like his brother. There was a mild physical resemblance between the two although Jerry had allowed the roast beef to pile up a little too much. He was a corporate lawyer who believed Shel had shuffled aimlessly through life, puttering away with notions that had no reality in the everyday world in which real people live. Even his brother's sudden wealth had not changed his opinion.

"I shouldn't speak ill of the dead," he told me that morning. "He was a decent man, had a lot of talent, but he never really made his life count for anything." Jerry sat behind a polished teak desk, guarded by an India rubber plant leaning toward a sun-filled window. The furniture was dark-stained, leather-padded, highly polished. Plaques covered the walls, appreciations from civic groups, awards from major corporations, various licenses and testaments. Photos of his two children were prominently displayed on the desk, a boy in a Little League uniform, a girl nuzzling a horse. His wife, who had left him years earlier, was missing.

"Actually," I said, "I thought he did pretty well."

"I don't mean money," he said. (I hadn't been thinking of money.) "But it seems to me a man has an obligation to live in his community. To make a contribution to it." He leaned back expansively and thrust a satisfied finger into a vest pocket. " 'To whom much is given,' " he said, " 'much shall be expected.' "

"I suppose," I said. "Anyway, I wanted to extend my sympathy."

"Thank you." Jerry rose, signaling that the interview was over.

We walked slowly toward the paneled door. "You know," I said, "this experience has a little bit of *déjà vu* about it."

He squinted at me. He didn't like me, and wasn't going to be bothered concealing it. "How do you mean?" I asked.

"There was a language preacher at Princeton, where I got my doctorate. Same thing happened to him. He lived alone and one night a gas main let go and blew up the whole house. They buried him, and then found out it wasn't him at all. He'd gone on an unannounced holiday to Vermont, and turned his place over to a friend. They didn't realize until several days after the funeral when he came home. Unsettled everybody.''

Jerry shook his head, amused at the colossal stupidity loose in the world. "Unfortunately," he said, "there's not much chance of that here. They tell me the dental records were dead on.''

■   ■   ■

I probably shouldn't have tried to see how Helen was doing, because my own emotions were still churning. But I called her from a drug store and she said yes, how about lunch? We met at an Applebee's in the Garden Square Mall.

She looked worn out. Her eyes were bloodshot, and she showed a tendency to lose the thread of the conversation. She and Shel had made no formal commitment, as far as I knew. But she had certainly believed they had a future together. Come what may. But Shel had been evasive. And there had been occasions when, discouraged that she got so little of his time, she'd opened up to me. I don't know if anything else in my life had ever been quite as painful as sitting with her, listening to her describe her frustration, watching the occasional tear roll down her cheek. She trusted me, absolutely.

"Are you all right?" she asked me.

"Yes," I said. "How about you?"

The talk was full of regrets, things not said, acts undone. The subject of the police suspicions came up, and we found it hard to subscribe to the burglar theory. "What kind of intruder," I asked, "kills a sleeping man, and then sets his house on fire?"

She was as soft and vulnerable that day as I've ever seen her. Ironically, by all the laws of nature, Shel was dead. Was I still bound to keep my distance? And the truth was that Shel did not even care enough to ease her suffering. I wondered how she would react if she knew Shel was probably sitting in my kitchen at that moment, making a submarine sandwich.

I wanted to tell her. There was a possibility that, when she *did* find out, she would hold it against *me*. I also wanted to keep Shel dead. That was hard to admit to myself, but it was true. I wanted nothing more than a clear channel with Helen Suchenko. But when I watched her bite down the pain, when the sobs began, when she excused herself with a shaky voice and hurried back to the ladies' room, I could stand it no more. "Helen," I said, "are you free this afternoon?"

She sighed. "I wanted to go into the office today, but people get nervous around weepy physicians. Yes, I'm more or less free. But I'm not in the mood to go anywhere."

"Can I persuade you to come out to my place?"

She looked desperately fragile. "I don't think so, Dave," she said. "I need some time."

A long silence fell between us. "Please," I said. "It's important."

        ■   ■   ■

More snow was coming. I watched it through the windshield, thick gray clouds drifting toward us. Approaching cars had their headlights on.

Helen followed me in her small blue Ford. I watched her in the mirror, playing back all possible scenarios on how to handle this. Tell her first, I finally decided. Leave out the time travel stuff. Use the story I'd told Jerry as an example of how misunderstandings can occur. *He's not dead, Helen.* She won't believe it, of course. But that's when I get him and bring him into the room. Best not to warn *him.* God knows how he would react. But get them together, present Shel with a *fait accompli,* and you will have done your self-sacrificial duty, Dave. You dumb bastard.

I pulled through blowing snow into my driveway, opened the garage, and went in. Helen rolled in beside me, and the doors closed. "Glad to be out of that," she said, with a brave smile that implied she had decided we needed something new to talk about.

The garage opened directly into the kitchen. I stopped before going through the door and listened. There were no sounds on the other side. "Helen," I said, "I've got something to tell you."

She pulled her coat around her. Her breath formed a mist. "We aren't going to go into it out here, I hope, are we?"

"No," I said, as if the notion were absurd, and opened the door. The kitchen was empty. I heard no sounds anywhere in the house.

"It's about Shel," I said.

She stepped past me and switched on the kitchen lights. "I know," she said. "What else could it be?"

A white envelope lay on the table, with my name on it, printed in his precise hand. I snatched it up, and she looked at me curiously. "What is it?" she asked.

"Just a list of things to do." I pushed it into my pocket. "How about some coffee?"

"Sure. Sounds good."

"It'll have to be instant," I said, putting a pot of water on the stove.

"Do you always do that?" she asked.

"Do what?"

"Write yourself notes?"

"It's my to-do list. It's the first thing I do every morning."

She got two cups down and I excused myself, slipped out, and opened the envelope.

∎   ∎   ∎

Dear Dave,

I don't know how to write this. But I have to think about what's happened, and figure out what I need to do. I don't want to jump the gun if it's not necessary. You understand.

I know this hasn't been easy for you. But I'm glad you were there. Thanks

Shel

P.S. I've left most of my estate to the Leukemia Foundation. That will generate a half-dozen lawsuits from my relatives. But if any of those vultures show signs of winning, I'll come back personally and deal with them.

I read it a half-dozen times. Then I crumpled it, tossed it, and went back to the kitchen.

She was looking out the window at the falling snow. Usually, my grounds were alive with blue jays and squirrels. But the critters were all tucked away now. "It's lovely," she said unexpectedly. And then: "So what's the surprise?"

Startled, I tried laughing to gain time. "Son of a gun," I said. "I went out to get it and came back without it." We strolled into the living room, where she sat down on the sofa. I hurried upstairs in search of an idea.

I think I mentioned that the wardrobe was also a small museum. There were items of inestimable value, but only if you knew their origin. We had scrolls from the library at Alexandria, a sextant designed and built by Leonardo, a silver bracelet that had once belonged to Calpurnia, a signed folio of *Hamlet*, a pocket watch that Leo Tolstoy had carried while writing *War and Peace.* There were photos of Martin Luther and Albert Schweitzer and Attila the Hun and Charles XII of Sweden. All more or less worthless.

I couldn't bear to give away Calpurnia's bracelet to someone who would not understand its true value. I settled instead for a gold medallion I'd bought from a merchant in Thebes during the fifth century, B.C. It carried a handsomely wrought likeness of a serpent. The Apollonian priest who was with me insisted that I had acquired a steal. At one time, he said, it had belonged to Aesculapius, the divine doctor, who had been so good he cured the dead. He backed up his view by trying to buy it from me, offering six times what I'd paid for it.

I carried it downstairs and gave it to Helen, telling her that Shel had wanted me to be sure she got it in the event anything happened to him. She glowed, and turned it over and over, unable to get enough of it. "It's exquisite," she said. And the tears came again.

If that thing had possessed any curative powers, I could have used them at that moment.

■ ■ ■

Snow filled the world. The stand of oaks bordering the approach to the house faded out. As did the stone wall along Carmichael Drive, and the hedges on the west side of the property. Gradually a heavy white curtain was drawn across the middle of the lawn. "I think we're going to get a foot before this is over," I told Helen.

She stood by the curtains, enjoying a glass of Chablis. I'd started the fire, and it crackled and popped comfortably. We added Mozart, and I hoped the storm would continue.

"I think so too," she said. A pair of headlights crept past, out beyond the stone wall. "I feel sorry for anybody out in this."

I stood beside her, and we talked inconsequentials. She had recovered herself, and I began to realize that it was her proximity to me, with all the baggage I brought to any meeting, that had triggered the emotional display earlier. I was not happy Shel was still in the field. But during that afternoon, I came to understand that even if Shel were safely in his grave, I might still be the embodiment of too many memories. The decent thing to do would be to fade out of her life, just as Carmichael Drive and the outer grounds were fading now. But I knew I could not bring myself to do that.

She talked about looking for a break in the weather so she could go home. But luck held and the break did not come. The snow piled up, and we stayed near the fire. I was alone at last with Helen Suchenko, and it was perhaps the most painful few hours of my life. Yet I would not have missed them, and I have replayed them countless times since, savoring every movement. Every word. *I feel sorry for anybody out in this.* I was out in it, and I believed I would never find shelter.

We watched the reports on the Weather Channel. It was a heavy system, moving down from Canada, low pressure and high pressure fronts colliding, eight inches predicted, which, on top of yesterday's storm, was expected to shut down the entire east coast from Boston to Baltimore.

She talked a lot about Shel that day. Periodically, she'd shake her head as if she'd remembered something, and then dismiss it. And she'd veer off onto some other subject, a movie she'd seen, the latest political scandal, a medical advance that held hope for a breakthrough in this or that. There were a couple of patients she was worried about, and a few hypochondriacs whose lives were centered on their imagined illnesses. I told her how much I missed teaching, which wasn't entirely true, but it's the sort of thing people expect you to say. What I really missed was a sense of purpose, a reason to exist. I had that upstairs, in notes detailing conversations with Rachmaninoff and Robert E. Lee and Oliver Cromwell and Aristotle and H. G. Wells. Those conversations would make the damnedest book the world had ever seen, reports by the principal actors on their ingenuity, their dreams, their follies. But it would never get written.

We lost the cable at four o'clock, and with it the Weather Channel.

Gradually, the light faded out of the sky. I put on steaks and Helen made up a salad. Our timing was perfect because the power failed just as we put everything on the table. I lit a couple of candles, and she sat in the flickering light and looked happy. If the clouds had not dissipated, at least for these few hours they had receded.

Afterward, we retreated into the living room. The music had been silenced by the power outage, so we sat listening to the fire and the whisper of snow against the house. Occasionally, I glanced up at the door of the wardrobe, half-expecting it to open. I tried to plan what I would do if Shel suddenly appeared on the landing. I was caught in the ultimate eternal triangle.

It did not happen. We talked into the early hours, until finally she gave out and fell asleep. I moved her to the sofa and went upstairs for blankets. The heating system, of course, was not working, nor was anything else in this all-electric house. The second floor was already cooling off, but I had plenty of firewood.

I settled into a large armchair and drifted into sleep. Somewhere around two, I woke and lay for a time, listening to the silence. The fire was low. I poked at it, and tossed on another log. Helen stirred but did not waken.

The storm must have passed over. Usually, even during the early morning hours, there are sounds: a passing car, the wind in the trees, a dog barking somewhere. But the world was absolutely still.

It was also absolutely dark. No stars. No lights of any kind.

I pointed a flashlight out the window. The night had closed in, wrapped itself around the house so tightly that the beam seemed to plunge into a black wall. I felt internal switches go to alert. It looked like an effect out of a Dracula film.

I picked up the phone to call the 24-hour weather line. But it was dead.

"What is it, Dave?" Helen's voice was soft in the dark.

"You awake?" I asked.

"Sort of."

"Come and take a look out the window."

She padded over. And caught her breath. "Where'd that come from?"

"I don't know."

We went outside. It was the thickest, darkest fog I'd ever seen. We didn't sleep well the rest of the night. At about six, Helen made toast over the fire, and I broke out some fruit juice. The lights were still off. More ominously, there was no sign of dawn.

I wondered about Ray White, my neighbor. Ray was a good guy, but he lived alone in a big house, and I thought of him over there wrapped in this goddamn black cloud with no power and maybe no food. He wasn't young, and I thought it would be a good idea to go check on him.

"I'll go with you," Helen said.

I got an extra flashlight, and we let ourselves out through the sliding door. I locked up, and we poked around until we found the pathway that leads down to the front gate. The flashlights didn't help much. There's a hundred-year-old oak midway between the house and the stone wall. It's only about ten feet off the walk, but we could not see it. I heard something stirring in its branches.

We picked our way to the front gate. I opened it, and we eased out onto the sidewalk. "The entrance to Ray's house is across the street, about twenty yards down," I said. "Stay close."

We stepped off the curb. Her hand tightened in mine. "Be careful," she said. "Somebody might be trying to drive."

We started across, but the snow cover stopped right in the middle of the street. It was the damnedest thing. There was no snow at all on the other side. There wasn't even *blacktop*. The surface had turned to rock. Where the hell was there rock on the other side of Carmichael Drive? A patch of grass, yes, and some concrete. But not rock.

Something in my voice scared her. "You sure you know where we are?"

"Yes," I said. "Of course."

The rock was black. It almost looked like marble.

We found no curb. No sidewalk. None of the trees that lined the far side of the street. No sign of the low wall that encloses Ray White's sprawling grounds and executive mansion.

We found nothing.

I tried calling White's name. But no one answered.

"Are you sure we came out the right way?" Helen asked.

4

Saturday, November 26. Late morning.

I woke up in a room lit only by a low fire. "You okay?" Helen asked. Her voice was thin.

I looked at the clock on the mantel. It was almost noon.

She came over and sat down beside me. "I've never seen weather like this," she said.

I got up, collected snow, and melted it to make water. (It's amazing how much snow you have to melt to get a little water.) I went into the bathroom, and, with the help of a flashlight, brushed my teeth. I tried to draw the bathroom around me, as a kind of shield against what was happening outside the house. The shower. The medicine cabinet. A couple of bars of soap. It was familiar, my anchor to reality.

When I returned downstairs, Helen was putting the phone back in the cradle. She shook her head no. It was still out. We opened a can of meat, added some vegetables, and cooked them over the fire. No matter what happened, we were in no personal danger. That was good to know, but it did not ease my fears.

Helen said she wasn't hungry, but she ate well anyhow. So did I.

It had to do with Shel. I knew that beyond any doubt. We were in the presence of the irrational. I wondered whether we had already done irreparable damage, whether the old world had already receded beyond recall. I was terrified.

When we'd finished eating, I went upstairs to the wardrobe. Shel would be easy to find.

■   ■   ■

He was standing where I knew he would be: on the slopes of Thermopolae watching the troops come in. He looked good. Tanned. Fit. Almost like a man on vacation. There were a few lines around the eyes, and I knew that, for him, several years had passed since the funeral.

"Shel," I said. "We need you."

"I know," he said gently. Below us, the Thespians were examining the ground on which they would fight. Out on the plain, north of the pass, we could see the Persian army. They stretched to the horizon. "I *will* go back."

"When?"

His eyes took on a haunted look. "When I'm ready. When I'm *able.* There's no hurry, Dave. We both know that."

"I'm not so sure," I said. "Something's wrong. We can't even *find* the rest of New Jersey."

"I'm trying to live my life," he said. "Be patient with me. I have a lot to do yet. But don't worry. You can count on me."

"When?"

"We have all the time in the world. Relax."

"Okay, Shel. Help me relax. If you're going to take care of everything, tell me what's causing the weather conditions back home? Why the power is out? Why I can't find my way across the street?"

"I know about all that," he said.

"And—?"

"Look. Maybe it has nothing to do with me."

The Hellenic squadrons were still filing in, their bright mail dusty from the journey north.

"I doubt it," I said.

He nodded. "As do I. But I've promised to go back. What more do you want?"

"Maybe you should do it now."

He glanced up at a promontory about a hundred feet over our heads. "What is *now* to you and me, Dave? What does the word mean?" When I did not respond, he knelt down and broke off a blade of grass. "Would you be willing to throw yourself from the top of that rock?"

"That has nothing to do with the business between us," I said.

"Not even if I pleaded with you to do so? If the world depended on it?"

I looked at him.

"What if it didn't matter whether you did it today or tomorrow? Or next month? Or forty years from now?"

"We don't *have* forty years."

"I'm not asking for forty of *your* years. I'm asking for forty of *mine*. I'll do it, Dave. God help me, I'll do it. But on my own schedule. Not yours."

I turned away from him, and he thought I was going to travel out. "Don't," he said. "Dave, try to understand. I'm scared of this."

"I know," I said.

"Good. I need you to know."

We passed ourselves off as traveling law-givers. We moved among the Hellenic troops, wishing them well, assuring them that Hellas would never forget them. We first glimpsed Leonidas sitting with his captains around a campfire.

People accustomed to modern security precautions would be amazed at how easy it was to approach him. He accepted our good wishes and observed that, considering our physical size, we would both have made excellent soldiers had we chosen that line of work. In fact, both Shel and I towered over him.

He had dark eyes and was only in his thirties. He brimmed with confidence, as did his men. There was no sense here of a doomed force.

He knew about the road that circled behind the pass, and he

had already dispatched troops to cover it. The Phoecians, as I recalled. Who would run at the first onset.

He invited us to share a meal. This was the third day of the standoff, before any blood had yet been spilt. We talked with him about Sparta's system of balancing the executive by crowning two kings. And whether democracy would really work in the long run. He thought not. "Athens cannot stay the course," he said. "They have no discipline, and their philosophers encourage them to put themselves before their country. God help us if the poison ever spreads to us." Later, over wine, he asked where we were from, explaining that he could not place the accent.

"America," I said.

He shook his head. "It must be far to the north. Or very small."

We each posed with Leonidas, and took pictures, explaining that it was a ritual that would allow us to share his courage. Sparks crackled up from the campfires, and the soldiers talked about home and the future.

Later, I traded a gold coin to one of the Thespian archers for an arrow. "I'm not sure that's a good idea," Shel said. "He may need the arrow before he's done."

I knew better. "One arrow more or less will make no difference. When the crunch comes, the Thespians will refuse to leave their Spartan allies. They'll die, too. All fifteen hundred of them."

And history will remember only the Spartans.

We watched them, exercising and playing games in full view of their Persian enemies. Shel turned to me, and his face was cold and hard. "You know, David," he said, "you are a monster."

5

Saturday, November 26. Mid-afternoon.

"This is not just heavy fog," she said. "It's *midnight* out there." Helen bit down on a grape.

I sat staring at the window, wondering what lay across Carmichael Drive.

She was lovely in the candlelight. "My guess is that a volcano erupted somewhere," she said. "I know that sounds crazy in South Jersey, but it's all I can think of." She was close to me. Warm and vulnerable and open. I reached out and touched her hair. Stroked it. She did not draw away. "I'm glad I was *here* when it happened, Dave. Whatever it is that's happened."

"So am I," I said.

She smiled appreciatively. And after a moment: "So what do *you* think?"

I took a deep breath. "I think I know what it is."

"I'm listening."

"Helen, there's a lot about Shel you don't know. To put it mildly." Her eyes widened. "Not other women," I added hurriedly. "Or anything like that."

That's not the kind of statement, I suppose, that gets any kind of reaction. Helen just froze in place. "I mean it," I said. "He has a working time machine." I was speaking of him in the present tense. With Shel it gets sort of confused.

"I could almost believe it," she said after a moment.

I'd been debating whether to destroy my own unit. It would have been the rational thing to do, and the day after Shel's death I'd even gone down to the river with it. But I hadn't been able to bring myself to throw it into the water. Next week, I'd thought. There's plenty of time. "Here," I said. "I'll show you one." I took it out of the desk and handed it to her. It looks like an oversized watch. "You just strap it on, connect it to the power pack, here. Set the destination, and punch the stem."

She looked at it curiously. "What *is* it really, Dave? A notebook TV?"

"Hell with this," I said. I have to keep my weight down. Three miles a day, every day. Other people walk around the block, or go down to a park. I like Ambrose, Ohio, near the beginning of the century. It's a pleasant little town with tree-lined streets and white picket fences, where straw hats are in vogue for the men, and bright ribbons for the ladies. Down at the barber's shop, the talk is mostly about the canal they're going to build through Panama.

I pulled Helen close, brought up Ambrose's coordinates, and told her to brace herself. "The sensation's a little odd at first. But it only lasts a few seconds. And I'll be with you."

The living room froze. She stiffened.

The walls and furniture faded to a green landscape with broad lawns and shingled houses and gas street lamps.

When we came out of it, she backed into me. "What happened?" she asked, looking wildly around.

"We've just gone upstream. Into the past. It's 1905. Theodore Roosevelt is President."

She didn't say anything for a long time. Birds sang, and in the distance we could hear the clean bang of church bells. We were standing outside a general store. About a block away there was a railroad siding.

The wind blew against us.

Her breathing had gone somewhat irregular. "It's okay," I said. "It just takes a little getting used to."

It was late September. People were working in yards, talking over back fences. "We're really here, aren't we?"

"Yes," I said. "We are."

"My God." She took a long, deep breath. The air smelled of burning leaves. I saw hurt come into her eyes. "Why didn't he ever say anything?"

"He kept it a secret for twenty years, Helen. It was habitual with him. He wanted to tell you, and he would have got around to it in his own good time." I shrugged. "Anyway, no one else knows. And no one should. I'll deny this whole thing if anyone ever asks."

She nodded. "Is this," lifting a hand in the general direction of the town, "connected with the problem at home? Is that what you're trying to say?"

"I think so." Cabbage was cooking somewhere. I told her about Shel, how he had died but was still alive. Her color changed and she moved closer to me. When I'd finished, she only stared straight ahead.

"He's still alive," she said at last.

In a way, he'll always be alive. "Yes," I said. "He's still out there." I explained about the funeral, and how he had reacted.

I could see her struggling to grasp the idea, and to control her anger. "Why didn't you tell me?"

"I didn't know how," I said numbly.

"You can take us back, right?"

"Home? Yes."

"And where else?"

"Anywhere. Well there are range limits, but nothing you'd care about."

A couple of kids with baseball gloves hurried past. "What you're saying," she said, "is that Shel should go back and walk into that fire. And if he doesn't, the black fog will not go away. Right? Is that what you're saying?"

"It's what I *think*. Yes, Helen, that's what he should do."

"But he's said he *would* do that? Right? And by the crazy logic of this business, it shouldn't matter when."

"But something's *wrong.* I think he never did go back. Never *will* go back. And I think that's the problem."

"I don't understand any of this," she said.

"I know." I watched a man with a handcart moving along the street, selling pickles and relishes. "I don't either. But there's a continuity. A track. Time flows along the track." I squeezed her hand. "We've torn out a piece of it."

"And—?"

"I think the locomotive went into the river."

She tried to digest that. "Okay," she said. "Grant the time machine. Dave, what you're asking him to do is unreasonable. I wouldn't go back either to get hit in the head and thrown into a fire. Would you?"

I got up. "Helen, what you or I would do doesn't matter much. I know this sounds cold, but I think we have to find a way to get Shel where he belongs."

She stood up, and looked west out of town. The fields were brown, dried out from the summer heat. "You know where to find him?"

"Yes."

"Will you take me to him?"

"Yes." And, after a pause: "Will you help me?"

She stared at the quiet little buildings. White clapboard houses. A carriage pulled by two horses just coming around a corner. "Nineteen-five," she said. "Shaw's just getting started."

I didn't push. I probably didn't need her to plead with him. Maybe just seeing her would jar something loose. And I knew where I wanted to confront him. At the one event in all of human history that might flay his conscience. "Let's go home," I said. "We need to do some sewing."

"Why?"

"You're going to need a costume."

She looked at me and her eyes were hooded. "Why don't we just shoot him?" she said. "And drag him back?"

■   ■   ■

"It seems that what you are really asking, Simmias, is whether death annihilates the soul?" Socrates looked from one to another of his friends.

The one who had put the question was, like most of the others, young and clear-eyed, but subdued in the shadow of the prison house. "It is an important matter," he said. "There is none of more importance. But we were reluctant—" He hesitated, his voice caught, and he could go no farther.

"I understand," said Socrates. "You fear this is an indelicate moment to raise such an issue. But if you would discuss it with me, we cannot very well postpone it, can we?"

"No, Socrates," said a thin young man with red hair. "Unfortunately, we cannot." This, I knew, was Crito.

Despite Plato's account, the final conversation between Socrates and his disciples did not take place in his cell. It might well have begun there, but they were in a wide, utilitarian meeting room when Helen and I arrived. Several women were present. Socrates, then seventy years old, sat at ease on a wooden chair, while the rest of us gathered around him in a half-circle. To my surprise and disappointment, I did not see Shel.

Socrates was, on first glance, a man of mundane appearance. He was of average height, for the time. He was clean-shaven, and he wore a dull red robe. Only his eyes were extraordinary, conveying the impression that they were lit from within. When they fell curiously on me, as they did from time to time, I imagined that he knew where I had come from, and why I was there.

Beside me, Helen writhed under the impact of conflicting emotions.

She had been ecstatic at the chance to see Shel again, although I knew she had not yet accepted the idea that he was alive. When he did not arrive, she looked at me as if to say she had told me so, and settled back to watch history unfold. She was, I thought, initially disappointed, in that the event seemed to be nothing more than a few people sitting around talking in an uncomfortable room in a prison. As if the scene should somehow be scored and choreographed and played to muffled drums. She had read Plato's account before we left. I tried to translate for her, but we gave it up. I was just getting in the way of the body language and the voices, which, she said, had a meaning and drama all their own.

"When?" she whispered, after we'd been there almost an hour. "When does it happen?"

"Sunset, I think," I said.

She made a noise deep in her throat.

"Why do men fear death?" Socrates asked.

"Because," said Crito, "they believe that it is the end of existence."

There were almost twenty people present. Most were young, but there was a sprinkling of middle-aged and elderly persons. The most venerable of these looked like Moses, a tall man with a white beard and expressive white eyebrows and a fierce countenance. He gazed intently at Socrates throughout, and periodically nodded when the philosopher hammered home a particularly salient point.

"And do all men fear death?" asked Socrates.

"Most assuredly, Socrates," said a boy, who could have been no more than eighteen.

Socrates addressed the boy. "Do even the brave fear death, Cebes?"

Cebes thought it over. "I have to think so, Socrates."

"Why then do the valiant dare death? Is it perhaps because they fear something else even more?"

"The loss of their honor," said Crito with conviction.

"Thus we are faced with the paradox that even the brave are driven by fear. Can we find no one who can face death with equanimity who is *not* driven by fear?"

Moses was staring at Helen. I moved protectively closer to her.

"Of all men," said Crito, "only you seem to show no concern at its approach."

Socrates smiled. "Of all men," he said, "only a philosopher can truly face down death. Because he knows quite certainly that the soul will proceed to a better existence. Provided he has maintained a lifelong pursuit of knowledge and virtue, and has not allowed his soul, which is his divine essence, to become entangled in concerns of the body. For when this happens, the soul takes on corporeal characteristics. And when death comes, it cannot escape. This is why cemeteries are restless at night."

"How can we be sure," asked a man in a blue toga who had not previously spoken, "that the soul, even if it succeeds in surviving the trauma of death, is not scattered by the first strong wind?"

It was not intended as a serious question, but Socrates saw that it affected the others. So he answered lightly, observing that it would be prudent to die on a calm day, and then undertook a serious response. He asked questions that elicited admissions that the soul was not physical and therefore could not be a composite object. "I think we need not fear that it will come apart," he said, with a touch of amusement.

One of the jailers lingered in the doorway throughout the long discussion. He seemed worried, and at one point cautioned Socrates against speaking so much, or getting excited. "If you get the heat up," he said, "the poison will not work well."

"We would not wish that," Socrates replied. But he saw the pained expression on the jailer's face, and I thought he immediately regretted the remark.

Women arrived with lunch, and several stayed, so that the room became more and more crowded. In fact, no doors were locked, and no guards, other than the reluctant jailer, were in evidence. Phaedo, who is the narrator of Plato's account, was beside me. He told me that the authorities had hoped profoundly that Socrates would run off. "They did everything they could to avoid this," he said. "There is even a rumor that last night they offered him money and transportation if he would leave."

Socrates saw us conversing, and he said, "Is there something in my reasoning that disturbs you?"

I'd lost the train of the discussion, but Phaedo said, "Yes, Socrates. However, I hesitate to put my objection to you."

Socrates turned a skeptical gaze on him. "Truth is what it is. Tell me what concerns you, Phaedo."

He swallowed to make sure of his voice. "Then let me ask," he said in a carefully neutral tone, "whether you are being truly objective on this matter. The sun is not far from the horizon and, although it grieves me to say it, were I in your position, I also would argue in favor of immortality."

"Were you in his position," said Crito, with a smile, "you would have taken the first ship to Syracuse." The company laughed, Socrates as heartily as any, and the strain seemed relieved for the moment.

"You are of course correct in asking, Phaedo. Am I seeking truth? Or trying to convince myself? I can only respond that, if my arguments are valid, then that is good. If they are false, and death does indeed mean annihilation, they nevertheless arm me to withstand its approach. And that too is good." He looked utterly composed. "If I'm wrong, it's an error that won't survive the sunset."

Simmias was seated immediately to the right of Moses. "I for one am convinced," he said. "Your arguments do not admit of refutation. And it is a comfort to me to believe that we have it in our power to draw this company together again in some place of the gods' choosing.''

"Yes," said Crito. "I agree. And, Socrates, we are fortunate to have you here to explain it to us."

"Anyone who has thought about these issues, should be able to reach, if not truth, at least a high degree of probability."

Moses seemed weighed down with the infirmities of age, and with the distress of the present calamity. Still, he continued to glance periodically at Helen. Now, for the first time, he spoke: "I very much fear, Socrates, that within a few hours there will be no one left anywhere in Hellas, or anywhere else for that matter, who will be able to make these matters plain."

"That's *Shel's* voice," Helen gasped, straining forward to see better. The light was not good, and he was turned away from us now, his face hidden in the folds of his hood.

Then he turned and looked openly at us. He smiled sadly at her. And his lips formed the English words *hello, Helen.*

She was getting to her feet.

At that moment, the jailer appeared with the poisoned cup, and the sight of him, and the silver vessel, froze everyone in the chamber. "I hope you understand, Socrates," he said, "this is not my doing."

"I know that, Thereus," said Socrates. "I am not angry with you."

"They always want to blame *me*," Thereus said.

Silence flowed through the chamber.

The jailer laid the cup on the table before him. "It is time," he said.

The rest of the company, following Helen's example, got one by one to their feet.

Socrates gave a coin to the jailer, squeezed his hand, thanked him, and turned to look at his friends one last time. "The world is very bright," he said. "But much of it is illusion. If we stare at it too long, in the way we look at the sun during an eclipse, it blinds us. Look at it only with the mind." He picked up the hemlock. Several in the assemblage started forward, but were restrained by their companions. Someone in back sobbed.

"Stay," a voice said sternly. "You have respected him all your life. Do so now."

He lifted the cup to his lips, and his hand trembled. It was the only time the mask slipped. Then he drank the hemlock down and laid the cup on the table. "I am sure Simmias is right," he said. "We shall gather again one day, as old friends should, in a far different chamber."

∎　∎　∎

Shel clasped Helen a long time in his big arms. "It's good to see you again," he said. Tears ran down his cheeks.

She shivered. "What happened to you?" she asked.

A smile flickered across his lips. "I've been traveling a long time." He stood silhouetted against the moon and the harbor. Behind us, the waterfront buildings of the Piraeus were illuminated by occasional lamps. He turned toward me. "David, you seem to have become my dark angel."

I was emotionally drained. "I'm sorry you feel that way," I said.

A gull wheeled overhead. "Socrates dies for a philosophical nicety. And Shelborne continues to run when all the world is at stake. Right?"

"That's right," I said.

Helen was still trembling. "I don't understand," she whispered.

His lips twitched, and he ran his hand over the long white whiskers. He looked haunted. "I haven't seen you for forty years," he said. "You have no idea how many times I've gone to sleep dreaming of you. And you are even lovelier than I remember."

I put a hand on her shoulder. Steadied her. "He's been out here a long time."

Her eyes blazed. "What happened to *my* Shel? What did you do with him?"

"He's been living his allotted years," he said. "Making them count for as much as he can as long as he can. Before my conscience here—" lifting his eyes and targeting me, "before my conscience succeeds in driving me into my grave."

She couldn't hold back any longer. Her tears flowed freely, and the water lapped against the piers. In that moment, I hated him.

"I've tried to go back," he said. "God help me, I've tried. But I could not bring myself to lie in that bed." Anger surfaced. I could not tell where it was directed. "Did you know that my skull was crushed?"

We knew.

He looked very old. And broken. He didn't seem to know what to do with his hands. The robes had no pockets. But he needed some kind of defensive gestures, so he folded his arms and turned to face the harbor. "I am not Socrates, Dave," he said. "I will not drink from his cup." His eyes locked on mine, and I could see him come to a decision. He drew us together, within the field of his Watch, and punched in a set of coordinates. "But I will settle the issue for you."

Helen shook her head no. No more surprises. And everything began to slow down. The harbor winked out, a ship's deck materialized underfoot, and the sky filled with fire.

■ ■ ■

We were on a Roman galley. The air was thick with powder and cinders, and the sails were down. We were pitching and rolling. The ocean broke across the deck, and men scrambled and swore at their stations. Below us, long oars dipped rhythmically into the waves. It was daylight, but we could not see more than twenty feet.

"How did you manage that?" I screamed at Shel over the hurricane of noise. The Watches had never possessed the precision to land people on a ship at sea.

"It's been a lot of years," he said. "Technology's better than it used to be."

"Where are we?" demanded Helen, barely able to make herself heard.

Shel was hanging onto a ladder. His clothes were drenched. "A.D. 79," he said. "Just west of Pompeii."

His eyes were afire. His silver hair was already streaked with black ash, and I began to suspect he had lost whatever anchor he might have had to reality. Time had become perhaps too slippery for him at last.

The ship rolled to starboard, and would have dumped Helen into the sea had the old man not grabbed her, and hung on, pushing me aside. "Isn't this glorious?" he asked.

"Why are we here?" Helen demanded, wiping her eyes.

The sea and the wind roared, and the dust was blinding.

"*I* will pick the time of my death," he cried. "And its manner."

I was trying to scramble toward him, but I could do no more than hang on.

"I am uniquely qualified—"

We went down into a trough, and I thought the sea was going to bury us.

"—To make that choice," he continued, ignoring the ocean. "My death will be an appropriate finale to the symphony of my life."

A fireball roared overhead, and plowed into the water.

"Don't do it," I cried.

"Have no fear, David. I'm not ready yet. But when I am, this will be the way of it." He smiled at me and touched the Watch. "What better end for a time traveler than sailing with Pliny the Elder?" And he was gone.

"What was that all about?" called Helen. We dipped again and salt water poured across the deck. "Maybe we ought to get out of here too."

I agreed, and wrapped one arm around a stanchion, something to hang onto while I set the Watch.

"Wait," she said. "Do you know who Pliny the Elder is?"

"A Roman philosopher."

"I did a paper on him once. He was an essayist and moralist. Fought a lot for the old values."

"Helen, can we talk about it later?"

"He was also a naval officer. He's trying to rescue survivors. Dave, if Shel meant what he said, he'll be back."

"I understand that."

"He'll be older. But he'll be back."

"We can't do anything about that. I don't think we want to wait around here."

We were on the starboard side, near the beam. The sails were down, and a few shadowy figures were moving through the volcanic haze. (I would have expected to hear the roar of the volcano, of Vesuvius, but the only noise came from the sea and the warm dry wind that blew across the deck.) "Let's try the other side," I said.

He was there, on the port quarter, clinging to a line, while the wind howled. Even more ancient this time, frail, weary, frightened. Dressed differently than he had been, in slacks and a green pullover that might have come out of the 1930s.

Cinders stung my eyes.

He saw us and waved. "I've been looking for you." His gaze lingered on Helen, and then drifted toward the sea. His eyes seemed utterly devoid of reasoning. Nothing of the old Shelborne seemed to be left.

"Don't," I cried.

She let go her handhold and tried to scramble across the pitching deck.

He was hanging onto a hawser, balanced near the rail.

The ship pitched, went up the front of a wave and down the back. He raised his hand in a farewell gesture, and the sea broke across the deck. I was thrown hard against a gunwale. The night was filled with water.

When it ended, Shel was gone. The rail was clear, and the line to which he'd clung whipped back and forth.

Helen shouted and pointed. I saw him briefly, rising over a swell, clutching a board and struggling to stay afloat, his white hair trailing in the water. But another wave broke over him and moments later the board popped to the surface, and drifted into the haze.

Something in the ship gave way with a loud crack, and the crewmen cried out. I pulled Helen close.

"Dead again," she said.

Maybe this time for good. I pressed the stem.

6

Saturday, November 26. Mid-afternoon.

We returned to the wardrobe in separate, but equally desperate, moods.

Helen could not connect the wild man on the galley with Shel, or even the moody septuagenarian on the dock at the Piraeus. Furthermore, she had not yet accepted either the reality or the implications of time travel. Yet, on a primal level, she had seen him. And for the second time during two weeks, she mourned him.

And I? I'd lost all feeling. How could I reconcile two graves? I collapsed into a chair and stared helplessly at the costumes, hanging neatly, marked off by period. Damn them. I remembered the planning and research that had gone into their creation. We had felt so well organized in those days. Prepared for anything.

I let it go.

And then I noticed that I was *seeing* the costumes. There was *light* in the room. It was gray, not bright, but it meant that the black mist was gone. I threw the curtains back, the walkway, the garage, were visible, huddled together in the storm. The wall still circled the property. And beyond the wall, I could see most of Carmichael Drive. *Most of it.* But Ray White's house was gone. As was the rest of the world over there. Carmichael Drive now skirted the edge of a precipice, its far side missing, broken off into a void. Beyond, I could see only gray sky.

Terrified, we went from room to room. Everywhere, in all directions, the picture was the same. On the east, where my property was most extensive, even the wall was gone. A seldom-used patio had been cut in half, and the stand of elms that used to provide shade for it now lined the limits of the world.

We opened a bottle of brandy and drew all the blinds in the house.

"Can't we replay that last scene?" she asked. "Go back and rescue him? I mean, that's the whole point of a time machine, isn't it? Nothing's ever irrevocable. You make a mistake, you go back and fix it."

I was tired and my head hurt and at that moment I hated Adrian Shelborne with every fiber of my being. "No," I said. "It would just make everything worse. We know what happened. We can't change *that*."

"Dave," she said, "how could we possibly make things *worse?*"

That was a pretty good question.

She eased onto a sofa and closed her eyes. "Time travel," she said, "isn't all it's cracked up to be, is it?"

Rain rattled against the windows. "We need to find a way to eliminate the paradox."

"Okay," she said. "What exactly is the paradox?"

I thought it over. "Adrian Shelborne has two graves. One out on Monument Hill. And the other in the Tyrrhenian Sea. We have to arrange things so that there is only one."

"Can we go back and stop the Friday night fire?"

"Same problem as trying a rescue on the galley. The Friday night fire has already happened, and if you prevent it, then what was the funeral all about?"

"It's like a big knot," she said. "No matter where you try to pull, everything just gets tighter."

We were still wearing our Hellenic robes, which were torn and soiled. And we both needed a shower, but there was no water. On the other hand, we *did* have rain. And as much privacy as we could ever want.

I got soap, towels, and wash cloths. She took the backyard, which was more sheltered (as if that mattered), and I stood out front. It was late November, but the weather had turned unseasonably warm nevertheless. Hot water would have been nice, but

I felt pretty good anyway after I'd dried off and changed into clean clothes.

Then we sat, each in a kind of private cocoon, thinking about options. Or things lost. The rain continued through the afternoon. I watched rivulets form and wondered how much soil was being washed over the edge. Where? Where would it be going? When the weather cleared, I promised myself that I would walk out and look down.

"Who's buried in the grave on Monument Hill?" she asked.

"Shel."

"How do we know? The body was burned beyond recognition."

"They checked his dental records. We can't *change* that."

She was sitting on the sofa with her legs drawn up under her. "We also can't recover the body from the Tyrrhenian Sea. We have to work on Monument Hill. What can we do about the dental records?"

I looked at her. "I don't think I understand."

"We have a time machine. Use your imagination."

Chain-reaction collisions have become an increasingly dangerous occurrence on limited-access highways around the world. Hundreds die every year, several thousand are injured, and property damage usually runs well into the millions. On the day that we buried Shel, there had been a pile-up in California. It had happened a little after eight o'clock in the morning under conditions of perfect visibility when a pickup rear-ended a station wagon full of kids headed for breakfast and Universal Studios.

We materialized by the side of the road moments after the chain reaction had ended. The highway and the shoulder were littered with wrecked vehicles. Some people were out of their cars trying to help; others were wandering dazed through the carnage. The morning air was filled with screams and the smell of burning oil.

"I'm not sure I can do this," Helen said, spotting a woman bleeding in an overturned Buick. She went over, got the door open, and motioned me to assist. The woman was unconscious, and her right arm was bent in an awkward manner.

"Helen," I said. "We have a bigger rescue to make."

She shook her head. No. This first.

She stopped the bleeding and I got someone to stay with the victim. We helped a few other people, pulled an elderly couple out of a burning van, got one man with two broken legs off the road. (I was horrified. She and I had always maintained a strict hands-off policy.) "We don't have time for this," I pleaded.

"I don't have time for anything else," she said.

Sirens were approaching. I let her go, concentrating on finding what we'd come for.

He was alone in a blue Toyota that had rolled over onto its roof. The front of the car was crumpled, a door was off, and the driver looked dead. He was bleeding heavily from a head wound. One tire was spinning slowly. I could find no pulse.

He was about the right size, tangled in a seat belt. When Helen got there, she confirmed that he was dead. I used a jack knife to cut him free. EMT's had arrived and were spreading out among the wrecked cars. Stretchers were appearing.

Helen could not keep her mind on what we were doing. "Your oath doesn't count," I said. "Not here. Let it go."

She looked at me out of empty eyes.

"Help me get him out," I said.

We wrapped him in plastic and laid him in the road. "He does look a little like Shel," she said in a small voice.

"Enough to get by."

Footsteps were approaching. Someone demanded to know what we were doing.

"It's okay," I said, "we're doctors." I pushed the stem and we were out of there.

．　．　．

His name was Victor Randall. His wallet carried pictures of an attractive woman with cropped brown hair seated with him in a front porch swing. And two kids. The kids were smiling up at the camera, one boy, one girl, both around seven or eight. "Maybe," Helen said, "when this is over, we can send them a note to explain things."

"We can't do that," I said.

"They'll never know what happened to him."

"That's right. And there's no way around it."

There was also about two hundred cash. Later, I would mail that back to the family.

We carried him down to the garage and put him in the Porsche. I adjusted the temporal sweep to maximum, so that when we went the car would go with us.

7

Thursday, November 10. Near midnight.

Mark S. Hightower had been Shel's dentist for seven years. He operated out of a medical building across the street from Friendship Hospital, where Helen had interned, and where she still served as a consultant.

I'd met Hightower once. He was short, barrel-chested, flat-skulled, a man who looked more like a professional wrestler than a dentist. But he was soft-spoken and, according to Shel, particularly good with kids.

We materialized on a lot down on Penrod Avenue, which was in the commercial district. The area was always deserted at night. Ten minutes later, we approached the hospital and pulled into the parking lot at the Forest Elm Medical Center. Hightower was located in back, well away from the street.

Victor was in the front seat, supported from behind by Helen. He was wrapped in plastic. He'd stopped bleeding, and we had cleaned him up as much as we could. "Are you sure you know how to do this?" I asked.

"Of course not, Dave," she said. "I'm not a dentist. But the equipment shouldn't be hard to figure out. How do we get inside?"

She looked dismayed. "I thought you could manage something a little more sophisticated than that. Why can't you just use that thing on your wrist and put us right inside the building?"

"Because it's not very precise. We could be here all night." I was thinking of Shel's trick in moving us from the Piraeus to the quarter-deck on Pliny's galley. If I'd tried that, we'd have gone into the ocean.

We put on gloves, and walked around the building, looking for an open window. There was none, but we found a rear exit that did not seem very sturdy. I wedged the tire iron between the door and the jamb, worked it back and forth, and felt the lock give. The door all but came off the hinges. I held my breath, waiting for the screech of a burglar alarm. It didn't come, and we were past the first hurdle.

We went back to the Porsche, got Victor out of the back seat and half-carried, half-dragged him around to the open door. Once inside, we set him in a chair. Then we turned on penlights and looked around. A half-dozen rooms were designated for patients, opening off a corridor that looped around to the reception area. I wandered from office to office, not really knowing what I was looking for. But Helen did one quick turn through the passageway and pointed at a machine tucked away in a corner. "This is it," she said. The manufacturer's label said it was an orthopantomograph. "It does panoramic X-rays," Helen said.

"Panoramic? What's that?"

"Full mouth. It should be all we'll need."

The idea was that the person being X-rayed placed his forehead against a plastic rest, and his chin in a cup-shaped support. The camera was located inside a cone which was mounted on a rotating arm. The arm and cone would traverse the head, and produce a single panoramic image of the teeth. The only problem was that the patient normally stood during the procedure.

"It'll take six to eight minutes," said Helen. "During that time we have to keep him absolutely still. Think you can do it?"

"I can do it," I said.

"Okay." She checked to make sure there was a film cassette in the machine. "Let's get him."

We carried Victor to the orthopantomograph. At Helen's suggestion, we'd brought along some cloth strips that we now used to secure him to the device. It was an uncomfortable and clumsy business, and he kept sliding away from us. Working in the dark complicated the procedure, but after about twenty minutes we had him in place.

"Okay," she said. "He should be all right now. Don't touch him. Right?"

I backed away.

"Something just occurred to me," I said. "Victor Randall already has the head wound."

Her eyes closed momentarily. "You're suggesting the arsonist didn't hit Shel in the head after all?"

"That's what I think."

She considered that piece of data. "This keeps getting weirder," she said.

A mirror was mounted on the machine directly in front of the patient's face. Helen pressed a button and a light went on in the center of the mirror. "They would tell the patient to watch the light," she said. "That's how they're sure they've got it lined up."

"How are *we* sure?"

"What's the term? 'Dead reckoning'?" She punched another button. A motor started, and the cone began to move.

Ten minutes later we took the cassette in back, carefully leaving Victor in place until we were sure we had good pictures. The developer was located in a windowless storage room. Helen removed the film from the cassette and ran it through the machine. When the finished picture came out, she handed it to me without looking at it. "What do you think?"

The entire mouth, uppers and lowers, was clear. "Looks good," I said.

She held it against the light. "Plenty of fillings on both sides. Let's see how it compares."

The records were maintained in manila folders behind the reception desk, where the counter hid her from anyone passing outside.

The folder was filled with records of Shel's visits. "He goes every three months," she said. "That's not bad." (She also tended to talk about him in the present tense.) The results of his most recent checkup were clipped on the right side. In the middle of the sheet was a panoramic picture, like the one we had just taken, and several smaller photos of individual sections. "I think they call these 'wings' " she said. "But when they bring a dentist in to identify a body, they do it with *these.*" She held up the panoramic and compared the two. "They don't look much alike in detail. And if they ever get around to comparing it with the wings, they'll notice something's wrong. But we should have enough to get by."

She removed Shel's panoramic, and substituted the one we had just taken. Then she replaced the folder. We wiped off the headrest and checked the floor to be sure we'd spilled no blood. "One more thing," said Helen. She inserted a fresh cassette into the orthopantomograph. "Okay. We've done what we came to do. Let's clear out."

"Wait a minute," I said. "They're going to know we broke in. We need to do something to make this look like a burglary." As far as I could see, there wasn't much worth stealing. Magazines. Cheap landscape prints on the walls. "How about a drill?" I asked. "They look expensive."

She squeezed my arm. "What kind of burglar would steal a *drill?*" She went on another tour of the office. Moments later, I heard glass breaking, and she came back with a couple of plastic bottles filled with pills. "Valium," she said.

8

Saturday, November 12. 1:15 A.M.

I had the coordinates for Shel's workshop, so we were able to go right in.

It was located in the basement of the townhouse, a small, cramped, cluttered place that had a Cray computer front and center, banks of displays, and an array of experimental equipment I had never begun to understand. Moments after we'd arrived, his oil heater came on with a thump.

Helen grumbled that we would have to carry the body up to the second floor. But I had done the best I could. The math had always been Shel's job, and the only place in the house I could get to was the workshop. So we dragged Victor up two flights of stairs to the master bedroom, dressed him in Shel's pajamas, turned back the sheets, and laid him in bed. We put his clothes into a plastic bag.

We also had a brick in the bag. Shel kept his car keys in the middle drawer of a desk on the first floor. We had debated just leaving the clothes to burn, but I wanted to leave nothing to chance. Despite what you might think about time travel, what we were doing was forever. We could not come back and undo it, because we were *here*, and we knew what the sequence of events was, and you couldn't change that without paying down the road. If we knew anything for sure now, we knew *that*.

I had left the Porsche at home this time. So we had to borrow Shel's green Pontiac. It had a vanity plate reading SHEL, and a lot of mileage. But he took good care of it. We drove down to the river. At the two-lane bridge that crosses the Narrows, we pulled off and waited until there was no traffic. Then we pulled onto the bridge, went out to the middle, where we presumed the water was deepest, and dropped the bag over the side. We still had Victor's wallet and ID, which I intended to burn.

We returned Shel's car to the garage. By now it was about a quarter to two, forty-eight minutes before a Mrs. Wilma Anderson would call to report a fire at the townhouse. I was a little concerned that we had cut things too close, and that the intruder might already be in the house. But the place was still quiet when I returned the car keys to the desk.

We locked the house, front and back, which was how we had

found it, and retired across the street, behind a hedge. We were satisfied with our night's work, and curious only to see who the criminal was. The neighborhood was tree-lined, well-lighted, quiet. The houses were middle-class, fronted by small yards that were usually fenced. Cars were parked on either side of the street. There was no traffic, and somewhere in the next block we could hear a cat yowling.

Two o'clock arrived.

"Getting late," Helen said.

Nothing stirred. "He's going to have to hurry up," I said.

She looked at me uncomfortably. "What happens if he doesn't come?"

"He *has* to come."

"Why?"

"Because that's the way it happened. We know that for an absolute fact."

She looked at her watch. Two-oh-one.

"I just had a thought," I said.

"Let's hear it."

"Maybe you're right. Maybe there is no firebug. Or rather, maybe *we* are the firebugs. After all, we already know where the fractured skull came from."

She nodded slowly. "Yeah," she said. "Maybe."

I left the shelter of the hedge and walked quickly across the street, entered Shel's driveway, and went back into the garage. There were several gas cans. They were all empty.

I needed the car keys. But I was locked out now. I used a rock to break a window, got in, and retrieved the keys. I threw the empty cans into the trunk of his Pontiac. "Wait here," I told Helen as I backed out onto the street. "Keep an eye open in case someone *does* show up."

"Where are you going?"

"To get some gas."

There was an all-night station down on River Road, only a few blocks away. It was one of those places where, after eleven o'clock, the cashier locks himself into a glass cage. He was a middle-aged, worn-out guy sitting in a cloud of cigarette smoke. A toothpick rolled relentlessly from one side of his mouth to the other. I filled three cans, paid, and drove back to the townhouse.

It was 2:17 when we began sloshing the gasoline around the basement. We emptied a can on the stairway and another upstairs, taking particular care to drench the master bedroom, where Victor Randall lay. We poured the rest of it on the first floor, and so thoroughly soaked the entry that I was afraid to go near it with a lighted match. But at 2:25 we touched it off.

Helen and I watched for a time from a block away. The flames cast a pale glare in the sky, and sparks floated overhead. We didn't know much about Victor Randall, but what we did know maybe was enough. He'd been a husband and a father. In their photos, his wife and kids had looked happy. And he got a Viking's funeral.

"What do you think?" asked Helen. "Will it be all right now?"

"Yeah," I said. "I hope so."

9

Sunday, November 27. Mid-morning.

In the end, the Great November Delusion was written off as precisely that, a kind of mass hysteria that settled across a substantial chunk of New Jersey, Pennsylvania, Maryland, and Delaware. Elsewhere, life had gone on as usual, except that the affected area seemed to have vanished behind a black shroud that turned back all attempts at entry, and admitted no signals.

Fortunately, it had lasted only a few hours. When it ended, persons who had been inside emerged with a range of stories. They had been stranded on rocky shores or amid needle peaks or in gritty wastes where nothing grew. One family claimed to have been inside a house that had an infinite number of stairways and chambers, but no doors or windows. Psychologists pointed out that the one element that appeared in all accounts was isolation. Sometimes it had been whole communities that were isolated; sometimes families. Occasionally it had been individuals. The general consensus was that, whatever the cause, therapists would be assured of a handsome income for years to come.

My first act on returning home was to destroy Victor Randall's wallet and ID. The TV was back with full coverage of the phenomenon. The National Guard was out, and experts were already appearing on talk shows. I would have been ecstatic with the way things had turned out, except that Helen had sunk into a dark mood. She was thinking about Shel.

"We saved the world," I told her. I showered and changed and put on some bacon and eggs. By the time she came downstairs it was ready. She ate, and cried a little, and congratulated me. "We were brilliant," she said.

After breakfast she seemed reluctant to leave, as if something had been left undone. But she announced finally that she needed to get back to her apartment and see how things were.

She had just started for the door when we heard a car pull up. "It's a woman," she said, looking out the window. "Friend of yours?"

It was Sgt. Lake. She was alone this time.

We watched her climb the porch steps. A moment later the door bell rang.

"This won't look so good," Helen said.

"I know. You want to duck upstairs?"

She thought about it. "No. What are we hiding?"

The bell sounded again. I crossed the room and opened up.

"Good morning, Dr. Dryden," said the detective. "I'm glad to see you came through it all right. Everything is okay?"

"Yes," I said. "How about you?"

Her cheeks were pale. "Good," she said. "I hope it's over." She seemed far more human than during her earlier visit.

"Where's your partner?" I asked.

She smiled. "Everything's bedlam downtown. A lot of people went berserk during that *thing*, whatever it was. We're going to be busy for a while." She took a deep breath and, for the moment at least, some unconscious communication passed between us. "I wonder if I could talk with you?"

"Of course." I stepped back and she came in.

"It's chaos." She seemed not quite able to focus. "Fires, people in shock, heart attacks everywhere. It hasn't been good." She saw Helen and her eyes widened. "Hello, Doctor. I didn't expect to see you here. I expect you're in for a busy day too."

Helen nodded. "You okay?" she asked.

"Yeah. Thanks. I'm fine." She stared out over my shoulder. Then, with a start, she tried to wave it all away.

We sat down. "What was it like here?" she asked.

I described what I'd seen. While I was doing so, Helen poured her some coffee and she relaxed a little. She had been caught in her car during the event on a piece of rain-swept foggy highway that just went round and round, covering the same ground. "Damnedest thing," she said. "No matter what I did, I couldn't get off." She shook her head and drank coffee.

"I could prescribe a sedative," said Helen.

"No, thank you," Lake said. "I should be one my way anyhow." She patted my shoulder in a comradely way and let herself out.

Lake turned her attention to me. "Doctor," she said, "you've informed us that you were home in bed at the time of Dr. Shelborne's death. Do you stand by that statement?"

"Yes," I said, puzzled. "I do."

"Are you sure?"

The question hung in the sunlit air. "Of course I am. Why do you ask?"

I could read nothing in her expression. "Someone answering your description was seen in the neighborhood of the townhouse shortly before the fire."

"It wasn't *me*," I said, suddenly remembering the man at the gas station. And I'd been driving Shel's car. With his vanity plate on the front to underscore the point.

"Okay," she said. "I wonder if you'd mind coming down to the station with me, so we can clear the matter up. Get it settled."

"Sure. Be glad to."

We stood up. "Could I have a moment, please?"

"Certainly," she said, and went outside.

I called Helen on her cellular. "Don't panic," she said. "All you need is a good alibi."

"I don't *have* an alibi."

"For God's sake, Dave. You've got something better. You have a *time machine*."

"Okay. Sure. But if I go back and set up an alibi, why didn't I tell them the truth in the beginning?"

"Because you were protecting a woman's reputation," she said. "What else would you be doing at two o'clock in the morning? Get out your little black book." It might have been my imagination, but I thought the reference to my little black book angered her slightly.

10

Friday, November 11. Early evening.

The problem was that I didn't have a little black book. I've never been all that successful with women. Not to the extent, certainly, that I could call one up with a reasonable hope of finishing the night in her bed.

What other option did I have? I could try to find someone in a bar, but you didn't really lie to the police in a murder case to protect a casual pickup.

I pulled over to the curb beside an all-night restaurant, planning to go in and talk to the waitress a lot. Give her a huge tip so she couldn't possibly forget me. But then, how would I explain why I had lied?

The restaurant was close to the river, a rundown area lined with crumbling warehouses. A police cruiser slowed down and pulled in behind the Porsche. The cop got out and I lowered the window.

"Anything wrong, Officer?" I asked. He was small, black, well-pressed.

"I was going to ask you the same thing, sir. This is not a good neighborhood."

"I was just trying to decide whether I wanted a hamburger."

"Yes, sir," he said. I could hear the murmur of his radio. "Well, listen, I'd make up my mind, one way or the other. I wouldn't hang around out here if I were you."

I smiled and gave him the thumbs-up. "Thanks," I said.

He got back in his cruiser and pulled out. I watched his lights turn left at the next intersection. And I knew what I was going to do.

■   ■   ■

I drove south on route 130 for about three-quarters of an hour, and then turned east on a two-lane. Somewhere around eleven, I entered Clovis, New Jersey, and decided it was just what I was looking for.

The Clovis police station occupied a small two-story building beside the post office. The Red Lantern Bar was located about two blocks away, on the other side of the street.

I parked in a lighted spot close to the police station, walked to the bar, and went inside. It was smoky, subdued, and reeking with the smell of dead cigarettes and stale beer. Most of the action was over around the dart board.

I settled in at the bar and commenced drinking Scotch. I stayed with it until the bartender suggested I'd had enough, which usually wouldn't have taken long because I don't have much capacity for alcohol. But that night my mind stayed clear. Not my motor coordination, though. I paid up, eased off the stool, and negotiated my way back onto the street.

I turned right and moved methodically toward the police station, putting one foot in front of the other. When I got close, I added a little panache to my stagger, tried a couple of practice giggles to warm up, and lurched in through the front door.

A man with two stripes came out of a back room.

"Good evening, Officer," I said, with exaggerated formality and the widest grin I could manage, which was then pretty wide. "Can you give me directions to Atlantic City?"

The corporal shook his head sadly. "Do you have some identification, sir?"

"Yes, I do," I said. "But I don't see why my name is any business of yours. I'm in a hurry."

He sighed. "Where are you from?"

"Two weeks from Sunday," I said. "I'm a time traveler."

11

Sunday, November 27. Late evening.

Sgt. Lake was surprised and, I thought, disappointed to learn that I had been in jail on the night of the fire. She said that she understood why I had been reluctant to say anything, but admonished me on the virtues of being honest with law enforcement authorities.

I called Helen, looking forward to an evening of celebration. But I only got her recording machine. "Call me when you get in," I told it.

The call never came. Just before midnight, when I'd given up and was getting ready to go to bed, I noticed a white envelope on the kitchen table.

My name was printed on it in neat, spare characters.

Dear Dave (it read),

Shel is back! My Shel. The real one. He wants to take me off somewhere, and I don't know where, but I can't resist. Maybe we will live near the Parthenon, or maybe Paris during the 1920s. I don't know. But I do know you will be happy for me.

I will never forget you, Dave.

> *Love,*
> *Helen*

P.S. We left something for you. In the wardrobe.

I read it several times, and finally crumpled it.

They'd left the *Hermes*. They had positioned it carefully under the light, to achieve maximum effect. Not that it needed it.

I stood a long time admiring the piece. It was Michelangelo at his most brilliant. But it wasn't Helen.

I went downstairs and wandered through the house. It was empty, full of echoes and the sound of the wind. More desolate now than it had been when it was the only thing in the universe.

I remembered how Helen had sounded when she thought she was sending me back to sleep with another woman. And I wondered why I was so ready to give up.

I did some quick research, went back to the wardrobe, scarcely noticing the statue, and put on turn-of-the-century evening clothes.

Next stop: The Court Theater in Sloane Square, London, to watch the opening performance of *Man and Superman*.

You're damned right, Shelborne.

Time travelers never die.

Larry Niven

Rotating Cylinders
and the
Possibility of Global Causality Violation

From *Microcosmic Tales*, 1978

Perhaps the greatest discovery in history is the discovery that time travel is possible. For the Emperor, time travel could be the way to finally destroy the Hallane Regency, by wiping out their ancestors.

But it is the second greatest discovery in history that is truly the most amazing: Time travel doesn't work. While time travel is a mathematical possibility, because time travel would violate the principle of causality—that an event cannot occur before the event that caused it—time travel is outlawed by the Universe.

But the Hallane Regency doesn't know this, so the Emperor leaks the secret of time travel to the Hallanes—and they waste their resources trying to perfect time travel so they can destroy the Emperor. But in the ultimate time travel paradox, the Hallanes come too close to perfecting time travel, and the Universe does what the Universe has always done when somebody has been close to attempting to travel in time: It boldly terminates the attempt, with dire consequences for all.

B. A.

"THREE HUNDRED YEARS WE'VE BEEN AT WAR," SAID QUIFTING, "and I have the means to end it. I can destroy the Hallane Regency." He seemed very pleased with himself, and not at all awed at being in the presence of the emperor of seventy worlds.

The aforementioned emperor said, "That's a neat trick. If you can't pull it off, you can guess what penalties I might impose. None of my generals would dare such a brag."

"Their tools are not mine." Quifting shifted in a valuable antique massage chair. He was small and round and completely hairless: the style of the nonaristocratic professional. He should have been overawed, and frightened. "I'm a mathematician. Would you agree that a time machine would be a useful weapon of war?"

"I would," said the emperor. "Or I'd take a faster-than-light starship, if you're offering miracles."

"I'm offering miracles," said Quifting, "but to the enemy."

The emperor wondered if Quifting was mad. Mad or not, he was hardly dangerous. The emperor was halfway around the planet from him, on the night side. His side of the meeting room was only a holographic projection, though Quifting wouldn't know that.

Half a dozen clerks and couriers had allowed this man to reach the emperor's ersatz presence. Why? Possibly Quifting had useful suggestions, but not necessarily. Sometimes they let an entertaining madman through, lest the emperor grow bored.

"It's a very old idea," Quifting said earnestly. "I've traced it back three thousand years, to the era when space-flight itself was only a dream. I can demonstrate that a massive rotating cylinder, infinite in length, can be circled by closed timelike paths. It seems reasonable that a long but finite—"

"Wait. I must have missed something."

"Take a massive cylinder," Quifting said patiently, "and put a rapid spin on it. I can plot a course for a spacecraft that will bring it around the cylinder and back to its starting point in space and time."

"Ah. A functioning time machine, then. Done with relativity, I expect. But must a cylinder be infinitely long?"

"I wouldn't think so. A long but finite cylinder ought to show the same behavior, except near the endpoints."

"And when you say you can demonstrate this . . ."

"To another mathematician. Otherwise I would not have been allowed to meet Your Splendor. In addition, there are historical reasons to think that the cylinder need not be infinite."

Now the emperor was jolted. "Historical? Really?"

"That's surprising, isn't it? But it's easy to design a time machine, given the Terching Effect. You know about the Terching Effect?"

"It's what makes a warship's hull so rigid," confirmed the emperor.

"Yes. The cylinder must be very strong to take the rotation without flying apart. Of course it would be enormously expensive to build. But others have tried it. The Six Worlds Alliance started one during the Free Trade period."

"Really?"

"We have the records. Archeology had them fifty years ago, but they had no idea what the construct was intended to do. Idiots." Quifting's scowl was brief. "Never mind. A thousand years later, during the One Race Wars, the Mao Buddhists started to build such a time machine out in Sol's cometary halo. Again, behind the Coal Sack is a long, massive cylinder, a quasi-Terching-Effect shell enclosing a neutronium core. We think an alien race called the Kchipreesee built it. The ends are flared, possibly to compensate for edge effects, and there are fusion rocket motors in orbit around it, ready for attachment to spin it up to speed."

"Did nobody ever finish one of these, ah, time machines?"

Quifting pounced on the word. "Nobody!" and he leaned forward, grinning savagely at the emperor. No, he was not awed. A mathematician rules his empire absolutely, and it is more predictable, easier to manipulate, than any universe an emperor would dare believe in.

"The Six Worlds Alliance fell apart before their project was barely started. The Mao Buddhist attempt—well, you know what happened to Sol system during the One Race Wars. As for the Kchipreesee, I'm told that many generations of space travel killed them off through biorhythm upset."

"That's ridiculous."

"It may be, but they are certainly extinct, and they certainly left their artifact half-finished."

"I don't understand," the emperor admitted. He was tall, muscular, built like a middleweight boxer. Health was the mark of aristocracy in this age. "You seem to be saying that building a time machine is simple but expensive, that it would handle any number of ships—it would, wouldn't it?"

"Oh, yes."

"—and send them back in time to exterminate one's enemies' ancestors. Others have tried it. But in practice, the project is always interrupted or abandoned."

"Exactly."

"Why?"

"Do you believe in cause and effect?"

"Of course. I . . . suppose that means I don't believe in time travel, doesn't it?"

"A working time machine would destroy the cause-and-effect relationship of the universe. It seems the universe resists such meddling. No time machine had ever been put into working condition. If the Hallane Regency tries it something will stop them. The Coal Sack is in Hallane space. They need only attach motors to the Kchipreesee device and spin it up."

"Bringing bad luck down upon their foolish heads. Hubris. The pride that challenges the gods. I like it. Yes. Let me see . . ." The emperor generally left war to his generals, but he took a high interest in espionage. He tapped at a pocket computer and said, "Get me Director Chilbreez."

To Quifting he said, "The director doesn't always arrest enemy spies. Sometimes he just watches 'em. I'll have him pick one and give him a lucky break. Let him stumble on a vital secret, as it were."

"You'd have to back it up—"

"Ah, but we're already trying to recapture Coal Sack space. We'll step up the attacks a little. We should be able to convince the Hallanes that we're trying to take away their time machine. Even if you're completely wrong—which I suspect is true—we'll have them wasting some of their industrial capacity. Maybe start some factional disputes, too. Pro-and anti-time-machine. Hah!" The emperor's smile suddenly left him. "Suppose they actually build a time machine?"

"They won't."

"But a time machine is possible? The mathematics works?"

"But that's the point, Your Splendor. The universe itself resists such things." Quifting smiled confidently. "Don't you believe in cause and effect?"

"Yes."

Violet-white light blazed through the windows behind the mathematician, making of him a star-edged black shadow. Quifting ran forward and smashed into the holograph wall. His eyes were shut tight, his clothes were afire. "What is it?" he screamed. "What's happening?"

"I imagine the sun has gone nova," said the emperor.

The wall went black.

A dulcet voice spoke. "Director Chilbreez on the line."

"Never mind." There was no point now in telling the director how to get an enemy to build a time machine. The universe protected its cause-and-effect basis with humorless ferocity. Director Chilbreez was doomed; and perhaps Quifting had ended the war after all. The emperor went to the window. A churning aurora blazed bright as day, and grew brighter still.

Derryl Murphy

What Goes Around
1997

When Henry, a washed-up actor who played "Space Cop" in his heyday, now adrift in booze and shattered ambition, is visited by a ghost from the future, he wonders if he has lost his mind. But when the once-scandalized television "Space Cop" travels forward in time, he finds that his most irrelevant, and painful, role has affected tens of millions and has made him a star. But how? And why?

B. A.

Episode One: We meet our hero, learn a bit of his background, and leap wildly back and forth through time

THE OPENING SEQUENCE OF "SPACE COPS" VIRTUALLY GUARANteed a great audience from the very beginning. Special effects that were extremely sophisticated for the time, exciting music and fast-paced action, and of course the handsome face of star and producer Henry Angel made for great television appeal, a very new concept at the time. As well, the series was true to the beliefs of the 1950's; while fear of nuclear destruction hung over the heads of millions of Americans, the family, strong values and mostly a bright future were what they wanted to see on their primitive picture tubes each week.

Witness this portion of the opening. Before credits roll, Captain Maxwell (played by Angel) and his sidekick Corporal Exeter (played by former child radio actor Spike Chapman) board their space car and launch from the asteroid they use as headquarters.

Flames jet out from the exhaust, the car tumbles wildly, bucking and heaving until, through sheer physical might, Captain Maxwell rights it and flies into the camera, the dissolve moving from space car to Maxwell to space car to Maxwell almost seamlessly.

Is it any wonder that such a nation, influenced so mightily by one show, would become the single most dominant space-faring country right into the late twenty-first century?

From "Space Cops": *A Modern History,*
An AmeriNet 46 production

■   ■   ■

Captain Michael Davis of Sector Seven pulls himself along the rails, eschewing the artificial gravity available to him at the wave of a hand. There is an emergency in his sector, a civilian ship overrun by criminals and pirates, and he needs to get to his space car as quickly as possible. Red lights flash and alarms ring all around him.

"Davis, you there?"

Captain Davis taps his wrist, activates his comm. "Here, Slam." Slam Rankin is the dispatch officer for Sector Seven.

"There are three of them, rogues that spilled over from the Belt Wars. We managed to get good pictures before they downed the emergency activator. One of them is Marcus Heimdal."

"Thanks, Slam. Over." Heimdal! Davis picks up speed. Heimdal was the scourge of the force, but he'd gone missing four years before. Apparently to pull mercenary duty in the Belt. What was he doing back?

Private Eddie Stern is waiting in his seat in the space car when Davis arrives. They quickly check all the functions, then get clearance to launch. The roar is momentarily deafening, and they are punched back into their seats as they clear Sector Seven H.Q. The car bucks and rocks and rolls for a moment, but Davis pulls it back under control and they head off to intercept the civilian ship and the pirates aboard it.

Private Stern occupies himself with readying the weapons and checking his helmet. Nerves of steel, that boy.

They approach the civilian ship.

■   ■   ■

Henry sits in his living room, black and white TV screen flickering silently in the background, bottle of beer in hand, waiting for another visit. He knows that if he goes into his bedroom, it will happen right away, but he does not want that. In a perfect world, none of this would be happening, he wouldn't be afraid that he was losing his sanity, he wouldn't be losing himself in three cases of beer a day. In a perfect world he would have made it, wouldn't have been caught with that lighting tech and fallen into a daze of beer and whiskey, paid for by hocking furniture and crappy little jobs for shithead directors in films that no one will ever see, or ever want to see.

And a fucking crazy ghost from the future wouldn't be visiting him.

■   ■   ■

As we see in this colorized footage of him signing autographs, Henry Angel was not only remarkably successful and popular, he was also very genial. He was especially fond of children, and often broke off early from public functions if he knew of a pick-up game of baseball being played in some nearby neighborhood.

But, it must be admitted, there was a dark side to Henry Angel. He was twice-divorced, and records show that he once received a speeding ticket from the California Highway Patrol (*see: CHiPs*; Erik Estrada; 1970's). But this did not ever get in the way of his popularity.

■   ■   ■

"Found him!" The voice is distant, kind of muffled.

"Hmm?"

"I said I found him. He's locked, Michael, settled and ready to pull!"

Michael switches on slomo/delay, tunes half of his view to see a representation of Arnold's face; a little fuzzy, motion not quite realtime, little mem going into receiving the visit, most being kept for the standard functions. "You're serious?"

Arnold's face jumps about as he nods; his scalp slides off and floats momentarily through the air before settling in again on his chin, a new beard. "I found him at the address we got from those old files."

"Does he know?"

A herky-jerky smile, teeth dancing a chorus line, all dressed up in perfect little tuxes. "I've been there three times now, tried to talk to him. He doesn't want to hear it, so I figure I should do the pull, explain from this side. *Fait accompli*, as it were."

"Good idea," says Mike. "I'll be out as soon as I finish running this mission."

■   ■   ■

When the ghost comes the last time for him, Henry is ready. Good and pissed, but ready. He stands, a little shakily, brushes pretzel crumbs from his shirt and pants, then stumbles forward into the receptor, glaring white light and screaming winds pounding his senses, scaring him so bad he shits his pants as he steps in and falls through time.

I mean, why the fuck not?

Episode Two: Our hero begins to see the future as it might really be

(POV Shift: Pull camera back, encompassing view of large office area. Tangled mass of wires lead from deposit site to fuser and two well-used pocket supercomputers sitting on otherwise empty desk, walls a nondescript and unadorned brown, doors occupying three of them)

Henry staggered as he hit the floor, shuffled drunkenly for a second or two, then fell flat on his face. A pair of hands gently grabbed him around the waist and lifted him up, helped him shuffle along the floor and through a door, where he was sat upon a cot. He blinked fiercely the whole time, trying to shake the vicious light from his head, the spinning of the decades and more from his eyes.

"There's a toilet behind you," said a voice, presumably belonging to the hands. "I'll leave you for a few minutes, let you clean up. You can drop your clothes in the basket by the sink; there's a fresh uniform for you, hanging on the wall behind me." A door shut.

Henry sat for another moment to let his eyes clear, uncomfortable with the lump of stool in his pants, unable to convince himself to get up. As things slipped back into focus, he took notice of what surrounded him in the room. It was small, maybe ten feet by twelve, the walls a quiet shade of brown and the door an off-white. The cot was small, low to the ground, and didn't seem to have springs or any other metal; he felt with his hands and bent over to look, but couldn't tell what it was made of. The toilet and sink were in plain view, no door or walls to block it off. Like a prison.

The clothing hanging on the wall looked familiar. Henry stood up, with some trouble, and shuffled over to have a look.

Aw, fuck!

It was the uniform, that fucking uniform from that fucking show, the one that busted him, that caused so much shit and grief in his life. One episode and marked for life, even though couldn't be more than a few dozen people even saw the thing. Stupid show, stupid tech, stupid booze, stupid everything!

He went to the toilet, puked up the last dregs of his liquid supper, pissed, then cleaned himself. He stood there, looking at the uniform, trying to keep from shaking, and desperately wanting a beer.

■ ■ ■

"Here we see the U.S.S. *Spelling* as it drifts silently through deep space, well beyond the orbit of Jupiter. Note the sleekness of her design, the fins and grids, pods and wires, that dance from her hull like leaping, shining metallic rainbows. The gun and missile placements bristle angrily, ready to take on any and all comers, looking for an excuse to put down further armed rebellion.

"This newest ship in the fleet, the pride of our armed might in space, is the replacement for the late, great U.S.S. *Tesh,* sadly lost with all hands in the gravity well of Saturn after a cowardly attack by . . .

"Jesus, I'm getting all, all emotional. I'm sorry, I'm sorry, I'll be all right, but . . . those boys, they died for our country."

From AmeriNet 46 *News at 0336*

■ ■ ■

After much hesitation, Henry decided to put the uniform on. It fit well, better than that piece of crap that the costume designers had come up with for the pilot. It also had the added advantage that it didn't stink like shit.

Shortly after dressing, the door cracked open tentatively, then opened wide. A man stood there, the oddest-looking man Henry had ever seen.

He was wearing a dull grey sweater that every few seconds rippled with what looked like tiny waves of oil-slick water, running in a different direction each time. His slacks were dark blue, almost black, and appeared to stiffen as the man stood still and then crack in a wild pattern of shiny crow's feet whenever he shifted a leg; he wore pale green sandals and matching socks.

He wasn't tall, this man. Maybe five foot six at best. His skin was darker than Henry's, but not so dark that he could be called a negro. Small, glittery things, like slivers of a shattered mirror, protruded from his tall forehead. He wore dark glasses that obliterated any view of his eyes, quite possibly from any angle. And his hair . . .

His hair was a wild conglomeration of wires, tubes, strings of tiny blinking lights, plastic and metal and maybe even some real hair hidden in there someplace, dark and stringy and matted in bunches under the foreign material. It was, thought Henry, as if this man had embedded his head in a Christmas tree just after a horrible soldering accident.

Upon seeing that Henry was wearing the uniform, the man broke into a huge, unrestrained grin. "Oh, this is so good to see!" said the man, accent unidentifiable but language definitely English, and he danced a few strange steps right there, Christmas lights bobbing in asympathetic rhythm. Then he stopped and saluted Henry, a salute modeled after the style created for that stupid show; right fist to left shoulder, then open palm out, fingers facing left, elbow crooked to keep the arm half extended (didn't want to look too much like a Nazi thing).

Henry nodded in return, cautious and a little scared, especially now that the booze seemed to have unfortunately deserted his system. "Are you . . ." His voice was scratchy, so he paused to swallow, to breathe and clear some of that shit from his skull. "Are you the guy who was visiting me? From the future?"

"No!" shouted the man, sounding excruciatingly delighted and excited at this riddle. "I'm the man who visited you from the present!" At this he giggled and danced a little more; the blinking lights on his head seemed to take up a more frantic pattern, pants cracking and resetting with each step.

Episode Three: More thrilling scenes
from this week's episode

Captain Michael Davis, fresh from his heroic encounter with Marcus Heimdal (currently on his way to serving a thirty-year sentence at the Charon Penal Colony—let's see him bust out of there!) has raced back to Earth with the aid of the newest in space travel technology. Less than a day to get there, as opposed to the two months it used to take, laughing in the face of modern physics.

A quick slingshot around the Moon, using its gravity to slow down rather than speed up (trust us on this), then captured by the Earth's gravity, sinking into a low orbit that makes parking on a dime after slowing down from 300 miles per hour in only four feet look easy. Private Stern gives him the thumbs-up. Perfect positioning.

A quick check of instruments, and then communicate with headquarters back in good old U.S. of A. Salt Lake City, to be exact, taking over where Hollywood left off *after it sank beneath the waves.*

"Captain Michael Davis, Sector Seven, to Sector One Headquarters, requesting permission to land."

A brief pause, and then, "Permission granted, Captain Davis. And congratulations on a job well done."

■   ■   ■

The strange man interrupted his equally strange dance to mumble something unintelligible, the Christmas lights blinking ever more fiercely. Then he grinned at Henry. "Come with me, please."

Henry followed him out of the room, shuffling along nervously. They walked through another room (previously described) and the strange man (whose name was Arnold, although there is no way that Henry could yet know that), bypassed the desk and the mass of wires and opened the door on the far side of that room.

Still following, Henry saw that another man was there, similarly attired and wearing dark and very large goggles, sitting in something like a dentist's chair, more wires and gimracks protruding from his head, as well as several tubes leading from his arms and one even coming from his belly. The wires led to a receptacle in the wall, the tubes to a metal and plastic and something-else contraption sitting hunched beside the chair, humming along to itself in ever-changing pitches.

■   ■   ■

Private Stern disappears, replaced by Arnold, all fuzzy and grainy and jerky again, a cheap representation of his real self. Bits of skin slag off and drift for a moment before reattaching themselves; one eyeball drifts away for a moment, before Arnold can capture it with his tongue, all four feet of it.

"Darn it, I wish you wouldn't do that!"

"He's here, Michael," says Arnold, ignoring the admonition. "Time to come on down."

■   ■   ■

Arnold reached over and touched a button on the humming machine. "He's here, Michael. Time to come on down." The machine shuddered and spit and whistled and belched and even barfed some sort of greyish fluid onto the floor, which was promptly cleaned up by four small cartoonish brooms with arms, each carrying two very real wooden buckets. Henry blinked his eyes, unsure where they had come from, and when he looked again they were gone, as was the barf.

The tubes withdrew, some going from arms to machine and some from machine into the arms, the (slightly larger) one in the belly pulling out from there and being sucked into the machine, accompanied by the sort of slurping noise one associates with a child eating spaghetti. The wires disentangled themselves, and pulled into a slot in the wall or else wrapped themselves around Michael's skull, a cheerful rainbow of Medusan snakes settling in for a nap.

■ ■ ■

The space car lands, magnificent Salt Lake City's towers thrusting into the sky all around it, like fingers reaching for God. Captain Michael Davis reaches out, touches a button, and watches the car and the city dissolve around him, fading to nothing. He turns his head, gazes with fondness and consternation at Arnold, with definite capital-A Awe at Henry. Time to sit up.

Episode Four: A brief hysterical interlude

(POV Shift: Swing camera in close, closer, closest. Burrow deep into the skull, sneak the camera past the blood-brain barrier, find your way along the neurons, synapses firing and sparking at a savage rate, pretend you have a wondrous device to translate what follows)

—*Oh God oh Christ I can't believe what the fuck is happening to me here. Maybe maybe maybe this is only a dream, maybe I got the fucking DT's, maybe I'm gonna wake up in a few minutes and laugh at all this. Noise in my head buzzing that's gotta be it—*

—*Shit no I'm still here these guys are for real maybe they aren't even from the future maybe they're aliens or something, come to grab me from their flying saucer—*

—*Calm down, don't let them see you scared. Maybe they can smell fear like dogs or something—*

—*Shit—*

Episode Five: Your trip to the outer reaches made easy

Michael stood up, pants cracking to allow him access to the floor, stiffening to keep him up. He hawked and spat on the floor, phlegm and a little bit of blood mixing, but not enough to worry about, cleared his throat a couple of times.

"Tired?" ventured Arnold.

Michael nodded. "Long trip," he rasped. "Good one, though." They hugged.

"Mmm," said Arnold, pulling away after a second. "Michael, I would like you to meet Henry Angel, himself. Mr. Angel, this is Michael Davis, your number one fan, I am sure."

Henry reached out a hand to shake, stared at empty air for a moment as Michael did not proffer his own. Then he dropped his arm and nodded. "Please. Call me Henry." *What the hell is going on here?*

"I am delighted to meet you, Henry," said Michael. "Your life as Captain Maxwell has been an inspiration to me and to tens of millions of other Americans."

Henry couldn't take it any longer. "What are you talking about? I played in that stupid show for one fucking episode! No one saw it except for some jerks at the network who decided that it would cost too much and I was too big a risk!"

Both men smiled. Arnold nodded sagely and said, "Experience is every bit as fluid as time, Henry." This seemed to greatly amuse both of them. Arnold danced that little dance, and Michael jigged for a brief moment as well, though it seemed to tire him out quite quickly.

Episode Six: Henry's life as it otherwise might have been

With the help of two of his few remaining good friends, Henry was taken to a doctor who saw fit to enroll him in a health spa that specialized in people with Henry's problem. Three months of intense physical and emotional work paid off, and Henry left the spa drier than he'd ever been since coming to Hollywood.

Rumors stuck like glue, however, and Hollywood would have nothing to do with him, so he left town and moved back home, lived in the basement of his mother's house on a farm in Sonoma County. By day he did carpentry, working for an old friend of his father's who built houses. By night, he put together a small community theater, put on some performances that were okay, some that were pretty awful, and a few that were terrific.

In the early seventies some of his roles in some especially atrocious B-grade horror films were rediscovered, and he was invited back to Hollywood to do some work in a few small productions, even some guest spots on some series television. He wanted more, however, and couldn't attain it.

Resentment of his situation and fear about his true self served to put him back on the downward spiral. Booze showed up again, this time accompanied by cocaine and other drugs.

Henry died of heart failure in 1976, two days after he had begun filming a guest spot in a popular detective series. Seven people attended his funeral.

■   ■   ■

Henry dried up, got some great parts, ended up copping an Oscar for a supporting role, went on to a life of acclaim as a character actor. A few months after coming out of the closet, he died at age sixty-eight, drowned in a boating accident.

■   ■   ■

Henry stayed in Sonoma County, got the house when his mother died, married his childhood sweetheart, raised a good family, then, still lost in his past and confused about who he really was, blew his brains out in 1972.

■   ■   ■

Henry stayed in Sonoma County, got the house, married his childhood sweetheart, raised a good family, then got a divorce. He died at age eighty-five, his two surviving children at his bedside. The construction company he had built with his father's old friend was worth tens of millions.

Episode Seven: Why Part Six doesn't really matter

The explanation is almost more than Henry can bear. He has been flung through time and greeted by people who, while undeniably human, have more than a few weird things counting as strikes against them.

And now he has heard a tale unlike anything he ever expected to hear: Now, in this future, Henry Angel is a hero. Honest to God, bigger than life. Michael and Arnold show him little snippets of television, or at least something very similar to it, shows that concentrate on him, but on a life he never led.

But how could he have led this life? Henry asks this, but the answers are not remotely satisfactory.

It is a fluid life, Arnold says, or a neurologically experiential one. It has been created, says Michael, with the aid of the Net. Michael doesn't elaborate.

Besides, says Arnold, time is what you make of it. And we are running out of time to make, so we need you here. He pauses, grins, dances a little bit more, and then asks if Henry would like to experience the Net.

Um, delays Henry, does experiencing this net have anything to do with those things in my body and on my head?

Another dance, and then heads nod gleefully, lights and wires bobbing.

Henry turns and runs, not knowing where the hell he's going, but knowing it has to be away from here.

Episode Eight: Henry's visit to the big city and a partial inventory of the things he sees

Buildings. Buildings, buildings, buildings and buildings. Some abandoned machines, look sort of like cars or something. More buildings.

Some streetlights. None of them working, though.

Pavement, cracked and weathered. Weeds growing out of the cracks. No people, no birds, no insects.

The sky, what Henry can see with all the tall buildings (did we mention all the buildings?) in the way, is grey, disturbed, distant and cold.

No sound, aside from a far-off hum, alien and probably unattainable.

Once, maybe, a person, far away down a street, half hidden in shadows. Said person doesn't respond to shouts, and, exhausted after running and yelling the entire distance, Henry's arrival at the approximate location reveals nothing.

Except for more buildings.

Episode Nine: The real world

Henry sat on the cold pavement, leaning against one of the grey buildings that marched down the streets like so many monoliths. Shaking from exhaustion and fear, he leaned his head back and watched the sky for a few moments, wondering at the total absence of blue sky, of clouds.

He may have fallen asleep. The new sound seemed to intrude on his dreams first, unsettled visions of dancing Christmas trees and much-needed bottles of beer. A growl superseded that, distant and dream-like at first, then persistent enough to get his attention.

"Henry."

He blinked his eyes open, stood up with a start. In front of him, on the street, was a vehicle of some sort.

"Henry," came the voice again. It was Arnold, inside the vehicle.

"What?"

"Oh, thank goodness, it *is* you. It took me forever to find this cab, and it isn't hooked up as well as it might have been a few decades ago. Please climb in." A side door slid open.

"Why? Why should I go back?"

"You can't go back, Henry. That's the problem. We pulled you up, but it was a one way trip. You are stuck now, and you're going to have to live with it."

Henry shook his head. "Then why'd you bring me here? This is hell!"

Arnold chuckled, a gentle sound this time. "You were in hell before, Henry. You weren't going to live for much longer. Please climb in and I'll explain."

Perhaps relieved to get away from the oppressive bulk of the buildings and from the all-encompassing greyness that surrounded him, Henry complied. He sat down, the door sliding shut behind him. But there was no one else in the vehicle.

"Where are you?" he asked as it started to move.

"Back where I've always been," said Arnold. "That's why it took so long to find you. I couldn't track down a cab that was operable. Most of them have just been sitting and rusting for years, decades, centuries even."

Henry nodded, not exactly sure of what Arnold was saying but not wanting any more details. "You said you'd explain."

"I did indeed," said Arnold, his voice coming from in front as well as to the sides. The vehicle grumbled and complained for a second, and then lurched forward. Peaceful piano music played from somewhere behind Henry's head.

"We live in tough times, Henry. Very difficult for all of us. The world that you knew came to an end a very long time ago, and our struggles to make do have pretty much been for nothing." The vehicle turned a corner a little too hard. "Sorry about that," said Arnold. "These mesh controls are old and rusty, and covered with dust and dead bugs. I'm just surprised they were never cannibalized."

"You were saying . . ." prompted Henry.

"Oh yes. Your future, my past, we fucked up. I won't go into a litany of things that went wrong. If you want you can do your own investigating when the time comes. Let's just say that this isn't a very pretty world.

"People being people, they want to hide from things when they aren't very pretty. Hiding in your time meant beer, whiskey, that sort of thing. Right?"

Henry nodded. He'd been good at hiding near the end, there.

"Well, these days people have stories, events, whole lives they lead outside of reality. This thing we call the Net—and no, I have no idea why we call it that—takes people into these lives, lets them experience them just like they were real."

Another corner. The background piano music swelled briefly, then faded back again. Arnold continued.

"Someone, many years ago, got their hands on the pilot you made, the "Space Cops" thing. Turned it into a whole event, this grand series that changed the way America and the world was." He sighed. "A lovely story, really. There was even a fabulous version of you wandering around the Net, interacting with all sorts of people whenever they wanted, although most people were happy being the heroes themselves.

"Not all of us were caught up in the scenario, however, although I must admit even for people like me it is difficult to spend more than a few hours away from it. I myself worked with some others on a device to bring someone through time, a kind of a hobby thing based on some old math one of us found drifting in a file somewhere, which explains how you got here. Not that any of us actually expected it to work."

"Where are the other people you worked with?" asked Henry.

Arnold chuckled. "I don't know. To tell you the truth, the chances are very good that they don't exist, or perhaps they did, but now they don't."

"Huh?"

"Never mind," said Arnold. "I'm just finding it harder and harder to figure out who's who these days. Maybe because I'm thinking about it now. I don't know."

"Why'd you bring me here?" Henry was feeling very confused.

"To put it bluntly, Henry, I'm losing Michael. He's spending more and more time away from me, and I don't have the energy in me to traipse all the way around a virtual solar system trying to keep up with him. I was kind of hoping your presence would be a nifty gift for him."

"A gift? You brought me forward in time to be a present?" Henry shook his head, feeling a dull ache beginning to creep up from his shoulders to his skull. Nothing in his life had been as confusing as the way Arnold behaved and spoke.

"Well, that and something for all of our society to look to. We need inspiration, Henry, inspiration to make more of ourselves. You can be that inspiration!"

The vehicle stopped and the door slid open. They were in a large empty warehouse, parked under a feeble pool of light cast by the only two fitfully-working bulbs that were hanging from the high ceiling. Arnold walked into the light to greet Henry as he got up from his seat and stepped out.

"How can a broken-down drunk be inspiration?" asked Henry.

"You can be so because we made you so!" said Arnold. "Come join us." He almost whispered this last.

Henry shook his head. "No. I want to go home."

Arnold grimaced. "You can't, even if I could let you. I'm sorry that's your answer."

There was a distant whine near Henry's ear, a mosquito maybe, although he'd not seen or heard any insects up until now, and then he felt a small sting in his neck. He swatted at it, but already things were going dim. As he fell forward, he managed to focus for a brief second on the gurney that rushed up to break his fall.

Episode Ten: The Henry Effect

The space car comes in for as smooth a landing as can be expected, considering the circumstances. "You're in," comes the distant voice of Slam Rankin, now promoted to Sector One. "Good luck."

"Thanks."

He steps out, views the unfamiliar landscape, almost alien in proportions. Buildings are too small and spaced too far apart, the riot of colors is almost too much for his unaccustomed eyes.

And there are more lights here than last time—a bad sign. Too many more joining this and the Space Cops will collapse. There is also no movement at all, and the silence is a different sort of quiet, unlike anything he has ever experienced in his life.

The walk is a short one, due to the space car being able to land in such small areas. Trees, scorched by the passing rockets, are already healing themselves, fast motion, almost liquid as they turn from shriveled and black to grey to erect and brown and green.

The entrance is open to him. After a pause to collect his thoughts, he steps across the threshold and into the room. They are there, the two of them, sitting as he expected to find them.

Henry looks up. "Arnold! So good to see you! Come in, come in."

Michael looks up from the nonsense patterns playing on the screen, smiles when he sees Arnold. He waves the hand that is not holding the bottle of beer, grinning. "Hiya Arnold. Been watching you on TV." With the hand holding the beer he gestures at the black and white screen.

Henry gets up and walks to another room, comes out holding a second bottle of beer, which he hands to Arnold. Arnold's protests that he is on duty are ignored.

When they are all settled in on the couch and chairs Henry smiles and says, "Good life you brought me to, Arnold. And I sure like what you've done to my old show."

Arnold is about to say something, but the nonsense on the screen fades and he is hushed. "The show's back on," says Michael. "Wait until the next commercial."

Arnold shrugs his shoulders, takes a sip of the beer, and leans back to watch himself, Henry and Michael sitting in a room drinking beer and watching TV.

All up and down the street, thousands of others share in the experience. Ratings go through the roof.

Eventually, Arnold goes and grabs another beer, settles down to enjoy the show.

Robert Sawyer

You See, But You Do Not Observe

From *Sherlock Holmes in Orbit*, 1995

Are we alone in the universe? It is the year 2096 A.D. and this question still remains unanswered, much to the chagrin of Mycroft Holmes. Holmes is a citizen of the 21st century who, along with the best minds of his time, is stumped over the non-emergence of contact with alien life, a phenomena which, according to their calculations, should have taken place long ago. The solution? Transport the world's most famous sleuths from the past—Sherlock Holmes and the ever-present Watson. Sure enough, Sherlock's uncanny intellect can crack the case of the missing extraterrestrials—but at what cost?

B. A.

I HAD BEEN PULLED INTO THE FUTURE FIRST, AHEAD OF MY COMPANION. There was no sensation associated with the chronotransference, except for a popping of my ears which I was later told had to do with a change in air pressure. Once in the 21st century, my brain was scanned in order to produce from my memories a perfect reconstruction of our rooms at 221-B Baker Street. Details that I could not consciously remember or articulate were nonetheless reproduced exactly: the flock-papered walls, the bearskin hearthrug, the basket chair and the armchair, the coal-scuttle, even the view through the window—all were correct to the smallest detail.

I was met in the future by a man who called himself Mycroft Holmes. He claimed, however, to be no relation to my companion, and protested that his name was mere coincidence, although he allowed that the fact of it was likely what had made a study of my partner's methods his chief avocation. I asked him if he had a brother called Sherlock, but his reply made little sense to me: "My parents weren't *that* cruel."

191

In any event, this Mycroft Holmes—who was a small man with reddish hair, quite unlike the stout and dark ale of a fellow with the same name I had known two hundred years before—wanted all details to be correct before he whisked Holmes here from the past. Genius, he said, was but a step from madness, and although I had taken to the future well, my companion might be quite rocked by the experience.

When Mycroft did bring Holmes forth, he did so with great stealth, transferring him precisely as he stepped through the front exterior door of the real 221-B Baker Street and into the simulation that had been created here. I heard my good friend's voice down the stairs, giving his usual glad tidings to a simulation of Mrs. Hudson. His long legs, as they always did, brought him up to our humble quarters at a rapid pace.

I had expected a hearty greeting, consisting perhaps of an ebullient cry of "My Dear Watson," and possibly even a firm clasping of hands or some other display of bonhomie. But there was none of that, of course. This was not like the time Holmes had returned after an absence of three years during which I had believed him to be dead. No, my companion, whose exploits it has been my honor to chronicle over the years, was unaware of just how long we had been separated, and so my reward for my vigil was nothing more than a distracted nodding of his drawn-out face. He took a seat and settled in with the evening paper, but after a few moments, he slapped the newsprint sheets down. "Confound it, Watson! I have already read this edition. Have we not *today's* paper?"

And, at that turn, there was nothing for it but for me to adopt the unfamiliar role that queer fate had dictated I must now take: our traditional positions were now reversed, and I would have to explain the truth to Holmes.

"Holmes, my good fellow, I am afraid they do not publish newspapers anymore."

He pinched his long face into a scowl, and his clear, gray eyes glimmered. "I would have thought that any man who had spent as much time in Afghanistan as you had, Watson, would be immune to the ravages of the sun. I grant that today was unbearably hot, but surely your brain should not have addled so easily."

"Not a bit of it, Holmes, I assure you," said I. "What I say is true, although I confess my reaction was the same as yours when I was first told. There have not been any newspapers for seventy-five years now."

"Seventy-five years? Watson, this copy of *The Times* is dated August the fourteenth, 1899—yesterday."

"I am afraid that is not true, Holmes. Today is June the fifth, *anno Domini* two thousand and ninety-six."

"Two thou—"

"It sounds preposterous, I know—"

"It is preposterous, Watson. I call you 'old man' now and again out of affection, but you are in fact nowhere near two hundred and fifty years of age."

"Perhaps I am not the best man to explain all this," I said.

"No," said a voice from the doorway. "Allow me."

Holmes surged to his feet. "And who are you?"

"My name is Mycroft Holmes."

"Impostor!" declared my companion.

"I assure you that that is not the case," said Mycroft. "I grant I'm not your brother, nor a habitué of the Diogenes Club, but I do share his name. I am a scientist—and I have used certain scientific principles to pluck you from your past and bring you into my present."

For the first time in all the years I had known him, I saw befuddlement on my companion's face. "It is quite true," I said to him.

"But why?" said Holmes, spreading his long arms. "Assuming this mad fantasy is true—and I do not grant for an instant that it is—why would you thus kidnap myself and my good friend, Dr. Watson?"

"Because, Holmes, the game, as you used to be so fond of saying, is afoot."

"Murder, is it?" asked I, grateful at last to get to the reason for which we had been brought forward.

"More than simple murder," said Mycroft. "Much more. Indeed, the biggest puzzle to have ever faced the human race. Not just one body is missing. Trillions are. *Trillions.*"

"Watson," said Holmes, "surely you recognize the signs of madness in the man? Have you nothing in your bag that can help him? The whole population of the Earth is less than two thousand millions."

"In your time, yes," said Mycroft. "Today, it's about eight thousand million. But I say again, there are trillions more who are missing."

"Ah, I perceive at last," said Holmes, a twinkle in his eye as he came to believe that reason was once again holding sway. "I have read in *The Illustrated London News* of these *dinosauria*, as Professor Owen called them—great creatures from the past, all now deceased. It is their demise you wish me to unravel."

Mycroft shook his head. "You should have read Professor Moriarty's monograph called *The Dynamics of an Asteroid*," he said.

"I keep my mind clear of useless knowledge," replied Holmes curtly.

Mycroft shrugged. "Well, in that paper Moriarty quite cleverly guessed the cause of the demise of the dinosaurs: an asteroid crashing into earth kicked up enough dust to block the sun for months on end. Close to a century after he had reasoned out this hypothesis, solid evidence for its truth was found in a layer of clay. No, that mystery is long since solved. This one is much greater."

"And what, pray, is it?" said Holmes, irritation in his voice.

Mycroft motioned for Holmes to have a seat, and, after a moment's defiance, my friend did just that. "It is called the Fermi paradox," said Mycroft, "after Enrico Fermi, an Italian physicist who lived in the twentieth century. You see, we know now that this universe of ours should have given rise to countless planets, and that many of those planets should have produced intelligent civilizations. We can demonstrate the likelihood of this mathematically, using something called the Drake equation. For a century and a half now, we have been using radio—wireless, that is— to look for signs of these other intelligences. And we have found nothing—*nothing!* Hence the paradox Fermi posed: if the universe is supposed to be full of life, then where are the aliens?"

"Aliens?" said I. "Surely they are mostly still in their respective foreign countries."

Mycroft smiled. "The word has gathered additional uses since your day, good doctor. By aliens, I mean extraterrestrials—creatures who live on other worlds."

"Like in the stories of Verne and Wells?" asked I, quite sure that my expression was agog.

"And even in worlds beyond the family of our sun," said Mycroft.

Holmes rose to his feet. "I know nothing of universes and other worlds," he said angrily. "Such knowledge could be of no practical use in my profession."

I nodded. "When I first met Holmes, he had no idea that the

Earth revolved around the sun." I treated myself to a slight chuckle. "He thought the reverse to be true."

Mycroft smiled. "I know of your current limitations, Sherlock." My friend cringed slightly at the overly familiar address. "But these are mere gaps in knowledge; we can rectify that easily enough."

"I will not crowd my brain with useless irrelevancies," said Holmes. "I carry only information that can be of help in my work. For instance, I can identify one hundred and forty different varieties of tobacco ash—"

"Ah, well, you can let that information go, Holmes," said Mycroft. "No one smokes anymore. It's been proven ruinous to one's health." I shot a look at Holmes, whom I had always warned of being a self-poisoner. "Besides, we've also learned much about the structure of the brain in the intervening years. Your fear that memorizing information related to fields such as literature, astronomy, and philosophy would force out other, more relevant data, is unfounded. The capacity for the human brain to store and retrieve information is almost infinite."

"It is?" said Holmes, clearly shocked.

"It is."

"And so you wish me to immerse myself in physics and astronomy and such all?"

"Yes," said Mycroft.

"To solve this paradox of Fermi?"

"Precisely!"

"But why me?"

"Because it is a *puzzle,* and you, my good fellow, are the greatest solver of puzzles this world has ever seen. It is now two hundred years after your time, and no one with a facility to rival yours has yet appeared."

Mycroft probably could not see it, but the tiny hint of pride on my longtime companion's face was plain to me. But then Holmes frowned. "It would take years to amass the knowledge I would need to address this problem."

"No, it will not." Mycroft waved his hand, and amidst the homely untidiness of Holmes's desk appeared a small sheet of glass standing vertically. Next to it lay a strange metal bowl. "We have made great strides in the technology of learning since your day. We can directly program new information into your brain."

Mycroft walked over to the desk. "This glass panel is what we call a *monitor*. It is activated by the sound of your voice. Simply ask it questions, and it will display information on any topic you wish. If you find a topic that you think will be useful in your studies, simply place this helmet on your head" (he indicated the metal bowl), "say the say the words 'load topic,' and the information will be seamlessly integrated into the neural nets of your very own brain. It will at once seem as if you know, and have always known, all the details of that field of endeavor."

"Incredible!" said Holmes. "And from there?"

"From there, my dear Holmes, I hope that your powers of deduction will lead you to resolve the paradox—and reveal at last what has happened to the aliens!"

■   ■   ■

"Watson! Watson!"

I awoke with a start. Holmes had found this new ability to effortlessly absorb information irresistible and he had pressed on long into the night, but I had evidently fallen asleep in a chair. I perceived that Holmes had at last found a substitute for the sleeping fiend of his cocaine mania: with all of creation at his fingertips, he would never again feel that emptiness that so destroyed him between assignments.

"Eh?" I said. My throat was dry. I had evidently been sleeping with my mouth open. "What is it?"

"Watson, this physics is more fascinating than I had ever imagined. Listen to this, and see if you do not find it as compelling as any of the cases we have faced to date."

I rose from my chair and poured myself a little sherry—it was, after all, still night and not yet morning. "I am listening."

"Remember the locked and sealed room that figured so significantly in that terrible case of the Giant Rat of Sumatra?"

"How could I forget?" said I, a shiver traversing my spine. "If not for your keen shooting, my left leg would have ended up as gamy as my right."

"Quite," said Holmes. "Well, consider a different type of locked-room mystery, this one devised by an Austrian physicist named Erwin Schrödinger. Image a cat sealed in a box. The box is of such opaque material, and its walls are so well insulated, and the seal is so profound, that there is no way anyone can observe the cat once the box is closed."

"Hardly seems cricket," I said, "locking a poor cat in a box."

"Watson, your delicate sensibilities are laudable, but please, man, attend to my point. Imagine further that inside this box is a triggering device that has exactly a fifty-fifty chance of being set off, and that this aforementioned trigger is rigged up to a cylinder of poison gas. If the trigger is tripped, the gas is released, and the cat dies."

"Goodness!" said I. "How nefarious."

"Now, Watson, tell me this: without opening the box, can you say whether the cat is alive or dead?"

"Well, if I understand you correctly, it depends on whether the trigger was tripped."

"Precisely!"

"And so the cat is perhaps alive, and, yet again, perhaps it is dead."

"Ah, my friend, I knew you would not fail me: the blindingly obvious interpretation. But it is wrong, dear Watson, totally wrong."

"How do you mean?"

"I mean the cat is neither alive nor is it dead. It is a *potential* cat, an unresolved cat, a cat whose existence is nothing but a question of possibilities. It is neither alive nor dead, Watson— neither! Until some intelligent person opens the box and looks, the cat is unresolved. Only the act of looking forces a resolution of the possibilities. Once you crack the seal and peer within, the potential cat collapses into an actual cat. Its reality is a *result* of having been observed."

"That is worse gibberish than anything this namesake of your brother has spouted."

"No, it is not," said Holmes. "It is the way the world works. They have learned so much since our time, Watson—so very much! But as Alphonse Karr has observed, *Plus ça change, plus c'est la même chose.* Even in this esoteric field of advanced physics, it is the power of the qualified observer that is most important of all!"

■   ■   ■

I awoke again hearing Holmes crying out, "Mycroft! Mycroft!"

I had occasionally heard such shouts from him in the past, either when his iron constitution had failed him and he was feverish, or when under the influence of his accursed needle. But after a moment I realized he was not calling for his real brother but rather was shouting into the air to summon the Mycroft Holmes who was the 21st-century savant. Moments later, he was rewarded: the door to our rooms opened and in came the red-haired fellow.

"Hello, Sherlock," said Mycroft. "You wanted me?"

"Indeed I do," said Holmes. "I have absorbed much now on not just physics but also the technology by which you have recreated these rooms for me and the good Dr. Watson."

Mycroft nodded. "I've been keeping track of what you've been accessing. Surprising choices, I must say."

"So they might seem," said Holmes, "but my method is based on the pursuit of trifles. Tell me if I understand correctly that you reconstructed these rooms by scanning Watson's memories, then using, if I understand the terms, holography and micro-manipulated force fields to simulate the appearance and form of what he had seen."

"That's right."

"So your ability to reconstruct is not just limited to rebuilding these rooms of ours, but, rather, you could simulate anything either of us had ever seen."

"That's correct. In fact, I could even put you into a simulation of someone else's memories. Indeed, I thought perhaps you might like to see the Very Large Array of radio telescopes, where most of our listening for alien messages—"

"Yes, yes, I'm sure that's fascinating," said Holmes, dismissively. "But can you reconstruct the venue of what Watson so appropriately dubbed 'The Final Problem'?"

"You mean the Falls of Reichenbach?" Mycroft looked shocked. "My God, yes, but I should think that's the last thing you'd want to relive."

"Aptly said!" declared Holmes. "Can you do it?"

"Of course."

"Then do so!"

. . .

And so Holmes's and my brains were scanned and in short order we found ourselves inside a superlative recreation of the Switzerland of May, 1891, to which we had originally fled to escape Professor Moriarty's assassins. Our re-enactment of events began at the charming Englischer Hof in the village of Meiringen. Just as the original innkeeper had done all those years ago, the reconstruction of him exacted a promise from us that we would not miss the spectacle of the Falls of Reichenbach. Holmes and I set out for the falls, him walking with the aid of an Alpine stock.

Mycroft, I was given to understand, was somehow observing all this from afar.

"I do not like this," I said to my companion. " 'Twas bad enough to live through this horrible day once, but I had hoped I would never have to relive it again except in nightmares."

"Watson, recall that I have fonder memories of all this. Vanquishing Moriarty was the high point of my career. I said to you then, and say again now, that putting an end to the very Napoleon of crime would easily be worth the price of my own life."

There was a little dirt path cut out of the vegetation running halfway round the falls so as to afford a complete view of the spectacle. The icy green water, fed by the melting snows, flowed with phenomenal rapidity and violence, then plunged into a great, bottomless chasm of rock black as the darkest night. Spray shot up in vast gouts, and the shriek made by the plunging water was almost like a human cry.

We stood for a moment looking down at the waterfall, Holmes's face in its most contemplative repose. He then pointed further ahead along the dirt path. "Note, dear Watson," he said, shouting to be heard above the torrent, "that the dirt path comes to an end against a rock wall there." I nodded. He turned in the other direction. "And see that backtracking out the way we came is the only way to leave alive: there is but one exit, and it is coincident with the single entrance."

Again I nodded. But, just as had happened the first time we had been at this fateful spot, a Swiss boy came running along the path, carrying in his hand a letter addressed to me which bore the mark of the Englischer Hof. I knew what the note said, of course: that an Englishwoman, staying at that inn, had been overtaken by a hemorrhage. She had but a few hours to live, but doubtless would take great comfort in being ministered to by an English doctor, and would I come at once?

"But the note is a pretext," said I, turning to Holmes. "Granted, I was fooled originally by it, but, as you later admitted in that letter you left for me, you had suspected all along that it was a sham on the part of Moriarty." Throughout this commentary, the Swiss boy stood frozen, immobile, as if somehow Mycroft, overseeing all this, had locked the boy in time so that Holmes and I might consult. "I will not leave you again, Holmes, to plunge to your death."

Holmes raised a hand. "Watson, as always, your sentiments are laudable, but recall that this is a mere simulation. You will be of material assistance to me if you do exactly as you did before. There is no need, though, for you to undertake the entire arduous hike to the Englischer Hof and back. Instead, simply head back to the point at which you pass the figure in black, wait an additional quarter of an hour, then return to here.''

"Thank you for simplifying it,'' said I. "I am eight years older than I was then; a three-hour round trip would take a goodly bit out of me today.''

"Indeed,'' said Holmes. "All of us may have outlived our most useful days. Now, please, do as I ask.''

"I will, of course,'' said I, "but I freely confess that I do not understand what this is all about. You were engaged by this twenty-first-century Mycroft to explore a problem in natural philosophy— the missing aliens. Why are we even here?''

"We are here,'' said Holmes, "because I have solved that problem! Trust me, Watson. Trust me, and play out the scenario again of that portentous day of May 4th, 1891.''

■   ■   ■

And so I left my companion, not knowing what he had in mind. As I made my way back to the Englischer Hof, I passed a man going hurriedly the other way. The first time I had lived through these terrible events I did not know him, but this time I recognized him for Professor Moriarty: tall, clad all in black, his forehead bulging out, his lean form outlined sharply against the green backdrop of the vegetation. I let the simulation pass, waited fifteen minutes as Holmes had asked, then returned to the falls.

Upon my arrival, I saw Holmes's Alpine stock leaning against a rock. The black soil of the path to the torrent was constantly remoistened by the spray from the roiling falls. In the soil I could see two sets of footprints leading down the path to the cascade, and none returning. It was precisely the same terrible sight that greeted me all those years ago.

"Welcome back, Watson!''

I wheeled around. Holmes stood leaning against a tree, grinning widely.

"Holmes!'' I exclaimed. "How did you manage to get away from the falls without leaving footprints?''

"Recall, my dear Watson, that except for the flesh-and-blood you and me, all this is but a simulation. I simply asked Mycroft to prevent my feet from leaving tracks.'' He demonstrated this by walking back and forth. No impression was left by his shoes, and no vegetation was trampled down by his passage. "And, of course, I asked him to freeze Moriarty, as earlier he had frozen the Swiss lad, before he and I could become locked in mortal combat."

"Fascinating," said I.

"Indeed. Now, consider the spectacle before you. What do you see?"

"Just what I saw that horrid day on which I had thought you had died: two sets of tracks leading to the falls, and none returning."

Holmes's crow of "Precisely!" rivaled the roar of the falls. "One set of tracks you knew to be my own, and the others you took to be that of the black-clad Englishman—the very Napoleon of crime!"

"Yes."

"Having seen these two sets approaching the falls, and none returning, you then rushed to the very brink of the falls and found—what?"

"Signs of a struggle at the lip of the precipice leading to the great torrent itself."

"And what did you conclude from this?"

"That you and Moriarty had plunged to your deaths, locked in mortal combat."

"Exactly so, Watson! The very same conclusion I myself would have drawn based on those observations!"

"Thankfully, though, I turned out to be incorrect."

"Did you, now?"

"Why, yes. Your presence here attests to that."

"Perhaps," said Holmes. "But I think otherwise. Consider, Watson! You were on the scene, you saw what happened, and for three years—three years, man!—you believed me to be dead. We had been friends and colleagues for a decade at that point. Would the Holmes you knew have let you mourn him for so long without getting word to you? Surely you must know that I trust you at least as much as I do my brother Mycroft, whom I later told you was the only one I had made had privy to the secret that I still lived."

"Well," I said, "since you bring it up, I was slightly hurt by that. But you explained your reasons to me when you returned."

"It is a comfort to me, Watson, that your ill-feelings were assuaged. But I wonder, perchance, if it was more you than I who assuaged them."

"Eh?"

"You had seen clear evidence of my death, and had faithfully if floridly recorded the same in the chronicle you so appropriately dubbed 'The Final Problem.' "

"Yes, indeed. Those were the hardest words I had ever written."

"And what was the reaction of your readers once this account was published in the *Strand?*"

I shook my head, recalling. "It was completely unexpected," said I. "I had anticipated a few polite notes from strangers mourning your passing, since the stories of your exploits had been so warmly received in the past. But what I got instead was mostly anger and outrage—people demanding to hear further adventures of yours."

"Which of course you believed to be impossible, seeing as how I was dead."

"Exactly. The whole thing left a rather bad taste, I must say. Seemed very peculiar behavior."

"But doubtless it died down quickly," said Holmes.

"You know full well it did not. I have told you before that the onslaught of letters, as well as personal exhortations wherever I would travel, continued unabated for years. In fact, I was virtually at the point of going back and writing up one of your lesser cases I had previously ignored as being of no general interest simply to get the demands to cease, when, much to my surprise and delight—"

"Much to your surprise and delight, after an absence of three years less a month, I turned up in your consulting rooms, disguised, if I recall correctly, as a shabby book collector. And soon you had fresh adventures to chronicle, beginning with that case of the infamous Colonel Sebastian Moran and his victim, the Honorable Ronald Adair."

"Yes," said I. "Wondrous it was."

"But Watson, let us consider the facts surrounding my apparent death at the Falls of Reichenbach on May 4th, 1891. You, the observer on the scene, saw the evidence, and, as you wrote in 'The Final Problem,' many experts scoured the lip of the falls and came to precisely the same conclusion you had—that Moriarty and I had plunged to our deaths."

"But that conclusion turned out to be wrong."

Holmes beamed intently. "No, my Good Watson, it turned out to be *unacceptable*—unacceptable to your faithful readers. And that is where all the problems stem from. Remember Schrödinger's cat in the sealed box? Moriarty and I at the falls present a very similar scenario: he and I went down the path into the cul-de-sac, our footprints leaving impressions in the soft earth. There were only two possible outcomes at that point: either I would exit alive, or I would not. There was no way out, except to take that same path back away from the falls. Until someone came and looked to see whether I had re-emerged from the path, the outcome was unresolved. I was both alive and dead—a collection of possibilities. But when you arrived, those possibilities had to collapse into a single reality. You saw that there were no footprints returning from the falls—meaning that Moriarty and I had struggled until at last we had both plunged over the edge into the icy torrent. It was your act of seeing the results that forced the possibilities to be resolved. In a very real sense, my good, dear friend, you killed me."

My heart was pounding in my chest. "I tell you, Holmes, nothing would have made me more happy than to have seen you alive!"

"I do not doubt that, Watson—but you had to see one thing or the other. You could not see both. And, having seen what you saw, you reported your findings: first to the Swiss police, and then to the reporter for the *Journal de Genève*, and lastly in your full account in the pages of the *Strand*."

I nodded.

"But here is the part that was not considered by Schrödinger when he devised the thought experiment of the cat in the box. Suppose you open the box and find the cat dead, and later you tell your neighbor about the dead cat—and your neighbor refuses to believe you when you say that the cat is dead. What happens if you go and look in the box a second time?"

"Well, the cat is surely still dead."

"Perhaps. But what if thousands—nay, millions!—refuse to believe the account of the original observer? What if they deny the evidence? What then, Watson?"

"I—I do not know."

"Through the sheer stubbornness of their will, they reshape reality, Watson! Truth is replaced with fiction! They *will* the cat back to life. More than that, they attempt to believe that the cat never died in the first place!"

"And so?"

"And so the world, which should have one concrete reality, is rendered unresolved, uncertain, adrift. As the first observer on the scene at Reichenbach, your interpretation should take precedence. But the stubbornness of the human race is legendary, Watson, and through that sheer cussedness, that refusal to believe what they have been plainly told, the world gets plunged back into being a wavefront of unresolved possibilities. We exist in flux—to this day, the whole world exists in flux—because of the conflict between the observation you really made at Reichenbach, and the observation the world *wishes* you had made."

"But this is all too fantastic, Holmes!"

"Eliminate the impossible, Watson, and whatever remains, however improbable, must be the truth. Which brings me now to the question we were engaged by this avatar of Mycroft to solve: this paradox of Fermi. Where are the alien beings?"

"And you say you have solved that?"

"Indeed I have. Consider the method by which mankind has been searching for these aliens."

"By wireless, I gather—trying to overhear their chatter on the ether."

"Precisely! And when did I return from the dead, Watson?"

"April of 1894."

"And when did that gifted Italian, Guglielmo Marconi, invent the wireless?"

"I have no idea."

"In eighteen hundred and ninety-*five*, my good Watson. The following year! In all the time that mankind has used radio, our entire world has been an unresolved quandary! An uncollapsed wavefront of possibilities!"

"Meaning?"

"Meaning the aliens are there, Watson—it is not they who are missing, it is us! Our world is out of synch with the rest of the universe. Through our failure to accept the unpleasant truth, we have rendered ourselves *potential* rather than *actual*."

I had always thought my companion a man with a generous regard for his own stature, but surely this was too much. "You are suggesting, Holmes, that the current unresolved state of the world hinges on the fate of you yourself?"

"Indeed! Your readers would not allow me to fall to my death, even if it meant attaining the very thing I desired most, namely the elimination of Moriarty. In this mad world, the observer has lost control of his observations! If there is one thing my life stood for—my life prior to that ridiculous resurrection of me you recounted in your chronicle of 'The Empty House'—it was reason! Logic! A devotion to observable fact! But humanity has abjured that. This whole world is out of whack, Watson—so out of whack that we are cut off from the civilizations that exist elsewhere. You tell me you were festooned with demands for my return, but if people had really understood me, understood what my life represented, they would have known that the only real tribute to me possible would have been to accept the facts! The only real answer would have been to leave me dead!''

■ ■ ■

Mycroft sent us back in time, but rather than returning us to 1899, whence he had plucked us, at Holmes's request he put us back eight years earlier in May of 1891. Of course, there were younger versions of ourselves already living then, but Mycroft swapped us for them, bringing the young ones to the future, where they could live out the rest of their lives in simulated scenarios taken from Holmes's and my minds. Granted, we were each eight years older than we had been when we had fled Moriarty the first time, but no one in Switzerland knew us and so the aging of our faces went unnoticed.

I found myself for a third time living that fateful day at the Falls of Reichenbach, but this time, like the first and unlike the second, it was real.

I saw the page boy coming, and my heart raced. I turned to Holmes, and said, "I can't possibly leave you."

"Yes, you can, Watson. And you will, for you have never failed to play the game. I am sure you will play it to the end." He paused for a moment, then said, perhaps just a wee bit sadly, "I can discover facts, Watson, but I cannot change them." And then, quite solemnly, he extended his hand. I clasped it firmly in both of mine. And then the boy, who was in Moriarty's employ, was upon us. I allowed myself to be duped, leaving Holmes alone at the falls, fighting with all my might to keep from looking back as I hiked onward to treat the nonexistent patient at the Englischer Hof. On my way, I passed Moriarty going in the other direction. It was all I could do to keep from drawing my pistol and putting an end to the blackguard, but I knew Holmes would consider robbing him of his own chance at Moriarty an unforgivable betrayal.

It was an hour's hike down to the Englischer Hof. There I played out the scene in which I inquired about the ailing Englishwoman, and Steiler the Elder, the innkeeper, reacted, as I knew he must, with surprise. My performance was probably half-hearted, having played the role once before, but soon I was on my way back. The uphill hike took over two hours, and I confess plainly to being exhausted upon my arrival, although I could barely hear my own panting over the roar of the torrent.

Once again, I found two sets of footprints leading to the precipice, and none returning. I also found Holmes's Alpine stock, and, just as I had the first time, a note from him to me that he had left with it. The note read just as the original had, explaining that he and Moriarty were about to have their final confrontation, but that Moriarty had allowed him to leave a few last words behind. But it ended with a postscript that had not been in the original:

> *My dear Watson* [it said], *you will honor my passing most of all if you stick fast to the powers of observation. No matter what the world wants, leave me dead.*

I returned to London, and was able to briefly counterbalance my loss of Holmes by reliving the joy and sorrow of the last few months of my wife Mary's life, explaining my somewhat older face to her and others as the result of shock at the death of Holmes. The next year, right on schedule, Marconi did indeed invent the wireless. Exhortations for more Holmes adventures continued to pour in, but I ignored them all, although the lack of him in my life was so profound that I was sorely tempted to relent, recanting my observations made at Reichenbach. Nothing would have pleased me more than to hear again the voice of the best and wisest man I had ever known.

In late June of 1907, I read in *The Times* about the detection of intelligent wireless signals coming from the direction of the star Altair. On that day, the rest of the world celebrated, but I do confess I shed a tear and drank a special toast to my good friend, the late Mr. Sherlock Holmes.

Geoffrey A. Landis

Ripples in the Dirac Sea

From *Asimov's Science Fiction*, 1988

When a mathematician invents a time machine he learns that there are physical laws that cannot be changed, including "Actions in the past cannot change the future." But what happens then, if you try to use your own time machine to escape your own frightening destiny? What is life like hanging on to the infinite moments in time between when you are, and where you must inevitably be?

B. A.

MY DEATH LOOMS OVER ME LIKE A TIDAL WAVE, RUSHING TOWARD me with inexorable slow-motion majesty. And yet I flee, pointless though it may be.

I depart and my ripples diverge into infinity, like waves smoothing out the footprints of forgotten travelers.

■ ■ ■

We were so careful to avoid any paradox, the day we first tested my machine. We pasted a duct-tape cross onto the concrete floor of a windowless lab, placed an alarm clock on the mark, and locked the door. An hour later we came back, removed the clock, and put the experimental machine back in the room with a super-eight camera set in the coils. I aimed the camera at the x, and one of my grad students programmed the machine to send the camera back half an hour, stay in the past five minutes then return. It left and returned without even a flicker. When we developed the film, the time on the clock was half an hour before we loaded the camera. We'd succeeded in opening the door into the past. We celebrated with coffee and champagne.

Now that I understand more about time, I understand our mistake, that we had not thought to put a movie camera in the room with the clock to photograph the machine as it arrived from the future. But what is obvious to me now, was not obvious then.

■ ■ ■

I arrive, and the ripples converge to the instant now from the vastness of the infinite sea.

To San Francisco, June 8, 1965. A warm breeze riffles across dandelion-speckled grass, while puffy white clouds form strange and wondrous shapes for our entertainment. Yet so very few people pause to enjoy it. They scurry about, diligently preoccupied, believing that if they act busy enough, they must be important. "They hurry so," I say "Why can't they slow down, sit back, enjoy the day?"

"They're trapped in the illusion of time," says Dancer. He lies on his back and blows a soap bubble, his hair flopping back long and brown in a time when "long" hair meant anything below the ear. A puff of breeze takes the bubble down the hill and into the stream of pedestrians. They uniformly ignore it. "They're caught in the belief that what they do is important to some future goal." The bubble pops against a briefcase, and Dancer blows another. "You and I, we know how false an illusion that is. There is no past, no future, only the now, eternal."

He was right, more right than he could have possibly imagined. Once I, too, was preoccupied and self-important. Once I was brilliant and ambitious. I was twenty-eight years old, and I'd made the greatest discovery in the world.

■ ■ ■

From my hiding place I watched him come up the service elevator. He was thin almost to the point of starvation, a nervous man with stringy blond hair and an armless white T-shirt. He looked up and down the hall, but failed to see me hidden in the janitor's closet. Under each arm was a two-gallon can of gasoline, in each hand another. He put down three of the cans and turned the last one upside down, then walked down the hall, spreading a pungent trail of gasoline. His face was blank. When he started on the second can, I figured it was about enough. As he passed my hiding spot, I walloped him over the head with a wrench, and called hotel security. Then I went back to the closet and let the ripples of time converge.

I arrived in a burning room, flames licking forth at me, the

heat almost too much to bear. I gasped for breath—a mistake—
and punched at the keypad.

NOTES ON THE THEORY AND PRACTICE
OF TIME TRAVEL

1. Travel is possible only into the past.
2. The object transported will return to exactly the time
   and place of departure.
3. It is not possible to bring objects from the past to the
   present.
4. Actions in the past cannot change the present.

One time I tried jumping back a hundred million years, to the
Cretaceous, to see dinosaurs. All the picture books show the landscape as being covered with dinosaurs. I spent three days wandering around a swamp—in my new tweed suit—before catching
even a glimpse of any dinosaur larger than a basset hound. That
one—a theropod of some sort, I don't know which—skittered
away as soon as it caught a whiff of me. Quite a disappointment.

My professor in transfinite math used to tell stories about a
hotel with an infinite number of rooms. One day all the rooms
are full, and another guest arrives. "No problem," says the desk
clerk. He moves the person in room one into room two, the person in room two into room three, and so on. Presto! A vacant
room.

A little later, an infinite number of guests arrive. "No problem," says the dauntless desk clerk. He moves the person in room
one into room two, the person in room two into room four, the
person in room three into room six, and so on. Presto! An infinite
number of rooms vacant.

My time machine works on just that principle.

．　．　．

Again I return to 1965, the fixed point, the strange attractor to
my chaotic trajectory. In years of wandering, I've met countless
people, but Daniel Ranien-Dancer was the only one who truly had
his head together. He had a soft, easy smile, a battered second-
hand guitar, and as much wisdom as it has taken me a hundred
lifetimes to learn. I've known him in good times and bad, in summer days with blue skies that we swore would last a thousand years,
in days of winter blizzards with drifted snow piled high over our

heads. In happier times we have laid roses into barrels of rifles, we have laid our bodies across the city streets in the midst of riots, and have not been hurt. And I have been with him when he died, once, twice, a hundred times over.

He died on February 8, 1969, a month into the reign of King Richard the Trickster and his court fool Spiro, a year before Kent State and Altamont and the secret war in Cambodia slowly strangled the summer of dreams. He died, and there was—is—nothing I can do. The last time he died I dragged him to the hospital where I screamed and ranted until finally I convinced them to admit him for observation, though nothing seemed wrong with him. With x-rays and arteriograms and radioactive tracers, they found the incipient bubble in his brain; they drugged him, shaved his beautiful long brown hair, and operated on him, cutting out the offending capillary and tying it off neatly. When the anesthetic wore off, I sat in the hospital room and held his hand. There were big purple blotches under his eyes. He gripped my hand and stared, silent, into space. Visiting hours or no, I didn't let them throw me out of the room. He just stared. In the gray hours just before dawn he sighed softly and died. There was nothing at all I could do.

. . .

Time travel is subject to two constraints: conservation of energy, and causality. The energy to appear in the past is only borrowed from the Dirac sea, and since ripples in the Dirac sea propagate in the negative t direction, transport is only into the past. Energy is conserved in the present as long as the object transported returns with zero time delay, and the principle of causality assures that actions in the past cannot change the present. For example, what if you went into the past and killed your father? Who, then, would invent the time machine?

Once I tried to commit suicide by killing my father, before he met my mother, twenty-three years before I was born. It changed nothing, of course, and even when I did it I knew it would change nothing. But you have to try these things. How else could I know for sure?

. . .

Next we tried sending a rat back. It made the trip through the Dirac sea and back undamaged. Then we tried a trained rat, one we borrowed from the psychology lab across the green without telling them what we wanted it for. Before its little trip it had been taught to run through a maze to get a piece of bacon. Afterwards, it ran the maze as fast as ever.

We still had to try it on a human. I volunteered myself and didn't allow anyone to talk me out of it. By trying it on myself, I dodged the University regulations about experimenting on humans.

The dive into the negative energy sea felt like nothing at all. One moment I stood in the center of the loop of Renselz coils, watched by my two grad students and a technician; the next I was alone, and the clock had jumped back exactly one hour. Alone in a locked room with nothing but a camera and a clock, that moment was the high point of my life.

The moment when I first met Dancer was the low point. I was in Berkeley, a bar called "Trisha's," slowly getting trashed. I'd been doing that a lot, caught between omnipotence and despair. It was 1967. 'Frisco then—it was the middle of the hippie era— seemed somehow appropriate.

There was a girl, sitting at a table with a group from the university. I walked over to her table and invited myself to sit down. I told her that she didn't exist, that her whole world didn't exist, it was all created by the fact that I was watching, and would disappear into the sea of unreality as soon as I stopped looking. Her name was Lisa, and she argued back. Her friends, bored, wandered off, and in a little while Lisa realized just how drunk I was. She dropped a bill on the table and walked out into the foggy night.

I followed her out. When she saw me following, she clutched her purse and bolted.

He was suddenly there under the street light. For a second I thought he was a girl. He had bright blue eyes and straight brown hair down to his shoulders. He wore an embroidered Indian shirt, with a silver and torquoise medallion around his neck and a guitar slung across his back. He was lean, almost stringy, and moved like a dancer, or a karate master. But it didn't occur to me to be afraid of him.

He looked me over. "That won't solve your problem, you know," he said.

And instantly I was ashamed. I was no longer sure exactly what I'd had in mind or why I'd followed her. It had been years since I first fled my death, and I had come to think of others as unreal, since nothing I could do would permanently affect them. My head was spinning. I slid down the wall and sat down, hard, on the sidewalk. What had I come to?

He helped me back into the bar, fed me orange juice and pretzels, and got me to talk. I told him everything. Why not, since I could unsay anything I said, undo anything I did? But I had no urge to. He listened to it all, saying nothing. No one had ever listened to the whole story before. I can't explain the effect it had on me. For uncountable years I'd been alone, and then, if only for a moment . . . it hit me with the intensity of a tab of acid. If only for a moment, I was not alone.

We left arm in arm. Half a block away, Dancer stopped, in front of an alley. It was dark.

"Something not quite right here." His voice had a puzzled tone.

I pulled him back. "Hold on. You don't want to go down there—" He pulled free and walked in. After a slight hesitation I followed.

The alley smelled of old beer, mixed with garbage and stale vomit. In a moment, my eyes became adjusted to the dark.

Lisa was cringing in the corner behind some trash cans. Her clothes had been cut away with a knife, and lay scattered around. Blood showed dark on her thighs and one arm. She didn't seem to see us. Dancer squatted down next to her and said something soft. She didn't respond. He pulled off his shirt and wrapped it around her, then cradled her in his arms, and picked her up. "Help me get her to my apartment."

"Apartment hell. We'd better call the police," I said.

"Call the pigs? Are you crazy? You want them to rape her, too?"

I'd forgotten; this was the sixties. Between the two of us, we got her to Dancer's VW bug and took her to his apartment in The Hashbury. He explained it to me quietly as we drove, a dark side of the summer of love that I'd not seen before. It was greasers, he said. They come down to Berkeley because they heard hippie chicks gave it away free, and they'd get nasty when they met one who thought otherwise.

Her wounds were mostly superficial. Dancer cleaned her, put her in bed, and stayed up all night beside her, talking and crooning and making little reassuring noises. I slept on one of the mattresses in the hall. When I woke up in the morning, they were both in his bed. She was sleeping quietly. Dancer was awake, holding her. I was aware enough to realize that that was all he was doing, holding her, but still I felt a sharp pang of jealousy, and didn't know which one of them it was that I was jealous of.

NOTES FOR A LECTURE ON TIME TRAVEL

The beginning of the twentieth century was a time for intellectual giants, whose likes will perhaps never again be equaled. Einstein had just invented relativity, Heisenberg and Schrödinger quantum mechanics, but nobody yet knew how to make the two theories consistent with each other. In 1930, a new person tackled the problem. His name was Paul Dirac. He was twenty-eight years old. He succeeded where others had failed.

His theory was an unprecedented success, except for one small detail. According to Dirac's theory, a particle could have either positive or negative energy. What did this mean, a particle of negative energy? How could something have negative energy? And why didn't ordinary—positive energy—particles fall down into these negative energy states, releasing a lot of free energy in the process?

You or I might have merely stipulated that it was impossible for an ordinary positive energy particle to make a transition to negative energy. But Dirac was not an ordinary man. He was a genius, the greatest physicist of all, and he had an answer. If every possible negative energy state was already occupied, a particle couldn't drop into a negative energy state. Ah ha! So Dirac postulated that the entire universe is entirely filled with negative energy particles. They surround us, permeate us, in the vacuum of outer space and in the center of the earth, every possible place a particle could be. An indefinitely dense "sea" of negative energy particles. The Dirac sea.

His argument had holes in it, but that comes later.

■ ■ ■

Once I went to visit the crucifixion. I took a jet from Santa Cruz to Tel Aviv, and a bus from Tel Aviv to Jerusalem. On a hill outside the city, I dove through the Dirac sea.

I arrived in my three-piece suit. No way to help that, unless I wanted to arrive naked. The land was surprisingly green and fertile, more so than I expected. The hill was now a farm, covered with grape arbors and olive trees. I hid the coils behind some rocks and walked down the road. I didn't get far. Five minutes on the road, I ran into a group of people. They had dark hair, dark skin, and wore clean, white tunics. Romans? Jews? Egyptians? How could I tell? They spoke to me, but I couldn't understand a word. After a while two of them held me, while a third searched me. Were they robbers, searching for money? Romans, searching for some kind of identity papers? I realized how naive I'd been to think I could just find appropriate dress and somehow blend in with the crowds. Finding nothing, the one who'd done the searching carefully and methodically beat me up. At last he pushed me face down in the dirt. While the other two held me down, he pulled out a dagger and slashed through the tendons on the back of each leg. They were merciful, I guess. They left me with my life. Laughing and talking incomprehensibly among themselves, they walked away.

My legs were useless. One of my arms was broken. It took me four hours to crawl back up the hill, dragging myself with my good arm. Occasionally people would pass by on the road, studiously ignoring me. Once I reached the hiding place, pulling out the Renselz coils and wrapping them around me was pure agony. By the time I entered return on my keypad I was wavering in and out of consciousness. I finally managed to get it entered. From the Dirac sea the ripples converged . . .

and I was in my hotel room in Santa Cruz. The ceiling had started to fall in where the girders had burned through. Fire alarms shrieked and wailed, there was no place to run. The room was filled with a dense, acrid smoke. Trying not to breathe, I punched out a code on the keypad, somewhere, anywhere other than that one instant . . .

and I was in the hotel room, five days before. I gasped for breath. The woman in the hotel bed shrieked and tried to pull the covers up. The man screwing her was too busy to pay any mind. They weren't real anyway. I ignored them and paid a little more attention to where to go next. Back to '65, I figured. I punched in the combo . . .

and was standing in an empty room on the thirtieth floor of a hotel just under construction. A full moon gleamed on the silhouettes of silent construction cranes. I flexed my legs experimentally. Already the memory of pain was beginning to fade. That was reasonable, because it never happened. Time travel. It's not immortality, but it's got to be the next best thing.

You can't change the past, no matter how you try.

■   ■   ■

In the morning I explored Dancer's pad. It was crazy, a small third floor apartment a block off Haight Ashbury that had been converted into something from another planet. The floor of the apartment had been completely covered with old mattresses, on top of which was a jumbled confusion of quilts, pillows, Indian blankets, stuffed animals. You took off your shoes before coming in—Dancer always wore sandals, leather ones from Mexico with soles cut from old tires. The radiators, which didn't work anyway, were sprayed in Dayglo colors. The walls were plastered with posters: Peter Max prints, brightly colored Eschers, poems by Allen Ginsberg, record album covers, peace rally posters, a "Haight is Love" sign, FBI ten-most-wanted posters torn down from a post office with the photos of famous antiwar activists circled in Magic Marker℠, a huge peace symbol in passion pink. Some of the posters were illuminated with black light and luminesced in impossible colors. The air was musty with incense and the banana sweet smell of dope. In one corner a record player played "Sergeant Pepper's Lonely Heart's Club Band" on infinite repeat. Whenever one copy of the album got too scratchy, inevitably one of Dancer's friends would bring in another.

He never locked the door. "Somebody wants to rip me off, well, hey, they probably need it more than I do anyway, okay? It's cool." People dropped by any time of day or night.

I let my hair grow long. Dancer and Lisa and I spent that summer together, laughing, playing guitar, making love, writing silly poems and sillier songs, experimenting with drugs. That was when LSD was blooming onto the scene like sunflowers, when people were still unafraid of the strange and beautiful world on the other side of reality. That was a time to live. I knew that it was Dancer that Lisa truly loved, not me, but in those days free love was in the air like the scent of poppies, and it didn't matter. Not much, anyway.

NOTES FOR A LECTURE ON TIME TRAVEL
(continued)

Having postulated that all of space was filled with an infinitely dense sea of negative energy particles, Dirac went on further and asked if we, in the positive-energy universe, could interact with this negative energy sea. What would happen, say, if you added enough energy to an electron to take it out of the negative energy sea? Two things: first, you would create an electron, seemly out of nowhere. Second, you would leave behind a "hole" in the sea. The hole, Dirac realized, would act as if it were a particle itself, a particle exactly like an electron except for one thing: it would have the opposite charge. But if the hole ever encountered an electron, the electron would fall back into the Dirac sea, annihilating both electron and hole in a bright burst of energy. Eventually they gave the hole in the Dirac sea a name of its own: "positron." When Anderson discovered the positron two years later to vindicate Dirac's theory, it was almost an anticlimax.

And over the next fifty years, the reality of the Dirac sea was almost ignored by physicists. Antimatter, the holes in the sea, was the important feature of the theory; the rest was merely a mathematical artifact.

Seventy years later, I remembered the story my transfinite math teacher told and put it together with Dirac's theory. Like putting an extra guest into a hotel with an infinite number of rooms, I figured out how to borrow energy from the Dirac sea. Or, to put it another way: I learned how to make waves.

And waves on the Dirac sea travel backward in time.

•   •   •

Next we had to try something more ambitious. We had to send a human back further into history, and obtain proof of the trip. Still we were afraid to make alterations in the past, even though the mathematics stated that the present could not be changed. We pulled out our movie camera and chose our destinations carefully.

In September of 1853 a traveler named William Hapland and his family crossed the Sierra Nevadas to reach the California coast. His daughter Sarah kept a journal, and in it she recorded how, as they reached the crest of Parker's ridge, she caught her first glimpse of the distant Pacific ocean exactly as the sun touched the horizon, "in a blays of cryms'n glorie," as she wrote. The journal still exists. It was easy enough for us to conceal ourselves and a movie camera in the cleft of rocks above the pass, to photograph the weary travelers in the ox-drawn wagon as they crossed.

The second target was the great San Francisco earthquake of 1906. From a deserted warehouse that would survive the quake—but not the following fire—we watched and took movies as buildings tumbled down around us and embattled firemen in horse-drawn fire trucks strove in vain to quench a hundred blazes.

Moments before the fire reached our building, we fled into the present.

The films were spectacular.

We were ready to tell the world.

There was a meeting of the AAAS in Santa Cruz in a month. I called the program chairman and wangled a spot as an invited speaker without revealing just what we'd accomplished to date. I planned to show those films at the talk. They were to make us instantly famous.

■ ■ ■

The day that Dancer died we had a going away party, just Lisa and Dancer and I. He knew he was going to die; I'd told him and somehow he believed me. He always believed me. We stayed up all night, playing Dancer's second-hand mandolin, painting psychedelic designs on each other's bodies with grease paint, competing against each other in a marathon game of cut-throat Monopoly, doing a hundred silly, ordinary things that took meaning only from the fact that it was the last time. About four in the morning, as the glimmer of false-dawn began to show in the sky, we went down to the bay and, huddling together for warmth, went tripping. Dancer took the largest dose, since he wasn't going to return. The last thing he said, he told us not to let our dreams die; to stay together.

We buried Dancer, at city expense, in a welfare grave. We split up three days later.

I kept in touch with Lisa, vaguely. In the late seventies she went back to school, first for an MBA, then law school. I think she was married for a while. We wrote each other on Christmas for a while, then I lost track of her. Years later, I got a letter from her. She said that she was finally able to forgive me for causing Dan's death.

It was a cold and foggy February day, but I knew I could find warmth in 1965. The ripples converged.

Anticipated questions from the audience:

Q (old, stodgy professor): It seems to me this proposed temporal jump of yours violates the law of conservation of mass/energy. For example, when a transported object is transported into the past, a quantity of mass will appear to vanish from the present, in clear violation of the conservation law.

A (me): Since the return is to the exact time of departure, the mass present is constant.

Q: Very well, but what about the arrival in the past? Doesn't this violate the conservation law?

A: No. The energy needed is taken from the Dirac sea, by the mechanism I explained in detail in the Phys. Rev. paper. When the object returns to the "future," the energy is restored to the sea.

Q (intense young physicist): Then doesn't Heisenberg uncertainty limit the amount of time that can be spent in the past?

A: A good question. The answer is yes, because we borrow an infinitesimal amount of energy from an infinite number of particles, the amount of time spent in the past can be arbitrarily large. The only limitation is that you must leave the past an instant before you depart from the present.

In half an hour I was scheduled to present the paper that would rank my name with Newton's and Galileo's—and Dirac's. I was twenty-eight years old, the same age that Dirac was when he announced his theory. I was a firebrand, preparing to set the world aflame. I was nervous, rehearsing the speech in my hotel room. I took a swig out of an old Coke that one of my grad students had left sitting on top of the television. The evening news team was babbling on, but I wasn't listening.

I never delivered that talk. The hotel had already started to burn; my death was already foreordained. Tie neat, I inspected myself in the mirror, then walked to the door. The doorknob was warm. I opened it onto a sheet of fire. Flame burst through the opened door like a ravenous dragon. I stumbled backward, staring at the flames in amazed fascination.

Somewhere in the hotel I heard a scream, and all at once I broke free of my spell. I was on the thirtieth story; there was no way out. My thought was for my machine. I rushed across the room and threw open the case holding the time machine. With swift, sure fingers I pulled out the Renselz coils and wrapped them around my body. The carpet had caught on fire, a sheet of flame between me and any possible escape. Holding my breath to avoid suffocation, I punched an entry into the keyboard and dove into time.

I return to that moment again and again. When I hit the final key, the air was already nearly unbreathable with smoke. I had about thirty seconds left to live, then. Over the years I've nibbled away my time down to ten seconds or less.

I live on borrowed time. So do we all, perhaps. But I know when and where my debt will fall due.

■   ■   ■

Dancer died on February 9, 1969. It was a dim, foggy day. In the morning he said he had a headache. That was unusual, for Dancer. He never had headaches. We decided to go on a walk through the fog. It was beautiful, as if we were alone in a strange formless world. I'd forgotten about his headache altogether, until, looking out across the sea of fog from the park over the bay, he fell over. He was dead before the ambulance came. He died with a secret smile on his face. I've never understood that smile. Maybe he was smiling because the pain was gone.

Lisa committed suicide two days later.

■   ■   ■

You ordinary people, you have the chance to change your future. You can father children, write novels, sign petitions, invent new machines, go to cocktail parties, run for president. You affect the future with everything you do no matter what. No matter what I do, I cannot. It is too late for that, for me. My actions are written in flowing water. And having no effect, I have no responsibilities. It makes no difference what I do, not at all.

When I fled the fire into the past, I tried everything I could to change it. I stopped the arsonist, I argued with mayors, I even went to my house and told myself not to go to the conference.

But that's not how time works. No matter what I do, talk to a governor or dynamite the hotel, when I reach that critical moment—the present, my destiny, the moment I have left—I vanish from whenever I was, and return to the hotel room, the fire approaching ever closer. I have about ten seconds left. Every time I dive through the Dirac sea, everything I changed in the past vanishes. Sometimes I pretend that the changes I make in the past create new futures, though I know this is not the case. When I return to the present, all the changes are wiped out by the ripples of the converging wave, like erasing a blackboard after a class.

Someday I will return and meet my destiny. But for now, I live in the past. It's a good life, I suppose. You get used to the fact that nothing you do will ever have any effect on the world. It gives you a feeling of freedom. I've been places no one has ever been, seen things no one alive has ever seen. I've given up physics, of course. Nothing I discover could endure past that fatal night in Santa Cruz. Maybe some people would continue for the sheer joy of knowledge. For me, the point is missing.

But there are compensations. Whenever I return to the hotel room, nothing is changed but my memories. I am again twenty-eight, again wearing the same three-piece suit, again have the fuzzy taste of stale cola in my mouth. Every time I return, I use up a bit of time. One day I will have no time left.

Dancer, too, will never die. I won't let him. Every time I get to that final February morning, the day he died, I return to 1965, to that perfect day in June. He doesn't know me, he never knows me. But we meet on that hill, the only two willing to enjoy the day doing nothing. He lies on his back, idly fingering chords on his guitar, blowing bubbles and staring into the clouded blue sky. Later I will introduce him to Lisa. She won't know us either, but that's okay. We've got plenty of time.

"Time," I say to Dancer, lying in the park on the hill. "There's so much time."

"All the time there is," he says.

Rod Serling

The Odyssey of Flight 33

From *Twilight Zone stories*, 1962; also aired on CBS in 1961

On a flight to New York, a Boeing 707 mysteriously picks up speed. The captain tries to radio Idlewild, but there's no answer. When Flight 33 breaks through the clouds, it finds New York below—but the buildings are gone. Flight 33 arrives in New York, but it is some 200 million years ahead of schedule.

B. A.

THEY DON'T TALK ABOUT THE FLIGHT MUCH ANYMORE—AT LEAST the pros don't. On occasion a vastly theoretical article will appear in a Sunday supplement or mention will be made in a book on air disasters but, by and large, the world's day-to-day catastrophes are sufficient in scope and number to take even the loss of a giant airliner off the agenda.

But with the pros it's different. It isn't that other flight talk takes precedence. It's simply that Flight 33, and what did or didn't happen to it, carries a chill. Even now, just eleven months later, you never hear it mentioned in the Ops Rooms, where the pilots chain-smoke and watch the weather reports, nor in the control towers, when the tense and tired men who talk planes down get a respite for a quick cup of coffee and a smoke.

There are other cases of disappearing aircraft on record, of course. There was Amelia Earhart, who took off from New Guinea for the mid-Pacific island of Howland, and was never heard from again. There was the less well-known, but equally tragic case of the two U.S. Navy AD6 Sky Raiders, in a flight for Fallon, Nevada, who neither arrived nor left a clue as to what happened to them. There was the mysterious case of the two British airliners, the Star Ariel and a sister ship the Star Tiger. Tiger vanished over that sea of weeds called Sargasso which lies in the Atlantic off the Bahamas. Thirteen days later Ariel followed her into oblivion. No trace of either plane was ever found.

But Flight 33 was different. It was a jet airliner. Beautiful, graceful, full of incredible power, as safe as any plane could be. And it simply had no business disappearing. It was too fine an aircraft. And whatever yanked it out of the skies was a power that couldn't be reckoned with in a design board or in an engineer's manual. That's why you rarely hear of it where pilots and crews congregate.

Call it superstition, vestiges of black magic. Call it that strange and unspoken mysticism that somehow, incongruously, is to be found among the highly scientific body of men who fight gravity for a living. But whatever you call it, don't ever ask a captain, a first officer or any crew member to talk about the Trans-Ocean flight that disappeared between London and New York on a quiet, otherwise uneventful June afternoon. They'll pretend they didn't hear you.

■   ■   ■

Trans-Ocean 33 was airborne at eight-thirty a.m. and left a fog-shrouded London International Airport under normal and routine circumstances. It was marshmallow and drifting whip cream until the 707 reached 21,000 feet and broke into that incredibly clear blue sky, the vast universe that hangs perpetually and majestically above the crowded, dingy world.

Three hours later the aircraft was a thousand miles from the Atlantic seaboard. The crew and the one hundred and three passengers aboard had enjoyed a pleasant, unruffled flight. They were on course and on time and estimated arrival at Idlewild, New York, within a couple of hours.

Inside the cockpit Captain William Farver, a ruddy-faced, forty-five-year-old pilot with several hundred thousand hours of flying time, made a visual sweep of the instrument panel, a ritual he performed every thirty or forty minutes. His practiced glance took in the altimeter, the Mach meter, the rate-of-climb indicator, the Ram air indicator, and two dozen other instruments whose dials, levels, and tabs were as familiar to him as shirt buttons to the average male. At his right side sat the first officer, Joe Craig, tall, youngish, blond. Craig had a tendency to quick anger, but he was a good pilot with know-how and a mind not a half a beat from that of the captain. Farver looked over his shoulder toward the navigator.

"Hey, Magellan," he said, using the sobriquet common to navigators, "how about a flight progress report?"

"Coming up, Skipper," Hatch, the navigator, answered him. "We'll be about four minutes behind flight plan at thirty degrees west."

"Advise Gander negative," Farver responded.

Hatch took a sheet of paper off a clip-board and handed it across to Purcell, the Flight Engineer, who scanned it briefly and gave it to Farver. Farver checked it, then grinned around the tiny, instrument-packed cubbyhole.

"Gentlemen," he said happily, "you'll be pleased to know that thanks to the quality of this aircraft, the fine weather and my brilliant flying, we'll hit Idlewild on schedule if our speed holds up." He handed the report over his shoulder to Wyatt the second officer. "Send it in, Wyatt," he ordered.

Wyatt put on his earphones, flicked a switch on the complex radio equipment and spoke into the mike. "Shannon, Shannon," he said over the whistling jet engines, "Copy Gander . . . Trans-Ocean Flight 33, position 50 north, 30 west, time 14-OH-3. . . . flight level 35,000. Estimating Idlewild 18–30. Endurance (by this he meant fuel) 7-9-5-6-OH. Temperature minus 47. Acknowledge, Shannon." He listened for a moment, heard the muffled voice at the other end, then flicked the switch. "Report received, Skipper," he announced.

Through the flight-deck door in the rear of the compartment, Jane Braden, the senior stewardess, entered, carrying her one hundred and twelve pounds like a Rockette. Her shoulder-length blond hair was pulled back severely in a bun, but she still looked like a Rockette and was built, in the memorable words of Flight Engineer Purcell, overheard in a bar one evening, "like a steel-girdered, two-funneled ship of the line on her inaugural sailing day." Jane leaned against the navigator's chair and Craig spoke to her without turning.

"How we doin' back there, Janie?"

"Your passengers are highly content. But on behalf of the stewardesses, we would like to respectfully request that we get to New York as soon as possible." She smiled and the smile was bright and beautiful, much like the rest of her. "One's going to the opera," she continued, "three have heavy dates, and the fourth is available to any honorable and single crew member."

There was laughter at this. Purcell half-rose in his seat to announce his qualifications in a piping voice that always made him sound like a bosun with a built-in claghorn. Farver, laughing with the rest of them, suddenly broke off and stared out into space.

Like many pilots, somewhere along the line the captain had developed a sixth sense for anything amiss. It could be a slightly laboring engine that skipped once in a thousand revolutions. It could be a stodgy rudder that an engineer wouldn't pick up with a microscope—but a pilot could feel. Or it could be a sensation of something . . . something indefinable . . . something without a precedent that would suddenly blanket him with a packed-ice feeling of impending trouble. And, at thirty-five thousand feet in a six hundred-miles-an-hour airplane, trouble wore a thousand masks, a million disguises. It could creep out of a crevice at any point along the one-hundred-and-forty-six-foot fuselage of a 707. Farver had that feeling.

"Hold it a minute," he said. He stared off to the left of the instrument panel, obviously listening, then he turned to Craig.

"You feel anything?" he asked.

Craig too listened. "Feel anything? No. What do you mean, Skipper?"

Farver shook his head. "I don't know. I felt something. Something funny. A sensation of speed." His eyes ran hurriedly across the instrument panel. "I . . . I can't even put my finger on it." Then he took a deep breath and seemed to relax. "I guess I'm getting old."

Craig glanced at the instruments. "True airspeed, 540, Skipper. We're level. Do you suppose we picked up a tail wind?"

Farver shook his head. "Maybe. Those jetstreams are tricky. I remember a TWA guy once told me he hit one that he figured was adding two hundred knots to his ground speed. This is a crazy feeling I can't shake. You can't feel a tail wind. But I feel something!"

Craig shook his head. "Everything looks fine, Skipper."

"Magellan," Farver said to the navigator, "give us a speed check with your Loran."

"Right," Hatch answered. He watched the grid lines of the black box in front of him, where the two pinpoints of light appeared and disappeared. His jaw tightened and perspiration appeared on his forehead. "I'd better do it again," he said.

"What's going on—" Jane began.

Hatch waved her quiet. "Hold it a minute." Again he studied the Loran. "Skipper," he said tersely, "Loran indicates a ground speed of 830 knots." He shook his head, mystified. "I've never heard of a tail wind like that."

Farver's voice was tight. "Check it again." Then he turned to Wyatt, "See if you can raise the OSV Charlie, air defense radar. Ask them to give us a fix and check our ground speed." Then he turned back toward the navigator. "Hatch, you sure about that Loran?"

Hatch's eyes were glazed with concentration as he studied the instrument. "Skipper, I'm not only sure—but we're still accelerating. 980 now." He hunched closer over the Loran. "1120. 1500." His lips began to tremble and his face suddenly looked white. "Jesus God," he half-shouted, "I can't even keep up with it."

"Anything from air defense?" Farver barked at Wyatt.

"No, sir," was the answer. "I can't raise them."

Hatch half-rose in his seat, his voice trembling. "2100. Honest to God . . . 2100 . . . and still increasing."

"I hope the wings stay on." It was more than just a statement from Craig. It was like a prayer.

"They will," Farver answered grimly. "Don't worry about the wings. Just watch that true airspeed. Ground speed doesn't mean a Goddamned thing. We're just in one helluva jetstream." He looked down at the instruments and then shook his head in total disbelief which was almost shock. "Magellan," he said, his voice raised. "My needle just reversed on Gander Omni." He looked up. "How in God's name could we get past Gander? Give me a fast position check."

Hatch stood on his seat in order to put his head into the tiny astrodome over the cockpit. He took a fast fix on the sun. For a moment he was silent. Then he said, "Skipper—we are past Gander. We must be doing 3,000 knots."

Taut, suddenly lined faces looked at one another and fear, like an air-borne virus, infected the room. Farver's voice cut into the silence.

"Try to raise Harmon control," he ordered Wyatt. "If you can't raise them try Moncton or Boston. And at this speed . . . you might as well try to get Idlewild!"

Wyatt again went on the radio. "Trans-Ocean 33," he said, his voice trembling slightly. "Trans-Ocean 33. Harmon Control, come in please . . . Harmon, please acknowledge. Trans-Ocean 33 Moncton. Trans-Ocean 33 Boston control, come in please . . . Trans-Ocean 33 Idlewild control . . . can you hear us, please?" Wyatt lowered the mike. "No soap," he said quietly. "I can't raise anyone."

Fear was the silence that followed the announcement. It was the sweat on Wyatt's forehead. It was the firm set to Craig's face. It was the panicky fluttering of Jane Braden's heart. And to Captain Farver it was an interloper threatening his coolness, his presence of mind, his ability to think and make decisions. The instruments in front of his eyes told him a lie. They couldn't be going that fast. Not and stay in one piece. Not and have the wings remain on the aircraft. Not without being shaken to pieces and disintegrating into so many tons of falling metal.

And yet they were continuing to accelerate. And the big 707 shot through the sky in a denial of logic and truth and mathematical equations. And inside its aluminum hull, the five crew members stared at their instruments. Deep inside they acknowledged their fears and gave silent assent to their helplessness.

A few moments later Jane Braden closed the flight-deck door behind her and went into the lounge. Her assistant, Paula Temple, a short, attractive brunette, was putting coffee on a tray in a small gallery adjoining the lounge. Paula looked up and winked.

"I hope you prodded the fly people. I'm seeing the 'Ride of the Valkyrie' tonight." Then she saw the look on Jane's face. "What's the matter?" she whispered.

Jane Braden entered the galley and pulled the curtain around them, closing them off to the lounge.

"Janie," Paula persisted. "I've always had a thing about Valhalla." Her voice shook slightly. "Be a good egg and tell me if I'll be there in time for the curtain."

Jane leaned closer to her. "Let me put it to you this way," she said. "It's my most earnest wish that the Valhalla you're talking about is at the Metropolitan Opera in little old New York."

"Instead of?" Paula's voice was a whisper.

"Instead of a . . . conducted tour into the real thing. We're in trouble, Paula."

"How bad?" Paula asked.

"They don't know yet." She looked down at Paula's tray. "Go ahead and serve it."

Paula lifted up the tray in shaking hands and started to pull the curtains apart."

"Paula—" Jane said to her.

Paula turned.

The beautiful blonde winked at her. "Like . . . coffee, tea or milk . . . and with a smile!"

Paula nodded, forcing a tight smile of her own as she gripped the tray tighter. "You got a deal," she announced, "but I wish to God I'd gone to acting school!"

She pulled the curtain apart and carried the tray past the lounge into the first-class compartment. She walked down the aisle conscious of the faces on either side. Men, women, a sleeping infant, an RAF officer. Innocent, guileless faces of human beings who felt a total trust in the omniscient father-figure at the controls of this complex vehicle. They felt safe because the alternative was a panicky insanity.

A stout, mouth-flapping, middle-aged woman, who was every tourist who'd ever complained about cold water in a London hotel and trumpeted America's pre-eminence in the field of plumbing fixtures, spewed out a monologue to the tall, gray-haired RAF pilot beside her.

"It's as my late husband used to say," she gurgled. "The only problem with the British, aside from the fact that you're perhaps a little behind the times, is this awful coldness of you people. You just don't seem to . . . to emotionalize anything. You're such cold fish about everything. And you know it's a fact—a person gets sick holding things in." She swept on without dropping a beat. "You know, you talk about ailments—I had an aunt once in Boise, Idaho. She had one of the worst livers in the medical history of the state. When that woman passed on, rest her soul, would you believe it? There were five medical associations bidding just to get her liver in a bottle on display. But her mother . . . my father's sister . . . absolutely refused to let them show her liver. And it's like I always said to my late husband—" She broke off suddenly and stared at the epaulets on the officer's shoulders. "What did you say you were?" she inquired.

The officer, with tired eyes, smiled thinly. "A captain, madam. I'm in a military attache to our British Consulate in Los Angeles."

"Now isn't that wonderful," the woman gushed at him. "Nephew of mine was in the navy during the Second World War. He was on a cruiser, or PT boat or something like that. Or was it a battleship?"

The RAF officer suddenly stared straight ahead. He first looked down at the floor then out toward the wing. There was no loss of power. No tell-tale shimmying. No flame or smoke. Nothing. And yet there was this feeling . . . this feeling that he couldn't describe even to himself. There was something wrong. This he knew. It was simple and unequivocal. There was something going wrong with this plane.

He turned to look down the aisle at the stewardess who was picking up coffee trays. Were her hands shaking as she went by him? Was there an odd look on her face? Imagination can spawn one nightmarish hallucination after another. This he knew. But the sensation persisted. And there was an odd look on the stewardess's face as she passed him.

"What's the matter?" his stout seatmate asked. "Air sickness? I've got some wonderful pills in my bag here—"

"Do you feel anything?" he interrupted her.

The woman stared at him blankly. "Feel anything? Like what?"

The RAF captain averted her look. "Nothing," he said softly. "I . . . ah . . . I just thought I felt something." He looked at the woman briefly out of the corner of his eye and decided that he'd keep this one to himself. He smiled at her and said, "What about this nephew of yours in the Navy?"

In the rear seat of the first-class compartment, a middle-aged man smiled at his wife. "Notice how nervous that little stewardess was? Probably got some kind of big heavy date or something when we land in New York."

His wife nodded sleepily and closed her eyes. The man picked up a magazine and began to read.

■   ■   ■

In the cockpit of Flight 33 the tension was like a big block of some material that could be cut with a saw. At intervals each man looked toward Farver, hunched over his instruments, and then to Hatch the navigator who continued to study the Loran, shaking his head in disbelief as each moment passed. Second Officer Wyatt fiddled with the radio and kept speaking quietly into the mike.

"What about it?" Farver asked him.

Wyatt shook his head. "Not a thing, sir. Not a bloody thing.

Either they're off whack . . . everybody out there," his voice was meaningful, "or we are."

Craig whirled around in his seat. "Why the hell don't you check your equipment—"

"I checked it four times," Wyatt shouted back.

"Knock it off," Farver interrupted. "We'll just have to bull it through and see if anything—"

He never completed his sentence. Not then or ever. There was a sudden, blinding flash of hot, white light. For one fragment of a second they seemed caught up in some kind of giant picture negative in reverse polarization. They looked foggy and indistinct. Then the cockpit shuddered and bucked. Purcell was flung from his seat. The clip-boards overhead tumbled down on Hatch's head. Both Farver and Craig instinctively reached for the controls, but the light had dissipated and the plane was once again in easy, level flight.

"Did we hit something?" Craig asked, breathlessly.

"I don't know," Farver answered briefly. "Check for damage."

Craig looked out the side window. "Numbers three and four are still on the wing," he announced. "They look okay."

Farver turned from studying the left wing. "Ditto one and two," he said tersely. "Everything seems in one piece. Purcell, go aft and check for any cabin damage. Report back as fast as you can. I'll get on the horn and try to calm everybody down if they need calming. Tell the girls to stay with it." He turned back to the instrument panel and his eyes traversed the maze of levers and dials. "We're in trouble," he said softly, as if to himself, "but I'll be Goddamned if I know what kind of trouble!"

"That light," Hatch said in a strained, tight voice. "That crazy light. What was it?"

"That's something we'll have to find out," Farver said. He turned to Craig. "And quick too."

"What was the shaking?" Craig asked. "Turbulence?"

Farver shook his head. "I doubt it. It was more like a . . . like a . . ."

"Like a what?" Craig asked impatiently.

"Like a sound wave," Farver said. "As if we'd gone past the speed of sound."

Craig was incredulous. "You mean we hit Mach 1? We broke the sound barrier? But how the hell could that happen? We didn't get any Mach 1 warning."

"We probably wouldn't," Farver said, "not with a true airspeed of only 440. I don't know what it was. I just don't know. Magellan's last speed check showed 3,000 knots. We could have broken some kind of sound barrier, but . . ." He hesitated. "But not any sound barrier I've ever heard of before. Magellan, can you give me a Loran fix now?"

Hatch checked his equipment. "Whatever that bump was, Skipper," he said, "it's really knocked out everything. Loran's inoperative."

"Altimeter and rate of climb steady, Skipper," Craig announced, checking the dials in front of him.

Behind them, Wyatt fiddled with the radio. "Skipper," he said, "I still can't raise Gander or Moncton or Boston or any place. It's like I said . . . either they're off the air or we are . . . or both!"

Farver took a deep breath. "Hatch, give me a sun fix. I'll need a heading to Idlewild from our last known position. If we can't raise anybody, we'll have to go down and establish visual contact!"

Craig looked at him, amazed. "Skipper," he said, "we can't do that. If we leave this altitude we'll land smack dab in the middle of twenty other flights."

"Anybody got an alternative?" Farver asked. "Sooner or later we're going to have to find a landmark or go VFR. With no radio control we're like a dead leaf and dumb man. As long as we stay up here we're also blind."

Purcell entered from the flight deck. "No damage aft, Skipper," he announced. "Everybody's shook up a bit, and they're curious. A few of them are plenty scared too!"

Farver took a deep breath. "Them and me both!" He reached for the hand mike. "Ours not to reason why. Ours but to do or die . . . into the valley of public relations." He flicked the cabin P.A. switch and wondered how his voice sounded as he spoke into the mike. "Ladies and gentlemen, this is Captain Farver, I want to assure you that everything is fine."

Craig closed his eyes and shook his head.

Farver grinned, but his mouth looked as if it had been cut out of paper with a scissors. "There is no danger," he continued on the mike. "We encountered a little clear air turbulence back there along with some kind of . . . atmospheric phenomena. There's been no damage to the aircraft."

His eyes moved up over the mike to scan the cockpit. The radio equipment. The silent black box that had once told them precisely where they were and where they were heading.

"I repeat," he said, "there is no cause for alarm. We'll keep you posted. If we run according to schedule, we should be landing in Idlewild inside of the next forty minutes."

He flicked off the switch, put the mike aside. Jesus God, he said to himself, I should put on a gray flannel suit and sell toothpaste. There was a point, he thought, where the passengers and crew should link arms and face whatever there was to face. They could be milk-fed and reassured to a degree. But then you had to come clean and tell them it was altogether probable that catastrophe was about two city blocks away, and all of them had better start making their peace. This is what he thought, but what he said was "Purcell—what's our fuel?"

Purcell checked his instruments. "29,435 pounds," was the answer.

Farver shook his head, scratched his jaw. "With that Loran out I don't know what our ground speed is. But I've got a feeling we've left that tail wind. I don't have that feeling of speed anymore. Do you, Craig?"

Craig shook his head.

Farver looked over his shoulder. "How about the heading to Idlewild, Magellan?"

Hatch scribbled furiously on a clip-board, adding, subtracting, estimating, and guessing. "Part of this is scientific," he announced finally. "Part of it's Kentucky windage. Try two-six-two. That's as close as I can make it."

Again the silent faces stared toward the captain. The whistling of the jet engines sounded normal and natural and yet strangely foreboding. Farver took a long, deep breath, like a man heading into an icy shower.

"All right, gentlemen," he announced, keeping his eyes straight ahead. "You know what we're up against. We have no radios. We're apparently out of touch with all ground radar points. We don't know where we are. We don't even know if we're on airways. The beast gulps fuel—you know that only too well. We've got one chance—go down through this overcast and look for something familiar. It's very possible, not to say probable . . . we may hit something on the way down, but we've got to take that chance." He paused.

"I just want you to know where we stand. Everyone keep a

sharp look out for other traffic and keep your fingers crossed."
He reached over and flicked on the seat-belt sign. His fingers
tightened on the wheel in front of him and he said quietly, "I
don't think a few prayers would be out of order either." Then
his voice was a clipped command. "All right, Craig . . . we're going down!"

The 707 raised its right wing and, like a monstrous yet beautiful
bird, nosed down through the clouds and headed toward the
earth. Inside the cockpit no one spoke a word. Eyes stared
through the small windows—eyes that strained like overworked
optical machines, desperately trying to x-ray through the billowing
clouds. It was as if, by some miracle of concentration and effort,
they hoped to see another airplane in time to avoid the blinding
hell of a mid-air collision. But there were no other aircraft. There
was nothing—only clouds that gradually became thinner and
more transparent. Suddenly they had broken through, and below
there was land.

Purcell spoke first. He shook his big, curly head, looked sar-
donically over toward Hatch and said, "Hatch, you dumb silly
bastard! Who the hell taught you to navigate?"

Wyatt kept shaking his head as he stared out of the window. "I
don't under—"

Purcell cut him off. "Two-six-two," Purcell mimicked fero-
ciously, "and that's supposed to take us over New York. Why this
dumb bastard couldn't navigate a kite across the living room!"

Hatch was stunned. Before he could answer Farver called the
shot. The captain was staring out toward his left wing and the
land mass that loomed beneath it.

"Hold it a minute," he said quietly. Then to Craig, "Level her
off."

It was incredible. It was really a monstrous practical joke. It was
a bad dream that followed a late lobster snack and an extra quart
of beer. But there it was down beneath them, stretched out in
sharp and clear relief.

"I don't get it," Farver said, shaking his head. "But that's Manhattan Island!"

"Manhattan Island," Purcell whispered, standing up to look
over Craig's shoulder. "How can it be Manhattan Island? Where
the hell's the skyline? Where are the buildings?"

"I don't know where they are," Farver said, "But we're over
New York City. There's only one small item amiss here."

Jane Braden entered from the gallery. "The passengers are—" she began.

"I don't blame them," Purcell interrupted.

"We're over land," Jane persisted, "but I don't see any—"

Farver turned and stared directly at her. "Any what, Janie? Any city?" He shook his head. "We don't either." He jerked his thumb toward the windshield. "That's Manhattan Island down there. There's the East River and the Hudson River. There's Montauk Point and every other topographical clue we need." He paused. "The problem is . . . the real estate's there. It's just that the city and eight million people seem to be missing. In short . . . there isn't any New York. It's disappeared!"

Craig grabbed Farver's arm. "Skipper, verify something for me, would you? And in a hurry? Look!"

Purcell and Hatch left their seats to look over the shoulders of the pilot and copilot.

"It's not possible," Hatch announced.

"What in the name of God is going on?" Purcell asked.

Down below, under the left wing of the 707, was a wild, tangled jungle, but something else was clearly visible even from three thousand feet, through the window of a speeding airplane. It was a dinosaur nibbling some leaves off the top branch of a giant tree. That's what it was. A dinosaur. And when Flight 33 banked around to make another pass over the area, it looked up with huge, blinking eyes, perhaps thinking in its tiny mind that this was some big, strange bird. But it continued to feed.

In the first-class passenger cabin, the RAF pilot started at what he thought he saw sweep by underneath him. The fat lady asked him what was the matter, but he did not answer her. A tourist passenger in the rear of the plane, a zoology professor coming back from a sabbatical, gulped and marred the bridge of his nose, as he thrust his face against the glass to stare down at what appeared to be an extinct animal he had lectured about a thousand times. But a 707 is a rapid piece of machinery. Within moments it had left Manhattan Island far behind and headed north toward Albany. But Albany, like New York, did not exist. It was a jungle and swamp and a maze of low-slung mountains. The plane headed inland toward what should have been Buffalo, then Lake Erie and Detroit. None of it was there. No cities. No buildings. No people. Just a vast expanse of prehistoric land.

Captain William Farver announced to nobody in particular,

"We've gone back in time. Somehow, some way, when we went through the speed of sound . . . we went back in time!"

Silence from the crew.

Silence from Jane Braden who, in this crazy, illogical moment, wanted to cry.

Silence from Farver, though his mind worked and probed and sifted and tried to formulate a plan.

Any eventuality. That, in a sense, was the Hippocratic oath of the airline pilot. Be prepared for any eventuality and be ready to meet it in a fraction of an instant without panic or indecision. But "any eventuality" did not include this. It meant a flame-out of an engine. It meant a runaway prop. It meant a hydraulic system gone awry. But the nightmare that was moving underneath the aircraft in the form of the eastern section of the North American continent, five million years earlier—this was an eventuality not planned for in any manual.

It was Craig who finally spoke. "What do we do about it, Skipper?"

Purcell looked at the fuel indicator. "Skipper, we're down to 19,000 pounds," he said.

Farver scanned his instruments. "Here's what we do about it. We rev this baby up until she's going as fast as she can. We'll climb upstairs until we hit that jetstream. And then . . ." He looked at the faces of the men and the girl. "Then we try to go back where we came from." He turned to Craig. "All right, First Officer," he said in a voice just loud enough to be heard, "Let's do it!"

The 707 pointed its nose toward the high layer of cumulus clouds and in a moment was immersed in them, pulling away from the earth that mocked them with its familiarity and with its strangeness.

Hatch suddenly noticed that his Loran was working again and he screamed out the airspeed as the ship climbed. "700 knots," he announced. "780 knots. 800 knots. 900 knots." He looked up excitedly. "Skipper . . . we're doing it, I think. Honest to God, I think we're doing it—"

The plane screamed through the sky like a projectile from some massive gun. In thirty-eight seconds it was up to 4,000 knots. Farver suddenly looked up, the sweat pouring down his face.

"We're picking it up again. Feel it? We're picking it up again."

They all felt it now. A sensation of such incredible speed . . . a feeling of propulsion beyond any experience they'd ever had before. And then the white light flashed in front of their faces. Once again the cockpit bucked and lurched and then the light was dissipated and the plane was level, its jet engines sucking in the air and roaring with unfettered power. But the blinding speed had gone. The plane intercom buzzed furiously and when Craig picked it up, he heard the frightened voice of one of the two stewardesses in the tourists' section at the rear of the plane. The girl was trying to keep the hysteria out of her voice and it took Craig a minute to calm her down long enough for him to tell her that they were all right. It was the jetstream again.

Paula Temple came through the flight-deck door, her face white. "Look, I know you've got your hands full . . . but somebody get on that pipe and in a hurry! I've got at least three people back there who are close to hysteria and—" She stopped abruptly, staring toward the front of the cockpit through the glass. Before she could say anything, Craig was half out of his seat, pointing.

"Look," he shouted. "Skipper, look. We made it! We're back! Look!"

Through a break in the heavy overcast they all saw it then. It was the skyline of New York, its tall spires shooting up toward the sky. Hatch closed his eyes and mumbled a prayer. Farver felt the sweat clammy on his forehead and for the first time noticed that his hands were shaking. He reached for the loudspeaker microphone, grinned around the cockpit, then pushed the button.

"Ladies and gentlemen, this is Captain Farver. We had some momentary difficulty back there, but as you can see we're now over New York and we should be landing in just a few minutes. Thank you."

Paula leaned against the bulkhead, tears in her eyes, her lips trembling. Jane held her tightly for a moment, kissed her on the cheek.

Jane said, "Come on partner, let's go back and make believe nothing happened."

The two girls left, and the captain of Flight 33 breathed deeply. He was conscious of a tightness in the chest suddenly unraveling itself. He checked the instruments, made a few adjustments, then spoke to Wyatt.

"How about Idlewild?"

Wyatt was already fiddling with the radio. "Nothing doing." He shook his head. "Our VFH is still out."

"Maybe Ildlewild's is too," Farver suggested. "Try using high frequency."

"I did already, Skipper. Nothing from Idlewild."

"How about La Guardia? Keep using high frequency. Somebody should hear us."

Wyatt spoke into the mike. "La Guardia, this is TransOcean 33. La Guardia, TransOcean 33."

There was some static and then a metallic voice that came from the other end. "This is La Guardia," the voice said. "Who's calling please?"

There was a whoop of unbridled delight from Purcell. Craig pounded the captain on the back, and Hatch kept applauding as if some unseen dance band had just finished a concert on the wing.

Wyatt held up his hand for silence and went back on the mike. "This is Trans-Ocean 33, La Guardia," he said. "We're on the northeast leg of the La Guardia range. Both our ILS and VOR appear inoperative. Request radar vector to Idlewild ILS."

There was a pause at the other end and then the voice came back, impatient and belligerent. "What are you, a wise guy? You'd like what?"

Wyatt's face sobered. "A radar vector to Idlewild ILS," he repeated.

"What flight did you say this was?" the La Guardia tower asked.

Wyatt's voice took on a tenseness. "Trans-Ocean 33. Come on, La Guardia, quit fooling around. We're low on fuel."

The other four men in the cockpit leaned forward toward Wyatt, a tiny, errant fear building in each mind as to what new devilment . . . what new incredible and wild deviation from the norm they were moving against now.

Then the La Guardia tower voice came back on. "Trans-Ocean airlines?" it asked. "What kind of aircraft is this?"

"This is Trans-Ocean 33," Wyatt said into the mike. "A Boeing 707 and we—"

A voice interrupted him. "Did you say a Boeing 247?"

Farver bit his lip, feeling anger and impatience surge through him. He plugged in his own mike. "Let me handle it," he said tersely to Wyatt. Then he held the mike close to his mouth. "La Guardia, this is Boeing 707, and every five-second period you keep this aircraft up in the air, you're shortening the odds on its ever getting back on the ground. Now don't give us this two-four-seven jazz. You're only about twenty years behind the times. This is a 707, La Guardia. A jet. Four big, lovely Pratt & Whitney turbines, only they're getting hungry. We're low on fuel and all we want is a radar vector to Idlewild. Now Goddamn it, do you have us in radar contact or don't you?''

There was a pause and then the La Guardia voice came back on, still sullen, but with just a shade of concern. "I don't know who you guys are," the tower said, "and we don't know anything at all about radar, jets, or anything else. We've never heard of a 707 aircraft. But if you're really low on fuel, we'll clear you to land."

Craig, who'd been consulting an approach chart during this exchange, leaned over to Farver and pointed to it. "Captain," he said, "their longest runway is less than five thousand feet. Can we take a chance?''

The La Guardia voice came back on. "Trans-Ocean 33, you're cleared to land on runway 22. Altimeter two nine eight eight, wind south 10 miles per hour. The Captain is to report to the CAA office immediately after landing.''

"Roger," Farver said tersely into the mike. "We'll stay in touch." He removed the microphone plug, then suddenly frowned. "CAA?" he asked aloud. "Why, they haven't called the Federal Aviation CAA—''

It was part of a pattern, he thought to himself. Part of a routine they had been going through for the past hour. A jigsaw puzzle perfect in every detail except every now and then a round peg appeared and didn't fit the square hole. Then he shook his head and pushed it out of his mind as he turned to Craig.

"We'll bring her down, Craig," he said. "It'll be like landing in a phone booth, but—''

Hatch, who was standing up between his seat and the two pilot's chairs, suddenly pointed out the window, his eyes wide.

"Captain," he said, pointing a shaking finger toward the left window. "Circle again, will you?" He wet his lips. "And then look!''

Farver winged the plane over gently, circled in as short an arc as he could and then came back, following the trembling finger of Hatch. And then they all saw it. The scene whisked past their eyes in less than a second, but it registered. It was an indelible

shock that made itself known optically, but then entered the mind
of every one of the crew members to infiltrate their brains and
corrode the lines to sanity.

Yes, they had all seen it. And when Farver turned the aircraft
to retrace the flight path, they saw it again. A trylon and peris-
phere were set in the middle of what appeared from the air to
be a giant fair or carnival. And they all knew what it was.

Craig's hands dropped from the controls and he had to press
them to his sides to keep from shaking. "Skipper," he said, "do
you know what—"

Farver, hunched forward in his seat, kept shaking his head from
side to side.

Wyatt said in a small, strained voice, "It's the New York World's
Fair. That's what it is. The New York World's Fair. But that means
we're in—"

"1939," Hatch interrupted him. "We came back . . . we came
back . . . but dear God . . . we didn't come back far enough!"

They all turned toward Farver. What was happening was more
than they could handle. For more than even their better-than-
average minds could assimilate. And they did what any human
being should do. They looked up and away, abdicated all decisions, and threw the massive dead weight of responsibility on the
number one man in the cabin.

Farver felt it press down on him. The prerogative of command
. . . but worse, the responsibility. They all wanted to know what to
do and he was the one man who would have to tell them.

And what do you tell them? What is the procedure? What is the
command that is right and proper to cover a situation that has
no precedent, no logic, and no reason. For one panicky moment
Farver's mind went blank and he felt like turning on them and
screaming, "Goddamn it, don't look at me. Don't wait to hear
what I say. Don't hang on the next command that's supposed to
come from this airplane pilot!"

Holy Mother—it was too much to expect that any human being
could rise up in the middle of this nightmare and point the way
to an awakening or anything even resembling it. But after a moment, whatever was the invisible challenge that was thrown at him
by the frightened faces, he responded. He was the captain of this
aircraft. And though reality and logic were cracking up and falling
to pieces all around him—by God he would command!

"We can't land," Farver said finally, his voice soft. He shook his head. We can't land in La Guardia . . . and we can't land back in 1939. We've got to try again. That's all that's left. Try again."

Craig nodded toward the flight-deck door. "What about the passengers?"

"I think we had better let them in on it now." Farver flicked on the P.A. system and reached for the mike. "Ladies and gentlemen," he said, his voice firm, full of resolve, no condescension, no fake optimism. "What I'm going to tell you is something I can't explain. The crew is as much in the dark as you are. Because if you look out on the left-hand side of the aircraft . . . you'll see directly below us an area called Lake Success. And those buildings down there aren't called the United Nations. They happen to be . . ." his voice faltered for a moment and then came back on. "They happen to be the World's Fair."

Down the length of the plane the loudspeaker carried Captain William Farver's voice and the passengers listened as a nightmare began to close in on them.

"What I'm trying to tell you," Farver's voice told them, "is that somehow, some way . . . this aircraft has gone back in time and it's 1939. What we're going to do now is increase our speed, get into the same jetstream and attempt to go through the sound barrier we've already broken twice before. I don't know if we can do it. All I ask of you is that you remain calm . . . and pray."

In the cockpit, Farver pulled the yoke forward and the 707 once again pointed toward the sky.

The giant aircraft disappeared through the heavy overcast. Its rotating engines grew indistinct and faded out, leaving a silence in its wake and a long jet trail that was picked up by the wind and carried away.

Thirty thousand feel below, it was 1939 and people gaped at the wondrous exhibits. There was the waterfall in front of the Italian building; the beautiful marble statuary that fronted the Polish pavilion; the exquisite detail of the tapestry and wood carvings shown by the smiling Japanese. And the people walked happily through a warm June afternoon, seeing only the sunlight and not knowing that darkness was falling over the world.

■   ■   ■

She was a Trans-Ocean jet airliner on her way from London to New York, on an uneventful June afternoon in the year 1961. She was last heard from six hundred miles south of Newfoundland, then somehow she was swallowed up into the vast design of things, to be searched for on land, sea, and in the air by anguished human beings, fearful of what they might find.

You and I, however, know where she is. You and I know what happened. So if some moment . . . any . . . you hear the sound of jet engines flying atop the overcast . . . engines that sound searching and lost . . . engines that sound desperate . . . shoot up a flare. Or do something. That would be Trans-Ocean 33 trying to get home . . . from The Twilight Zone.

Connie Willis

Fire Watch

From *Asimov's Science Fiction*, February 1982

A time-traveling Oxford student journeys back to London during World War II to observe the Blitz—and more.

B. A.

"History hath triumphed over time, which besides it nothing but eternity hath triumphed over."

—Sir Walter Raleigh

SEPTEMBER 20—OF COURSE THE FIRST THING I LOOKED FOR was the firewatch stone. And of course it wasn't there yet. It wasn't dedicated until 1951 . . . accompanying speech by the Very Reverend Dean Walter Matthews . . . and this is only 1940. I knew that. I went to see the firewatch stone only yesterday, with some kind of misplaced notion that seeing the scene of the crime would somehow help. It didn't.

The only things that would have helped were a crash course in London during the Blitz and a little more time. I had not gotten either.

"Traveling in time is not like taking the tube, Mr. Bartholomew," the esteemed Dunworthy had said, blinking at me through those antique spectacles of his. "Either you report on the twentieth or you don't go at all."

"But I'm not ready," I'd said. "Look, it took me four years to get ready to travel with St. Paul. *St. Paul.* Not St. Paul's. You can't expect me to get ready for London in the Blitz in two days."

"Yes," Dunworthy had said. "We can." End of conversation.

241

"Two days!" I had shouted at my roommate Kivrin. "All because some computer adds an 'apostrophe s'. And the esteemed Dunworthy doesn't even bat an eye when I tell him. 'Time travel is not like taking the tube, young man,' he says. 'I'd suggest you get ready. You're leaving day after tomorrow.' The man's a total incompetent."

"No," she said. "He isn't. He's the best there is. He wrote the book on St. Paul's. Maybe you should listen to what he says."

I had expected Kivrin to be at least a little sympathetic. She had been practically hysterical when she got her practicum changed from fifteenth to fourteenth century England, and how did either century qualify as a practicum? Even counting infectious diseases they couldn't have been more than a five. The Blitz is an eight, and St. Paul's itself is, with my luck, a ten.

"You think I should go see Dunworthy again?" I said.

"Yes."

"And then what? I've got two days. I don't know the money, the language, the history. Nothing."

"He's a good man," Kivrin said. "I think you'd better listen to him while you can." Good old Kivrin. Always the sympathetic ear.

The good man was responsible for my standing just inside the propped-open west doors, gawking like the country boy I was supposed to be, looking for a stone that wasn't there. Thanks to the good man, I was about as unprepared for my practicum as it was possible for him to make me.

I couldn't see more than a few feet into the church. I could see a candle gleaming feebly a long way off and a closer blur of white moving toward me. A verger, or possibly the Very Reverend Dean himself. I pulled out the letter from my clergyman uncle in Wales that was supposed to gain me access to the Dean, and patted my back pocket to make sure I hadn't lost the microfiche *Oxford English Dictionary, Revised, with Historical Supplements*, I'd smuggled out of the Bodleian. I couldn't pull it out in the middle of the conversation, but with luck I could muddle through the first encounter by context and look up the words I didn't know later.

"Are you from the ayarpee?" he said. He was no older than I am, a head shorter and much thinner. Almost ascetic looking. He reminded me of Kivrin. He was not wearing white, but clutching it to his chest. In other circumstances I would have thought it was a pillow. In other circumstances I would know what was being said to me, but there had been no time to unlearn sub-Mediterranean Latin and Jewish law and learn Cockney and air-raid procedures. Two days, and the esteemed Dunworthy, who wanted to talk about the sacred burdens of the historian instead of telling me what the ayarpee was.

"Are you?" he demanded again.

I considered slipping out the OED after all on the grounds that Wales was a foreign country, but I didn't think they had microfilm in 1940. Ayarpee. It could be anything, including a nickname for the fire watch, in which case the impulse to say no was not safe at all. "No," I said.

He lunged suddenly toward and past me and peered out the open doors. "Damn," he said, coming back to me. "Where are they then? Bunch of lazy bourgeois tarts!" And so much for getting by on context.

He looked at me closely, suspiciously, as if he thought I was only pretending not to be with the ayarpee. "The church is closed," he said finally.

I held up the envelope and said, "My name's Bartholomew. Is Dean Matthews in?"

He looked out the door a moment longer, as if he expected the lazy bourgeois tarts at any moment and intended to attack them with the white bundle, then he turned and said, as if he were guiding a tour, "This way; please," and took off into the gloom.

He led me to the right and down the south aisle of the nave. Thank God I had memorized the floor plan or at that moment, heading into total darkness, led by a raving verger, the whole bizarre metaphor of my situation would have been enough to send me out the west doors and back to St. John's Wood. It helped a little to know where I was. We should have been passing number twenty-six: Hunt's painting of "The Light of the World"—Jesus with his lantern—but it was too dark to see it. We could have used the lantern ourselves.

He stopped abruptly ahead of me, still raving. "We weren't asking for the bloody Savoy, just a few cots. Nelson's better off than we are—at least he's got a pillow provided." He brandished the white bundle like a torch in the darkness. It was a pillow after all. "We asked for them over a fortnight ago, and here we still are, sleeping on the bleeding generals from Trafalgar because those bitches want to play tea and crumpets with the tommies at Victoria and the Hell with us!''

He didn't seem to expect me to answer his outburst, which was good, because I had understood perhaps one key word in three. He stomped on ahead, moving out of sight of the one pathetic altar candle and stopping again at a black hole. Number twenty-five: stairs to the Whispering Gallery, the Dome, the library (not open to the public). Up the stairs, down a hall, stop again at a medieval door and knock. ''I've got to go wait for them,'' he said. ''If I'm not there they'll likely take them over to the Abbey. Tell the Dean to ring them up again, will you?'' and he took off down the stone steps, still holding his pillow like a shield against him.

He had knocked, but the door was at least a foot of solid oak, and it was obvious the Very Reverend Dean had not heard. I was going to have to knock again. Yes, well, and the man holding the pinpoint had to let go of it, too, but even knowing it will all be over in a moment and you won't feel a thing doesn't make it any easier to say, ''Now!'' So I stood in front of the door, cursing the history department and the esteemed Dunworthy and the computer that had made the mistake and brought me here to this dark door with only a letter from a fictitious uncle that I trusted no more than I trusted the rest of them.

Even the old reliable Bodleian had let me down. The batch of research stuff I cross-ordered through Balliol and the main terminal is probably sitting in my room right now, a century out of reach. And Kivrin, who had already done her practicum and should have been bursting with advice, walked around as silent as a saint until I begged her to help me.

''Did you go to see Dunworthy?'' she said.

''Yes. You want to know what priceless bit of information he had for me? 'Silence and humility are the sacred burdens of the historian.' He also told me I would love St. Paul's. Golden gems from the master. Unfortunately, what I need to know are the times and places of the bombs so one doesn't fall on me.'' I flopped down on the bed. ''Any suggestions?''

''How good are you at memory retrieval?'' she said.

I sat up. ''I'm pretty good. You think I should assimilate?''

''There isn't time for that,'' she said. ''I think you should put everything you can directly into long-term.''

''You mean endorphins?'' I said.

The biggest problem with using memory-assistance drugs to put information into your long-term memory is that it never sits, even for a micro-second, in your short-term memory, and that makes retrieval complicated, not to mention unnerving. It gives you the most unsettling sense of *déjà vu* to suddenly know something you're positive you've never seen or heard before.

The main problem, though, is not eerie sensations but retrieval. Nobody knows exactly how the brain gets what it wants out of storage, but short-term is definitely involved. That brief, sometimes microscopic, time information spends in short-term is apparently used for something besides tip-of-the-tongue availability. The whole complex sort-and-file process of retrieval is apparently centered in short-term; and without it, and without the help of the drugs that put it there or artificial substitutes, information can be impossible to retrieve. I'd used endorphins for examinations and never had any difficulty with retrieval, and it looked like it was the only way to store all the information I needed in anything approaching the time I had left, but it also meant that I would never have known any of the things I needed to know, even for long enough to have forgotten them. If and when I could retrieve the information, I would know it. Till then I was as ignorant of it as if it were not stored in some cobwebbed corner of my mind at all.

"You can retrieve without artificials, can't you?" Kivrin said, looking skeptical.

"I guess I'll have to."

"Under stress? Without sleep? Low body endorphin levels?" What exactly had her practicum been? She had never said a word about it, and undergraduates are not supposed to ask. Stress factors in the Middle Ages? I thought everybody slept through them.

"I hope so," I said. "Anyway, I'm willing to try this idea if you think it will help."

She looked at me with that martyred expression and said, "Nothing will help." Thank you, St. Kivrin of Balliol.

But I tried it anyway. It was better than sitting in Dunworthy's rooms having him blink at me through his historically accurate eyeglasses and tell me I was going to love St. Paul's. When my Bodleian requests didn't come, I overloaded my credit and bought out Blackwell's. Tapes on World War II, Celtic literature, history of mass transit, tourist guidebooks, everything I could think of. Then I rented a high-speed recorder and shot up. When

I came out of it, I was so panicked by the feeling of not knowing any more than I had when I started that I took the tube to London and raced up Ludgate Hill to see if the firewatch stone would trigger any memories. It didn't.

"Your endorphin levels aren't back to normal yet," I told myself and tried to relax, but that was impossible with the prospect of the practicum looming up before me. And those are real bullets, kid. Just because you're a history major doing his practicum doesn't mean you can't get killed. I read history books all the way home on the tube and right up until Dunworthy's flunkies came to take me to St. John's Wood this morning.

Then I jammed the microfiche OED in my back pocket and went off feeling as if I would have to survive by my native wit and hoping I could get hold of artificials in 1940. Surely I could get through the first day without mishap, I thought; and now here I was, stopped cold by almost the first word that was spoken to me.

Well, not quite. In spite of Kivrin's advice that I not put anything in short-term, I'd memorized the British money, a map of the tube system, a map of my own Oxford. It had gotten me this far. Surely I would be able to deal with the Dean.

Just as I had almost gotten up the courage to knock, he opened the door, and as with the pinpoint, it really was over quickly and without pain. I handed him my letter, and he shook my hand and said something understandable like, "Glad to have another man, Bartholomew." He looked strained and tired as if he might collapse if I told him the Blitz had just started. I know, I know: Keep your mouth shut. The sacred silence, etc.

He said, "We'll get Langby to show you round, shall we?" I assumed that was my Verger of the Pillow, and I was right. He met us at the foot of the stairs, puffing a little but jubilant.

"The cots came," he said to Dean Matthews. "You'd have thought they were doing us a favor. All high heels and hoity-toity. 'You made us miss our tea, luv,' one of them said to me. 'Yes, well, and a good thing, too,' I said. 'You look as if you could stand to lose a stone or two.' "

Even Dean Matthews looked as though he did not completely understand him. He said, "Did you set them up in the crypt?" and then introduced us. "Mr. Bartholomew's just got in from Wales," he said. "He's come to join our volunteers." Volunteers, not fire watch.

Langby showed me around, pointing out the various dimnesses

in the general gloom and then dragged me down to see the ten folding canvas cots set up among the tombs in the crypt, also in passing Lord Nelson's black marble sarcophagus. He told me I didn't have to stand a watch the first night and suggested I go to bed, since sleep is the most precious commodity in the raids. I could well believe it. He was clutching that silly pillow to his breast like his beloved.

"Do you hear the sirens down here?" I asked, wondering if he buried his head in it.

He looked round at the low stone ceilings. "Some do, some don't. Brinton has to have his Horlich's. Bence-Jones would sleep if the roof fell in on him. I have to have a pillow. The important thing is to get your eight in no matter what. If you don't, you turn into one of the walking dead. And then you get killed."

On that cheering note he went off to post the watches for tonight, leaving his pillow on one of the cots with orders for me to let nobody touch it. So here I sit, waiting for my first air-raid siren and trying to get all this down before I turn into one of the walking or non-walking dead.

I've used the stolen OED to decipher a little Langby. Middling success. A tart is either a pastry or a prostitute (I assume the latter, although I was wrong about the pillow). Bourgeois is a catchall term for the faults of the middle class. A tommy's a soldier. Ayarpee I could not find under any spelling and I had nearly given up when something in long-term about the use of acronyms and abbreviations in wartime popped forward (bless you, St. Kivrin) and I realized it must be an abbreviation. ARP. Air Raid Precautions. Of course. Where else would you get the bleeding cots from?

■ ■ ■

September 21—Now that I'm past the first shock of being here, I realize that the history department neglected to tell me what I'm supposed to do in the three-odd months of this practicum. They handed me this journal, the letter from my uncle, and a ten-pound note, and sent me packing into the past. The ten pounds (already depleted by train and tube fares) is supposed to last me until the end of December and get me back to St. John's Wood for pickup when the second letter calling me back to Wales to my sick uncle's bedside comes. Till then I live here in the crypt with Nelson, who, Langby tells me, is pickled in alcohol inside his coffin. If we take a direct hit, will he burn like a torch or simply trickle out in a decaying stream onto the crypt floor, I wonder. Board is provided by a gas ring, over which are cooked wretched tea and indescribable kippers. To pay for all this luxury I am to stand on the roofs of St. Paul's and put out incendiaries.

I must also accomplish the purpose of this practicum, whatever it may be. Right now the only purpose I care about is staying alive until the second letter from uncle arrives and I can go home.

I am doing makework until Langby has time to "show me the ropes." I've cleaned the skillet they cook the foul little fishes in, stacked wooden folding chairs at the altar end of the crypt (flat instead of standing because they tend to collapse like bombs in the middle of the night), and tried to sleep.

I am apparently not one of the lucky ones who can sleep through the raids. I spent most of the night wondering what St. Paul's risk rating is. Practica have to be at least a six. Last night I was convinced this was a ten, with the crypt as ground zero, and that I might as well have applied for Denver.

The most interesting thing that's happened so far is that I've seen a cat. I am fascinated, but trying not to appear so since they seem commonplace here.

■   ■   ■

September 22—Still in the crypt. Langby comes dashing through periodically cursing various government agencies (all abbreviated) and promising to take me up on the roofs. In the meantime, I've run out of makework and taught myself to work a stirrup pump. Kivrin was overly concerned about my memory retrieval abilities. I have not had any trouble so far. Quite the opposite. I called up fire-fighting information and got the whole manual with pictures, including instructions on the use of the stirrup pump. If the kippers set Lord Nelson on fire, I shall be a hero.

Excitement last night. The sirens went early and some of the chars who clean offices in the City sheltered in the crypt with us. One of them woke me out of a sound sleep, going like an air raid siren. Seems she'd seen a mouse. We had to go whacking at tombs and under the cots with a rubber boot to persuade her it was gone. Obviously what the history department had in mind: murdering mice.

■   ■   ■

September 24—Langby took me on rounds. Into the choir, where I had to learn the stirrup pump all over again, assigned rubber boots and a tin helmet. Langby says Commander Allen is getting us asbestos firemen's coats, but hasn't yet, so it's my own wool coat and muffler and very cold on the roofs even in September. It feels like November and looks it, too, bleak and cheerless with no sun. Up to the dome and onto the roofs which should be flat, but in fact are littered with towers, pinnacles, gutters, and statues, all designed expressly to catch and hold incendiaries out of reach. Shown how to smother an incendiary with sand before it burns through the roof and sets the church on fire. Shown the ropes (literally) lying in a heap at the base of the dome in case somebody has to go up one of the west towers or over the top of the dome. Back inside and down to the Whispering Gallery.

Langby kept up a running commentary through the whole tour, part practical instruction, part church history. Before we went up into the Gallery he dragged me over to the south door to tell me how Christopher Wren stood in the smoking rubble of Old St. Paul's and asked a workman to bring him a stone from the graveyard to mark the cornerstone. On the stone was written in Latin, "I shall rise again," and Wren was so impressed by the irony that he had the words inscribed above the door. Langby looked as smug as if he had not told me a story every first-year history student knows, but I suppose without the impact of the firewatch stone, the other is just a nice story.

Langby raced me up the steps and onto the narrow balcony circling the Whispering Gallery. He was already halfway round to the other side, shouting dimensions and acoustics at me. He stopped facing the wall opposite and said softly, "You can hear me whispering because of the shape of the dome. The sound waves are reinforced around the perimeter of the dome. It sounds like the very crack of doom up here during a raid. The dome is one hundred and seven feet across. It is eighty feet above the nave."

I looked down. The railing went out from under me and the black-and-white marble floor came up with dizzying speed. I hung onto something in front of me and dropped to my knees, staggered and sick at heart. The sun had come out, and all of St. Paul's seemed drenched in gold. Even the carved wood of the choir, the white stone pillars, the leaden pipes of the organ, all of it golden, golden.

Langby was beside me, trying to pull me free. "Bartholomew," he shouted, "What's wrong? For God's sake, man."

I knew I must tell him that if I let go, St. Paul's and all the past would fall in on me, and that I must not let that happen because I was an historian. I said something, but it was not what I intended because Langby merely tightened his grip. He hauled me violently free of the railing and back onto the stairway, then let me collapse limply on the steps and stood back from me, not speaking.

"I don't know what happened in there," I said. "I've never been afraid of heights before."

"You're shaking," he said sharply. "You'd better lie down." He led me back to the crypt.

■ ■ ■

September 25—Memory retrieval: ARP manual. Symptoms of bombing victims. Stage one—shock; stupefaction; unawareness of injuries; words may not make sense except to victim. Stage two—shivering; nausea; injuries, losses felt; return to reality. Stage three—talkativeness that cannot be controlled; desire to explain shock behavior to rescuers.

Langby must surely recognize the symptoms, but how does he account for the fact there was no bomb? I can hardly explain my shock behavior to him, and it isn't just the sacred silence of the historian that stops me.

He has not said anything, in fact assigned me my first watches for tomorrow night as if nothing had happened, and he seems no more preoccupied than anyone else. Everyone I've met so far is jittery (one thing I had in short-term was how calm everyone was during the raids) and the raids have not come near us since I got here. They've been mostly over the East End and the docks.

There was a reference tonight to a UXB, and I have been thinking about the Dean's manner and the church being closed when I'm almost sure I remember reading it was open through the entire Blitz. As soon as I get a chance, I'll try to retrieve the events of September. As to retrieving anything else, I don't see how I can hope to remember the right information until I know what it is I am supposed to do here, if anything.

There are no guidelines for historians, and no restrictions either. I could tell everyone I'm from the future if I thought they would believe me. I could murder Hitler if I could get to Germany. Or could I? Time paradox talk abounds in the history department, and the graduate students back from their practica don't say a word one way or the other. Is there a tough, immutable past? Or is there a new past every day and do we, the historians, make it? And what are the consequences of what we do, if there are consequences? And how do we dare do anything without knowing them? Must we interfere boldly, hoping we do not bring about all our downfalls? Or must we do nothing at all, not interfere, stand by and watch St. Paul's burn to the ground if need be so that we don't change the future?

All those are fine questions for a late-night study session. They do not matter here. I could no more let St. Paul's burn down than I could kill Hitler. No, that is not true. I found out yesterday in the Whispering Gallery. I could kill Hitler if I caught him setting fire to St. Paul's.

■ ■ ■

September 26—I met a young woman today. Dean Matthews has opened the church, so the watch have been doing duties as chars and people have started coming in again. The young woman reminded me of Kivrin, though Kivrin is a good deal taller and would never frizz her hair like that. She looked as if she had been crying. Kivrin has looked like that since she got back from her practicum. The Middle Ages were too much for her. I wonder how she would have coped with this. By pouring out her fears to the local priest, no doubt, as I sincerely hoped her lookalike was not going to do.

"May I help you?" I said, not wanting in the least to help. "I'm a volunteer."

She look distressed. "You're not paid?" she said, and wiped her reddened nose with a handkerchief. "I read about St. Paul's and the fire watch and all and I thought, perhaps there's a position there for me. In the canteen, like, or something. A paying position." There were tears in her red-rimmed eyes.

"I'm afraid we don't have a canteen," I said as kindly as I could, considering how impatient Kivrin always makes me, "and it's not actually a real shelter. Some of the watch sleep in the crypt. I'm afraid we're all volunteers, though."

"That won't do, then," she said. She dabbed at her eyes with the handkerchief. "I love St. Paul's, but I can't take on volunteer work, not with my little brother Tom back from the country." I was not reading this situation properly. For all the outward signs of distress, she sounded quite cheerful and no closer to tears than when she had come in. "I've got to get us a proper place to stay. With Tom back, we can't go on sleeping in the tubes."

A sudden feeling of dread, the kind of sharp pain you get sometimes from involuntary retrieval, went over me. "The tubes?" I said, trying to get at the memory.

"Marble Arch, usually," she went on. "My brother Tom saves us a place early and I go—" She stopped, held the handkerchief close to her nose, and exploded into it. "I'm sorry," she said, "this awful cold!"

Red nose, watering eyes, sneezing. Respiratory infection. It was a wonder I hadn't told her not to cry. It's only by luck that I haven't made some unforgivable mistake so far, and this is not because I can't get at the long-term memory. I don't have half the information I need even stored: cats and colds and the way St. Paul's looks in full sun. It's only a matter of time before I am stopped cold by something I do not know. Nevertheless, I am going to try for retrieval tonight after I come off watch. At least I can find out whether and when something is going to fall on me.

I have seen the cat once or twice. He is coal-black with a white patch on his throat that looks as if it were painted on for the blackout.

■   ■   ■

September 27—I have just come down from the roofs. I am still shaking.

Early in the raid the bombing was mostly over the East End. The view was incredible. Searchlights everywhere, the sky pink from the fires and reflecting in the Thames, the exploding shells sparkling like fireworks. There was a constant, deafening thunder broken by the occasional droning of the planes high overhead, then the repeating stutter of the ack-ack guns.

About midnight the bombs began falling quite near with a horrible sound like a train running over me. It took every bit of will I had to keep from flinging myself flat on the roof, but Langby was watching. I didn't want to give him the satisfaction of watching a repeat performance of my behavior in the dome. I kept my head up and my sand-bucket firmly in hand and felt quite proud of myself.

The bombs stopped roaring past about three, and there was a lull of about half an hour, and then a clatter like hail on the roofs. Everybody except Langby dived for shovels and stirrup pumps. He was watching me. And I was watching the incendiary.

It had fallen only a few meters from me, behind the clock tower. It was much smaller than I had imagined, only about thirty centimeters long. It was sputtering violently, throwing greenish-white fire almost to where I was standing. In a minute it would simmer down into a molten mass and begin to burn through the roof. Flames and frantic shouts of firemen, and then the white rubble stretching for miles, and nothing, nothing left, not even the firewatch stone.

It was the Whispering Gallery all over again. I felt that I had said something, and when I looked at Langby's face he was smiling crookedly.

"St. Paul's will burn down," I said. "There won't be anything left."

"Yes," Langby said. "That's the idea, isn't it? Burn St. Paul's to the ground? Isn't that the plan?"

"Whose plan?" I said stupidly.

"Hitler's, of course," Langby said. "Who did you think I meant?" and, almost casually, picked up his stirrup pump.

The page of the ARP manual flashed suddenly before me. I poured the bucket of sand around the still sputtering bomb, snatched up another bucket and dumped that on top of it. Black smoke billowed up in such a cloud that I could hardly find my shovel. I felt for the smothered bomb with the tip of it and scooped it into the empty bucket, then shovelled the sand in on top of it. Tears were streaming down my face from the acrid smoke. I turned to wipe them on my sleeve and saw Langby.

He had not made a move to help me. He smiled. "It's not a bad plan, actually. But of course we won't let it happen. That's what the fire watch is here for. To see that it doesn't happen. Right, Bartholomew?"

I know now what the purpose of my practicum is. I must stop Langby from burning down St. Paul's.

∎   ∎   ∎

September 28—I try to tell myself I was mistaken about Langby last night, that I misunderstood what he said. Why would he want to burn down St. Paul's unless he is a Nazi spy? How can a Nazi spy have gotten on the fire watch? I think about my faked letter of introduction and shudder.

How can I find out? If I set him some test, some fatal thing that only a loyal Englishman in 1940 would know, I fear I am the one who would be caught out. I *must* get my retrieval working properly.

Until then, I shall watch Langby. For the time being at least that should be easy. Langby has just posted the watches for the next two weeks. We stand every one together.

▪   ▪   ▪

September 30—I know what happened in September. Langby told me.

Last night in the choir, putting on our coats and boots, he said, "They've already tried once, you know."

I had no idea what he meant. I felt as helpless as that first day when he asked me if I was from the ayarpee.

"The plan to destroy St. Paul's. They've already tried once. The tenth of September. A high explosive bomb. But of course you didn't know about that. You were in Wales."

I was not even listening. The minute he had said, "high explosive bomb," I had remembered it all. It had burrowed in under the road and lodged on the foundations. The bomb squad had tried to defuse it, but there was a leaking gas main. They decided to evacuate St. Paul's, but Dean Matthews refused to leave, and they got it out after all and exploded it in Barking Marshes. Instant and complete retrieval.

"The bomb squad saved her that time," Langby was saying. "It seems there's always somebody about."

"Yes," I said. "There is," and walked away from him.

▪   ▪   ▪

October 1—I thought last night's retrieval of the events of September tenth meant some sort of breakthrough, but I have been lying here on my cot most of the night trying for Nazi spies in St. Paul's and getting nothing. Do I have to know exactly what I'm looking for before I can remember it? What good does that do me?

Maybe Langby is not a Nazi spy. Then what is he? An arsonist? A madman? The crypt is hardly conducive to thought, being not at all as silent as a tomb. The chars talk most of the night and the sound of the bombs is muffled, which somehow makes it worse. I find myself straining to hear them. When I did get to sleep this morning, I dreamed about one of the tube shelters being hit, broken mains, drowning people.

▪   ▪   ▪

October 4—I tried to catch the cat today. I had some idea of persuading it to dispatch the mouse that has been terrifying the chars. I also wanted to see one up close. I took the water bucket I had used with the stirrup pump last night to put out some burning shrapnel from one of the anti-aircraft guns. It still had a bit of water in it, but not enough to drown the cat, and my plan was to clamp the bucket over him, reach under, and pick him up, then carry him down to the crypt and point him at the mouse. I did not even come close to him.

I swung the bucket, and as I did so, perhaps an inch of water splashed out. I thought I remembered that the cat was a domesticated animal, but I must have been wrong about that. The cat's wide complacent face pulled back into a skull-like mask that was absolutely terrifying, vicious claws extended from what I had thought were harmless paws, and the cat let out a sound to top the chars.

In my surprise I dropped the bucket and it rolled against one of the pillars. The cat disappeared. Behind me, Langby said, "That's no way to catch a cat."

"Obviously," I said, and bent to retrieve the bucket.

"Cats hate water," he said, still in that expressionless voice.

"Oh," I said, and started in front of him to take the bucket back to the choir. "I didn't know that."

"Everybody knows it. Even the stupid Welsh."

. . .

October 8—We have been standing double watches for a week—bomber's moon. Langby didn't show up on the roofs, so I went looking for him in the church. I found him standing by the west doors talking to an old man. The man had a newspaper tucked under his arm and he handed it to Langby, but Langby gave it back to him. When the man saw me, he ducked out. Langby said, "Tourist. Wanted to know where the Windmill Theater is. Read in the paper the girls are starkers."

I know I looked as if I didn't believe him because he said, "You look rotten, old man. Not getting enough sleep, are you? I'll get somebody to take the first watch for you tonight."

"No," I said coldly. "I'll stand my own watch. I like being on the roofs," and added silently, *where I can watch you.*

He shrugged and said, "I suppose it's better than being down in the crypt. At least on the roofs you can hear the one that gets you."

. . .

October 10—I thought the double watches might be good for me, take my mind off my inability to retrieve. The watched pot idea. Actually, it sometimes works. A few hours of thinking about

something else, or a good night's sleep, and the fact pops forward
without any prompting, without any artificials.

The good night's sleep is out of the question. Not only do the
chars talk constantly, but the cat has moved into the crypt and
sidles up to everyone, making siren noises and begging for kippers. I am moving my cot out of the transept and over by Nelson
before I go on watch. He may be pickled, but he keeps his mouth
shut.

■   ■   ■

October 11—I dreamed Trafalgar, ships' guns and smoke and
falling plaster and Langby shouted my name. My first waking
thought was that the folding chairs had gone off. I could not see
for all the smoke.

"I'm coming," I said, limping toward Langby and pulling on
my boots. There was a heap of plaster and tangled folding chairs
in the transept. Langby was digging in it. "Bartholomew!" he
shouted, flinging a chunk of plaster aside. "Bartholomew!"

I still had the idea it was smoke. I ran back for the stirrup pump
and then knelt beside him and began pulling on a splintered
chair back. It resisted, and it came to me suddenly, There is a
body under here. I will reach for a piece of the ceiling and find
it is a hand. I leaned back on my heels, determined not to be
sick, then went at the pile again.

Langby was going far too fast, jabbing with a chair leg. I
grabbed his hand to stop him, and he struggled against me as if
I were a piece of rubble to be thrown aside. He picked up a
large flat square of plaster, and under it was the floor. I turned
and looked behind me. Both chars huddled in the recess by the
altar. "Who are you looking for?" I said, keeping hold of
Langby's arm.

"Bartholomew," he said, and swept the rubble aside, his hands
bleeding through the coating of smoky dust.

"I'm here," I said. "I'm all right." I choked on the white dust.
"I moved my cot out of the transept."

He turned sharply to the chars and then said quite calmly,
"What's under here?"

"Only the gas ring," one of them said timidly from the shad-
owed recess, "and Mrs. Galbraith's pocketbook." He dug through
the mess until he had found them both. The gas ring was leaking
at a merry rate, though the flame had gone out.

"You've saved St. Paul's and me after all," I said, standing there in my underwear and boots, holding the useless stirrup pump. "We might all have been asphyxiated."

He stood up. "I shouldn't have saved you," he said.

Stage one: Shock, stupefaction, unawareness of injuries, words may not make sense except to victim. He would not know his hand was bleeding yet. He would not remember what he had said. He had said he shouldn't have saved my life.

"I shouldn't have saved you," he repeated. "I have my duty to think of."

"You're bleeding," I said sharply. "You'd better lie down." I sounded just like Langby in the Gallery.

. . .

October 13—It was a high explosive bomb. It blew a hole in the choir roof; and some of the marble statuary is broken; but the ceiling of the crypt did not collapse, which is what I thought at first. It only jarred some plaster loose.

I do not think Langby has any idea what he said. That should give me some sort of advantage, now that I am sure where the danger lies, now that I am sure it will not come crashing down from some other direction. But what good is all this knowing, when I do not know what he will do? Or when?

Surely I have the facts of yesterday's bomb in long-term, but even falling plaster did not jar them loose this time. I am not even trying for retrieval now. I lie in the darkness waiting for the roof to fall in on me. And remembering how Langby saved my life.

. . .

October 15—The girl came in again today. She still has the cold, but she has gotten her paying position. It was a joy to see her. She was wearing a smart uniform and open-toed shoes, and her hair was in an elaborate frizz around her face. We are still cleaning up the mess from the bomb, and Langby was out with Allen getting wood to board up the choir, so I let the girl chatter at me while I swept. The dust made her sneeze, but at least this time I knew what she was doing.

She told me her name is Enola and that she's working for the WVS, running one of the mobile canteens that are sent to the fires. She came, of all things, to thank me for the job. She said that after she told the WVS that there was no proper shelter with a canteen for St. Paul's, they gave her a run in the City. "So I'll just pop in when I'm close and let you know how I'm making out, won't I just?"

She and her brother Tom are still sleeping in the tubes. I asked
her if that was safe and she said probably not, but at least down
there you couldn't hear the one that got you and that was a blessing.

■ ■ ■

October 18—I am so tired I can hardly write this. Nine incendiaries tonight and a land mine that looked as though it was going
to catch on the dome till the wind drifted its parachute away from
the church. I put out two of the incendiaries. I have done that at
least twenty times since I got here and helped with dozens of
others, and still it is not enough. One incendiary, one moment
of not watching Langby, could undo it all.

I know that is partly why I feel so tired. I wear myself out every
night trying to do my job and watch Langby, making sure none
of the incendiaries falls without my seeing it. Then I go back to
the crypt and wear myself out trying to retrieve something, anything, about spies, fires, St. Paul's in the fall of 1940, anything. It
haunts me that I am not doing enough, but I do not know what
else to do. Without the retrieval, I am as helpless as these poor
people here, with no idea what will happen tomorrow.

If I have to, I will go on doing this till I am called home. He
cannot burn down St. Paul's so long as I am here to put out the
incendiaries. "I have my duty," Langby said in the crypt.

And I have mine.

■ ■ ■

October 21—It's been nearly two weeks since the blast and I just
now realized we haven't seen the cat since. He wasn't in the mess
in the crypt. Even after Langby and I were sure there was no one
in there, we sifted through the stuff twice more. He could have
been in the choir, though.

Old Bence-Jones says not to worry. "He's all right," he said.
"The jerries could bomb London right down to the ground and
the cats would waltz out to greet them. You know why? They don't
love anybody. That's what gets half of us killed. Old lady out in
Stepney got killed the other night trying to save her cat. Bloody
cat was in the Anderson."

"Then where is he?"

"Someplace safe, you can bet on that. If he's not around St.
Paul's, it means we're in for it. That old saw about the rats de-
serting a sinking ship, that's a mistake, that is. It's cats, not rats."

■ ■ ■

October 25—Langby's tourist showed up again. He cannot still be looking for the Windmill Theatre. He had a newspaper under his arm again today, and he asked for Langby, but Langby was across town with Allen, trying to get the asbestos firemen's coats. I saw the name of the paper. It was *The Worker*. A Nazi newspaper?

■ ■ ■

November 2—I've been up on the roofs for a week straight, helping some incompetent workmen patch the hole the bomb made. They're doing a terrible job. There's still a great gap on one side a man could fall into, but they insist it'll be all right because, after all, you wouldn't fall clear through but only as far as the ceiling, and "the fall can't kill you." They don't seem to understand it's a perfect hiding place for an incendiary.

And that is all Langby needs. He does not even have to set a fire to destroy St. Paul's. All he needs to do is let one burn uncaught until it is too late.

I could not get anywhere with the workmen. I went down into the church to complain to Matthews, and saw Langby and his tourist behind a pillar, close to one of the windows. Langby was holding a newspaper and talking to the man. When I came down from the library an hour later, they were still there. So is the gap. Matthews says we'll put planks across it and hope for the best.

■ ■ ■

November 5—I have given up trying to retrieve. I am so far behind on my sleep I can't even retrieve information on a newspaper whose name I already know. Double watches the permanent thing now. Our chars have abandoned us altogether (like the cat), so the crypt is quiet, but I cannot sleep.

If I do manage to doze off, I dream. Yesterday I dreamed Kivrin was on the roofs, dressed like a saint. "What was the secret of your practicum?" I said. "What were you supposed to find out?"

She wiped her nose with a handkerchief and said, "Two things. One, that silence and humility are the sacred burdens of the historian. Two," she stopped and sneezed into the handkerchief. "Don't sleep in the tubes."

My only hope is to get hold of an artificial and induce a trance. That's a problem. I'm positive it's too early for chemical endorphins and probably hallucinogens. Alcohol is definitely available, but I need something more concentrated than ale, the only alcohol I know by name. I do not dare ask the watch. Langby is suspicious enough of me already. It's back to OED, to look up a word I don't know.

. . .

November 11—The cat's back. Langby was out with Allen again, still trying for the asbestos coats, so I thought it was safe to leave St. Paul's. I went to the grocer's for supplies and hopefully, an artificial. It was late, and the sirens sounded before I had even gotten to Cheapsie, but the raids do not usually start until after dark. It took awhile to get all the groceries and to get up my courage to ask whether he had any alcohol—he told me to go to a pub—and when I came out of the shop, it was as if I had pitched suddenly into a hole.

I had no idea where St. Paul's lay, or the street, or the shop I had just come from. I stood on what was no longer the sidewalk, clutching my brown-paper parcel of kippers and bread with a hand I could not have seen if I held it up before my face. I reached up to wrap my muffler closer about my neck and prayed for my eyes to adjust, but there was no reduced light to adjust to. I would have been glad of the moon, for all St. Paul's watch curses it and calls it a fifth columnist. Or a bus, with its shuttered headlights giving just enough light to orient myself by. Or a searchlight. Or the kickback flare of an ack-ack gun. Anything.

Just then I did see a bus, two narrow yellow slits a long way off. I started toward it and nearly pitched off the curb. Which meant the bus was sideways in the street, which meant it was not a bus. A cat meowed, quite near, and rubbed against my leg. I looked down into the yellow lights I had thought belonged to the bus. His eyes were picking up light from somewhere, though I would have sworn there was not a light for miles, and reflecting it flatly up at me.

"A warden'll get you for those lights, old tom," I said, and then as a plane droned overhead, "Or a jerry."

The world exploded suddenly into light, the searchlights and a glow along the Thames seeming to happen almost simultaneously, lighting my way home.

"Come to fetch me, did you, old tom?" I said gaily. "Where've you been? Knew we were out of kippers, didn't you? I call that loyalty." I talked to him all the way home and gave him half a tin of the kippers for saving my life. Bence-Jones said he smelled the milk at the grocer's.

• • •

November 13—I dreamed I was lost in the blackout. I could not see my hands in front of my face, and Dunworthy came and shone a pocket torch at me, but I could only see where I had come from and not where I was going.

"What good is that to them?" I said. "They need a light to show them where they're going."

"Even the light from the Thames? Even the light from the fires and the ack-ack guns?" Dunworthy said.

"Yes. Anything is better than this awful darkness." So he came closer to give me the pocket torch. It was not a pocket torch, after all, but Christ's lantern from the Hunt picture in the south nave. I shone it on the curb before me so I could find my way home, but it shone instead on the firewatch stone and I hastily put the light out.

• • •

November 20—I tried to talk to Langby today. "I've seen you talking to the old gentleman," I said. It sounded like an accusation. I meant it to. I wanted him to think it was and stop whatever he was planning.

"Reading," he said. "Not talking." He was putting things in order in the choir, piling up sandbags.

"I've seen you reading then," I said belligerently, and he dropped a sandbag and straightened.

"What of it?" he said. "It's a free country. I can read to an old man if I want, same as you can talk to that little WVS tart."

"What do you read?" I said.

"Whatever he wants. He's an old man. He used to come home from his job, have a bit of brandy and listen to his wife read the papers to him. She got killed in one of the raids. Now I read to him. I don't see what business it is of yours."

It sounded true. It didn't have the careful casualness of a lie, and I almost believed him, except that I had heard the tone of truth from him before. In the crypt. After the bomb.

"I thought he was a tourist looking for the Windmill," I said.

He looked blank only a second, and then he said, "Oh, yes, that. He came in with the paper and asked me to tell him where it was. I looked it up to find the address. Clever, that. I didn't guess he couldn't read it for himself." But it was enough. I knew that he was lying.

He heaved a sandbag almost at my feet. "Of course you

wouldn't understand a thing like that, would you? A simple act of human kindness?''

"No," I said coldly. "I wouldn't."

None of this proves anything. He gave away nothing, except perhaps the name of an artificial, and I can hardly go to Dean Matthews and accuse Langby of reading aloud.

I waited till he had finished in the choir and gone down to the crypt. Then I lugged one of the sandbags up to the roof and over to the chasm. The planking has held so far, but everyone walks gingerly around it, as if it were a grave. I cut the sandbag open and spilled the loose sand into the bottom. If it has occurred to Langby that this is the perfect spot for an incendiary, perhaps the sand will smother it.

■   ■   ■

November 21—I gave Enola some of "uncle's" money today and asked her to get me the brandy. She was more reluctant than I thought she'd be so there must be societal complications I am not aware of, but she agreed.

I don't know what she came for. She started to tell me about her brother and some prank he'd pulled in the tubes that got him in trouble with the guard, but after I asked her about the brandy, she left without finishing the story.

■   ■   ■

November 25—Enola came today, but without bringing the brandy. She is going to Bath for the holidays to see her aunt. At least she will be away from the raids for a while. I will not have to worry about her. She finished the story of her brother and told me she hopes to persuade this aunt to take Tom for the duration of the Blitz but is not at all sure the aunt will be willing.

Young Tom is apparently not so much an engaging scapegrace as a near-criminal. He has been caught twice picking pockets in the Bank tube shelter, and they have had to go back to the Marble Arch. I comforted her as best I could, told her all boys were bad at one time or another. What I really wanted to say was that she needn't worry at all, that young Tom strikes me as a true survivor type, like my own tom, like Langby, totally unconcerned with any-body but himself, well-equipped to survive the Blitz and rise to prominence in the future.

Then I asked her whether she had gotten the brandy.

She looked down at her open-toed shoes and muttered unhap-pily, "I thought you'd forgotten all about that."

I made up some story about the watch taking turns buying a bottle, and she seemed less unhappy, but I am not convinced she will not use this trip to Bath as an excuse to do nothing. I will have to leave St. Paul's and buy it myself, and I don't dare leave Langby alone in the church. I made her promise to bring the brandy today before she leaves. But she is still not back, and the sirens have already gone.

■   ■   ■

November 26—No Enola, and she said their train left at noon. I suppose I should be grateful that at least she is safely out of London. Maybe in Bath she will be able to get over her cold.

Tonight one of the ARP girls breezed in to borrow half our cots and tell us about a mess over in the East End where a surface shelter was hit. Four dead, twelve wounded. "At least it wasn't one of the tube shelters!" she said. "Then you'd see a real mess, wouldn't you?"

■   ■   ■

November 30—I dreamed I took the cat to St. John's Wood.

"Is this a rescue mission?" Dunworthy said.

"No, sir," I said proudly. "I know what I was supposed to find in my practicum. The perfect survivor. Tough and resourceful and selfish. This is the only one I could find. I had to kill Langby, you know, to keep him from burning down St. Paul's. Enola's brother has gone to Bath, and the others will never make it. Enola wears open-toed shoes in the winter and sleeps in the tubes and puts her hair up on metal pins so it will curl. She cannot possibly survive the Blitz."

Dunworthy said, "Perhaps you should have rescued her instead. What did you say her name was?"

"Kivrin," I said, and woke up cold and shivering.

■   ■   ■

December 5—I dreamed Langby had the pinpoint bomb. He carried it under his arm like a brown-paper parcel, coming out of St. Paul's Station and up Ludgate Hill to the west doors.

"This is not fair," I said, barring his way with my arm. "There is no fire watch on duty."

He clutched the bomb to his chest like a pillow. "That is your fault," he said, and before I could get to my stirrup pump and bucket, he tossed it in the door.

The pinpoint was not even invented until the end of the twentieth century, and it was another ten years before the dispossessed

Communists got hold of it and turned it into something that could be carried under your arm. A parcel that could blow a quarter-mile of the City into oblivion. Thank God that is one dream that cannot come true.

It was a sunlit morning in the dream and this morning when I came off watch the sun was shining for the first time in weeks. I went down to the crypt and then came up again, making the rounds of the roofs twice more, then the steps and the grounds and all the treacherous alleyways between where an incendiary could be missed. I felt better after that, but when I got to sleep I dreamed again, this time of fire and Langby watching it, smiling.

■ ■ ■

December 15—I found the cat this morning. Heavy raids last night, but most of them over towards Canning Town and nothing on the roofs to speak of. Nevertheless the cat was quite dead. I found him lying on the steps this morning when I made my own, private rounds. Concussion. There was not a mark on him anywhere except the white blackout patch on his throat, but when I picked him up, he was all jelly under the skin.

I could not think what to do with him. I thought for one mad moment of asking Matthews if I could bury him in the crypt. Honorable death in war or something. Trafalgar, Waterloo, London, died in battle. I ended by wrapping him in my muffler and taking him down Ludgate Hill to a building that had been bombed out and burying him in the rubble. It will do no good. The rubble will be no protection from dogs or rats, and I shall never get another muffler. I have gone through nearly all of uncle's money.

I should not be sitting here. I haven't checked the alleyways or the rest of the steps, and there might be a dud or a delayed incendiary or something that I missed.

When I came here, I thought of myself as a noble rescuer, the savior of the past. I am not doing very well at the job. At least Enola is out of it. I wish there were some way I could send St. Paul's to Bath for safekeeping. There were hardly any raids last night. Bence-Jones said cats can survive anything. What if he was coming to get me, to show me the way home? All the bombs were over Canning Town.

■ ■ ■

December 16—Enola has been back a week. Seeing her, standing on the west steps where I found the cat, sleeping in Marble Arch and not safe at all, was more than I could absorb. "I thought you were in Bath," I said stupidly.

"My aunt said she'd take Tom but not me as well. She's got a houseful of evacuation children, and what a noisy lot. Where is your muffler?" she said. "It's dreadful cold up here on the hill."

"I . . ." I said, unable to answer, "I lost it."

"You'll never get another one," she said. "They're going to start rationing clothes. And wool, too. You'll never get another one like that."

"I know," I said blinking at her.

"Good things just thrown away," she said. "It's absolutely criminal, that's what it is."

I don't think I said anything to that, just turned and walked with my head down, looking for bombs and dead animals.

■   ■   ■

December 20—Langby isn't a Nazi. He's a Communist. I can hardly write this. A Communist.

One of the chars found *The Worker* wedged behind a pillar and brought it down to the crypt as we were coming off the first watch.

"Bloody Communists," Bence-Jones said. "Helping Hitler, they are. Talking against the king, stirring up trouble in the shelters. Traitors, that's what they are."

"They love England same as you," the char said.

"They don't love nobody but themselves, bloody selfish lot. I wouldn't be surprised to hear they were ringing Hitler up on the telephone," Bence-Jones said. " 'Ello, Adolf, here's where to drop the bombs."

The kettle on the gas ring whistled. The char stood up and poured the hot water into a chipped tea pot, then sat back down. "Just because they speak their minds don't mean they'd burn down old St. Paul's, does it now?"

"Of course not," Langby said, coming down the stairs. He sat down and pulled off his boots, stretching his feet in their wool socks. "Who wouldn't burn down St. Paul's?"

"The Communists," Bence-Jones said, looking straight at him, and I wondered if he suspected Langby, too.

Langby never batted an eye. "I wouldn't worry about them if I were you," he said. "It's the jerries that are doing their bloody best to burn her down tonight. Six incendiaries so far, and one almost went into that great hole over the choir." He held out his cup to the char, and she poured him a cup of tea.

I wanted to kill him, smashing him to dust and rubble on the floor of the crypt while Bence-Jones and the char looked on in helpless surprise, shouting warnings to them and the rest of the watch. "Do you know what the Communists did?" I wanted to shout. "Do you? We have to stop him." I even stood up and started toward him as he sat with his feet stretched out before him and his asbestos coat still over his shoulders.

And then the thought of the Gallery drenched in gold, the Communist coming out of the tube station with the package so casually under his arm, made me sick with the same staggering vertigo of guilt and helplessness, and I sat back down on the edge of my cot and tried to think what to do.

They do not realize the danger. Even Bence-Jones, for all his talk of traitors, thinks they are capable only of talking against the king. They do not know, cannot know, what the Communists will become. Stalin is an ally. Communists mean Russia. They have never heard of Karinsky or the New Russia or any of the things that will make "Communist" into a synonym for "monster." They will never know it. By the time the Communists become what they became, there will be no fire watch. Only I know what it means to hear the name "Communist" uttered here, so carelessly, in St. Paul's.

A Communist. I should have known. I should have known.

■   ■   ■

December 22—Double watches again. I have not had any sleep, and I am getting very unsteady on my feet. I nearly pitched into the chasm this morning, only saved myself by dropping to my knees. My endorphin levels are fluctuating wildly, and I know I must get some sleep soon or I will become one of Langby's walking dead; but I am afraid to leave him alone on the roofs, alone in the church with his Communist party leader, alone anywhere. I have taken to watching him when he sleeps.

If I could just get hold of an artificial, I think I could induce a trance, in spite of my poor condition. But I cannot even go out to a pub. Langby is on the roofs constantly, waiting for his chance. When Enola comes again, I must convince her to get the brandy for me. There are only a few days left.

■   ■   ■

December 28—Enola came this morning while I was on the west porch, picking up the Christmas tree. It has been knocked over three nights running by concussion. I righted the tree and was bending down to pick up the scattered tinsel when Enola appeared suddenly out of the fog like some cheerful saint. She stopped quickly and kissed me on the cheek. Then she straightened up, her nose red from her perennial cold, and handed me a box wrapped in colored paper.

"Merry Christmas," she said. "Go on then, open it. It's a gift."

My reflexes are almost totally gone. I knew the box was far too shallow for a bottle of brandy. Nevertheless, I believed she had remembered, had brought me my salvation. "You darling," I said, and tore it open.

It was a muffler. Gray wool. I stared at it for fully half a minute without realizing what it was. "Where's the brandy?" I said.

She looked shocked. Her nose got redder and her eyes started to blur. "You need this more. You haven't got any clothing coupons and you have to be outside all the time. It's been so dreadful cold."

"I *needed* the brandy," I said angrily.

"I was only trying to be kind," she started, and I cut her off.

"Kind?" I said. "I asked you for brandy. I don't recall ever saying I needed a muffler." I shoved it back at her and began untangling a string of colored lights that had shattered when the tree fell.

She got that same holy martyr look Kivrin is so wonderful at. "I worry about you all the time up here," she said in a rush. "They're *trying* for St. Paul's you know. And it's so close to the river. I didn't think you should be drinking. I . . . it's a crime when they're trying so hard to kill us all that you won't take care of yourself. It's like you're in it with them. I worry someday I'll come up to St. Paul's and you won't be here."

"Well, and what exactly am I supposed to do with a muffler? Hold it over my head when they drop the bombs?"

She turned and ran, disappearing into the gray fog before she had gone down two steps. I started after her, still holding the string of broken lights, tripped over it, and fell almost all the way to the bottom of the steps.

Langby picked me up. "You're off watches," he said grimly.

"You can't do that," I said.

"Oh, yes, I can. I don't want any walking dead on the roofs with me."

I let him lead me down here to the crypt, make me a cup of tea, put me to bed, all very solicitous. No indication that this is

what he has been waiting for. I will lie here until the sirens go.
Once I am on the roofs he will not be able to send me back
without seeming suspicious. Do you know what he said before he
left, asbestos coat and rubber boots, the dedicated fire watcher?
"I want you to get some sleep." As if I could sleep with Langby
on the roofs. I would be burned alive.

■ ■ ■

December 30—The sirens woke me, and old Bence-Jones said,
"That should have done you some good. You've slept the clock
round."

"What day is it?" I said, going for my boots.

"The twenty-ninth," he said, and as I dived for the door, "No
need to hurry. They're late tonight. Maybe they won't come at
all. That'd be a blessing, that would. The tide's out."

I stopped by the door to the stairs, holding onto the cool stone.
"Is St. Paul's all right?"

"She's still standing," he said. "Have a bad dream?"

"Yes," I said, remembering the bad dreams of all the past
weeks—the dead cat in my arms in St. John's Wood, Langby with
his parcel and his *Worker* under his arm, the firewatch stone gar-
ishly lit by Christ's lantern. Then I remembered I had not
dreamed at all. I had slept the kind of sleep I had prayed for, the
kind of sleep that would help me remember.

Then I remembered. Not St. Paul's, burned to the ground by
the Communists. A headline from the dailies. "Marble Arch hit.
Eighteen killed by blast." The date was not clear except for the
year. 1940. There were exactly two more days left in 1940. I
grabbed my coat and muffler and ran up the stairs and across the
marble floor.

"Where the hell do you think you're going?" Langby shouted
to me. I couldn't see him.

"I have to save Enola," I said, and my voice echoed in the dark
sanctuary. "They're going to bomb Marble Arch."

"You can't leave now," he shouted after me, standing where
the firewatch stone would be. "The tide's out. You dirty . . ."

I didn't hear the rest of it. I had already flung myself down the
steps and into a taxi. It took almost all the money I had, the
money I had so carefully hoarded for the trip back to St. John's
Wood. Shelling started while we were still in Oxford Street, and
the driver refused to go any farther. He let me out into pitch
blackness, and I saw I would never make it in time.

Blast. Enola crumpled on the stairway down to the tube, her open-toed shoes still on her feet, not a mark on her. And when I try to lift her, jelly under the skin. I would have to wrap her in the muffler she gave me, because I was too late. I had gone back a hundred years to be too late to save her.

I ran the last blocks, guided by the gun emplacement that had to be in Hyde Park, and skidded down the steps into Marble Arch. The woman in the ticket booth took my last shilling for a ticket to St. Paul's Station. I stuck it in my pocket and raced toward the stairs.

"No running," she said placidly. "To your left, please." The door to the right was blocked off by wooden barricades, the metal gates beyond pulled to and chained. The board with names on it for the stations was X-ed with tape, and a new sign that read, "All trains," was nailed to the barricade, pointing left.

Enola was not on the stopped escalators or sitting against the wall in the hallway. I came to the first stairway and could not get through. A family had set out, just where I wanted to step, a communal tea of bread and butter, a little pot of jam sealed with waxed paper, and a kettle on a ring like the one Langby and I had rescued out of the rubble, all of it spread on a cloth embroidered at the corners with flowers. I stood staring down at the layered tea, spread like a waterfall down the steps.

"I . . . Marble Arch . . ." I said. Another twenty killed by flying tiles. "You shouldn't be here."

"We've as much right as anyone," the man said belligerently, "and who are you to tell us to move on?"

A woman lifting saucers out of a cardboard box looked up at me, frightened. The kettle began to whistle.

"It's you that should move on," the man said. "Go on then." He stood off to one side so I could pass. I edged past the embroidered cloth apologetically.

"I'm sorry," I said. "I'm looking for someone. On the platform."

"You'll never find her in there, mate," the man said, thumbing in that direction. I hurried past him, nearly stepping on the teacloth, and rounded the corner into hell.

It was not hell. Shopgirls folded coats and leaned back against them, cheerful or sullen or disagreeable, but certainly not damned. Two boys scuffled for a shilling and lost it on the tracks. They bent over the edge, debating whether to go after it, and the

station guard yelled to them to back away. A train rumbled
through, full of people. A mosquito landed on the guard's hand
and he reached out to slap it and missed. The boys laughed. And
behind and before them, stretching in all directions down the
deadly tile curves of the tunnel like casualties, backed into the
entrance-ways and onto the stairs, were people. Hundreds and
hundreds of people.

I stumbled back into the hall, knocking over a teacup. It spilled
like a flood across the cloth.

"I told you, mate," the man said cheerfully. "It's Hell in there,
ain't it? And worse below."

"Hell," I said. "Yes." I would never find her. I would never
save her. I looked at the woman mopping up the tea, and it came
to me that I could not save her either. Enola or the cat or any of
them, lost here in the endless stairways and cul-de-sacs of time.
They were already dead a hundred years, past saving. The past is
beyond saving. Surely that was the lesson the history department
sent me all this way to learn. Well, fine, I've learned it. Can I go
home now?

Of course not, dear boy. You have foolishly spent all your money
on taxicabs and brandy, and tonight is the night the Germans burn
the City. (Now it is too late, I remember it all. Twenty-eight incendiaries on the roofs.) Langby must have his chance, and you must
learn the hardest lesson of all and the one you should have known
from the beginning. You cannot save St. Paul's.

I went back out onto the platform and stood behind the yellow
line until a train pulled up. I took my ticket out and held it in
my hand all the way to St. Paul's Station. When I got there, smoke
billowed toward me like an easy spray of water. I could not see
St. Paul's.

"The tide's out," a woman said in a voice devoid of hope, and
I went down in a snake pit of limp cloth hoses. My hands came
up covered with rank-smelling mud, and I understood finally (and
too late) the significance of the tide. There was no water to fight
the fires.

A policeman barred my way and I stood helplessly before him
with no idea what to say. "No civilians allowed up there," he said.
"St. Paul's is in for it." The smoke billowed like a thundercloud,
alive with sparks, and the dome rose golden above it.

"I'm fire watch," I said, and his arm fell away, and then I was
on the roofs.

My endorphin levels must have been going up and down like an air raid siren. I do not have any short-term from then on, just moments that do not fit together: the people in the church when we brought Langby down, huddled in a corner playing cards, the whirlwind of burning scraps of wood in the dome, the ambulance driver who wore open-toed shoes like Enola and smeared salve on my burned hands. And in the center, the one clear moment when I went after Langby on a rope and saved his life.

I stood by the dome, blinking against the smoke. The City was on fire and it seemed as if St. Paul's would ignite from the heat, would crumble from the noise alone. Bence-Jones was by the northwest tower, hitting at an incendiary with a spade. Langby was too close to the patched place where the bomb had gone through, looking toward me. An incendiary clattered behind him. I turned to grab a shovel, and when I turned back, he was gone.

"Langby!" I shouted, and could not hear my own voice. He had fallen into the chasm and nobody saw him or the incendiary. Except me. I do not remember how I got across the roof. I think I called for a rope. I got a rope. I tied it around my waist, gave the ends of it into the hands of the fire watch, and went over the side. The fires lit the walls of the hole almost all the way to the bottom. Below me I could see a pile of whitish rubble. He's under there, I thought, and jumped free of the wall. The space was so narrow there was nowhere to throw the rubble. I was afraid I would inadvertently stone him, and I tried to toss the pieces of planking and plaster over my shoulder, but there was barely room to turn. For one awful moment I thought he might not be there at all, that the pieces of splintered wood would brush away to reveal empty pavement, as they had in the crypt.

I was numbed by the indignity of crawling over him. If he was dead I did not think I could bear the shame of stepping on his helpless body. Then his hand came up like a ghost's and grabbed my ankle, and within seconds I had whirled and had his head free.

He was the ghastly white that no longer frightens me. "I put the bomb out," he said. I stared at him, so overwhelmed with relief I could not speak. For one hysterical moment I thought I would even laugh, I was so glad to see him. I finally realized what it was I was supposed to say.

"Are you all right?" I said.

"Yes," he said, and tried to raise himself on one elbow. "So much the worse for you."

He could not get up. He grunted with pain when he tried to shift his weight to his right side and lay back, the uneven rubble crunching sickeningly under him. I tried to lift him gently so I could see where he was hurt. He must have fallen on something.

"It's no use," he said, breathing hard. "I put it out."

I spared him a startled glance, afraid that he was delirious, and went back to rolling him onto his side.

"I know you were counting on this one," he went on, not resisting me at all. "It was bound to happen sooner or later with all these roofs. Only I went after it. What'll you tell your friends?"

His asbestos coat was torn down the back in a long gash. Under it his back was charred and smoking. He had fallen on the incendiary. "Oh, my God," I said, trying frantically to see how badly he was burned without touching him. I had no way of knowing how deep the burns went, but they seemed to extend only in the narrow space where the coat had torn. I tried to pull the bomb out from under him, but the casing was as hot as a stove. It was not melting, though. My sand and Langby's body had smothered it. I had no idea if it would start up again when it was exposed to the air. I looked around, a little wildly, for the bucket and stirrup pump Langby must have dropped when he fell.

"Looking for a weapon?" Langby said, so clearly it was hard to believe he was hurt at all. "Why not just leave me here? A bit of overexposure and I'd be done for by morning. Or would you rather do your dirty work in private?"

I stood up and yelled to the men on the roof above us. One of them shone a pocket torch down at us, but its light didn't reach.

"Is he dead?" somebody shouted to me.

"Send for an ambulance," I said. "He's been burned."

I helped Langby up, trying to support his back without touching the burn. He staggered a little and then leaned against the wall, watching me as I tried to bury the incendiary, using a piece of the planking as a scoop. The rope came down and I tied Langby to it. He had not spoken since I helped him up. He let me tie the rope around his waist, still looking steadily at me. "I should have let you smother in the crypt," he said.

He stood leaning easily, almost relaxed against the wood supports, his hands holding him up. I put his hands on the slack rope and wrapped it once around them for the grip I knew he didn't have. "I've been on to you since that day in the Gallery. I knew you weren't afraid of heights. You came down here without any fear of heights when you thought I'd ruined your precious plans. What was it? An attack of conscience? Kneeling there like a baby, whining, 'What have we done? What have we done?' You made me sick. But you know what gave you away first. The cat. Everybody knows cats hate water. Everybody but a dirty Nazi spy."

There was a tug on the rope. "Come ahead," I said, and the rope tautened.

"That WVS tart? Was she a spy, too? Supposed to meet you in Marble Arch? Telling me it was going to be bombed. You're a rotten spy, Bartholomew. Your friends already blew it up in September. It's open again."

The rope jerked suddenly and began to lift Langby. He twisted his hands to get a better grip. His right shoulder scraped the wall. I put up my hands and pushed him gently so that his left side was to the wall. "You're making a big mistake, you know," he said. "You should have killed me. I'll tell."

I stood in the darkness, waiting for the rope. Langby was unconscious when he reached the roof. I walked past the fire watch to the dome and down to the crypt.

This morning the letter from my uncle came and with it a ten-pound note.

■   ■   ■

December 31—Two of Dunworthy's flunkies met me in St. John's Wood to tell me I was late for my exams. I did not even protest. I shuffled obediently after them without considering how unfair it was to give an exam to one of the walking dead. I had not slept in—how long? Since yesterday when I went to find Enola. I had not slept in a hundred years.

Dunworthy was at his desk, blinking at me. One of the flunkies handed me a test paper and the other one called time. I turned the paper over and left an oily smudge from the ointment on my burns. I stared uncomprehendingly at them. I had grabbed at the incendiary when I turned Langby over, but these burns were on the backs of my hands. The answer came to me suddenly in Langby's unyielding voice. "They're rope burns, you fool. Don't they teach you Nazi spies the proper way to come up a rope?"

I looked down at the test. It read, "Number of incendiaries that fell on St. Paul's. Number of land mines. Number of high explosive bombs. Method most commonly used for extinguishing incendiaries. Land mines. High explosive bombs. Number of volunteers on first watch. Second watch. Casualties. Fatalities." The questions made no sense. There was only a short space, long enough for the writing of a number, after any of the questions. Method most commonly used for extinguishing incendiaries. How would I ever fit what I knew into that narrow space. Where were the questions about Enola and Langby and the cat?

I went up to Dunworthy's desk. "St. Paul's almost burned down last night," I said. "What kind of questions are these?"

"You should be answering questions, Mr. Bartholomew, not asking them."

"There aren't any questions about the people," I said. The outer casing of my anger began to melt.

"Of course there are," Dunworthy said, flipping to the second page of the test. "Number of casualties, 1940. Blast, shrapnel, other."

"Other?" I said. At any moment the roof would collapse on me in a shower of plaster dust and fury. "Other? Langby put out a fire with his own body. Enola has a cold that keeps getting worse. The cat . . ." I snatched the paper back from him and scrawled "one cat" in the narrow space next to "blast." "Don't you care about them at all?"

"They're important from a statistical point of view," he said, "but as individuals, they are hardly relevant to the course of history."

My reflexes were shot. It was amazing to me that Dunworthy's were almost as slow. I grazed the side of his jaw and knocked his glasses off. "Of course they're relevant!" I shouted. "They *are* the history, not all these bloody numbers!"

The reflexes of the flunkies were very fast. They did not let me start another swing at him before they had me by both arms and were hauling me out of the room.

"They're back there in the past with nobody to save them. They can't see their hands in front of their faces and there are bombs falling down on them and you tell me they aren't important? You call that being an historian?"

The flunkies dragged me out the door and down the hall. "Langby saved St. Paul's. How much more important can a person get? You're no historian! You're nothing but a . . ." I wanted to call him a terrible name, but the only curses I could summon up were Langby's. "You're nothing but a dirty Nazi spy!" I bellowed. "You're nothing but a lazy bourgeois tart!"

They dumped me on my hands and knees outside the door and slammed it in my face. "I wouldn't be an historian if you paid me!" I shouted, and went to see the firewatch stone.

. . .

December 31—I am having to write this in bits and pieces. My hands are in pretty bad shape, and Dunworthy's boys didn't help matters much. Kivrin comes in periodically, wearing her St. Joan look, and smears so much salve on my hands that I can't hold a pencil.

St. Paul's Station is not there, of course, so I got out at Holborn and walked, thinking about my last meeting with Dean Matthews on the morning after the burning of the City. This morning.

"I understand you saved Langby's life," he said. "I also understand that between you, you saved St. Paul's last night."

I showed him the letter from my uncle and he stared at it as if he could not think what it was. "Nothing stays saved forever," he said, and for a terrible moment I thought he was going to tell me Langby had died. "We shall have to keep on saving St. Paul's until Hitler decides to bomb the countryside."

The raids on London are almost over, I wanted to tell him. He'll start bombing the countryside in a matter of weeks. Canterbury, Bath, aiming always at cathedrals. You and St. Paul's will both outlast the war and live to dedicate the firewatch stone.

"I am hopeful, though," he said. "I think the worst is over."

"Yes, sir." I thought of the stone, its letters still readable after all this time. No, sir, the worst is not over.

I managed to keep my bearings almost to the top of Ludgate Hill. Then I lost my way completely, wandering about like a man in a graveyard. I had not remembered that the rubble looked so much like the white plaster dust Langby had tried to dig me out of. I could not find the stone anywhere. In the end I nearly fell over it, jumping back as if I had stepped on a grave.

It is all that's left. Hiroshima is supposed to have had a handful of untouched trees at ground zero, Denver the capitol steps. Neither of them says, "Remember the men and women of St. Paul's Watch who by the grace of God saved this cathedral." The grace of God.

Part of the stone is sheared off. Historians argue there was an-

other line that said, "for all time", but I do not believe that, not
if Dean Matthews had anything to do with it. And none of the
watch it was dedicated to would have believed it for a minute. We
saved St. Paul's every time we put out an incendiary, and only
until the next one fell. Keeping watch on the danger spots, putting out the little fires with sand and stirrup pumps, the big ones
with our bodies, in order to keep the whole vast complex structure
from burning down. Which sounds to me like a course description
for History Practicum 401. What a fine time to discover what historians are for when I have tossed my chance for being one out
the windows as easily as they tossed the pinpoint bomb in! No,
sir, the worst is not over.

There are flash burns on the stone, where the legend says the
Dean of St. Paul's was kneeling when the bomb went off. Totally
apocryphal, of course, since the front door is hardly an appropriate place for prayers. It is more likely the shadow of a tourist
who wandered in to ask the whereabouts of the Windmill Theatre,
or the imprint of a girl bringing a volunteer his muffler. Or a cat.

Nothing is saved forever, Dean Matthews; and I knew that when
I walked in the west doors that first day, blinking into the gloom,
but it is pretty bad nevertheless. Standing here knee-deep in rubble out of which I will not be able to dig any folding chairs or
friends, knowing that Langby died thinking I was a Nazi spy, knowing that Enola came one day and I wasn't there. It's pretty bad.

But it is not as bad as it could be. They are both dead, and
Dean Matthews too; but they died without knowing what I knew
all along, what sent me to my knees in the Whispering Gallery,
sick with grief and guilt: that in the end none of us saved St.
Paul's. And Langby cannot turn to me, stunned and sick at heart,
and say, "Who did this? Your friends the Nazis?" And I would
have to say, "No. The Communists." That would be the worst.

I have come back to the room and let Kivrin smear more salve
on my hands. She wants me to get some sleep. I know I should
pack and get gone. It will be humiliating to have them come and
throw me out, but I do not have the strength to fight her. She
looks so much like Enola.

■   ■   ■

January 1—I have apparently slept not only through the night,
but through the morning mail drop as well. When I woke up just
now, I found Kivrin sitting on the end of the bed holding an
envelope. "Your grades came," she said.

I put my arm over my eyes. "They can be marvelously efficient when they want to, can't they?"

"Yes," Kivrin said.

"Well, let's see it," I said, sitting up. "How long do I have before they come and throw me out?"

She handed the flimsy computer envelope to me. I tore it along the perforation. "Wait," she said. "Before you open it, I want to say something." She put her hand gently on my burns. "You're wrong about the history department. They're very good."

It was not exactly what I expected her to say. "Good is not the word I'd use to describe Dunworthy," I said and yanked the inside slip free.

Kivrin's look did not change, not even when I sat there with the printout on my knees where she could surely see it.

"Well," I said.

The slip was hand-signed by the esteemed Dunworthy. I have taken a first. With honors.

．．．

January 2—Two things came in the mail today. One was Kivrin's assignment. The history department thinks of everything—even to keeping her here long enough to nursemaid me, even to coming up with a prefabricated trial by fire to send their history majors through.

I think I want to believe that was what they had done, Enola and Langby only hired actors, the cat a clever android with its clockwork innards taken out for the final effect, not so much because I wanted to believe Dunworthy was not good at all, but because then I would not have this nagging pain at not knowing what had happened to them.

"You said your practicum was England in 1300?" I said, watching her as suspiciously as I had watched Langby.

"1349," she said, and her face went slack with memory. "The plague year."

"My God," I said. "How could they do that? The plague's a ten."

"I have a natural immunity," she said, and looked at her hands.

Because I could not think of anything to say, I opened the other piece of mail. It was a report on Enola. Computer-printed, facts and dates and statistics, all the numbers the history department so dearly loves, but it told me what I thought I would have to go without knowing: that she had gotten over her cold and survived the Blitz. Young Tom had been killed in the Baedaker raids on Bath, but Enola had lived until 2006, the year before they blew up St. Paul's.

I don't know whether I believe the report or not, but it does not matter. It is, like Langby's reading aloud to the old man, a simple act of human kindness. They think of everything.

Not quite. They did not tell me what happened to Langby. But I find as I write this that I already know: I saved his life. It does not seem to matter that he might have died in hospital next day; and I find, in spite of all the hard lessons the history department has tried to teach me, I do not quite believe this one: that nothing is saved forever. It seems to me that perhaps Langby is.

■   ■   ■

January 3—I went to see Dunworthy today. I don't know what I intended to say—some pompous drivel about my willingness to serve in the fire watch of history, standing guard against the falling incendiaries of the human heart, silent and saintly.

But he blinked at me nearsightedly across his desk, and it seemed to me that he was blinking at that last bright image of St. Paul's in sunlight before it was gone forever and that he knew better than anyone that the past cannot be saved, and I said instead, "I'm sorry that I broke your glasses, sir."

"How did you like St. Paul's?" he said, and like my first meeting with Enola, I felt I must be somehow reading the signals all wrong, that he was not feeling loss, but something quite different.

"I loved it, sir," I said.

"Yes," he said. "So do I."

Dean Matthews is wrong. I have fought with memory my whole practicum only to find that it is not the enemy at all, and being an historian is not some saintly burden after all. Because Dunworthy is not blinking against the fatal sunlight of the last morning, but into the gloom of that first afternoon, looking in the great west doors of St. Paul's at what is, like Langby, like all of it, every moment, in us, saved forever.

Isaac Asimov

What If

From *Nightfall and Other Stories*, 1952

Time moves in mysterious ways. Some people believe that time is linear; that time moves in one direction only, like a beam of light shooting out of a powerful flashlight. Others propose that time can have many branches or currents, and that journey through time may be very different from another journey, depending on how the current flows. Isaac Asimov's "What If" shows how variable and fragile time can be. Are our own personal lives controlled by seminal events, or do minor disturbances in time—random acts of chance—affect our lives in ways that are far more powerful than we wish to acknowledge?

B. A.

NORMAN AND LIVVY WERE LATE, NATURALLY, SINCE CATCHING A train is always a matter of last-minute delays, so they had to take the only available seat in the coach. It was the one toward the front, the one with nothing before it but the seat that faced the wrong way, with its back hard against the front partition. While Norman heaved the suitcase onto the rack, Livvy found herself chafing a little.

If a couple took the wrong-way seat before them, they would be staring self-consciously into each other's faces all the hours it would take to reach New York; or else, which was scarcely better, they would have to erect synthetic barriers of newspaper. Still, there was no use in taking a chance on there being another unoccupied double seat elsewhere in the train.

Norman didn't seem to mind, and that was a little disappointing to Livvy. Usually they held their moods in common. That, Norman claimed, was why he remained sure that he had married the right girl.

He would say, "We fit each other, Livvy, and that's the key fact.

279

When you're doing a jigsaw puzzle and one piece fits another, that's it. There are no other possibilities, and of course there are no other girls."

And she would laugh and say, "If you hadn't been on the street-car that day, you would probably never have met me. What would you have done then?"

"Stayed a bachelor. Naturally. Besides, I would have met you through Georgette another day."

"It wouldn't have been the same."

"Sure it would."

"No, it wouldn't. Besides, Georgette would never have introduced me. She was interested in you herself, and she's the type who knows better than to create a possible rival."

"What nonsense."

Livvy asked her favorite question: "Norman, what if you had been one minute later at the streetcar corner and had taken the next car? What do you suppose would have happened?"

"And what if fish had wings and all of them flew to the top of the mountains? What would we have to eat on Fridays then?"

But they had caught the streetcar, and fish didn't have wings, so that now they had been married for five years and ate fish on Fridays. And because they had been married five years, they were going to celebrate by spending a week in New York.

Then she remembered the present problem. "I wish we could have found some other seat."

Norman said, "Sure. So do I. But no one has taken it yet, so we'll have relative privacy as far as Providence, anyway."

Livvy was unconsoled, and felt herself justified when a plump little man walked down the central aisle of the coach. Now, where had he come from? The train was halfway between Boston and Providence, and if he had had a seat, why hadn't he kept it? She took out her vanity and considered her reflection. She had a theory that if she ignored the little man, he would pass by. So she concentrated on her light-brown hair which, in the rush of catching the train, had become disarranged just a little; at her blue eyes, and at her little mouth with the plump lips which Norman said looked like a permanent kiss.

Not bad, she thought.

Then she looked up, and the little man was in the seat opposite. He caught her eye and frowned widely. A series of lines curled about the edges of his smile. He lifted his hat hastily and put it down beside him on top of the little black box he had been carrying. A circle of white hair instantly sprang up stiffly about the large bald spot that made the center of his skull a desert.

She could not help smiling back a little, but then she caught sight of the black box again and the smile faded. She yanked at Norman's elbow.

Norman looked up from his newspaper. He had startlingly dark eyebrows that almost met above the bridge of his nose, giving him a formidable first appearance. But they and the dark eyes beneath bent upon her now with only the usual look of pleased and somewhat amused affection.

He said, "What's up?" He did not look at the plump little man opposite.

Livvy did her best to indicate what she saw by a little unobtrusive gesture of her hand and head. But the little man was watching and she felt a fool, since Norman simply stared at her blankly.

Finally she pulled him closer and whispered, "Don't you see what's printed on his box?"

She looked again as she said it, and there was no mistake. It was not very prominent, but the light caught it slantingly and it was a slightly more glistening area on a black background. In flowing script it said, "What If."

The little man was smiling again. He nodded his head rapidly and pointed to the words and then to himself several times over.

Norman put his paper aside. "I'll show you." He leaned over and said, "Mr. If?"

The little man looked at him eagerly.

"Do you have the time, Mr. If?"

The little man took out a large watch from his vest pocket and displayed the dial.

"Thank you, Mr. If," said Norman. And again in a whisper, "See, Livvy."

He would have returned to his paper, but the little man was opening his box and raising a finger periodically as he did so, to enforce their attention. It was just a slab of frosted glass that he removed—about six by nine inches in length and width and perhaps an inch thick. It had beveled edges, rounded corners, and was completely featureless. Then he took out a little wire stand on which the glass slab fitted comfortably. He rested the combination on his knees and looked proudly at them.

Livvy said, with sudden excitement, "Heavens, Norman, it's a picture of some sort."

Norman bent close. Then he looked at the little man. "What's this? A new kind of television?"

The little man shook his head, and Livvy said, "No, Norman, it's us."

"What?"

"Don't you see? That's the streetcar we met on. There you are in the back seat wearing that old fedora I threw away three years ago. And that's Georgette and myself getting on. The fat lady's in the way. Now! Can't you see us?"

He muttered, "It's some sort of illusion."

"But you see it too, don't you? That's why he calls this, 'What If.' It will *show* us what if. What if the streetcar hadn't swerved . . ."

She was sure of it. She was very excited and very sure of it. As she looked at the picture in the glass slab, the late afternoon sunshine grew dimmer and the inchoate chatter of the passengers around and behind them began fading.

How she remembered that day. Norman knew Georgette and had been so embarrassed that he was forced into gallantry and then into conversation. An introduction from Georgette was not even necessary. By the time they got off the streetcar, he knew where she worked.

She could still remember Georgette glowering at her, sulkily forcing a smile when they themselves separated. Georgette said, "Norman seems to like you."

Livvy replied, "Oh, don't be silly! He was just being polite. But he is nice-looking isn't he?"

It was only six months after that that they married.

And now here was that same streetcar again, with Norman and herself and Georgette. As she thought that, the smooth train noises, the rapid clack-clack of wheels, vanished completely. Instead, she was in the swaying confines of the streetcar. She had just boarded it with Georgette at the previous stop.

Livvy shifted weight with the swaying of the streetcar, as did forty others, sitting and standing, all to the same monotonous and rather ridiculous rhythm. She said, "Somebody's motioning at you, Georgette. Do you know him?"

"At me?" Georgette directed a deliberately casual glance over her shoulder. Her artificially long eyelashes flickered. She said, "I know him a little. What do you suppose he wants?"

"Let's find out," said Livvy. She felt pleased and a little wicked.

Georgette had a well-known habit of hoarding her male acquaintances, and it was rather fun to annoy her this way. And besides, this one seemed quite . . . interesting.

She snaked past the lines of standees, and Georgette followed without enthusiasm. It was just as Livvy arrived opposite the young man's seat that the streetcar lurched heavily as it rounded a curve. Livvy snatched desperately in the direction of the straps. Her fingertips caught and she held on. It was a long moment before she could breathe. For some reason, it had seemed that there were no straps close to be reached. Somehow, she felt that by all the laws of nature she should have fallen.

The young man did not look at her. He was smiling at Georgette and rising from his seat. He had astonishing eyebrows that gave him a rather competent and self-confident appearance. Livvy decided that she definitely liked him. Georgette was saying, "Oh no, don't bother. We're getting off in about two stops."

They did. Livvy said, "I thought we were going to Sachs."

"We are. There's just something I remember having to attend to here. It won't take but a minute."

"Next stop, Providence!" the loud-speakers were blaring. The train was slowing and the world of the past had shrunk itself into the glass slab once more. The little man was still smiling at them.

Livvy turned to Norman. She felt a little frightened. "Were you through all that, too?"

He said, "What happened to the time? We can't be reaching Providence yet?" He looked at his watch. "I guess we are." Then, to Livvy, "You didn't fall that time."

"Then you did see it?" She frowned. "Now, that's like Georgette. I'm sure there was no reason to get off the streetcar except to prevent my meeting you. How long had you known Georgette then, Norman?"

"Not very long. Just enough to be able to recognize her at sight and to feel that I ought to offer her my seat."

Livvy curled her lip.

Norman grinned, "You can't be jealous of a might-have-been, kid. Besides, what difference would it have made? I'd have been sufficiently interested in you to work out a way of meeting you."

"You didn't even look at me."

"I hardly had the chance."

"Then how would you have met me?"

"Some way. I don't know how. But you'll admit this is a rather foolish argument we're having."

They were leaving Providence. Livvy felt a trouble in her mind. The little man had been following their whispered conversation, with only the loss of his smile to show that he understood. She said to him, "Can you show us more?"

Norman interrupted, "Wait now, Livvy. What are you to try to do?"

She said, "I want to see our wedding day. What it would have been if I hadn't caught the strap."

Norman was visibly annoyed. "Now, that's not fair. We might not have been married on the same day, you know."

But she said, "Can you show it to me, Mr. If?" and the little man nodded.

The slab of glass was coming alive again, glowing a little. Then the light collected and condensed into figures. A tiny sound of organ music was in Livvy's ears without there actually being sound.

Norman said with relief, "Well, there I am. That's our wedding. Are you satisfied?"

The train sounds were disappearing again, and the last thing Livvy heard was her own voice saying, "Yes, there you are. But where am I?"

．　．　．

Livvy was well back in the pews. For a while she had not expected to attend at all. In the past months she had drifted further and further away from Georgette, without quite knowing why. She had heard of her engagement only through a mutual friend, and, of course, it was to Norman. She remembered very clearly that day, six months before, when she had first seen him on the streetcar. It was the time Georgette had so quickly snatched her out of sight. She had met him since on several occasions, but each time Georgette was with him, standing between.

Well, she had no cause for resentment; the man was certainly none of hers. Georgette, she thought, looked more beautiful than she really was. And he was very handsome indeed.

She felt sad and rather empty, as though something had gone wrong— something that she could not quite outline in her mind. Georgette had moved up the aisle without seeming to see her, but earlier she had caught his eyes and smiled at him. Livvy thought he had smiled in return.

．

She heard the words distantly as they drifted back to her, "I now pronounce you—"

The noise of the train was back. A woman swayed down the aisle, herding a little boy back to their seats. There were intermittent bursts of girlish laughter from a set of four teenage girls halfway down the coach. A conductor hurried past on some mysterious errand.

Livvy was frozenly aware of it all.

She sat there, staring straight ahead, while the trees outside blended into a fuzzy, furious green and the telephone poles galloped past.

She said, "It was she you married."

He stared at her for a moment and then one side of his mouth quirked a little. He said lightly, "I didn't really, Olivia. You're still my wife, you know. Just think about it for a few minutes."

She turned to him. "Yes, you married me—because I fell in your lap. If I hadn't, you would have married Georgette. If she hadn't wanted you, you would have married someone else. You would have married anybody. So much for your jigsaw-puzzle pieces."

Norman said very slowly, "Well-I'll-be-darned!" He put both hands to his head and smoothed down the straight hair over his ears where it had a tendency to tuft up. For the moment it gave him the appearance of trying to hold his head together. He said, "Now, look here, Livvy, you're making a silly fuss over a stupid magician's trick. You can't blame me for something I haven't done."

"You would have done it."

"How do you know?"

"You've seen it."

"I've seen a ridiculous piece of—hypnotism, I suppose." His voice suddenly raised itself into anger. He turned to the little man opposite. "Off with you, Mr. If, or whatever your name is. Get out of here. We don't want you. Get out before I throw your little trick out the window and you after it."

Livvy yanked at his elbow. "Stop it. Stop it! You're in a crowded train."

The little man shrank back into the corner of the seat as far as he could go and held his little black box behind him. Norman looked at him, then at Livvy, then at the elderly lady across the way who was regarding him with patent disapproval.

He turned pink and bit back a pungent remark. They rode in frozen silence to and through New London.

Fifteen minutes past New London, Norman said, "Livvy!"

She said nothing. She was looking out the window but saw nothing in the glass.

He said again, "Livvy! Livvy! Answer me!"

She said dully, "What do you want?"

He said, "Look, this is all nonsense. I don't know how the fellow does it, but even granting it's legitimate, you're not being fair. Why stop where you did? Suppose I had married Georgette, do you suppose you would have stayed single? For all I know, you were already married at the time of my supposed wedding. Maybe that's why I married Georgette."

"I wasn't married."

"How do you know?"

"I would have been able to tell. I knew what my own thoughts were."

"Then you would have been married within the next year."

Livvy grew angrier. The fact that a sane remnant within her clamored at the unreason of her anger did not soothe her. It irritated her further, instead. She said, "And if I did, it would be no business of yours, certainly."

"Of course it wouldn't. But it would make the point that in the world of reality we can't be held responsible for the 'what ifs.' "

Livvy's nostrils flared. She said nothing.

Norman said, "Look! You remember the big New Year's celebration at Winnie's place year before last?"

"I certainly do. You spilled a keg of alcohol all over me."

"That's beside the point, and besides, it was only a cocktail shaker's worth. What I'm trying to say is that Winnie is just about your best friend and had been long before you married me."

"What of it?"

"Georgette was a good friend of hers too, wasn't she?"

"Yes."

"All right, then. You and Georgette would have gone to the party regardless of which one of you I had married. I would have had nothing to do with it. Let him show us the party as it would have been if I had married Georgette, and I'll bet you'd be there with either your fiancée or your husband."

Livvy hesitated. She felt honestly afraid of that.

He said, "Are you afraid to take the chance?"

And that, of course, decided her. She turned on him furiously, "No, I'm not! And I hope I am married. There's no reason I should pine for you. What's more, I'd like to see what happens when you spill the shaker all over Georgette. She'll fill both your ears for you, and in public, too. I know her. Maybe you'll see a certain difference in the jigsaw pieces then." She faced forward and crossed her arms angrily and firmly across her chest.

Norman looked across at the little man, but there was no need to say anything. The glass slab was on his lap already. The sun slanted in from the west, and the white foam of hair that topped his head was edged with pink.

Norman said tensely, "Ready?"

Livvy nodded and let the noise of the train slide away again.

■   ■   ■

Livvy stood, a little flushed with recent cold, in the doorway. She had just removed her coat, with its sprinkly of snow, and her bare arms were still rebelling at the touch of open air.

She answered the shouts that greeted her with "Happy New Year's" of her own, raising her voice to make herself heard over the squealing of the radio. Georgette's shrill tones were almost the first thing she heard upon entering, and now she steered herself toward her. She hadn't seen Georgette, or Norman, in weeks.

Georgette lifted an eyebrow, a mannerism she had lately culti-vated, and said, "Isn't anyone with you, Olivia?" Her eyes swept the immediate surroundings and then returned to Livvy.

Livvy said indifferently, "I think Dick will be around later. There was something or other he had to do first." She felt as indifferent as she sounded.

Georgette smiled tightly. "Well, Norman's here. That ought to keep you from being lonely, dear. At least, it's turned out that way before."

As she said so, Norman sauntered in from the kitchen. He had a cocktail shaker in his hand, and the rattling of ice cubes casta-netted his words. "Line up, you rioting revelers, and get a mixture that will really revel your riots—Why, Livvy!"

He walked toward her, grinning his welcome, "Where've you been keeping yourself? I haven't seen you in twenty years, seems like. What's the matter? Doesn't Dick want anyone else to see you?"

"Fill my glass, Norman," Georgette said sharply.

"Right away," he said, not looking at her. "Do you want one too, Livvy? I'll get you a glass." He turned, and everything happened at once.

Livvy cried, "Watch out!" She saw it coming, even had a vague feeling that all this had happened before, but it played itself out inexorably. His heel caught the edge of the carpet; he lurched, tried to right himself, and lost the cocktail shaker. It seemed to jump out of his hands, and a pint of ice-cold liquor drenched Livvy from shoulder to hem.

She stood there, gasping. The noises muted about her, and for a few intolerable moments she made futile brushing gestures at her gown, while Norman kept repeating "Damnation!" in rising tones.

Georgette said coolly, "It's too bad, Livvy. Just one of those things. I imagine the dress can't be very expensive."

Livvy turned and ran. She was in the bedroom, which was at least empty and relatively quiet. By the light of the fringe-shaded lamp on the dresser, she poked among the coats on the bed, looking for her own.

Norman had come in behind her. "Look, Livvy, don't pay any attention to what she said. I'm devilishly sorry. I'll pay—"

"That's all right. It wasn't your fault." She blinked rapidly and didn't look at him. "I'll just go home and change."

"Are you coming back?"

"I don't know. I don't think so."

"Look, Livvy . . ." His warm fingers were on her shoulders—

Livvy felt a queer tearing sensation deep inside her, as though she were ripping away, clinging cobwebs and—

∎   ∎   ∎

—and the train noises were back.

Something did go wrong with the time when she was in there—in the slab. It was deep twilight now. The train lights were on. But it didn't matter. She seemed to be recovering from the wrench inside her.

Norman was rubbing his eyes with thumb and forefinger. "What happened?"

Livvy said, "It just ended. Suddenly."

Norman looked uneasily, "You know, we'll be putting into New Haven soon." He looked at his watch and shook his head.

Livvy said wonderingly, "You spilled it on me."

"Well, so I did in real life."

"But in real life I was your wife. You ought to have spilled it on Georgette this time. Isn't that queer?" But she was thinking of Norman pursuing her; his hands on her shoulders . . .

She looked up at him and said with warm satisfaction, "I wasn't married."

"No, you weren't. But was that Dick Reinhardt you were going around with?"

"Yes."

"You weren't planning to marry him, were you, Livvy?"

"Jealous, Norman?"

Norman looked confused. "Of that? Of a slab of glass? Of course not."

"I don't think I would have married him."

Norman said, "You know, I wish it hadn't ended when it did. There was something that was about to happen, I think." He stopped, then added slowly, "It was as though I would rather have done it to anybody else in the room."

"Even to Georgette."

"I wasn't giving two thoughts about Georgette. You don't believe me, I suppose."

"Maybe I do." She looked up at him. "I've been silly, Norman. Let's—let's live our real life. Let's not play with all the things that just might have been."

But he caught her hands. "No, Livvy. One last time. Let's see what we would have been doing right now, Livvy! This very minute! If I had married Georgette."

Livvy was a little frightened. "Let's not, Norman." She was thinking of his eyes, smiling hungrily at her as he held the shaker, while Georgette stood beside her, and regarded. She didn't want to know what happened afterward. She just wanted this life now, this good life.

New Haven came and went.

Norman said again, "I want to try, Livvy."

She said, "If you want to, Norman." She decided fiercely that it wouldn't matter. Nothing would matter. Her hands reached out and encircled his arm. She held it tightly, and while she held it she thought: "Nothing in make-believe can take him from me."

Norman said to the little man, "Set 'em up again."

In the yellow light the process seemed to be slower. Gently the frosted slab cleared, like clouds being torn apart and dispersed by an unfelt wind.

Norman was saying, "There's something wrong. That's just the two of us, exactly as we are now."

He was right. Two little figures were sitting in a train on the seats which were the farthest toward the front. The field was enlarging now—they were merging into it. Norman's voice was distant and fading.

"It's the same train," he was saying. "The window in back is cracked just as—"

∎ ∎ ∎

Livvy was blindingly happy. She said, "I wish we were in New York."

He said, "It will be less than an hour, darling." Then he said, "I'm going to kiss you." He made a movement, as though he were about to begin.

"Not here! Oh, Norman, people are looking."

Norman drew back. He said, "We should have taken a taxi."

"From Boston to New York?"

"Sure. The privacy would have been worth it."

She laughed. "You're funny when you try to act ardent."

"It isn't an act." His voice was suddenly a little somber. "It's not just an hour, you know. I feel as though I've been waiting five years."

"I do, too."

"Why couldn't I have met you first. It was such a waste."

"Poor Georgette," Livvy sighed.

Norman moved impatiently. "Don't be sorry for her, Livvy. We never really made a go of it. She was glad to get rid of me."

"I know that. That's why I say 'Poor Georgette.' I'm just sorry for her for not being able to appreciate what she had."

"Well, see to it that you do," he said. "See to it that you're immensely appreciative, infinitely appreciative—or more than that, see that you're at least half as appreciative as I am of what I've got."

"Or else you'll divorce me, too?"

"Over my dead body," said Norman.

Livvy said, "It's all so strange. I keep thinking, What if you hadn't spilt the cocktails on me that time at the party? You wouldn't have followed me out; you wouldn't have told me; I wouldn't have known. It would have been so different . . . everything."

"Nonsense. It would have been just the same. It would have all happened another time."

"I wonder," said Livvy softly.

■   ■   ■

Train noises merged into train noises. City lights flickered outside, and the atmosphere of New York was about them. The coach was astir with travelers dividing the baggage among themselves.

Livvy was an island in the turmoil until Norman shook her.

She looked at him and said, "The jigsaw pieces fit after all."

He said, "Yes."

She put a hand on his. "But it wasn't good, just the same. I was very wrong. I thought that because we had each other, we should have all the possible each others. But all of the possibilities are none of our business. The real is enough. Do you know what I mean?"

He nodded.

She said, "There are millions of other what ifs. I don't want to know what happened in any of them. I'll never say, 'What if,' again."

Norman said, "Relax, dear. Here's your coat." And he reached for the suitcases.

Livvy said with sudden sharpness, "Where's Mr. If?"

Norman turned slowly to the empty seat that faced them. Together they scanned the rest of the coach.

"Maybe," Norman said, "he went into the next coach."

"But why? Besides, he wouldn't leave his hat." And she bent to pick it up.

Norman said, "What hat?"

And Livvy stopped her fingers hovering over nothingness. She said, "It was here—I almost touched it." She straightened and said, "Oh, Norman, what if—"

Norman put a finger on her mouth. "Darling . . ."

She said, "I'm sorry. Here, let me help you with the suitcases."

The train dived into the tunnel beneath Park Avenue, and the noise of the wheels rose to a roar.

Steven Utley

There and Then

From *Asimov's Science Fiction*, 1993

What does living in prehistoric times bring to mind? Lush vegetation? Massive cold-blooded carnivores? For Kevo and his small team of colleagues living in the Paleozoic period of history, those developments are a long way off. Still, this quiet, untouched world, millions of years in the past, is home. But for how long? The government has its eye on saving the future by stripping the past of its most precious resources. Can tampering with the past destroy our future . . . or save it?

B. A.

THE WIND HAD SHIFTED, AND THE NIGHT WAS FULL OF LAND smells, estuarine smells, green slime, black mud, rotten eggs. The only sounds were ship and sea sounds; occasionally, there was also a murmur of conversation in the shadow beneath the eaves of the helicopter deck. Chamberlain's two assistants were back there somewhere, tending equipment, their voices muffled as if by layers of flannel. The moon had vanished into a vast, dense cloud bank. The fantail was so dark that I could see little of Chamberlain except his glowing red eye and, intermittently, red-tinged highlights of his face and hands. He looked devilish in those moments. He held the glowing eye sometimes between his fingers and sometimes between his lips. Every so often, its glow would expire, and he'd fumble with his pockets, there'd be a sputter of flame, the thick smells coming off the land would momentarily mix with that of burning tobacco. I wonder again how he got his ancient and disagreeable vice past screening.

Chamberlain sat in his beat-up deck chair, surrounded by a mutant-toadstool growth of meteorological godknowswhat. I leaned against the rail. Hundreds of people lived and worked abroad, but late at night it was easy to get the feeling, and hard to get rid of it, that we were the only human beings in all the world. Actually, we represented a few tenths of a percent of present world population.

After a while, I said, "You should come."

"Too much work to do here."

"Oh, come on. We've both been cooped up here too long. We could both use some excitement."

"Hm." Hm was the sound Chamberlain made when he meant to laugh. "I hear they could use some excitement ashore, too. There's none of the tumult and squawk you just naturally associate with prehistoric times."

"You don't think a live sex act with trilobites will be exciting? Come on. A walk on the beach'll do you good."

"This the beach I smell? Ew."

"We'll be on a different beach. What you smell is blowing off the estuary. We'll be way around the coast from here."

"Still." The old deck chair squeaked unhappily as he shifted his weight. "I'm a meteorologist. Meteorologists aren't supposed to have to smell bad smells."

"Then don't smoke."

He called me a body Nazi and ignited a new cigarette off the old. "Sure smells like the honey pot got kicked over."

"Gripe, gripe," I said. "You have it made. The weather never does anything here. The only forecast you ever make is warm, east wind, possibility of showers. You sleep when you want, come out and play with your expensive toys when you want—"

"You've got no damn idea what my workload's like. Anybody has it made on this boat, it's you."

"—sit back and watch the sunset and drink till you nod off!"

He made a rumbling noise deep inside himself. "You know as well as I do that nothing enhances a sunset better'n a drink. And nothing enhances a drink better'n a nap." The glowing eye moved away from his face in the direction of his invisible assistants, Immelmanned, and went back to his face. When he spoke again, his voice was so quiet that I had to lean down into his nimbus of smoke to hear his words. "Those two wait till I'm asleep and then sneak away to fool around. If you know what I mean."

"How simply, terribly shocking."

"It's true. Had my eye on 'em for a while." The eye brightened for a moment, fell away in his hand. "Definitely something going on between 'em."

"Well," I said, "what could be more romantic than holding hands under a prehistoric moon? Ooh woo, what a little moonlight can do."

"That from one of your damned old songs? Of course it is, got to be. I forgot, you're one of them. Listen, it's past the handholding stage with those two. They're up to the bucking-and-grunting stage."

I couldn't recall having seen either of Chamberlain's assistants in good light. Now, in my imagination, they appeared as shadows, rubbing against each other. I said, "Well, it's still most people's favorite way to pair-bond."

"Fat lot of good pair-bonding ever did you, Kev. None of your ex-wives has spoken to you in years."

"They've hardly been able to, under the circumstances."

"Anyway, you think I want a couple of disgruntled ex-lovers on my team?" He made a disgusted sound. "When they fall out, this boat won't be big enough for the two of 'em."

"Ship. This is a ship, not a boat."

"Ship, boat," he said dismissively.

"Rain, dew," I said, in the same tone. "If Captain Kelly ever hears you call his ship a boat, he'll keelhaul you, hang you from the yardarm, and make you walk the plank all in the same afternoon."

"He makes allowances for dotty scientists. Point is—"

"The point is, your young honeys are happy together right now. Maybe they'll stay happy together. There's always the possibility that things'll work out, you know."

"Hm. That what you told yourself along about the third time you got married?"

"Sure was."

"You are such a dog with women," he said, and extinguished his latest cigarette. A moment later, I heard a faint click in the darkness. "Want another drink?"

"Sure."

He gave me another capful of brandy from his flask. Officially, it was a long walk from the Paleozoic to the nearest liquor store. In fact, there was probably enough booze on board to float us the thousand of kilometers to Caledonian Land-proto-Greenland, Kalaallitt Nunaat-to-be. Old hands know that when a body needs a drink, only a drink will do. Pleasantly abuzz, I peered off into the darkness toward the shore. Its smells were palpable, but it wasn't even a glimmer in the night. The moon gave no sign of coming out of its cocoon of clouds. After a time, I realized that Chamberlain had fallen asleep. I left him snoring harshly in his deck chair, and his assistants to their alleged smooching, and went up to the helicopter deck.

The helicopters sat there like big metal sculptures of dragonflies lighted for Christmas. Mechanics tinkered with the motors while people wearing overalls loaded equipment and supplies. A shirtsleeved man stood by with the unmistakable air of a junior supervisor. He looked my way as I passed and seemed about to ask if I was authorized to be there, but then two of the mechanics said hello to me and I said hello back, and you could see the wheel turn behind the shirtsleeved man's face: maybe I wasn't a scruffy old stowaway, maybe I was somebody eccentric but important. I knew the mechanics and loaders but had no idea who he was. So many similar-looking people had arrived in the past few weeks that I didn't know who a tenth of them were.

The ship's engines throbbed suddenly as Captain Kelly got us under way. I put strangers out of my mind and strolled all the way forward and halfway back. Ours was in no way a lovely vessel. It had originally been designed and built during the Oughts to deliver Marines to beachheads and provide support with Missiles and helicopter gunships. Not a lot had been done, or could have been done, to tone down its brooding militariness. The missile launchers were gone now, and the gun turret rebuilt to house one of the astronomy team's big telescopes, but the superstructure, helicopter deck, and boat bay had required no redesign. The forest of antennae, scanner, things, and stuff rising above the bridge looked formidably thorny. Except for human beings in helicopters, there wasn't an airborne creature on Earth, but still the dishes turned and cocked and listened, as intently as if swarms of kamikaze aircraft lurked over the horizon.

The task of renaming the vessel had fallen to a group of more or less prominent scientists, who duly voted to rechristen it the H. G. Wells. Some nasty hustling little demagogue in Congress scotched that on the grounds of Wells having been, besides a lousy stinking Brit—this, of course, was well after the end of the Special Relationship between the countries—a communist, or some closely related species of one-worlder. The story goes that, told to submit something "more patriotic and appropriate," most of the scientists next agreed that the vessel should be renamed after one or another of certain late-twentieth century-and-early-twenty-first-century presidents, because the ship, too, would move boldly into the past. "This kind of reckless sarcasm," a dissenter warned, "will backfire on us," and sure enough, it did. Most of us since neglected to call the ship anything except "here" when we were aboard and "the ship" when we weren't. And we did keep a big framed portrait of Bertie Wells hanging in the rec room, over his alleged epitaph: Dammit, I told you so!

The brandy and the stroll conspired to fill me with a luxurious sense of peace and belonging. When my pocketphone buzzed, I murmured absently into the mouthpiece.

"Kevo," said Ruth Lott, "you're up."

Peace and belonging fled. Ruth had the mellifluous Georgia-accented voice I hated to hear. I said, "Ruth, all decent people are asleep at this hour."

"That's how I knew you'd be up."

"Okay, I'm up. I just hope you're calling about something really interesting, like maybe an out-of-clothes experience you personally have had."

The phone barely did her great sweet laugh justice. "I have a little job for you." She always had a little job for me. "Come see me, I'll tell you all about it."

I knew and she knew that she had me, but even a rabbit struggles in a lion's grip. I said, "It really is kind of late."

"Won't take but a minute." When I hesitated long enough to make her impatient, she said, "Oh, and before I forget—" her voice was as dulcet-toned as before, but I wasn't fooled "—note on your calendar, extension review next month."

"Now that's low!"

"Why, whatever do you mean?"

"It's blackmail!"

"No, actually, Kevo, it's extortion. Bye."

"Go ahead," I said into a suddenly dead phone, "hang up on me, see what it gets you."

Then, having no choice, I did as I was told.

Ruth was a Junoesque fiftyish woman with the world's sliest smile. She trained it on me when I appeared in her hatchway. She said, "Are those the best clothes you have?"

"I was—I am going ashore when we get to Number Four camp."

"Please see if you can't make yourself just a teensy bit more presentable. I want you to meet a party at the jump station in a little while."

"Since when am I the official greeter? You break your legs off above the knee?"

"These are media types. You should get along."

"There's got to be someone else on this bucket who's—what am I supposed to do? It's not like these people will arrive in any condition to listen to me give a welcome speech."

"All you have to do is say hello, show them around when they're up to it, whatever. I'm making them your responsibility."

"But why me?"

"Because you are not snowed under with work, you bum. How often do you actually touch your wordboard?"

I gave her my most pained look. "Writing isn't just a matter of touching a wordboard. You'd know that if you'd ever had specialized training in the putting together of subjects and verbs so that they agree. The real work's mental."

"You're mental," and she laughed her laugh again. "How is the book coming along? Think you'll have it finished by the Mesozoic? Listen to me, and believe me when I tell you this, I'm doing you a favor. Once we're privatized—don't give me that look, we both know it's a done deal—once we're privatized, the new bosses will be looking very carefully at their assets and liabilities here. These include," and she ticked them off on her fingers, "one converted assault ship with some el strange-o scientists embarked, and some hired help, and you. You've been hanging on here for too long. It's time you had visible means of support. You need to be seen earning your keep. This little job won't take too much of a bite out of your life. Just till these newcomers get acclimated. Just make sure they have a good time."

"What, find them women, young boys?"

"I'm serious. Northemico's sponsoring them."

That impressed me. Northemico figured prominently in the push for privatization.

"Think of this," Ruth went on, "as sort of an opportunity to do what a writer's supposed to do, make all of this, this—" She gestured helplessly, unable to find a word that took in everything

from ship's routine to the reality of our surroundings and circumstances. I supplied it.

"Stuff," I said.

"Right. Make all of this stuff make sense to them." She eyed
my attire again. "It really will help if you try not to look so much
like a beachcomber."

"I am a beachcomber."

"Kevo, I put up with you because you make me laugh." She
leaned toward me confidentially. "Even Captain Kelly puts up
with you. He thinks of you as our resident artistic type and has
the weird idea that you're brilliant. God knows why. The new
bosses, when they get here, aren't going to put up with you unless
you seem to be of use around here. They'll probably institute a
dress code, too. Now go on, get to the jump station," and she
urged me on my way with the kind of little wave women use to
dry their fingernail polish.

The tang of ooze in the jump station was as sharp as an icepick
up the nose. I tried out looks and gestures of welcome on Cullum
and Summers, the two techs on duty. Summers appeared to think
I was pretty funny. Cullum appeared to think I thought I was
pretty funny. They did the synchronization countdown. The medical team stood around the rail-enclosed sending-and-receiving
platform and watched as its surface shimmered and grew bright.

First to arrive was a woman who was so shaken up by the experience that the medical team had to roll her away on a gurney.
The man who followed her looked gray but insisted that he was
okay, please take him topside. I couldn't talk him out of it. Cullum
and Summers exchanged looks with me and quietly made a bet
between themselves: I either would or would not get the fellow
out of the jump station, through a short companionway, and onto
the starboardside gangwalk before it was too late.

As it happened, I did, but just barely. The man made it the last
couple of steps with both hands clapped over his mouth. He
grabbed the rail, stood there uneasily for a moment, then leaned
out over the dark sea, out into the blackness, and retched at
length. He didn't actually lose his lunch because he hadn't any
lunch to lose. Only the first visitors to the Paleozoic hadn't known
not to eat before making the jump. They had gone about suited
as if for Mars—you weren't even supposed to breathe the air here,
let alone cough up your socks. The past was supposed to be as
brittle as a Ming vase—you didn't dare give it a cross look. It was

years before people got comfortable with the idea that if the past was resilient enough to accommodate an 8500-ton ship, it could probably accommodate the everyday stupidity of the species embarked.

I stood behind and slightly to one side of the newcomer. When he turned from the rail, I handed him a bottle of spring water and said, "This'll help." He took it, rinsed, spat over the side. When he tried to hand the bottle back, I declined as if I were doing him a favor. He pulled a handkerchief from the breast pocket of his jacket and wiped his mouth. He was in his late twenties or early thirties and well-built. He would have had, ordinarily, what I call friendly good looks. At the moment, in the light of the safety lamp, he had the color of oatmeal.

"If you want," he said, "you can say you told me so."

"That is our motto here."

He gingerly felt around the lower edge of his ribcage. His hands fell abruptly to his sides when he saw me watching him.

"I should introduce myself," I said, and did.

"Rick King," he said. I was grateful that he didn't offer to shake hands.

"Can't those technicians do something to make it so you don't get rattled apart when you come through?"

"They've been working on it forever."

"You want more folks to come and visit you here, you're going to have to make the trip more pleasant." I didn't reply to that. The last thing I wanted was for more folks to come and visit me here. "They told me all those drugs I had to take would help."

"They did help. Without them, you'd be feeling really bad right about now."

"And this smell. Hits you right in the face."

"Uh huh. But we're moving away from it. Anyway, you get used to it."

He shook his head. "Can't imagine how."

"If you're up for it, a turn around the deck might be a good way to start."

I led him up a deck and forward. His color slightly improved after a couple of minutes, but heat and humidity were taking the last measure of starch out of him. I figured he was about ready to collapse, and I'd be able to hustle him off to quarters, then slip ashore before Ruth knew what was up.

"Except for the stink," King said, "I could be on a boat in the

Caribbean or somewhere. With the stink," King said, "I guess I could be off the Texas coast. When I first heard about all this, I thought, wow, travel through time, see prehistoric monsters battling fang and claw, you bet!"

"Sorry, fang and claw haven't quite evolved yet."

"Well, so far, nothing's what I expected."

"Common observation." I had a niggling suspicion, founded on nothing more substantial than King's being some kind of filmmaker, that all of his expectations have been shaped by the movies, that he had come prepared to see, besides primordial ferocity, jump-station technicians who were prematurely balding men dressed in white coats and carrying clipboards, not guys who could have been mistaken for air-conditioner repairmen and displayed much hairy butt-crack whenever they hunkered down to fix stuff. I wondered what King would make of the scientists ashore, who wore big Kaiki pants and canvas shoes that made them resemble ducks. Still, if he had to have crewcuts and creased slacks, there were always the naval reservists who attended to the actual running of the ship.

Suddenly, though not exactly unexpectedly, King made a sound like ah-rurr and pressed both hands against his abdomen. His expression was alarm. "I think I better get to the restroom," he said.

"This way," I said, "to the head."

When he finished in there, I showed him where he was to bunk down. Someone had thoughtfully brought his gear from the jump station and stopped it for him. King took out an object the size of a wallet, unfolded it with the thoughtless ease of long practice, and slipped it over his close-cropped skull—a headheld camera. A long thin cable ran from the jawpiece to batteries and record-pack in his pocket; the headheld whirred faintly, and I pretended to become fascinated by the paint on the bulkhead. Headhelds disconcert me. I never knew whether to make eye contact with the wearer's natural eye or unnatural one.

"Be prepared is my motto," King said.

I looked at him in wonder. He was still a mess. I asked if he didn't really want to get some rest, and he said he was too excited. I sneaked a peek at my watch. The boat would be leaving soon, and I was bound and determined to be on it. I made my fateful decision and asked him, "Do you think you're up for a little boat ride and campout?"

"I'm up for anything."

I looked doubtful, and not just because I wanted to appear sincerely concerned about him. Then: "Okay, it's your funeral. I'll go get my things and meet you back here. We'll pop into sick bay to see how your friend's doing—" he had not once inquired about her in all this time "—and then we hit the beach."

"Great! D-day in the Devonian!"

Silurian, I thought as I turned away.

King's friend's name was Claire Duvall. Chance had treated him with kid gloves and smacked her upside the head: she had a mild concussion. King took the news well. I shouldn't have held that against him, because I was even more impatient than he to get to the boat bay, and with much better reason. Nevertheless, it rankled me.

The boat bay could have stood some redesign. The slap of waves against the hull reduced unamplified speech to so much mutter. You could ruin your voice working in this part of the ship. At night, you could ruin your eyes, too, and your shins if you weren't careful. Few lights showed. Captain Kelly, it was said, didn't like to excite the, understand, extremely limited imaginations of light-sensitive Paleozoic marine organisms. I could dimly see human figures working in and around a boat, and called down, "How soon till we leave?"

"Kev!" someone called back. "Come on if you're coming."

Someone else bawled out, "Will somebody up there please throw some goddamn light down here?" There ensued a bit of rude jawing back and forth, and then a shaft of stark white light suddenly spotlighted the ramp of the boat bay as if it were a stage. People froze like deer in traffic. I beheld the true object of my desire.

She looked like an ivory statuette from my vantage point. Up close and in good light, she had blue eyes and fair brown hair. She was wearing cut-offs and a T-shirt, and at any distance and in any light she had the best legs in the Paleozoic. Vicki Harris had been haunting my thoughts for some time. All at once, I had seen her, though I'd been looking at her for weeks, months, who knew how long? Sometimes it happens that way.

The light switched off. I remembered to breathe. King and I climbed down, and everybody found a place to sit amid the jumble of boxes in the boat. The motor coughed and gurgled as the pilot revved it. The sides of the bay loomed around us like im-

mense black cliffs. As we eased out, the almost-full moon emerged
from the purple clouds, suffusing the air with milky light. Above
the rhythmic prum-pum of the motor and the hiss of water parting before the prow, King said, "My God," and then, "Wow!"

"No kidding," said someone behind me.

I looked around and found that I could just make out the faces
of my companions. Cardwell and Jank were aft with Hirsch, the
pilot; Vicki Harris sat amidships. All of them except Hirsch gazed
upward. I'd have done so, too, but for the warm pleasure I got
from gazing at Vicki Harris. She noticed me staring at her and
cocked an index finger moonward to redirect my attention.

"Seen it," I said.

She flashed a grin. "Me too, but I never get over how it looks.
It's like it's almost but not quite the same moon. Like the features
I'm used to seeing don't exist yet."

"I asked Hill about that once. You know Sharon Hill? One of
the astronomers. She told me it's the same moon, less some impact craters. The main difference is in rotational velocity or some
such. We're seeing it sort of from behind and off to one side."

She directed a look past me. I heard a faint whirring and remembered King. I made introductions, and she reached around
me to offer him a hand and said, "Mister King."

"Please," King said, "Rick," and held on to her a beat or two
longer than I liked.

"Vick," she said.

"Vee for short," Jank said, behind her.

"Vee Vee," said Cardwell, "if you want to be really disarming."

"My delightful colleagues, Doctors Jankowski and Cardwell."
Her tone of voice fell somewhere in the middle of affection, tol-
erance, and reproach. I'd learned from Jank—who'd affected not
to find my sudden curiosity remarkable—that she hated her first
name. I have few opinions about what parents should call their
girl babies, though I know a trend when I see it: names ending
in i have become true artifacts; more and more young women are
answering to monikers that end in o, Fujiko, Tamiko. Still, I had
had a lovely, sweet girlfriend by the name of Vicki in high school
and was ever afterward kindly predisposed toward anyone who
bore it. Not, of course, that I didn't find Vicki Vick Vee Vee Harris
entirely attractive in her own right.

"It's Cardwell's performing trilobites," I said, "whose antics we
hope to see."

"I should get some great stuff," said King. He talked past me, to her. "I make documentaries and things." Talk about disarming. Documentaries and things.

She said, "Really?"

Vick and Rick, I suddenly thought, oh no.

Jank evidently thought it a bit much, too, for he said, "What other things," and paused, and added, "Rick?"

"Commercials," King said, "infotainment, that kind of thing." I could tell that he was slightly taken aback.

"So which is it this time," Jack demanded, "documentary or commercial?"

"Documentary, of course."

"Of course. And when do you start?"

King lightly touched the headheld. "I already have. You don't have any objection to being on television, do you?"

Now Jank was taken aback.

"We've been on television," Cardwell said. "Not lately, though. Been a while since we had a documentary crew through here." He had the same interested attitude he'd had the time he showed me my first prehistoric shellfish. He could have been joining in two colleagues' discussion of trilobites.

By the way Jank shifted in his seat, I could tell that he was buckling down for business. He said to King, "You seem a little underscrewed."

"My partner was badly shaken up by the jump. But what you mean, of course, is, why aren't I hauling around a lot of help? No one does that anymore unless they're making big Hollywood product."

Jank wouldn't let up. "What's your background."

"Media arts, of course."

"Of course. Aren't there any real scientists who can do documentaries anymore?"

"I took the famous crash course in rocks, bugs, and stones before I came." King laughed. "Whoa, Mister Overqualified, huh?"

"Yeah," said Jank, "thank goodness you're not just some facile slime-sucking adman."

Everyone lapsed into silence. Vick and I exchanged embarrassed smiles. The wind sweetened. Hirsch turned the boat and expertly took it in, bringing us to rest without so much as a bump alongside a natural stone jetty. We all scrambled ashore carrying something and were greeted by several of the semi-permanent residents of Number Four camp. The jetty dipped into the beach's sandy slope at the high-tide mark; the camp sat above. The moon was down and the sky was turning grey by the time we had the boat unloaded. I somehow found myself at Vick's side as we lugged the last of the cargo along the jetty. King and Caldwell were right behind us. Jank was already out of sight among the tents.

"Let's do breakfast," I said to Vick.

"Sounds good to me," and then, probably—I told myself—because she wanted to make up for Jank's rudeness, she said over her shoulder, "Join us, Mister King?"

"You bet." He obviously was happy that she'd asked, but sorry that she hadn't called him Rick.

We entered the camp, and Vick veered off. "Meet you at the mess tent," she said to no one of us in particular. I didn't care for how King watched her walk away.

I had Cardwell and Jank's standing invitation to share their tent space; a geologist named Crumhorn agreed to take King in, though it was on short notice. Cardwell and I delivered him to Crumhorn's tent and were about to move on when he said, "I don't believe I've actually sucked any slime since grade school. I'm just a film-maker, Kevin." When he spoke my name, I felt a sudden, irrational, tremendous urge to rub myself all over with hot sand or maybe ground glass. "If I said or did something to set Doctor Jankoski off—"

"Jankowshi," I said.

"Oh, Jank," Cardwell said, "Jank's just," and shrugged as if that explained everything. He had the dimensions and temperament of a bear.

"Breakfast," I told King, "is in the big tent over yonder," and set off to get mine and left him to get his as he would.

Vick had saved two places at the table. I settled into one of them and happily stirred my coffee. We listed to Rubenstein, a cartographer, who, two days before, had completed a trek overland from Stinktown, Number Two camp, on the estuary. "Only sign of life we saw the whole time," he said, "was one of our own 'coptors, headed inland."

Crumhorn dropped into a chair across from me and scooped up a piece of toast. I asked where his houseguest was, and he said, "Conked out. Just like that. Hi, how do you do, snork, zzz."

"I was wondering when it'd catch up with him. He jumped in

a few hours ago, and he's been going like a chipmunk on an exercise wheel ever since."

"So," said De La Cerda, another geologist, "he's, what, a video producer or something?"

"Or something."

She shook her head. "These people just keep trickling in."

Rubenstein said, "You say that about everybody."

"I'm part-Indian," De La Cerda said, "and Indians know about people who keep trickling in. The Sioux had a word for white people, wasichu. It means, you can't get rid of them."

Rubenstein looked at her askance for a moment. Then: "You're not a Sioux, you're mestizo or some goddamn something."

Hendryx, yet another geologist, said, "So sue her."

Amid the groans, Crumhorn observed that punning was a cry for help, and Westerman, the slight blond botanist seated next to Hendryx, said, "I used to love this man. Now I'm for feeding him to the fishes."

Hendryx looked smug. "No fishes this time of the Paleozoic, right, Vick?"

"Just some armored ones that look like tadpoles wearing football padding."

"They always looked kind of art deco to me," said De La Cerda.

"Well," said Vick. "you have to go to Stinktown to find them, and then they're only about as big as your hand."

"Are they edible?" I said. One thing I did miss in the Silurian was catfish sandwiches.

Vick made a face. "They've got a taste sort of between salt and mud."

"Vick Harris," Rubenstein murmured over the rim of his coffee cup, "girl ichthyologist and gourmet." He sipped and grimaced. "Talk about salt and mud. So where're all the big exciting fish? Where's old Dinowhatsit? You know the one, ten meters long, armored head. Mouth like a big ugly pinking shears."

"Dunkleosteus, alias Dinicthys."

"Yeah, that's the one, where's old Dunkywhatsit?"

"Not even a glimmer in his great-great-granddaddy's eye, I'm afraid."

"So," De La Cerda said to me, "what about this video guy?"

"Northemico sent him to make a documetary about you folks."

Both De La Cerda and Rubenstein gave me the same sharp look, and Westerman said, flatly, "Northemico."

In spite of myself, I spread my fingers in the air and said, "He's just a film-maker."

"You mean like you're just a writer, I'm just a botanist?" Westerman shook her head. "Nobody who's made the jump in the last month or so has been just anything. This guy's just not as obscurely specialized as the rest of them."

"Wait a minute," Vick began, but Rubenstein cut her off.

"If he really is a film guy. Probably a spy."

"I don't think you're being fair," said Vick. "You can't go around automatically assuming someone's a spy just because—"

"Vick," said Rubenstein, "you gotta admit, Northemico and the rest of that pack've been slavering to get in here from day one. There's money waiting to be made here."

She appeared doubtful. "I don't see trilobites and seaweed as the basis for growth industries."

"Try oil." De La Cerda gave her a not-unkindly look. "Something's sure going on. On the ship—" she nodded vaguely in the direction of the sea, "—we're suddenly cramped for space. Too many newcomers all at once. People I've never seen before are suddenly looking over my shoulder all the time. Suddenly it's harder to schedule the use of the helicopter. Then it's just impossible, because they're all the time flying people and surveying equipment into the interior."

"And we all know," Westerman said, "that there's nothing in the interior to survey."

"Sure," said Hendryx, "not if you're a botanist!"

Westerman laughed along with him and then made a face at him. They must have been a riot in bed.

Crumhorn rested his elbows on the table and steepled his fingers. "No reason to think there's suddenly something mysterious or sinister going on," he said. "We've been surveying the interior since we got here."

"Think about what you just said," said De La Cerda. "We've been surveying. We've been doing this, that, every other thing. We, us, the members of this expedition. These other people belong to some whole other expedition. It's riding piggy-back on ours. Gradually, it's displacing ours."

"They want to know everything," Westerman said. "They don't want to tell you anything in return. Look, I don't mind answering questions about my work, I like talking about it. But these people ask all the wrong questions."

"What questions are those?" Hendryx asked sharply.

"Tim," said Westerman. I looked at her in surprise. She was almost pleading with him. "We've talked about this."

"Bottom-line kind of questions," said De La Cerda. "Is there you-name-the-mineral here? Is there a lot of it? Things like that. And you can bet somebody's spent a lot of time calculating which natural resources might be safe to grab here and not have them missed for a hundred million years from now."

Hendryx's wedge-like jaw jutted belligerently forward. "Nothing ever was missed, was it? So they can't have taken anything out. Or maybe they did, maybe you can take out whatever you want, because the past takes care of itself. It has so far."

Westerman folded her thin arms across her chest and gave him an angry look. "I can't believe I'm hearing this from you."

"You should get used to the idea that not everybody thinks exactly the way you do. From time to time, you might even try rethinking a position."

"Tim, you know if Northemico gets loose here, it'll make the Antarctic feeding frenzy look like a model of responsible conservation."

"That was different."

Several people demanded in chorus, "How?"

The beleaguered geologist glowered. "What have we missed from the Paleozoic? Maybe the stripmine scars are buried deep inside the earth. Maybe they've eroded completely away. Maybe they've been deformed beyond recognition and understanding."

"Lots of maybe," muttered Rubenstein.

"We know the landmasses are drawing together, and that the collision'll fold this whole region over on itself."

Everyone at the table was regarding Hendryx very seriously. Westerman said, "Are you saying anything people do here's okay as long as they hide the evidence under a mountain range?"

"Listen, the bills have to be paid, or we have to go home."

"This is home," De La Cerda said, "for some of us."

"You think so." Hendryx patted his lips with a napkin. "But you can't live here without supplies from the future, and the pipeline stays open only so long as someone foots the bill to keep it open. If the government stops, then Northemico or somebody has to start, or that's all she wrote." He pushed his chair back, surveyed the semicircle of mostly hostile faces before him. Vick hung

back, and because she did, I hung back, too. "I want this expedition to continue as much as you do."

Westerman's mouth was set in a thin, straight line as she glared
at his retreating back. An almost identical line creased her forehead. "I sometimes wonder," she said, "if good sex is worth all
the aggravation."

After breakfast, Vick said she had to go with Cardwell to splash
around in tide pools and collect specimens. I passed what passed
for the cool part of the morning bringing whoever didn't have
work to do up to date with the latest shipboard gossip and scur-
rilous rumor. It got definitely hottish toward midday, but then
clouds scudded in at noon, dumped enough rain to cool things
off reasonably, and, mission accomplished, scudded away. I took
a long nap and was greatly improved for it. Rick King was up and
around by late afternoon—days were shorter in the Silurian, and
years consequently longer, by three dozen days—and looked
rested, fit, and out of place in what I took to be the latest thing
in twenty-first-century beachwear for men.

I had hoped simply to prowl on the beach, poke at the occasional lump of cast-up sea life, and just enjoy being on land for a
change. King, however, prevailed on me to steer him around and
make such introductions as I didn't have to disturb anyone's work
to make. Nearly everyone was polite, and De La Cerda, of all
people, actually seemed charmed. Westerman couldn't keep suspicion out of her face, and King, to give him what was due, received her chilly how-do-you-do and perfunctory handshake with
admirable grace.

While we had run through the possible introductions, King
studied the cliffs behind the camp. "What's up there?"

"More sand and rock."

"There a way up?"

I should have lied to him, but I didn't, so next I had to take
him up the path to the top. He looked like Tarzan going up; I
felt like Sisyphus. When we got up, he stood with his arms akimbo
and gazed off at the low mountains in the distance while I sat on
a rock and pretended that I wasn't panting for breath, that my
heart wasn't rattling loosely in its mountings. It was getting into
evening, and all of that bare jagged rock had begun to burn pret-
tily.

Number Four camp was located on a stretch of coastline where
erosion had cut away headlands to form slip-faulted cliffs. Detritus

littered the narrow scalloped beach below. This was a rough bit of seafront, but wherever you made landfall, you found yourself on an inhospitable shore. The one-day North American west was a volcano range; one-day Appalachia was a chain of islands; between the two stretched an unbroken shallow sea. Just so one's sense of direction would be utterly skewed, the equator bisected this sea from the future site of San Diego to that of Iceland. Equatorial North America was geologically part of the great northern landmass, Laurasia, whose southern counterpart was Gondwanaland, comprising South America, Africa, India, Australia, Anartica. In all the unsubmerged regions of the world there was very little soil, and what soil there was was thin, poor, and as vulnerable as life on land itself. Actual greenery existed only beside the waterways. It didn't measure up to the popular idea of a coal-forest, with gern trees, dragonflies big as crows, salamanders as big as sofas. None of the flora was more than waist-high; most were much shorter. Carpeting the lowest and moistest patches of the badlands was Cooksonia, a rootless, leafless plant, no more, really, than a forked stem, towering a mighty five centimeters above the ground. The giant sequoias of the day were comparatively sophisticated—stems with forked branches bearing clusters of small leaflets—but still fell short of what you'd call rank jungle growth. They didn't soften the land's serrate outline so much as make it look furry and itchy. Munching happily through all this green salad were millipedes, some of them big enough to provoke a shudder but all of them perfectly harmless. Munching happily through the millipedes were scorpions that looked and carried on as scorpions were always going to act and carry on. There were some book-gilled arthropods that rated the adjective "amphibious." There were no terrestrial vertebrates, excepting human beings. On the list of things yet to be were lungs, flowers, wings, thumbs, bark, milk, and penes. I was happier here than I'd ever been anywhere else.

King broke a long silence by saying, "This is good stuff." he patted the pocket containing the recordpack. "Long slow pan from the primordial ocean to the desert of barren rock and drifted sand." He fiddled with the headheld for another couple of seconds. "This world's one big still-life, though."

"Take it up with the folks who punched a hole in time. Maybe they can open up a more action-packed era for you. The Mesozoic, or World War Two."

"What do they do for excitement around here?"

I took my cue from his choice of pronouns. He excluded me from his subjects, to remind me, I suppose, that we were both media types, cousin—if not brother—professionals. I said, "That depends on who you talk to. For Cardwell, it's trilobites. For Westerman, it's club mosses."

"What is it for you?"

"Being here."

He brushed that away. "Being here isn't the be-all, end-all of our existence. You're a writer, writing a book."

I had come ostensibly to write a book about life on and around a research vessel embedded in mid-Paleozoic time. The book still wasn't finished, but, anymore, it was beside the point. I had lost all sense of urgency about finishing it. I didn't need the money. I didn't need anything to do with writing a book, except as an excuse to stay.

I said, "I'm here because this is my home."

"Is it, now?" He shook his head. "One day, this place will be home. People won't just work and live here, they'll be born and die here. That's what makes a place home. Right now, this is summer camp. People come here, do the equivalent of making baskets and looking for arrowheads, and when the time comes, they go home."

"Hardly anyone goes ho—back. Not if they can help it. They just have to keep passing their extension reviews. It's less trouble to maintain us here than to replace us."

"Still—"

I slid off the rock. "It'll be dark soon. I'm not going to negotiate that path in the dark. Wouldn't advise you to try it, either."

I started down without waiting to see if he would follow. Later, in the mess tent, I saw him schmoozing with Hendryx and thought, Kindred spirits. Then I took it back. Hendryx was one of us. King, I swore, would never belong.

Everyone scattered into the dusk after supper, most of them claiming to have work that absolutely had to be done before Cardwell's show started. I changed to my least-ratty attire and went down to the high-tide mark ahead of everyone else to find the best seat. My chip player was in my pocket. I took it out and pressed the go button, and merely ancient music floated out over the prehistoric sea. It was "Stardust," recorded by Artie Shaw and

His Orchestra in A.D. 1941. I stood wading in time, enthralled as always by Billy Butterfield's incandescent trumpet, Jack Jenny's smoky trombone, Shaw's own soaring clarinet. Then, as I waited for the next track to begin, I heard somebody behind me and put my thumb on the stop button. Vick paused a short distance away. She said, "I heard music."

"Yes, you did," I said, and then, even more inanely, "I don't have earphones, I hate earphones," and before I could stop myself, "If God'd intended for us to listen to music on earphones . . ." Babbling.

Fortunately, I relaxed my finger on the button, and Shaw's rendition of "I Surrender, Dear" throbbed out of the player and enveloped us like a smoky blue cloud. I was gratified to note that she listened almost all the way through the track before she said anything.

"What is this music?"

"Jazz. Swing. Music."

"It's," and she waited two whole seconds before finishing the sentence, "lovely." She waited again, listened some more. "Lovely and old."

"Barely pre-World War Two," I said, trying not to sound defensive.

"God, my grandmother wasn't even born then."

"Mine was a teenage girl in Indiana. She used to scrape up thirty-five cents somehow and go see Glenn Miller at the local theater. In those days, thirty-five cents was a lot of money for a teenage girl to scrape up."

"This is Glenn Miller?"

"A contemporary. Artie Shaw."

She looked like someone trying to decide if a name she'd never heard before meant anything to her. Then she admitted that it didn't.

"No need to apologize," I said. "I'd be fairly astonished if you had heard of him. Pop music before Elvis Presley, before rock and roll, was like the Precambrian to members of my own generation."

"I have heard of Elvis Presley."

I decided from the way she said it that she probably didn't have him confused with some other, subsequent Elvis—Costello, Hitler, Christ, one of those. We listened to "Moonglow," "Begin the Beg-

uine," and "Summit Ridge Drive." The chip contained dozens
of other tracks that I'd personally selected from Shaw's body of
work, but I didn't want to be a mere tune jockey. I thumbed the
stop button twice after "Summit Ridge Drive," to switch off the
player.

"Certainly does grow on you," she said.

"Uh huh. I have Goodman and Ellington, too. Cab Calloway,
Billie Holiday, dozens of—I think American pop music peaked
sometime between nineteen thirty-five and nineteen fifty." I
looked at her closely. "I wrote a book about it once. Am I getting
carried away here?"

She showed me a small gap between her thumb and forefinger.
"Only a little. I know people who'd make me listen to the whole
Flucks catalogue." My utter ignorance of even a portion of the
Flucks catalogue must have been obvious. "Flucks does a lot of
sub—and ultrasonic pieces. Some of them are said to make lis-
teners lose, ah, muscular control."

"Gosh, why couldn't Artie Shaw have recorded songs like
that?"

She laughed, "I don't see the fun in it either."

Other people had been drifting down from the camp all this
while. They made themselves comfortable, talked, drank, or simply stared out to sea and waited. Jank showed up with a bottle of
brandy, and the three of us passed it around and heckled Cardwell to get the show started. The level of brandy in the bottle got
lower and lower. Lulled by a murmur of waves and voices, I nodded off. When I awoke, with a start, the moon was out, the tide
was in, and it had become as chilly on the beach as it ever got.
Next to me, Jank was gently shaking Vick awake. Everyone else
was heading back to camp.

"Rise up, Lazarus," Jank said, "and walk."

I said, incredulously, "I missed the show? You let me miss the
show?"

"Wasn't any show." He nodded seaward, at Cardwell, who
stood in the foam at the water's edge, a master of ceremonies
whose star act had let him down. "Tomorrow night, maybe."

"Doesn't he know?"

"When they get here, they'll be here." Jank drew Vick to her
feet, and I made a point of helping. "Tomorrow night, the night
after—*some* night this week, anyway."

Between us, Vick nodded agreement, sleepily. "Moon's full. This is the season."

"How can even the trilobites know when it's time? There's only ever the one season."

"If it'll ease the pain of disappointment," Vick said, "why not come snorkeling with us tomorrow?"

"Love to."

Jank and I saw her to her tent flap like gentlemen. I started softly whistling "Embraceable You" as we moved on, and then King bounced up out of the darkness and announced that he had wangled us invitations to a poker game in Rubenstein's tent. He was disheveled and dirty. His shoes looked to be a total write-off, and his beachwear wasn't in much better shape. I couldn't decide whether that ought to raise or lower him in my estimation—the one because he didn't care that he had ruined his expensive outfit, the other because I imagined he could afford not to care. He was thoroughly pleased with himself. Through the simple expedient of spending a night on a beach, he had begun to prove me wrong and become one of the guys. I had never been so disappointed with the people at Number Four camp.

"In all this time," Jank said, "I never knew I had to have an invitation to play poker with Rubenstein." He looked at me. "How about you?"

I was dead tired, but something made me answer, "Oh, why not?"

"Sure," said Jank, "why not?"

Rubenstein poured each of us a drink and dealt us in. The drink was heavenly, the cards were trash. I looked across the table at him and demanded, "These all you have?" He asked how many I wanted and peeled them off. I looked at them and thought, Worse and worse.

"Yow," said Jank. "No cards."

"Yow indeed," said De La Cerda. "You're much too happy with your hand."

"Aah, he's bluffing," I said. "Jank always bluffs."

De La Cerda threw her cards down. "He wants you to think he's bluffing. I fold." The rest of us played out the hand, to our regret. De La Cerda looked smug as Jank raked in chips. "Told you so."

The deal passed to Jank. As he shuffled, he said, without quite looking at King, "How'd you get this assignment?"

After a second, King realized that he was the person being addressed. "Applied for it, how else?"

"Applied to Northemico?"

"Yes." A pause. "Much as you applied to the government."

Jank snapped a card down on the table in front of King. "I applied through the University of Texas."

"Play cards," Rubenstein growled.

We played. Jank won the hand again. The deal passed to me. As I shuffled, King said to Jank, "You talk like you think the government's one thing and Northemico's another. Like they're separate, and one's good and one's not." He shrugged. "Or one's bad and one's worse."

Jank stared determinedly at his cards. "Aren't they? Separate, I mean."

"Public government, what you think of as *the* government—its job is just to keep the citizenry in line, make sure they don't make trouble for the *real* government. Real government is *private* government. Its job is helping rich people to become more so."

We stared at him, all but gaped, in fact. Jank finally said, "If that's so, why the whole big show of keeping the corporations out of the Paleozoic all this time?"

"Takes a while to agree on how to cut up a pie so that everybody's happy."

De La Cerda nodded slowly, as if agreeing against her will. "Like carving up old gangland cities. It's just good practice to keep your trouble away from your money."

Rubenstein said, "Does anybody here want to play *poker*, for chrissake?"

"Just a sec." King shut his fan of cards and closed his hands around it. He looked straight at Jank. "You've got some grudge against Northemico, so, because I'm here making a documentary for Northemico, you've got a grudge against me. Lots of people get mad at the government. *I* get mad at it. Doesn't mean I'm mad at *you*, or anyone at this table, or anyone in this camp. I'm here to do my job, same as you."

"Remember the ad campaign," Jank said to nobody particularly, "when Antarctica finally got opened up?" I could tell from King's expression that he'd never imagined any connection between himself and Antarctica. "Yesterday's land of perpetual ice and snow, today's treasure chest of mineral wealth. My favorite was, What good is it to the penguins? Succinct. Punchy." He looked around at all our faces. "I'm willing to bet there's this bright entrepreneur somewhere who's seen pictures of the Silurian sea, how beautiful and serene it looks. He has a brainstorm. A luxury hotel in the prehistoric past. The Silurian Arms! Next thing you know, there's this whole big ad campaign pitched to assholes with money they don't know how to spend. The ads say crap like, Come back, come home, to a quiet and unspoiled world. Dine at Chez Paleozoic, gourmet cuisine from then to now."

King had sat back in his seat and folded his arms while Jank talked. Now he said, "You may have missed your true calling." He grinned to show that he really was trying to be a sport. "You'd have been an ace adman."

"No, I was born with a soul," and Jank grinned, too, like a carnivore. "About this luxury hotel. Hotels mean earth-moving equipment, mean draining all those smelly bayous. There'd have to be golf courses, too. Rich assholes can't live without golf. Golf courses mean landscaping Paleozoic Appalachia to resemble Palm Beach. There'd have to be colored people to work as caddies and groundskeepers and do all the crap jobs, and poor neighborhoods for them to go home to at night. And golf courses mean effluent runoff, and particularly they mean grass, which as Westerman will tell you is a flowering plant, not due to appear until half past the Cenozoic. Someone decides club mosses are boring and a few palm trees wouldn't hurt. So-called sportsmen won't get much of a kick out of a little jawless fish, hey, this is prehistory, let's liven it up! Bio-concoct some big placoderms like Dunkleosteus, maybe even some plesiosaurs. Or just import bass. Earth history's going to get really twisted when all the little improvements take hold here."

King raised a shoulder in a half-shrug. "Sounds pretty farfetched to me. This is what's real. On the other side of the hole is an exhausted planet with nine billion people on it. On this side is a whole untouched planet."

"It's the *same* planet," Jank said. "Let Northemico go mine the moon instead, it's already dead."

"Too dead," said King, "and too far away. The Paleozoic's alive, and it's *here*. Are you going to sit there and tell me we should let our whole civilization run down so a few thousand folks here can go on admiring the place's natural splendors? Face facts. The thing's inevitable. When a thing's inevitable, the best you can do is accept it and try to find the good in it."

"Yeah." Jank pushed back his chair and got to his feet. "Just look where accepting the inevitable has got us so far."

I stood up, too. The buzz the first drink had given me was long gone; a second drink hadn't brought it back. Rubenstein, who had sat fuming with his cards fanned in his hand throughout Jank and King's set-to, cursed and flung down a full house.

Jank and I wove our way among the tents and down to the beach. I was past being ready for bed, but felt he needed me to stay with him. "Well," I said, "he's right about one thing. The Silurian Arms does sound pretty farfetched."

"Like twenty-first-century America would have to De La Cerda's damn Indians? *They* never expected to get overtaken by events, either. People never do, and yet they always are. All of us here are going to be overtaken by events any day now. Any moment. We can't outrun them, can't duck them."

"Then what do we do?"

"Then we face a choice between, I guess, becoming some sort of revolutionaries or goddamn acquiescing in another Antarctica. Put *that* in your book, Kev."

"I guess," I said, "we'll all just acquiesce. What else could we do, really?"

"Toss certain parties through the hole and then wreck the jump station."

I looked at him unhappily. We weren't just talking about golf courses in the Paleozoic now. "They'd just open up another hole."

"You don't just 'open up' another hole. You have to find one and then widen it. They could look for a long, long time. Even if they found one they could use, the odds against it being one that would bring them right back *here* are billions, trillions to one. Even if they didn't miss by much, they could miss by five or ten million years."

"Which means," I said, "they don't play golf in the Silurian, they play it in the Ordovician or the Devonian."

"At least they couldn't mess up the Silurian. You can't save everything, you save what you can."

"Jank, the whole crew on the ship is Navy Reserve. They'd never throw in with the mutineers. And you know that mutiny *is* what you're talking about."

He was quiet for a moment. Then: "Yeah, hell, I know."

"Plus, the ship's not self-sustaining, and what is there to *eat* here? Trilobites, seaweed, bony fish Vick says taste like salt and mud. At least at your luxury hotel we could get a decent meal, and a drink besides."

He seemed unable to decide how much of what I said was serious and how much was meant to be funny. After a moment, he gave me a comradely punch on the arm and said, "Meet you on the jetty tomorrow A.M." He walked away, and I quickly lost sight of him in the gloom.

In the morning, it took a handful of aspirin to ease my aching head and three cups of burnt-tasting black coffee to get my eyes ungummed. The one other late-breakfaster was Rubenstein, who pointedly passed my table to sit at another one and hissed, by way of saying good morning, "A full house!"

I found Jank and Vick on the jetty, and King, too, all of them with masks and flippers in their hands. I hesitated when I saw King. He was an annoyance to Jank, but for me he was definitely shaping up as a rival. I was wearing faded cut-offs and suddenly became very conscious of the contrast provided by his sculpted thighs and calves and my scrawny knobby old-man's sticks. Vick, however, didn't recoil in horror when she looked at me, and I was further emboldened when she gave me a smile and a come-on shake of the head that a plaster saint couldn't have resisted. There is no way, I told myself, I'm *not* going into the water if King does.

Still, as Jank was getting me equipped, I said in an undertone, "What's he doing here?"

Jank shrugged helplessly. "He found out somehow and asked Vick if he could come along."

"You want to drown him?"

"Maybe something will eat him."

The four of us waded out until we had to swim, then swam out to where the water was six or seven meters deep. Sea and sky were warm, calm, and very clear. It was another perfect day in a ten-million-year summer.

The bottom reminded me of a *NatGeo* holo. Reef life only looks disorganized. Elsewhere in the world, coral polyps may already have been great, slow, patient architects, building barrier reefs the size of California; here, they were putting up lumpish, honeycombed bungalows. We passed over successive crescent-shaped zones dominated by gastropods, scalloped brachiopods, pink flower-like crinoids. In each zone, particular types of straight-shelled and slim tusk-shaped nautiloids jetted about above the bottom, looking like octopi in party hats. At their passing, particular types of elongate burrower disappeared under the sand with a minimum of fuss, and one or another variety of pillbug-shaped trilobite stopped grazing and dodged among the seaweed. The trilobites ranged from the fingernail- to the cracker-sized. There were prickly echinoderms, vase-shaped sponges, and limy stands of worm tubes. The first time I had ever seen any of these creatures, in clear, calf-deep water at low tide, with Cardwell standing beside me and pointing them out, I'd been disappointed. There's nothing *strange* about them, I'd thought, they're just these inoffensive little marine animals, going about their business. In spite of myself, I had, like King after me, expected more in the way of red-mawed ferocity, or of glandular imbalance, at the very least. None of these creatures was longer than my forearm. Most were smaller than my fingers.

This wasn't a scary sea by later standards. Most of the marine life that was equipped to bite hugged the bottom, where the food was, and, consequently, where the eating occurred. On dives, you stayed off the bottom and always scrupulously observed the rule against touching anything unfamiliar unless Jank or one of the other marine specialists handed it to you. We glided as huge, remote, and inaccessible as planets above the world of burrowers and scurriers. Only a few of the nautiloids seemed to notice, and all they did was track us as we passed overhead. Halfway through the Paleozoic Era, there was already that unnerving gleam of intelligence in cephalopod eyes. I glanced over my shoulder to see how my companions were doing and saw King watching, not the sea bottom, but Vick's. The headheld—I hadn't seem him without it since he donned it aboard the ship—made him look as if he were wearing an echinoderm for a cap.

Directly below us, the free-swimmers suddenly executed hard turns and rocketed away with their delicate pale tentacles fluttering behind. That spooked the more alert bottom-dwellers, and the nimbler of these made for cover among the corals. An instant later, something moved angularly across the feeding ground. It had many variously sized and shaped appendages sticking out from under its streamlined headpiece, which was adorned with two blister-like eyes as purposeful-looking as radar housings on fighter aircraft. One set of long appendages resembled nothing so much as vice-grips, another looked like sculls, and several short bristly pairs between the two were expressly for locomotion. The flattened body behind the head was divided into a dozen segments; the tail ended in an awl-like spike. The animal tore straight into a hapless trilobite. The vise-grips went to work, raising a swirl of mud and wreaking fearful havoc—the trilobite flew apart at the joints.

All of us remembered at the same moment that we occasionally had to bob up for air. We broke the surface together, and King spat out his mouthpiece and yelled, "What the hell *is* it?"

"Eurypterid!" Jank told him.

"Sea scorpion!" I put in.

We went back under. Below our waving flippers, the eurypterid swept bits of butchered trilobite under the front edge of its head. The victim's survivors had quit the area as fast as their zillions of tiny legs could carry them, or had wedged themselves into crevices in the coral. Only some cephalopods warily hovered close by, tasting blood.

The eurypterid ate as if it didn't have a care in the world. Maybe it really didn't. It was the biggest animal I had seen in all the time I'd sojourned here, and even I knew a thing or two about its tribe. Eurypterids—the term "sea scorpion" was misleading; the animals' closest relatives were horseshoe crabs—were the biggest arthropods of all time. The biggest ever found, *Pterygotus*, was two meters long, almost three with its main claws outstretched. The one before us measured only about half that, but we maintained our distance, and I personally would've preferred the view from a strong glass-bottomed boat.

The thing finished its repast and half-scuttered, half-swam into a dark space beneath a coral shelf. Jank signaled to King and me to stay where we were, and then he and Vick went down to where they could peer under the shelf. I was relieved when they kicked away and rose, and grateful, too. I was becoming fatigued. We swam until we could wade, then splashed toward the jetty. I noticed that I was going in faster than I had gone out, impelled, no doubt, by that silly fear some people have of getting a leg laid open by a flick of a marine monster's spiky tail. Unmindful of me, Jank and Vick were talking breathlessly of eurypterid body parts, the chelicerae and the telson, the proma this, the ophisthosoma that. King kept abreast of them, not so much listening to what they said as simply watching them say it. That damned headheld.

We flopped panting onto the rocks, and Jank grinned at me and said, "I spent a whole year at Stinktown trying to study big live eurypterids close-up. Came away with almost nothing to show for it except a scar this long." He held up his forefinger and thumb to show me how long.

"How do you mean," said King, "close-up?"

Jank's grin shrank to a smile, but he was too excited, he couldn't keep himself from answering, he'd have answered a blood enemy's questions about his specialty right then. "I tried nets and lobster pots. The varmints busted the lobster pots to pieces with their tails. I got this smallish one in a nylon net, almost a baby to the one we just saw, and had it half over the gunwale when it became annoyed and started taking the boat apart. It sideswiped me on its way back into the water."

"So, what, you just dived and looked at them?"

Jank shook his head. "Not at Stinktown. The water's too muddy. It would've been like diving in chocolate milk. With the possibility of blundering into a power saw thrown in."

"Well, I take it back," King said happily, "I really thought this place was empty," and he got up and strolled away.

"Empty," Jank breathed, "Jesus!" I tried to gauge Vick's re-action, but she was busy with her mask and flippers and didn't look up.

We were celebrities at suppertime. As happens with marine life that gets away, the eurypterid grew larger and more fearsome with each telling, until I capped matters by describing it as having been big enough to gut an orca and likening it to a lawn mower as it ripped through mats of hapless bottom-feeders. Spirits remained high as everyone collected on the beach afterward. Cardwell was having to put up with a lot of heckling and did so calmly, like Leonardo's man who knows the truth and doesn't have to shout. King kept circling him. Arty shot, I thought, and sort of happened upon Vick among the rocks at the base of the jetty. Before I could say a word to her, however, somebody on the beach shouted, "They're here!"

A foaming wave cast up a dozen glistening shoe-sized lumps almost at my feet. The next wave brought another dozen, and the one after that, scores, hundreds. I heard Cardwell give a whoop—it was more of a bellow, actually—and my first thought was that the sound would scare away the creatures we had gathered to watch. Then I remembered that eardrums, too, were on the list of the yet-to-be. Cardwell rose to his full height and spread his arms in welcome, and from around him came applause and a ragged chorus of male and female voices, *"Ta-dah!"* and one lone smart-aleck's demand, "Yeah, but what's your *next* trick going to be?" Everybody stood up and began moving noisily back and forth along the tide line. Almost at once I found King tagging along with Vick and me, but for at least a little while I didn't care. It was *showtime.*

Within twenty minutes, there were thousands of trilobites on the beach, females with males in tow. The females half-buried themselves in the wet sand and dumped their eggs while the males released sperm. It doesn't sound like anything you'd want to lose your head about, but trilobite males were as eager as males of any species—some females had three or four suitors tagging after them—and there were hazards such as never spiced up human procreation.

Sometimes a trilobite was overturned. It would kick a bit with its legs, then contract the muscles running along its back, roll itself into a ball, and let the next wave draw it into deeper water—where it was at considerable risk from cephalopods and other predators. The press of bodies behind pushed some overturned trilobites too far onto land for waves to pull them back. Vick picked up one of these and showed me the paired, jointed legs. King leaned in between us to capture the moment for posterity. Vick turned and lightly chucked the animal back into the water, and then several more after it. Otherwise, they'd have still been on the beach, dying, when the sun rose. King stayed with us and managed to stay with her in particular. I was thinking about chucking him into the water when he asked her, "Why do you throw them back in? What about natural selection and all that?"

"What about it?" she asked. "It's getting on toward the Devonian Period. Trilobites are on their way out anyway."

"Then why . . . ?"

I stopped, picked up a stranded animal, made an underhand toss seaward. After a moment, King did the same. Vick looked pleased with both of us, which of course only half-pleased me. I wondered how to get him to go be in somebody else's face for a while. God sent somebody—who didn't see and didn't care—to snag him by the arm and direct his attention to an especially

frenzied or imaginative expression of arthropod passion. I offered
up a prayer of thanks, motioned Vick to come with me, and offered up more thanks when she did. We strolled for a bit, saying
nothing, then climbed onto the jetty. The chip player was in my
pocket, loaded with a sampler program. We looked at the moon
and the sea and listened first to a Tommy Dorsey rendition of
"Moonlight in Vermont" and next to a "Moonglow" by one of
Benny Goodman's combos. She sighed. What a little moonlight
can do.

At length, she said, "Can you dance to this music?"

My heart raced. I had picked out these tracks myself, with serious kootchiness in mind. June moon spoon. I said, "Millions
did."

"No, can *you* dance to it?"

"I do what people've always done. I fake it. If all you want to
do is hold on to somebody and move in time with the music, it's
easy." I opened my arms. After a moment, she came into them.
"Okay, now put your left hand on my shoulder. I hold you lightly
at the waist. Now put the edge of your right foot against the inside
of my left foot, and the inside of your left foot against the outside
of my right foot."

"This is already starting to get complicated," but she leaned
away from me and looked down to position her feet. "Tab A into
slot A. Tab B into slot B. Got it."

"Don't press your feet against mine so tightly. Maintain the
contact lightly. Relax, stay loose."

She shifted on her feet and leaned back in against me. I was
happier for that.

"Now just glide with me when I move," I said. "I'm going to
lead with my right foot and follow with my left. We take one step
this way." We took the step that way, stiffly, like automatons.
"Then another. Then I angle off a bit and take one step back. I
learned how to do this in junior high school. It's served me well
for over fifty years."

I could have kicked myself for reminding her how old I was.

The jetty lay like a titan's vertebrae half-buried in the sand,
pitted and uneven and altogether not an ideal surface for what
we were about. Nevertheless, she began to get the hang of moving
with me, began to loosen up, and I held her close and as tightly
as I dared and got dizzy on her scent. After a minute or so of

that, I said, "Song's almost over." It was "Sleep Lagoon." "We're going to end with a dip."

"What's—*aieep!*"

"See?"

She was laughing and lost track of her feet and almost fell. I steadied her and didn't give her a chance to slip out of my arms, or to think about doing it. I'd picked these tracks and known what I was about when I picked them. Billie Holiday started singing "You're my Thrill," a performance that could raise goose pimples on a corpse. Vick made a sound like *ooh.* Then came an instrumental version of "Where or When" by Duke Ellington and His Orchestra; Paul Gonsalves's vaporous saxophone enfolded us. Behind us, somebody said, "Yo. Fred and Ginger. Want a drink?"

It was Cardwell, feet planted wide, face beatific in the moonlight. He held up a silver flask and offered us the screw-on cup. It looked like a thimble among his thick figures. We gave him a smart bit of applause, and I said, "Bravo, Doctor Cardwell!"

Vick asked him, "Who're Fred and Ginger?"

"Don't mind him," I said, "he's living in the past."

Cardwell, who was almost my age, snorted like a happy bull. "We're *all* living in the past!"

We sat down on the end of the jetty and proceeded to get pretty silly together. She was between us, and at some point she slipped her arms around our necks and gave us a squeeze. We talked about trilobites and about nothing in particular, or didn't talk at all but listened to "Happiness Is a Thing Called Joe" and "Blue Flame" by Woody Herman, "Body and Soul" by Benny Goodman, "Lover Man" by Holiday. We took turns dozing. It finally worked out, just at dawn, that Cardwell was dozing and Vick and I were watching the sea lighten and the night retreat to the west. She looked sleepy and content, past being drunk but still short of hungover. There was a small dab of mud on her neck. I brushed it away and said, "Doctor Harris."

She said, "Mister Barnett."

"How come both of us've been here as long as we have, and I've only recently realized what a swell person you are?"

A smile spread across her face. "You're slow."

Kiss her, moron, I told myself.

And at that very moment, King came scrambling up the side of the jetty like the evil monkey he was and dropped into a squat

before us. I heard the headheld's faint whir and saw its eye seek
Vick's face. I couldn't tell from her expression whether she, too,
was conscious of having been interrupted at a crucial moment.
"All I can say," he said, "is, wow!" Mister Articulate. Someone
on the beach hallooed and called him to breakfast by name.
Somehow, he was still one of the guys. It eluded me.

Not everyone had stayed up drinking for nights running, or was
old, so not everyone at breakfast felt entirely as washed out as I
did. I wanted to hang around, to head King off at the pass if the
need arose, but started to nod and almost face-dived into my food.
I bade Vick as gallant a farewell as I was able without being a total
clown and hobbled achingly off to my cot. The snoring hillock
on the next cot was Cardwell; he had almost the same beatific
look on his face. Jank, in skivvies, sat in a camp chair and
scratched his pectorals. He nodded at a scrap of paper on my cot.
"That came in from Sparks a couple minutes ago."

I carefully sat down on the cot. "You wouldn't have any hair of
the dog, would you?"

He looked around blearily. "Is it after noon yet?"

I looked at the writing on the paper. *Call me. Ruth.* "Later," I
said, and became unconscious.

Which was a mistake, because by the time I regained consciousness, Ruth, who was not someone who liked to be kept waiting,
had had time to put a fine vindictive edge on her plans for me.
Another mistake was concluding my account of King's impromptu
beach holiday by telling her that he seemed well on the way to
carving out a secure niche for himself in the camp and I therefore
ought to be relieved of all responsibility for him. She agreed.
Then, in as sweet-Southern-sexy a voice as though she were telling
me to go ahead, pick something out of the *Kama Sutra*, she added,
"This will allow you to devote your time to your *other* guest, Ms.
Duvall, when you get back to the ship tonight." I sputtered, protested, tried to argue. She wouldn't argue. "Just make sure you're
with Hirsch when she comes back," she said, "bye, hon," and
signed off.

I spent some time complaining to anybody who would listen,
but hardly anybody could listen. Everyone had work to do. Toward
sundown, however—by which time I was well past disbelief and
outrage and clear to the sullen cranks—Jank showed up at the
tent to watch me toss my meager gear into my threadbare seabag
and listen to me damn Ruth. When I had exhausted her as a

subject, I started in on King, whom I likened, in swift succession, to a burr under my saddle, a thorn in my side, and sand in my undershorts. Jank burst out laughing.

My surprise and pain at his unsympathetic reaction showed. He said, "Sorry. Don't mean to make light."

"Keep an eye on Mister Smarm while I'm off the beach, okay? Don't let him work his bolt too much." I closed the bag and looked around. "Are you all the send-off I'm getting?"

"It's not like you're going *back*, Kev."

"I don't suppose you know where Vick's got to."

"Off checking specimens with Cardwell, where else?"

We didn't shake hands. It wasn't as though I were going back. We separated outside the tent, and I walked disconsolately through the camp. There were voices in Rubenstein's tent: the poker game was gearing up. At the end of the jetty, I found Hirsch fiddling around in the boat. We exchanged nods, and I was about to get in when I heard my name called. I turned to see three people coming along the jetty, Vick and Cardwell dressed in hideous Hawaiian shirts—both his; there was sufficient material in the one Vick wore for five or six dresses in her size—and King tagging along, duded up as usual. He hung back as they approached the boat. Vick hugged me warmly, gave me a quick kiss on the corner of the mouth, and said, "Sorry we didn't get to see much of you today."

"Well, *you* have a day job."

"I just wanted to make sure you knew I had a wonderful time last night."

"Cardwell supplied the trilobites and the booze."

Cardwell sighed like an old steam engine and said, "I just catered. You guys danced." He handed me some old-fashioned letters, written on paper, sealed in envelopes with names and addresses inscribed on them in ink. "Didn't get these into the mail pouch in time."

"No problemo."

I stepped away, stepped down into the boat. King had got it all with the headheld. The boat pulled away from the jetty. Luminous in the golden light of evening, Vick and Cardwell waved to me, and I to them, and as far as I was concerned at that moment the only way the scene could have been improved—short, of course, of a last-minute reprieve for me and the simultaneous annihilation by lightning of Rick King—would have been for Cardwell to strum on a ukelele and Vick in a grass skirt to call out *aloha oe* while Bing Crosby crooned, Soon I'll be sailing. . . .

Back on the ship, I pointedly did not report immediately to Ruth. I unpacked, showered to sluice off beach grit and thwarted hopes, stretched out on my bunk, with an anthology of essays plugged into the machine so I wouldn't look just like some old bum taking a nap, and took a nap. I was awakened by the ship's getting under way and lay staring up at the major decorative touch in my little compartment.

It was a framed reproduction, given to me as a birthday present by my third wife shortly before she called me a bastard and threw the cat at my head, of a map of mid-Paleozoic North America as it had been reconstructed by Charles Schuchert and other early-twentieth-century, pre-plate-tectonics paleogeographers. They had, among other things, rather seriously underestimated the extent of continental inundation and postulated persistent border-lands separated by seaways. I'd always been drawn to the region labeled *Llanoria (Mexia)*, comprising what I regarded as home territory, northeastern Mexico, southern and southeastern Texas, Louisiana, bits of Oklahoma and Arkansas. Disappointingly, where Schuchert had postulated land, later, better-equipped geologists had found evidence only of muddy sea bottom. Yet I remained charmed by Llanoria and the other strangely shaped, exotically named land masses, *Laurentia (Canadia), Cordillera (Cascadia), Appalachia*, enclosing an inland sea studded with lesser lands, *Siouia, Wisconsin Isle, Adirondack Island*. I think the reason for the enduring appeal of this outmoded representation was that Schuchert and his colleagues must have approached their task not simply with the idea in mind of mapping a prehistoric continent according to the data available, but also with something like the pleasure Frank Baum and Edgar Rice Burroughs derived from filling in their maps of Oz and Barsoom.

I went to the mess and glumly ate. Then I sat thinking that I really ought to go see Ruth. *Then* I sat thinking that I really ought to go visit Chamberlain on the fantail, and wondered what I should say to him about Vick, and concluded that I didn't feel like being disapproved of by a solitary drunk who hadn't been involved with a woman since the Treaty of Ghent, who hadn't even been ashore in all the years he'd spent there. Then I went to see Ruth, who while waiting for me had thought up all sorts of little jobs for me to do.

The days dragged into a week. Claire Duvall got shakily back on her feet. I took her on brief tours, introduced her to various people, and disliked her a lot. She was attractive in her way, with eyes so blue they were almost violet and hair so black it was almost blue, like a comic-book character's, but I found her irritating company. All she could talk about was what a genius Rick was.

Ruth informed me that other newcomers, "important ones"— suits, in short—would soon be arriving, too, and maybe I should become the official greeter after all, since I was so good at it, and this was definitely the time to upgrade my wardrobe. I looked landward and burned with the torments of the damned. I couldn't even get a personal message to shore—Sparks regretfully informed me that radio traffic was at an all-time high, all day every day the air crackled with messages, either highly technical or else coded, from the interior. I was miserable enough to wonder if Ruth had somehow heard something about Vick and me, was keeping me on the ship and off the air out of spite, and more nonsense in that vein. The wasichu, those unsociable, obscurely specialized personnel who were taking over the expedition, continued to arrive and depart by helicopter, mysteriously, sinisterly. The suits didn't come and didn't come and didn't come.

On the afternoon of the eighth day, there was a knock, and Chamberlain appeared in the hatchway, flask in hand. He said, "I got tired of waiting for you to come visit me." He gave me a closer look. "You sulking alone in here, or you want someone to get you good and drunk and listen to your tale of woe?"

"I'm in no mood to be made fun of."

"Oh, come on." He was looking around for a place to sit. I moved a box of book chips, and he plopped himself down with a grunt. "Can I smoke?"

"I wish you wouldn't."

He heaved a sigh that was almost a whimper, fidgeted, remembered the flask. "Want a drink?"

I took a long swallow and handed the flask back to him. "I drink too much."

"Right now, you look like you can't drink enough."

"I'm about six minutes from going on a killing spree."

"Hm." He took a drink, stowed the flask, put his hands on his knees. "Our tail is tied in a knot today."

"You wouldn't understand."

"Welty, Eudora Welty, said that, whatever wonderful things we may do, fly to the moon, whatever—travel through time—we're driven by a small range of feelings. She said all our motives can still be counted on our fingers."

"You got that out of one of my books!"

"It matter where I got it if it's true?"

I regarded him sullenly.

"Man your age shouldn't pout," he said. He waited, heaved another sigh, slapped his thighs. "Well, I'm not going to try and pry it out of you. I'm your *friend*, schmuck. You need to talk, *talk*, I'll listen. You may find you're blowing whatever it is all out of proportion."

"I don't *have* a sense of proportion right now. Sorry, but there're just some things that're bigger than I am."

"Have it your way. I'm going back where I can smoke. Come join me when you feel better. You don't want to sweat out the storm of Silurian in this little box."

"What? Storm?"

Halfway through the hatchway, Chamberlain turned and gave me a big happy grin. "All signs meteorological point to a big 'un piling up in the east. They're evacuating the windward camps."

He almost didn't get through the hatchway before I did.

When the boat arrived with the contingent from Number Four camp, I spotted Vick at once. A moment later, I spotted King as well. He had shucked his fancy beachwear in favor of cut-offs and a T-shirt. He was sitting beside her in the boat. They were talking to each other. Whatever they were talking about, she looked as if she found it very interesting indeed. I told myself that it was only clinical interest, but even as I did, the sharp barb of jealousy sank into my aorta, as I saw, realized, that she was holding his hand, there was a sick awful sinking feeling in the pit of my stomach, I knew he had novelty going for him, and sculpted muscles, and youth, and he'd surely let only me see him sick and whiny, and I hardly counted. . . .

Everything looked so ordinary. Everyone was tired and dirty. No one paid any attention to the new lovers, regarded them strangely or enviously or hatefully or any way at all, not even Jank, who sat at the bow looking gloomily preoccupied. What really drove home the idea that, somehow, incredibly, she was *with* King was her looking up, seeing me, smiling, waving, calling out a friendly greeting. She was radiant with guiltless happiness. I moved my hand at my side, the best I could do by way of waving back. Suddenly desperate to escape from the boat bay, I turned to go, and there stood Claire Duvall, staring down at the two people among all the people in the boat, with an expression of disbelief on her face that was only beginning to yield to hurt and anger. She looked the way I felt. I brushed past her and stumbled numbly through the ship. Someone touched my arm and said, "Hey, Kev, you okay?" and I made a noise, slipped past, kept walking until I was in my cabin, shut in.

I sat down. I exhaled emphatically, as if that would take care of matters, let me go on with my day, my life. Of course it didn't. I promptly found myself trying to pinpoint in memory the instant when the spark must have leaped between them. I shook those thoughts out of my skull only so I could wonder if she let him wear the headheld when they had sex, and if this wasn't strictly a short-term pheromone-propelled kind of relationship anyway. It seemed to me that world-view had to matter even between the sheets, but then I thought of Westerman and Hendryx's relationship, which had endured for years, and even prospered at times, in the face of major differences of opinion on every subject imaginable. I'd made so bold as to ask them about that, one time when we were sitting around ruining our livers, and received for an answer giggles from her and a dreamy grin from him. Pheromones.

I decided I needed some music and stuck Coleman Hawkins into the player. "I'm Through With Love," "What Is There to Say?" I could have gone with Cab Calloway or Fats Waller, who would've worked hard to cheer me up; at least I didn't choose Holiday and "Good Morning, Heartache." For all the difference it made. I went right on foundering in my tarpit of self-pity. I'd always loved women and the company of women. I'd had girlfriends since I was in third grade, lovers since I was in my midteens, a lifetime of love's ups and downs, ins and outs. Yet I couldn't believe how awful I felt *now*. I felt every bit as awful now as when I'd been a high-school sophomore and Judy Biesemeyer had broken my heart. Nothing had a right, I told myself, to hurt me as much in my sixties as it had at fifteen, and yet why I asked myself, would I ever have thought that it *wouldn't?* To which I could only answer, duh, dunno, just stupid, I guess. And at last it struck me, I hadn't just been passed over, I wasn't just stupid, I was *ridiculous* was what I was, a lover boy trapped in a flabby, loose-skinned, wrinkling, balding, shrinking, crumbling body, and the best I could hope for was that she hadn't noticed how ridiculous I was, that she had thought of me the whole time merely as a sweet old gent, not as—

I glared at my antique map of Llanoria, land that never was, and decided what I really needed was a drink. I stood up and sat right back down again. The deck was tilted. Then it was level. Then it was tilted again, but in the opposite direction. I stuck my head into the companionway and yelled at the first person I saw, "The ship's pitching!"

"Storm," he said, as if replying to a child, and unhurriedly went on about his business.

On the fantail, Chamberlain was sitting in his deck chair and peering out to sea while his assistants busied themselves among the gadgets. I could hear people yelling at one another up on the helicopter deck as they lashed down aircraft. The ship raced with the sea and before a cool, moisture-heavy wind. Far astern, spanning the horizon, seeming to reach clear into the ionosphere, were sheer cliffs of dark gray cloud.

"Sweet Jesus," I said, "where did *that* come from?"

"If that's not a number twelve on the Beaufort scale, I'll eat my barometer." Chamberlain spared me a glance along his shoulder. "You look worse now than you did before."

I barely heard him. I couldn't take my eyes off the clouds. Then my pocketphone buzzed, and the bane of my existence said, "Kevo, get down to the jump station. Those vee-eye-pees are definitely on the way. You've got just enough time to change into some decent clothes."

"They're coming *now?*" I was holding on to the rail with one hand and needed two. "There's a big storm on the way, too."

"How're they supposed to know what they're jumping into? Twenty minutes, dear heart."

I screeched into the speaker and tossed the pocketphone overboard. Then I said, "Oh, hell, I shouldn't done that. Some rockhound'll find it."

Chamberlain said, "We won't leave a trace."

"Can I have a drink? I'm having a bad day? First—and now suits jumping in."

He handed me the flask. "Cheer up. You're probably going to be treated to the sight of some very self-important people puking like cats."

"Some treat."

He took a pack of cigarettes from his shirt pocket, shook out one of the nasty things, braced himself against the rail with his back to the wind to light up. "Hurry on back here when you can. You don't want to miss this, it's going to be quite a blow. We can't outrun it, despite what the Navy may let on. May not even be able to ride it out on the lee shore."

I said, "You'd be a much happier person if you'd get yourself a girlfriend," but the truth was, he looked happier at that moment than I'd ever seen him, as happy as Cardwell with his trilobites, Jank with his eurypterid—

—King with his ichthyologist.

I suddenly felt so tired. This was the last time, I thought, I don't have another good love affair left in me, or even a bad one. I saw the rest of my life. I'd spend my time drinking and listening to people argue whether or not it was a good idea to use the Paleozoic to keep the twenty-first century clanking and sputtering along. Not that argument would stop it from happening. I'd hear Holiday sing another few hundred or thousand times of how she covered the waterfront, be dazzled anew at every playing of the Shaw or the Goodman "Moonglow," and hum along whenever the morning found me miles away with still a million things to say. The long, quiet Silurian summer would wear on, Laurasia and Gondwanaland would draw inexorably together, and the solar system would continue its circuit of the outerreaches of the Milky Way. I'd do whatever I had to do for Ruth to go on being a hanger-on here, and I wouldn't write, and if ever I found myself *seeing* anyone else whom I'd only been looking at before, I'd throw myself overboard. . . .

"Feel that wind," Chamberlain murmured. His long, thin hair whipped about his skull. "I've been thinking a lot about fetch today."

"Huh? Like with a dog?"

"Idiot. Fetch is the extent of open water a wind can blow across. Here we've got a northern hemisphere that's almost nothing but fetch. Wind, waves could travel right around the planet. Storm comes along, whips together a bunch of mid-ocean waves traveling at different speeds, piles 'em up into big waves. *Big* waves. Back in the nineteen-thirties, a Navy ship in the Pacific sighted a wave over thirty-five meters high."

I was appalled. "You're hoping we break that record?"

"Hm. About time we had some excitement around here." He

regarded me with approximately equal parts of amusement and tenderness. "See how quickly your priorities are getting straightened out?"

"Okay," I said, "so there're things that're bigger than the things that're bigger than me."

"Hm. Mm hm." For Chamberlain, that was a gale of laughter.

Rudyard Kipling

Wireless

From *Traffics and Discoveries*, 1904

Time travel does not always require futuristic technology—sometimes the technology at hand is enough to blur the barriers between past, present, and future. Only the most simple elements are needed: a turn of the century chemist shop, a British seaside town, the poetry of John Keats, and a wireless that receives messages not from another place, but another time.

B. A.

"IT'S A FUNNY THING, THIS MARCONI BUSINESS, ISN'T IT?" SAID Mr. Shaynor, coughing heavily. "Nothing seems to make any difference, by what they tell me—storms, hills, or anything; but if that's true we shall know before morning."

"Of course it's true," I answered, stepping behind the counter. "Where's old Mr. Cashell?"

"He's had to go to bed on account of his influenza. He said you'd very likely drop in."

"Where's his nephew?"

"Inside, getting the things ready. He told me that the last time they experimented they put the pole on the roof of one of the big hotels here, and the batteries electrified all the water-supply, and—" he giggled— "the ladies got shocks when they took their baths."

"I never heard of that."

"The hotel wouldn't exactly advertise it, would it? Just now, by what Mr. Cashell tells me, they're trying to signal from here to Poole, and they're using stronger batteries than ever. But, you see, he being the guvnor's nephew and all that, (and it will be in the papers too), it doesn't matter how they electrify things in this house. Are you going to watch?"

"Very much. I've never seen this game. Aren't you going to bed?"

"We don't close till ten on Saturdays. There's a good deal of influenza in town, too, and there'll be a dozen prescriptions coming in before morning. I generally sleep in the chair here. It's warmer than jumping out of bed every time. Bitter cold, isn't it?"

"Freezing hard. I'm sorry your cough's worse."

"Thank you. I don't mind cold so much. It's this wind that fair cuts me to pieces." He coughed again hard and hackingly, as an old lady came in for ammoniated quinine. "We've just run out of it in bottles, madam," said Mr. Shaynor, returning to the professional tone, "but if you will wait two minutes, I'll make it up for you, madam."

I had used the shop for some time, and my acquaintance with the proprietor had ripened into friendship. It was Mr. Cashell who revealed to me the purpose and power of Apothecaries' Hall what time a fellow a chemist had made an error in a prescription of mine, had lied to cover his sloth, and when error and lie were brought home to him had written vain letters.

"A disgrace to our profession," said the thin, mild-eyed man, hotly, after studying the evidence. "You couldn't do a better service to the profession than report him to Apothecaries' Hall."

I did so, not knowing what djinns I should evoke; and the result was such an apology as one might make who had spent a night on the rack. I conceived great respect for Apothecaries' Hall, and esteem for Mr. Cashell, a zealous craftsman who magnified his calling. Until Mr. Shaynor came down from the North his assistants had by no means agreed with Mr. Cashell. "They forget," said he, "that, first and foremost, the compounder is a medicine-man. On him depends the physician's reputation. He holds it literally in the hollow of his hand, sir."

Mr. Shaynor's manners had not, perhaps, the polish of the grocery and Italian warehouse next door, but he knew and loved his dispensary work in every detail. For relaxation he seemed to go no farther afield than the romance of drugs—their discovery, preparation, packing, and export—but it led him to the ends of the earth, and on this subject, and the Pharmaceutical Formulary, and Nicholas Culpepper, most confident of physicians, we met.

Little by little I grew to know something of his beginnings and his hopes—of his mother, who had been a schoolteacher in one of the northern counties, and of his red-headed father, a small job-master at Kirby Moors, who died when he was a child; of the examinations he had passed and of their exceeding and increasing difficulty; of his dreams of a shop in London; of his hate for the price-cutting Co-operative stores; and, most interesting, of his mental attitude towards customers.

"There's a way you get into," he told me, "of serving them carefully, and I hope, politely, without stopping your own thinking. I've been reading Christy's *New Commercial Plants* all this autumn, and that needs keeping your mind on it, I can tell you. So long as it isn't a prescription, of course, I can carry as much as half a page of Christy in my head, and at the same time I could sell out all that window twice over, and not a penny wrong at the end. As to my prescriptions, I think I could make up the general run of 'em in my sleep, almost."

For reasons of my own, I was deeply interested in Marconi experiments at their outset in England; and it was of a piece with Mr. Cashell's unvarying thoughtfulness that, when his nephew the electrician appropriated the house for a long-range installation, he should, as I have said, invite me to see the result.

The old lady went away with her medicine, and Mr. Shaynor and I stamped on the tiled floor behind the counter to keep ourselves warm. The shop, by the light of the many electrics, looked like a Paris-diamond mine, for Mr. Cashell believed in all the ritual of his craft. Three superb glass jars—red, green, and blue—of the sort that led Rosamund to parting with her shoes—blazed in the broad plate-glass windows, and there was a confused smell of orris, Kodak films, vulcanite, tooth-powder, sachets, and almond-cream in the air. Mr. Shaynor fed the dispensary stove, and we sucked cayenne-pepper jujubes and menthol lozenges. The brutal east wind had cleared the streets, and the few passers-by were muffled to their puckered eyes. In the Italian warehouse next door some gay feathered birds and game, hung upon hooks, sagged to the wind across the left edge of our window-frame.

"They ought to take these poultry in—all knocked about like that," said Mr. Shaynor. "Doesn't it make you feel fair perishing? See that old hare. The wind's nearly blowing the fur off him."

I saw the belly-fur of the dead beast blown apart in ridges and streaks as the wind caught it, showing bluish skin underneath.

"Bitter cold," said Mr. Shaynor, shuddering. "Fancy going out on a night like this! Oh, here's young Mr. Cashell."

The door of the inner office behind the dispensary opened, and an energetic, spade-bearded man stepped forth, rubbing his hands.

"I want a bit of tinfoil, Shaynor," he said. "Good-evening. My uncle told me you might be coming." This to me, as I began the first of a hundred questions.

"I've everything in order," he replied. "We're only waiting until Poole calls us up. Excuse me a minute. You can come in whenever you like—but I better be with the instruments. Give me that tinfoil. Thanks."

While we were talking, a girl—evidently no customer—had come into the shop, and the face and bearing of Mr. Shaynor changed. She leaned confidently across the counter.

"But I can't," I heard him whisper uneasily—the flush on his cheek was dull red, and his eyes shone like a drugged moth's. "I tell you I'm alone in the place."

"No, you aren't. Who's *that?* Let him look after it for a half an hour. A brisk walk will do you good. Ah, come now, John."

"But he isn't—"

"I don't care. I want you to; we'll only go round by St. Agnes. If you don't—"

He crossed to where I stood in the shadow of the dispensary counter, and began some sort of broken apology about a lady-friend.

"Yes," she interrupted. "You take the shop for half an hour—to oblige *me*, won't you?"

She had a singularly rich and promising voice that well matched her outline.

"All right," I said. "I'll do it—but you'd better wrap yourself up, Mr. Shaynor."

"Oh, a brisk walk ought to help me. We're only going round by the church." I heard him cough grievously as they went out together.

I refilled the stove, and, after reckless expenditure of Mr. Cashell's coal, drove some warmth into the shop. I explored many of the glass-knobbed drawers that lined the walls, tasted some disconcerting drugs, and, by the aid of a few cardamoms, ground ginger, chloric-ether, and dilute alcohol, manufactured a new and wildish drink, of which I bore a glassful to young Mr. Cashell, busy in the back office. He laughed shortly when I told him that Mr. Shaynor had stepped out—but a frail coil of wire held all his attention, and he had no word for me bewildered among the batteries and rods. The noise of the sea on the beach began to make itself heard as the traffic in the street ceased. Then briefly, but very lucidly, he gave me the names and uses of the mechanisms that crowded the tables and the floor.

"When do you expect to get the message from Poole?" I demanded, sipping my liquor out of a graduated glass.

"About midnight, if everything is in order. We've got our installation-pole fixed to the roof of the house. I shouldn't advise you to turn on a tap or anything tonight. We've connected up with the plumbing, and all the water will be electrified." He repeated to me the history of the agitated ladies at the hotel at the time of the first installation.

"But what *is* it?" I asked. "Electricity is out of my beat altogether."

"Ah, if you knew *that* you'd know something nobody knows. It's just It—what we call Electricity, but the magic—the manifestations—the Hertzian waves—are all revealed by *this*. The coherer, we call it."

He picked up a glass tube not much thicker than a thermometer, in which, almost touching, were two tiny silver plugs, and between them an infinitesimal pinch of metallic dust. "That's all," he said, proudly, as though himself responsible for the wonder. "That is the thing that will reveal to us the Powers—whatever the Powers may be—at work—through space—a long distance away."

Just then Mr. Shaynor returned alone and stood coughing his heart out on the mat.

"Serves you right for being such a fool," said young Mr. Cashell, as annoyed as myself at the interruption. "Never mind—we've all the night before us to see wonders."

Shaynor clutched the counter, his handkerchief to his lips. When he brought it away I saw two bright red stains.

"I—I've got a bit of rasped throat from smoking cigarettes," he panted. "I think I'll try a cubeb."

"Better take some of this. I've been compounding while you've been away." I handed him the brew.

" 'Twon't make me drunk, will it? I'm almost a teetotaller. My word! That's grateful and comforting."

He set down the empty glass to cough afresh.

"Brr! But it was cold out there! I shouldn't care to be lying in my grave a night like this. Don't *you* ever have a sore throat from smoking?" He pocketed the handkerchief after a furtive peep.

"Oh, yes, sometimes," I replied, wondering, while I spoke, into what agonies of terror I should fall if ever I saw those bright-red danger-signals under my nose. Young Mr. Cashell among the batteries coughed slightly to show that he was quite ready to continue his scientific explanations, but I was thinking still of the girl with the rich voice and significantly cut mouth, at whose command I had taken charge of the shop. It flashed across me that she distantly resembled the seductive shape on a gold-framed toilet-water advertisement whose charms were unholily heightened by the glare from the red bottle in the window. Turning to make sure, I saw Mr. Shaynor's eyes bent in the same direction, and by instinct recognized that the flamboyant thing was to him a shrine. "What do you take for your—cough?" I asked.

"Well, I'm the wrong side of the counter to believe much in patent medicines. But there are asthma cigarettes, and there are pastilles. To tell you the truth, if you don't object to the smell, which is very like incense, I believe, though I'm not a Roman Catholic, Blaudett's Cathedral Pastilles relieve me as much as anything."

"Let's try." I had never raided a chemist's shop before, so I was thorough. We unearthed the pastilles—brown, gummy cones of benzoin—and set them alight under the toilet-water advertisement, where they fumed in thin blue spirals.

"Of course," said Mr. Shaynor, to my question, "what one uses in the shop for one's self comes out of one's pocket. Why, stock-taking in our business is nearly the same as with jewellers—and I can't say more than that. But one gets them"—he pointed to the pastille-box—"at trade prices." Evidently the censing of the gay, seven-tinted wench with the teeth was an established ritual which cost something.

"And when do we shut up shop?"

"We stay like this all night. The guv—old Mr. Cashell—doesn't believe in locks and shutters as compared with electric light. Besides it brings trade. I'll just sit here in the chair by the stove and write a letter, if you don't mind. Electricity isn't my prescription."

The energetic young Mr. Cashell snorted within, and Shaynor settled himself up in his chair over which he had thrown a staring red, black, and yellow Austrian jute blanket, rather like a table-cover. I cast about, amid patent—medicine pamphlets, for something to read, but finding little, returned to the manufacture of the new drink. The Italian warehouse took down its game and went to bed. Across the street blank shutters flung back the gas-light in cold smears; the dried pavement seemed to rough up in goose-flesh under the scouring of the savage wind, and we could hear, long ere he passed, the policeman flapping his arms to keep himself warm. Within, the flavors of cardamoms and chloric-ether disputed those of the pastilles and a score of drugs and perfume and soap scents. Our electric lights, set low down in the windows before the tun-bellied Rosamund jars, flung inward three monstrous daubs of red, blue, and green, that broke into kaleidoscopic lights on the faceted knobs of the drug-drawers, the cut-glass scent flagons, and the bulbs of the sparkly bottles. They flushed the white-tiled floor in gorgeous patches; splashed along the nickel-silver counter-rails, and turned the polished mahogany counter-panels to the likeness of intricate grained marbles—slabs of porphyry and malachite. Mr. Shaynor unlocked a drawer, and ere he began to write, took out a meager bundle of letters. From my place by the stove, I could see the scalloped edges of the paper with a flaring monogram in the corner and could even smell the reek of chypre. At each page he turned toward the toilet-water lady of the advertisement and devoured her with over-luminous eyes. He had drawn the Austrian blanket over his shoulders, and among those warring lights he looked more than ever the incarnation of a drugged moth—a tiger-moth as I thought.

He put his letter into an envelope, stamped it with stiff mechanical movements, and dropped it in the drawer. Then I became aware of the silence of a great city asleep—the silence that underlaid the quiet of warm life stilled down for its appointed time, and unconsciously I moved about the glittering shop as one moves in a sickroom. Young Mr. Cashell was adjusting some wire that crackled from time to time with the tense, knuckle-stretching sound of the electric spark. Upstairs, where a door shut and opened swiftly, I could hear his uncle coughing abed.

"Here," I said, when the drink was properly warmed, "take some of this, Mr. Shaynor."

He jerked in his chair with a start and a wrench, and held out his hand for the glass. The mixture, of a rich port-wine color, frothed at the top.

"It looks," he said, suddenly, "it looks—those bubbles—like a string of pearls winking at you—rather like the pearls round that young lady's neck." He turned again to the advertisement where the female in the dove-colored corset had seen fit to put on her pearls before she cleaned her teeth.

"Not bad, is it?" I said.

"Eh?"

He rolled his eyes heavily full on me, and, as I stared, I beheld all meaning and consciousness die out of the swiftly dilating pupils. His figure lost its stark rigidity, softened into the chair, and, chin on chest, hands dropped before him, he rested open-eyed, absolutely still.

"I'm afraid I've rather cooked Shaynor's goose," I said, bearing the fresh drink to young Mr. Cashell. "Perhaps it was the chloric-ether."

"Oh, he's all right." The spade-bearded man glanced at him pityingly. "Consumptives go off in those sort of doses very often. It's exhaustion . . . I don't wonder. I daresay the liquor will do him good. It's grand stuff," he finished his share appreciatively. "Well, as I was saying—before he interrupted—about this little coherer. The pinch of dust, you see, is nickel-filings. The Hertzian waves, you see, come out of space from the station that dispatches 'em, and all these little particles are attracted together—cohere, we call it—for just so long as the current passed through them. Now, it's important to remember that the current is an induced current. There are a good many kinds of induction—"

"Yes, but what *is* induction?"

"That's rather hard to explain untechnically. But the long and the short of it is that when a current of electricity passes through a wire there's a lot of magnetism present round that wire; and if you put another wire parallel to, and within what we call its magnetic field—why then, the second wire will also become charged with electricity."

"On its own account?"

"On its own account."

"Then let's see if I've got it correctly. Miles off, at Poole, or wherever it is—"

"It will be anywhere in ten years."

"You've got a charged wire—"

"Charged with Hertzian waves which vibrate, say, two hundred and thirty million times a second." Mr. Cashell snaked his forefinger rapidly through the air.

"All right—a charged wire at Poole, giving out these waves into space. Then this wire of yours sticking out into space—on the roof of the house—in some mysterious way gets charged with those waves from Poole—"

"Or anywhere—it only happens to be Poole tonight."

"And those waves set the coherer at work, just like an ordinary telegraph-office ticker?"

"No! That's where so many people make the mistake. The Hertzian waves wouldn't be strong enough to work a great heavy Morse instrument like ours. They can only just make that dust cohere, and while it coheres (a little while for a dot and a longer while for a dash) the current from this battery—the home battery"—he laid his hand on the thing—"can get through to the Morse printing-machine to record the dot or dash. Let me make it clearer. Do you know anything about steam?"

"Very little. But go on."

"Well, the coherer is like a steam-valve. Any child can open a valve and start a steamer's engines, because a turn of the hand lets in the main steam, doesn't it? Now, this home battery here ready to print is the main steam. The coherer is the valve, always ready to be turned on. The Hertzian wave is the child's hand that runs it."

"I see. That's marvelous."

"Marvelous, isn't it? And, remember, we're only at the beginning. There's nothing we shan't be able to do in ten years. I want to live—my God, how I want to live, and see it develop!" He looked through the door at Shaynor breathing lightly in his chair. "Poor beast! And he wants to keep company with Fanny Brand."

"Fanny *who*?" I said, for the name struck an obscurely familiar chord in my brain—something connected with a stained handkerchief, and the word "arterial."

"Fanny Brand—the girl you kept shop for." He laughed. "That's all I know about her, and for the life of me I can't see what Shaynor sees in her, or she in him."

"*Can't* you see what he sees in her?" I insisted.

"Oh, yes, if *that's* what you mean. She's a great, big, fat lump of a girl, and so on. I suppose that's why he's so crazy after her. She isn't his sort. Well, it doesn't matter. My uncle says he's bound to die before the year's out. Your drink's given him a good sleep, at any rate." Young Mr. Cashell could not catch Mr. Shaynor's face, which was half turned to the advertisement.

I stoked the stove anew, for the room was growing cold, and lighted another pastille. Mr. Shaynor in his chair, never moving, looked through and over me with eyes as wide and lusterless as those of a dead hare.

"Poole's late," said young Mr. Cashell, when I stepped back. "I'll just send them a call."

He pressed a key in the semidarkness, and with a rending crackle there leaped between two brass knobs a spark, streams of sparks, and sparks again.

"Grand, isn't it? *That's* the Power—our unknown Power—kicking and fighting to be let loose," said young Mr. Cashell. "There she goes—kick—kick—kick into space, I never get over the strangeness of it when I work a sending-machine-waves going into space, you know. T. R. is our call. Poole ought to answer with L. L. L."

We waited two, three, five minutes. In that silence, of which the boom of the tide was an orderly part, I caught the clear *"kiss— kiss—kiss"* of the halliards on the roof, as they were blown against the installation-pole.

"Poole is not ready. I'll stay here and call you when he is."

I returned to the shop, and set down my glass on a marble slab with a careless clink. As I did so, Shaynor rose to his feet, his eyes fixed once more on the advertisement, where the young woman bathed in the light from the red jar simpered pinkly over her pearls. His lips moved with cessation. I stepped nearer to listen. "And threw—and threw—and threw," he repeated, his face all sharp with some inexplicable agony.

I moved forward astonished. But it was then he found words— delivered roundly and clearly. These:—

And threw warm gules on Madeleine's young breast.

The trouble passed off his countenance, and he returned lightly to his place, rubbing his hands.

It had never occurred to me, though we had many times discussed reading and prize-competitions as a diversion, that Mr. Shaynor ever read Keats, or could quote him at all appositely. There was, after all, a certain stained-glass effect of light on the high bosom of the highly polished picture which might, by stretch of fancy, suggest, as a vile chromo recalls some incomparable canvas, the line he had spoken. Night, my drink, and solitude were evidently turning Mr. Shaynor into a poet. He sat down again and wrote swiftly on his villainous note-paper, his lips quivering.

I shut the door into the inner office and moved up behind him. He made no sign that he saw or heard. I looked over his shoulder, and read, amid half-formed words, sentences, and wild scratches:—

> —*Very cold it was. Very cold*
> *The hare—the hare—the hare—*
> *The birds—*

He raised his head sharply, and frowned toward the blank shutters of the poulterer's shop where they jutted out against our window. Then one clear line came:—

> *The hare, in spite of fur, was very cold.*

The head, moving machine-like, turned right to the advertisement where the Blaudett's Cathedral pastille reeked abominably. He grunted, and went on:—

> *Incense in a censer—*
> *Before her darling picture framed in gold—*
> *Maiden's picture—angel's portrait—*

"Hsh!" said Mr. Cashell guardedly from the inner office, as though in the presence of spirits. "There's something coming through from somewhere; but it isn't Poole." I heard the crackle of sparks as he depressed the keys of the transmitter. In my own brain, too, something crackled, or it might have been the hair on my head. Then I heard my own voice, in a harsh whisper: "Mr. Cashell, there is something coming through here, too. Leave me alone till I tell you."

"But I thought you'd come to see this wonderful thing—Sir," indignantly at the end.

"Leave me alone till I tell you. Be quiet."

I watched—I waited. Under the blue-veined hand—the dry hand of the consumptive—came away clear, without erasure:—

And my weak spirit fails
To think how the dead must freeze—

he shivered as he wrote—

Beneath the churchyard mold.

Then he stopped, laid the pen down, and leaned back.

For an instant, that was half an eternity, the shop spun before me in a rainbow-tinted whirl, in and through which my own soul most dispassionately considered my own soul as that fought with an over-mastering fear. Then I smelt the strong smell of cigarettes from Mr. Shaynor's clothing, and heard, as though it had been the rending of trumpets, the rattle of his breathing. I was still in my place of observation, much as one would watch a rifle-shot at the butts, half-bent, hands on my knees, and head within a few inches of the black, red, and yellow blanket of his shoulder. I was whispering encouragement, evidently to my other self, sounding sentences, such as men pronounce in dreams.

"If he has read Keats, it proves nothing. If he hasn't—like causes *must* beget like effects. There is no escape from this law. *You* ought to be grateful that you know 'St. Agnes' Eve' without the book; because, given the circumstances, such as Fanny Brand, who is the key of the enigma, and approximately represents the latitude and longitude of Fanny Brawne; allowing also for the bright red color of the arterial blood upon the handkerchief, which was just what you were puzzling over in the shop just now; and counting the effect of the professional environment, here almost perfectly duplicated—the result is logical and inevitable. As inevitable as induction."

Still, the other half of my soul refused to be comforted. It was cowering in some minute and inadequate corner—at an immense distance.

Hereafter, I found myself one person again, my hands still gripping my knees, and my eyes glued on the page before Mr. Shaynor. As dreamers accept and explain the upheaval of landscapes and the resurrection of the dead, with excerpts from the evening hymn or the multiplication-table, so I had accepted the facts, whatever they might be, that I should witness, and had devised a theory, sane and plausible to my mind, that explained them all. Nay, I was even in advance of my facts, walking hurriedly before them, assured that they would fit my theory. And all that I now recall of that epoch-making theory are the lofty words: "If he has read Keats it's the chloric-ether. If he hasn't, it's the identical bacillus, or Hertzian wave of tuberculosis, *plus* Fanny Brand the professional status, which, in conjunction with the mainstream of subconscious thought common to all mankind, has thrown up temporarily an induced Keats."

Mr. Shaynor returned to his work, erasing and rewriting as before with swiftness. Two or three blank pages he tossed aside. Then he wrote, muttering:—

The little smoke of a candle that goes out.

"No," he muttered. "Little smoke—little smoke—little smoke. What else?" He thrust his chin forward toward the advertisement, whereunder the last of the Blaudett's Cathedral pastilles fumed in its holder. "Ah!" Then with relief—

The little smoke that dies in moonlight cold.

Evidently he was snared by the rhymes of his first verse, for he wrote and rewrote "gold—cold—mold" many times. Again he sought inspiration from the advertisement, and set down, without erasure, the line I had overheard:—

And threw warm gules on Madeleine's young breast.

As I remembered the original it is "fair"—a trite word—instead of "young," and I found myself nodding approval, though I admitted that the attempt to reproduce "its little smoke in pallid moonlight died" was a failure.

Followed without a break ten or fifteen lines of bald prose—the naked soul's confession of its physical yearning for its beloved—unclean as we count uncleanliness; unwholesome, but human exceedingly; the raw material, so it seemed to me in that hour and in that place, whence Keats wove the twenty-sixth, seventh, and eighth stanzas of his poem. Shame I had none in overseeing this revelation; and my fear had gone with the smoke of the pastille.

"That's it," I murmured. That's how it's blocked out. Go on! Ink it in, man. Ink it in!"

Mr. Shaynor returned to broken verse wherein "loveliness" was made to rhyme with a desire to look upon "her empty dress." He picked up a fold of the gay, soft blanket, spread it over one hand, caressed it with infinite tenderness, thought, muttered, traced some snatches which I could not decipher, shut his eyes drowsily, shook his head, and dropped the stuff. Here I found myself at fault, for I could not then see (as I do now) in what manner a red, black, and yellow Austrian blanket colored his dreams.

In a few minutes he laid aside his pen, and, chin on hand, considered the shop with thoughtful and intelligent eyes. He threw down the blanket, rose, passed along a line of drug-drawers, and read the names on the labels aloud. Returning, he took from his desk Christy's *New Commercial Plants* and the old Culpepper that I had given him, opened and laid them side by side with a clerkly air, all trace of passion gone from his face, read first in one and then in the other, and paused with pen behind his ear.

"What wonder of Heaven's coming now?" I thought.

"Manna—manna—manna," he said at last, under wrinkled brows. "That's what I wanted. Good! Now then! Now then! Good! Good! Oh, by God, that's good!" His voice rose and he spoke rightly and fully without a falter:—

> *Candied apple, quince and plum and gourd,*
> *And jellies smoother than the creamy curd,*
> *And lucent syrups tinct with cinnamon,*
> *Manna and dates in Argosy transferred*
> *From Fez; and spiced dainties, every one*
> *From silken Samarcand to cedared Lebanon.*

He repeated it once more, using "blander" for "smoother" in the second line; then wrote it down without erasure, but this time (my set eyes missed no stroke of any word) he substituted "soother" for his atrocious second thought, so that it came away under his hand as it is written in the book—as it is written in the book.

A wind went shouting down the street, and on the heels of the wind followed a spurt and rattle of rain.

After a smiling pause—and good right had he to smile—he began anew, always tossing the last sheet over his shoulder:—

> *The sharp rain falling on the window-pane,*
> *Rattling sleet—the wind-blown sleet.*

Then prose: "It is very cold of mornings when the wind brings rain and sleet with it. I heard the sleet on the window-pane outside, and thought of you, my darling. I am always thinking of you. I wish we could both run away like two lovers into the storm and get that little cottage by the sea which we are always thinking about, my own dear darling. We could sit and watch the sea beneath our windows. It would be a fairyland all of our own—a fairy sea—a fairy sea. . . ."

He stopped, raised his head, and listened. The steady drone of the Channel along the seafront that had borne us company so long leaped up a note to the sudden fuller surge that signals the change from ebb to flood. It beat in like the change of step throughout an army—this renewed pulse of the sea—and filled our ears till they, accepting it, marked it no longer.

> *A fairyland for you and me*
> *Across the foam—beyond . . .*
> *A magic foam, a perilous sea.*

He grunted again with effort and bit his underlip. My throat dried, but I dared not gulp to moisten it lest I should break the spell that was drawing him nearer and nearer to the high-water mark but two of the sons of Adam have reached. Remember that in all the millions permitted there are no more than five—five little lines—of which one can say: "These are pure Magic. These are the clear Vision. The rest is only poetry." And Mr. Shaynor was playing hot and cold with two of them!

I vowed no unconscious thought of mine should influence the blindfold soul, and pinned myself desperately to the other three, repeating and re-repeating:—

> *A savage spot as holy and enchanted*
> *As e'er beneath a waning moon was haunted*
> *By woman wailing for her demon lover.*

But though I believed, my brain thus occupied, my every sense hung upon the writing under the dry, bony hand, all brown-fingered with chemicals and cigarette smoke.

> *Our windows fronting on the dangerous foam,*

(he wrote, after long, irresolute snatches), and then—

> *Our open casements facing desolate seas*
> *Forlorn—forlorn—*

Here again his face grew peaked and anxious with that sense of loss I had first seen when the Power snatched him. But this time the agony was tenfold keener. As I watched it mounted like mercury in the tube. It lighted his face from within till I thought the visibly scourged soul must leap forth naked between his jaws, unable to endure. A drop of sweat trickled from my forehead down my nose and splashed on the back of my hand.

> *Our windows facing on the desolate seas*
> *And pearly foam of magic fairyland—*

"Not yet—not yet," he muttered, "wait a minute. *Please* wait a minute. I shall get it then—

> *Our magic windows fronting on the sea,*
> *The dangerous foam of desolate seas..*
> *For aye.*

Ouh, my God!"
From head to heel he shook—shook from the marrow of his bones outwards—then leaped to his feet with raised arms, and slid the chair screeching across the tiled floor where it struck the drawers behind and fell with a jar. Mechanically, I stooped to recover it.
As I rose, Mr. Shaynor was stretching and yawning at leisure.
"I've had a bit of a doze," he said. "How did I come to knock the chair over? You look rather—"
"The chair startled me," I answered. "It was so sudden in this quiet."
Young Mr. Cashell behind his shut door was offendedly silent.
"I suppose I must have been dreaming," said Mr. Shaynor.
"I suppose you must," I said. "Talking of dreams—I—I noticed you writing—before—"

He flushed consciously.

"I meant to ask you if you've ever read anything written by a man called Keats."

"Oh! I haven't much time to read poetry, and I can't say that I remember the name exactly. Is he a popular writer?"

"Middling. I thought you might know him because he's the only poet who was ever a druggist. And he's rather what's called the lover's poet."

"Indeed. I must dip into him. What did he write about?"

"A lot of things. Here's a sample that may interest you."

Then and there, carefully, I repeated the verse he had twice spoken and once written not ten minutes ago.

"Ah! Anybody could see he was a druggist from that line about the tinctures and syrups. It's a fine tribute to our profession."

"I don't know," said young Mr. Cashell, with icy politeness, opening the door one half-inch, "if you still happen to be interested in our trifling experiments. But, should such be the case—"

I drew him aside, whispering, "Shaynor seemed going off into some sort of fit when I spoke to you just now. I thought, even at the risk of being rude, it wouldn't do to take you off your instruments just as the call was coming through. Don't you see?"

"Granted—granted as soon as asked," he said, unbending. "I *did* think it a shade odd at the time. So that was why he knocked the chair down?"

"I hope I haven't missed anything," I said.

"I'm afraid I can't say that, but you're just in time for the end of a rather curious performance. You can come in too, Mr. Shaynor. Listen, while I read it off."

The Morse instrument was ticking furiously. Mr. Cashell interpreted: " '*K.K.V. Can make nothing of your signals.*' " A pause. " '*M.M.V.M.M.V. Signals unintelligible. Purpose anchor Sandown Bay. Examine instruments tomorrow.*' " Do you know what that means? It's a couple of men-o'-war working Marconi signals off the Isle of Wight. They are trying to talk to each other. Neither can read the other's messages, but all their messages are being taken in by our receiver here. They've been going on for ever so long. I wish you could have heard it."

"How wonderful!" I said. "Do you mean we're overhearing Portsmouth ships trying to talk to each other—that we're eavesdropping across half South England?"

"Just that. Their transmitters are all right, but their receivers are out of order, so they only get a dot here and a dash there. Nothing clear."

"Why is that?"

"God knows—and Science will know tomorrow. Perhaps the induction is faulty; perhaps the receivers aren't tuned to receive just the number of vibrations per second that the transmitter sends. Only a word here and there. Just enough to tantalize."

Again the Morse sprang to life.

"That's one of 'em complaining now. Listen: *Disheartening— most disheartening.*' It's quite pathetic. Have you ever seen a spiritualistic seance? It reminds me of that sometimes—odds and ends of messages coming out of nowhere—a word here and there— no good at all."

"But mediums are all impostors," said Mr. Shaynor, in the doorway, lighting an asthma-cigarette. "They only do it for the money they can make. I've seen 'em."

"Here's Poole, at last—clear as a bell. L.L.L. *Now* we shan't be long." Mr. Cashell rattled the keys merrily. "Anything you'd like to tell 'em?"

"No, I don't think so," I said. "I'll go home and get to bed. I'm feeling a little tired."

Harry Turtledove

The Last Article

From *The Magazine of Fantasy & Science Fiction*, 1988.

Peaceful resistance worked in ending segregation in the American South, for the suffragettes in England, and for Gandhi against the British. But what if Gandhi had gone up against the Third Reich?

B. A.

Nonviolence is the first article of my faith. It is also the last article of my creed.

—Mohandas Gandhi

The one means that wins the easiest victory over reason: terror and force.

—Adolf Hitler, *Mein Kampf*

THE TANK RUMBLED DOWN THE RAJPATH, PAST THE RUINS OF THE Memorial Arch toward the India Gate. The gateway arch was still standing, although it had taken a couple of shell hits in the fighting before New Delphi fell. The Union Jack fluttered above it.

British troops lined both sides of the Rajpath, watching silently as the tank rolled past them. Their Khaki uniforms were filthy and torn; many wore bandages. They had the weary, past-caring stares of beaten men, though the Army of India had fought until flesh and munitions gave out.

The India gate drew near. A military bank smartened up for the occasion began to play as the tank went past. The bagpipes sounded thin and lost in the hot, humid air.

A single man stood waiting in the shadow of the gate. Field Marshal Walther Model leaned down into the cupola of the Panzer IV. "No one can match the British ceremonies of this sort," he said to his aide.

Major Dieter Lasch laughed, a bit unkindly. "They've had

enough practice, sir," he answered raising his voice to be heard over the flatulent roar of the tank's engine.

"What is that tune?" the field marshal asked. "Does it have a meaning?"

"It's called 'The World Turned Upside Down,' " said Lasch, who had been involved with his British opposite number in planning the formal surrender. "Lord Conwallis's army musicians played it when he yielded to the Americans at Yorktown."

"Ah, the Americans." Model was for a moment so lost in his own thoughts that his monocle threatened to slip from his right eye. He screwed it back in. The single lens was the only thing he shared with the clichéd image of a high German officer. He was no lean, hawk-faced Prussian. But his rounded features were unyielding, and his stocky body sustained the energy of his will better than the thin, dyspeptic frames of so many aristocrats. "The Americans," he repeated. "Well, that will be the next step, won't it? But enough. One thing at a time."

The panzer stopped. The driver switched off the engine. The sudden quiet was startling. Model leaped nimbly down. He had been leaping down from tanks for eight years now, since his days as a staff officer for the IV Corps in the Polish campaign.

The man in the shadows stepped forward, saluted. Flashbulbs lit his long, tired face as German photographers recorded the moment for history. The Englishman ignored the cameras and cameramen alike. "Field Marshal Model," he said politely. He might have been about to discuss the weather.

Model admired his sangfroid. "Field Marshal Auchinleck," he replied, returned the salute and giving Auchinleck a last few seconds to remain his equal. Then he came back to the matter at hand. "Field Marshal, have you signed the instrument of surrender of the British Army of India to the forces of the Reich?"

"I have," Auchinleck replied. He reached into the left pocket of his battle dress, removed a folded sheet of paper. Before handing it to Model, though, he said, "I should like to request your permission to make a brief statement at this time."

"Of course, sir. You may say what you like, at whatever length you like." In victory, Model could afford to be magnanimous. He had even granted Marshal Zhukov leave to speak in the Soviet capitulation at Kuibyshev, before the marshal was taken out and shot.

"I thank you." Auchinleck stiffly dipped his head. "I will say, then, that I find the terms I have been forced to accept to be cruelly hard on the brave men who have served under my command."

"That is your privilege, sir." But Model's round face was no longer kindly, and his voice had iron in it as he replied, "I must remind you, however, that my treating with you at all under the rules of war is an act of mercy for which Berlin may yet reprimand me. When Britain surrendered in 1941, all Imperial forces were also ordered to lay down their arms. I daresay you did not expect us to come so far, but I would be within my rights in reckoning you no more than so many bandits."

A slow flush darkened Auchinleck's cheeks. "We gave you a bloody good run for bandits."

"So you did." Model remained polite. He did not say he would ten times rather fight straight-up battles than deal with the partisans who to this day harassed the Germans and their allies in occupied Russia. "Have you anything further to add?"

"No, sir, I do not." Auchinleck gave the German the signed surrender, handed him his sidearm. Model put the pistol in the empty holster he wore for the occasion. It did not fit well; the holster was made for a Walther P-38, not this man-killing brute of a Webley and Scott. That mattered little, though—the ceremony was almost over.

Auchinleck and Model exchanged salutes for the last time. The British field marshal stepped away. A German lieutenant came up to lead him into captivity.

Major Lasch waved his left hand. The Union Jack came down from the flagpole on the India Gate. The swastika rose to replace it.

■ ■ ■

Lasch tapped discreetly on the door, stuck his head into the field marshal's office. "That Indian politician is here for his appointment with you, sir."

"Oh yes. Very well, Dieter, send him in." Model had been dealing with Indian politicians even before the British surrender, and with hordes of them now that the resistance was over. He had no more liking for the breed than for Russian politicians, or even German ones. No matter what pious principles they spouted, his experience was that they were all out for their own good first.

The small, frail brown man the aide showed in made him wonder. The Indian's emaciated frame and the plain white cotton

loincloth that was his only garment contrasted starkly with the
Victorian splendor of the Viceregal Palace from which Model was
administering the Reich's new conquest. "Sit down, Herr Gandi,"
the field marshal urged.

"I thank you very much, sir." As he took his seat, Gandhi
seemed a child in an adult's chair: it was much too wide for him,
and its soft, overstuffed cushions hardly sagged under his meager
weight. But his eyes, Model saw, were not child's eyes. They
peered with disconcerting keenness through his wire-framed spectacles as he said, "I have come to inquire when we may expect
German troops to depart from our country."

Model leaned forward, frowning. For a moment he thought he
had misunderstood Gandhi's Gujarati-flavored English. When he
was sure he had not, he said, "Do you think perhaps we have
come all this way as tourists?"

"Indeed I do not." Gandhi's voice was sharp with disapproval.
"Tourists do not leave so many dead behind them."

Model's temper kindled. "No, tourists do not pay such a high
price for the journey. Having come regardless of that cost, I assure
you we shall stay."

"I am very sorry, sir; I cannot permit it."

"You cannot?" Again, Model had to concentrate to keep his
monocle from falling out. He had heard arrogance from politicians before, but this scrawny old devil surpassed belief. "Do you
forget I can call my aide and have you shot behind this building?
You would not be the first, I assure you."

"Yes, I know that," Gandhi said sadly. "If you have that fate in
mind for me, I am an old man. I will not run."

Combat had taught Model a hard indifference to the prospect
of injury or death. He saw the older man possessed something of
the same sort, however he had acquired it. A moment later he
realized his threat had not only failed to frighten Gandhi, but had
actually amused him. Disconcerted, the field marshal said, "Have
you any serious issues to address?"

"Only the one I named just now. We are a nation of more than
300 million; it is no more just for Germany to rule us than for
the British."

Model shrugged. "If we are able to, we will. We have the
strength to hold what we have conquered, I assure you."

"Where there is no right, there can be no strength," Gandhi
said. "We will not permit you to hold us in bondage."

"Do you think to threaten me?" Model growled. In fact, though, the Indian's audacity surprised him. Most of the locals had fallen over themselves, fawning on their new masters. Here, at least, was a man out of the ordinary.

Gandhi was still shaking his head, although Model saw he had still not frightened him (a man out of the ordinary indeed, thought the field marshal, who respected courage when he found it). "I make no threats, sir, but I will do what I believe to be right."

"Most noble," Model said, but to his annoyance the words came out sincere rather than with the sardonic edge he had intended. He had heard such canting phrases before, from Englishmen, from Russians, yes, and from Germans as well. Somehow, though, this Gandhi struck him as one who always meant exactly what he said. He rubbed his chin, considering how to handle such an intransigent.

A large green fly came buzzing into the office. Model's air of detachment vanished the moment he heard that malignant whine. He sprang from his seat, swatted at the fly. He missed. The insect flew around awhile longer, then settled in the arm of Gandhi's chair. "Kill it," Model told him. "Last week one of those accursed things bit me on the neck, and I still have the lump to prove it."

Gandhi brought his hand down, but several inches from the fly. Frightened, it took off. Gandhi rose. He was surprisingly nimble for a man nearing eighty. He chivvied the fly out of the office, ignoring Model, who watched his performance in openmouthed wonder.

"I hope it will not trouble you again," Gandhi said, returning as calmly as if he had done nothing out of the ordinary. "I am one of those who practice ahimsa: I will do no injury to any living thing."

Model remembered the fall of Moscow, and the smell of burning bodies filling the chilly autumn air. He remembered machine guns knocking down cosack cavalry before they could close, and the screams of the wounded horses, more heartrending than any woman's. He knew of other things, too, things he had not seen for himself and of which he had no desire to learn more.

"Herr Gandhi," he said, "how do you propose to bend to your will someone who opposes you, if you will not use force for the purpose?"

"I have never said I will not use force, sir." Gandhi's smile invited the field marshal to enjoy with him the distinction he was making. "I will not use violence. If my people refuse to cooperate in any way with yours, how can you compel them? What choice will you have but to grant us leave to do as we will?"

Without the intelligence estimates he had read, Model would have dismissed the Indian as a madman. No madman, though, could have caused the British so much trouble. But perhaps the decadent Raj simply had not made them afraid enough. Model tried again. "You understand that what you have said is treason against the Reich," he said harshly.

Gandhi bowed in his seat. "You may, of course, do what you will with me. My spirit will in any case survive among my people."

Model felt his face heat. Few men were immune to fear. Just his luck, he thought sourly, to have run into one of them. "I warn you, *Herr* Gandhi, to obey the authority of the officials of the Reich, or it will be the worse for you."

"I will do what I believe to be right, and nothing else. If you Germans exert yourselves toward the freeing of India, joyfully will I work with you. If not, then I regret we must be foes."

The field marshal gave him one last chance to reason. "Were it you and I alone, there might be some doubt as to what would happen." Not much, he thought, not when Gandhi was twenty-odd years older and thin enough to break like a stick. He fought down the irrelevance, went on, "But where, *Herr* Gandhi, is your *Wehrmacht?*"

Of all things, he had least expected to amuse the Indian again. Yet Gandhi's eyes unmistakably twinkled behind the lenses of his spectacles. "Field Marshal, I have an army too."

Model's patience, never of the most enduring sort, wore thin all at once. "Get out!" he snapped.

Gandhi stood, bowed, and departed. Major Lasch stuck his head into the office. The field marshal's glare drove him out again in a hurry.

■   ■   ■

"Well?" Jawaharlal Nehru paced back and forth. Tall, slim, and saturnic he towered over Gandhi without dominating him. "Dare we use the same police against the Germans that we employed against the English?"

"If we wish our land free, dare we do otherwise?" Gandhi replied. "They will not grant our wish of their own volition. Model struck me as a man not much different from various British leaders whom we have succeeded in vexing in the past." He smiled at the memory of what passive resistance had done to officers charged with combating it.

"Very well, satyagraha it is." But Nehru was not smiling. He had less humor than his older colleague.

Gandhi teased him gently, "Do you fear another spell in prison, then?" Both men had spent time behind bars during the war, until the British released them in a last, vain effort to rally the support of the Indian people to the Raj.

"You know better." Nehru refused to be drawn, and persisted, "The rumors that come out of Europe frighten me."

"Do you tell me you take them seriously?" Gandhi shook his head in surprise and a little reproof. "Each side in any war will always paint its opponents as blackly as it can."

"I hope you are right, and that is all. Still, I confess I would feel more at ease with what we plan to do if you found me one Jew, officer or other rank, in the army now occupying us."

"You would be hard-pressed to find any among the forces they defeated. The British have little love for Jews, either."

"Yes, but I daresay it could be done. With the Germans, they are banned by law. The English would never make such a rule. And while the laws are vile enough, I think of the tales that man Wiesenthal told, the one who came here—the gods know how—across Russia and Persia from Poland."

"Those I do not believe," Gandhi said firmly. "No nation could act in that way and hope to survive. Where could men be found to carry out such horrors?"

"Azad Hind," Nehru said, quoting the "Free India" motto of the locals who had fought on the German side.

But Gandhi shook his head. "They are only soldiers, doing as soldiers have always done. Wiesenthal's claims are for an entirely different order of bestiality, one that could not exist without destroying the fabric of the state that gave it birth."

"I hope very much you are right," Nehru said.

■ ■ ■

Walther Model slammed the door behind him hard enough to make his aide, whose desk faced away from the field marshal's office, jump in alarm. "Enough of this twaddle for one day," Model said. "I need schnapps, to get the taste of these Indians out of my mouth. Come along if you care to, Dieter."

"Thank you, sir." Major Lasch threw down his pen, eagerly got to his feet. "I sometimes think conquering India was easier than ruling it will be."

Model rolled his eyes. "I know it was. I would ten times rather be planning a new campaign than sitting here bogged down in pettifogging details. The sooner Berlin sends me people trained in colonial administration, the happier I will be."

The bar might have been taken from an English pub. It was dark, quiet, and paneled in walnut; a dartboard still hung on the wall. but a German sergeant in field gray stood behind the bar, and, despite the lazily turning ceiling fan, the temperature was close to thirty-five Celsius. The one might have been possible in occupied London, the other not.

Model knocked back his first shot at a gulp. He sipped his second more slowly, savoring it. Warmth spread through him, warmth that had nothing to do with the heat of the evening. He leaned back in his chair, steepled his fingers. "A long day," he said.

"Yes, sir," Lasch agreed. "After the effrontery of that Gandhi, any day would seem a long one. I've rarely seen you so angry." Considering Model's temper, that was no small statement.

"Ah, yes, Ghandi." Model's tone was reflective rather than irate; Lasch looked at him curiously. The field marshal said, "For my money, he's worth a dozen of the ordinary sort."

"Sir?" The aide no longer tried to hide his surprise.

"He is an honest man. He tells me what he thinks, and will stick by that. I may kill him—I may have to kill him—but he and I will both know why, and I will not change his mind." Model took another sip of schnapps. He hesitated, as if unsure whether to go on. At last he did. "Do you know, Dieter, after he left I had a vision?"

"Sir?" Now Lasch was alarmed.

The field marshal might have read his aide's thoughts. He chuckled wryly. "No, no, I am not about to swear off eating beef-steak and wear sandals instead of my boots, that I promise. But I saw myself as a Roman procurator, listening to the rantings of some early Christian priest."

Lasch raised an eyebrow. Such musings were unlike Model, who was usually direct to the point of bluntness and altogether materialistic—assets in the makeup of a general officer. The major cautiously sounded these unexpected depths: "How do you suppose the Roman felt, facing that kind of man?"

"Bloody confused, I suspect," Model said, which sounded more like him. "And because he and his comrades did not know how to handle such fanatics, you and I are Christians today, Dieter."

"So we are." The major rubbed his chin. "Is that a bad thing?"

Model laughed and finished his drink. "From your point of view or mine, no. But I doubt that old Roman would agree with us, any more than Gandhi agrees with me over what will happen next here. But then, I have two advantages over the dead procurator." He raised his finger; the sergeant hurried over to fill his glass.

At Lasch's nod, the young man also poured more schnapps for him. The major drank, then said, "I should hope so. We are more civilized, more sophisticated, than the Romans ever dreamed of being."

But model was still in that fey mood. "Are we? My procurator was such a sophisticate that he tolerated anything, and never saw the danger in a few who would not do the same. Our Christian God, though, is a jealous god who puts up with no rivals. And one who is a National Socialist serves also the Volk, to whom he owes sole loyalty. I am immune to Gandhi's virus the way the Roman was not to the Christian's."

"Yes, that makes sense," Lasch agreed after a moment. "I had not thought of it in that way, but I see it is so. And what is our other advantage over the Roman procurator?"

Suddenly the field marshal looked hard and cold, much the way he had looked leading the tanks of the Third Panzer against the Kremlin compound. "The machine gun," he said.

■　■　■

The rising sun's rays made the sandstone of the Red Fort seem even more the color of blood. Gandhi frowned and turned his back on the fortress, not caring for that thought. Even at dawn the air was warm and muggy.

"I wish you were not here," Nehru told him. The younger man lifted his trademark fore-and-aft cap, scratched his graying hair, and glanced at the crowd growing around them. "The Germans' orders forbid assemblies, and they will hold you responsible for this gathering."

"I am, am I not?" Ghandi replied. "Would you have me send

my followers into danger I do not care to face myself? How would I presume to lead them afterward?"

"A general does not fight in the front ranks," Nehru came back. "If you are lost to our cause, will we be able to go on?"

"If not, then surely the cause is not worthy, yes? Now let us be going."

Nehru threw his hands in the air. Gandhi nodded, satisfied, and worked his way toward the head of the crowd. Men and women stepped aside to let him through. Still shaking his head, Nehru followed.

The crowd slowly began to march east up Chandni Chauk, the Street of Silversmiths. Some of the fancy shops had been wrecked in the fighting, more looted afterward. But others were opening up, their owners as happy to take German money as they had been to serve the British before.

One of the proprietors, a man who had managed to stay plump even through the past year of hardship, came rushing out of his shop when he saw the procession go by. He ran to the head of the march and spotted Nehru, whose height and elegant dress singled him out.

"Are you out of your mind?" the silversmith shouted. "The Germans have banned assemblies. If they see you, something dreadful will happen."

"Is it not dreadful that they take away the liberty that properly belongs to us?" Gandhi asked. The silversmith spun round. His eyes grew wide when he recognized the man who was speaking to him. Gandhi went on, "Not only is it dreadful, it is wrong. And so we do not recognize the Germans' right to ban anything we may choose to do. Join us, will you?"

"Great-souled one, I—I—," the silversmith spluttered. Then his glance slid past Ghandi. "The Germans!" he squeaked. He turned and ran.

Gandhi led the procession toward the approaching squad. The Germans stamped down Chandni Chauk as if they expected the people in front of them to melt from their path. Their gear, Ghandi thought, was not that much different from what British soldiers wore: ankle boots, shorts, and open-necked tunics. But their coal-scuttle helmets gave them a look of sullen, beetle-browed ferocity the British tin hat did not convey. Even for a man of Gandhi's equanimity, it was daunting, as no doubt it was intended to be.

"Hello, my friends," he said. "Do any of you speak English?"

"I speak it, a little," one of them replied. His shoulder straps had the twin pips of a sergeant major: he was the squad leader, then. He hefted his rifle, not menacingly, Gandhi thought, but to emphasize what he was saying. "Go to your homes back. This coming together is verboten."

"I am sorry, but I must refuse to obey your order," Gandhi said. "We are walking peacefully on our own street in our own city. We will harm no one, no matter what; this I promise you. But walk we will, as we wish." He repeated himself until he was sure the sergeant major understood.

The German spoke to his comrades in his own language. One of the soldiers raised his gun and with a nasty smile pointed at Gandhi. The Indian nodded politely. The German blinked to see him unafraid. The sergeant major slapped the rifle down. One of his men had a field telephone on his back. The sergeant major cranked it, waited for a reply, spoke urgently into it.

Nehru caught Gandhi's eye. His dark, tired gaze was full of worry. Somehow that nettled Gandhi more than the German's arrogance in ordering around his people. He began to walk forward again. The marchers followed him, flowing around the German squad like water flowing round a boulder.

The soldier who had pointed his rifle at Gandhi shouted in alarm. He brought up the weapon again. The sergeant major barked at him. Reluctantly, he lowered it.

"A sensible man," Gandhi said to Nehru. "He sees we do no injury to him or his, and so does none to us."

"Sadly, though, not everyone is so sensible," the younger man replied, "as witness his lance corporal there. And even a sensible man may not be well inclined to us. You notice he is still on the telephone."

■ ■ ■

The phone on Field Marshal Model's desk jangled. He jumped and swore; he had left orders he was to be disturbed only for an emergency. He had to find time to work. He picked up the phone. "This had better be good," he growled without preamble.

He listened, swore again, slammed the receiver down. "Lasch!" he shouted.

It was his aide's turn to jump. "Sir?"

"Don't just sit there on your fat arse," the field marshal said unfairly. "Call out my car and driver, and quickly. Then belt on your sidearm and come along. The Indians are doing something stupid. Oh yes, order out a platoon and have them come after us. Up on Chandni Chauk, the trouble is.''

■   ■   ■

Lasch called for the car and the troops, then hurried after Model. "A riot?" he asked as he caught up.

"No, no." Model moved his stumpy frame along so fast that the taller Lasch had to trot beside him. "Some of Gandhi's tricks, damn him."

The field marshal's Mercedes was waiting when he and his aide hurried out of the Viceregal palace. "Chandni Chauk," Model snapped as the driver held the door open for him. After that he sat in furious silence as the powerful car roared up Irwin road, round a third of Connaught circle, and north on Chelmsford road past the bombed out railway station until, for no reason Model could see, the street's name changed to Qutb road.

A little later the driver said, "Some kind of disturbance up ahead, sir."

"Disturbance?" Lasch echoed, leaned forward to peer through the windscreen. "It's a whole damned regiment's worth of Indians coming at us. Don't they know better than that? And what the devil," he added, his voice rising, "are so many of our men doing ambling along beside them? Don't they know they are supposed to break up this sort of thing?" In his indignation he did not notice he was repeating himself.

"I suspect they don't," Model said dryly. "Gandhi, I gather, can have that effect on people who aren't ready for his peculiar brand of stubbornness. That, however, does not include me." He tapped the driver on the shoulder. "Pull up about two hundred meters in front of the first rank of them, Joachim."

"Yes, sir."

Even before the car had stopped moving, Model jumped out of it. Lasch, hand on his pistol, was close behind, protesting, "What if one of those fanatics has a gun?"

"Then Colonel General Weilding assumes command, and a lot of Indians end up dead." Model strode toward Gandhi, ignoring the German troops who were drawing themselves to stiff, horrified attention at the sight of his field marshal's uniform. He would deal with them later. For the moment, Gandhi was more important.

He had stopped—which meant the rest of the marchers did,

too—and was waiting politely for Model to approach. The German commandant was not impressed. He thought Gandhi sincere, and could not doubt his courage, but none of that mattered at all. He said harshly, "You were warned against this sort of behavior."

Gandhi looked him in the eye. They were very much of a height. "And I told you, I do not recognize your right to give such orders. This is our country, not yours, and if some of us choose to walk on our streets, we will do so."

From behind Gandhi, Nehru's glance flicked worriedly from one of the antagonists to the other. Model noticed him only peripherally; if Nehru was already afraid, he could be handled whenever necessary. Gandhi was a tougher nut. The field marshal waved at the crowd behind the old man. "You are responsible for all these people. If harm comes to them, you will be to blame."

"Why should harm come to them? They are not soldiers. They do not attack your men. I told that to one of your sergeants, and he understood it, and refrained from hindering us. Surely you, sir, an educated, cultured man, can see that what I say is self-evident truth."

Model turned his head to speak to his aide in German: "If we did not have Goebbels, this would be the one for his job." He shuddered to think of the propaganda victory Gandhi would win if he got away with flouting German ordinances. The whole countryside would be boiling with partisans in a week. And he had already managed to hoodwink some Germans into letting him do it!

Then Gandhi surprised him again. "Ich danke Ihnen, Herr Generalfeldmarschall, aber das glaube ich kein Kompliment zu sein," he said in slow but clear German. "I thank you, field Marshal, but I believe that to be no compliment."

Having to hold his monocle in place helped Model keep his face straight. "Take it however you like," he said. "Get these people off the street, or they and you will face the consequences. We will do what you force us to."

"I force you to nothing. As for these people who follow, each does so of his or her own free will. We are free, and we will show it, not by violence, but through firmness of truth."

Now Model listened with only half an ear. He had kept Gandhi talking long enough for the platoon he had ordered to arrive. Half a dozen SdKfz 251 armored personnel carriers came clanking up. The men piled out of them. "Give me a firing line, three ranks deep," Model shouted. As the troops scrambled to obey, he waved the half-trucks into position behind them, all but blocking Qutb road. The half-trucks' commanders swiveled the machine guns at the front of the vehicles' troop compartments so they bore on the Indians.

Gandhi watched these preparations as calmly as if they had nothing to do with him. Again Model had to admire his calm. Gandhi's followers were less able to keep fear from their faces. Very few, though, used the pause to slip away. Gandhi's discipline was a long way from the military sort, but effective all the same.

"Tell them to disperse now, and we can still get away without bloodshed," the field marshal said.

"We will shed no one's blood, sir. But we will continue on our pleasant journey. Moving carefully, we will, I think be able to get between your large lorries there." Gandhi turned to wave his people foreword once more.

"You insolent—" Rage choked Model, which was as well, for it kept him from cursing Gandhi like a fishwife. To give him time to master his temper, he plucked his monocle from his eye and began polishing his lens with a silk handkerchief. He replaced his monocle, started to jam the handkerchief back into his trouser pocket, then suddenly had a better idea.

"Come Lasch," he said, and started toward the waiting German troops. About halfway to them, he dropped his handkerchief on the ground. He spoke in loud, simple German so his men and Gandhi could both follow: "If any Indians come past this spot, I wash my hands of them."

He might have known Gandhi would have a comeback ready. "That is what Pilate said also, you will recall, sir."

"Pilate washed his hands to avoid responsibility," the field marshal answered steadily; he was in control of himself again. "I accept it: I am responsible to my Fuhrer and to the Oberkommando-Wehrmacht for maintaining the Reich's control over India, and I will do what I see fit to carry out that obligation."

For the first time since they had come to know each other, Gandhi looked sad.

"I too, sir, have my responsibilities." He bowed slightly to Model.

Lasch chose that moment to whisper in his commander's ear:

"Sir, what of our men over there? Had you planned to leave them in the line of fire?"

The field marshal frowned. He had planned to do just that; the wretches deserved no better, for being taken in by Gandhi. But Lasch had a point. The platoon might balk at shooting countrymen, if it came to that. "You men," Model said sourly, jabbing his marshal's baton at them, "fall in behind the armored personnel carriers, at once."

The Germans' boots pounded on the macadam as they dashed to obey. They were still at right, then, with a clear order in front of them. Something, Model thought, but not much.

He had also worried that the Indians would take advantage of the moment of confusion to press forward, but they did not. Gandhi and Nehru and a couple of men were arguing among themselves. Model nodded once. Some of them knew he was earnest, then. And Gandhi's followers discipline, as the field marshal had thought a few minutes ago, was not of the military sort. He could not simply issue an order and know his will would be done.

■　■　■

"I issue no orders," Gandhi said "Let each man follow his conscience as he will—what else is freedom?"

"They will follow *you* if you go forward, great-souled one," Nehru replied, "and that German, I fear, means to carry out his threat. Will you throw your life away, and those of your countrymen?"

"I will not throw my life away," Gandhi said, but before the men around him could relax, he went on, "I will gladly give it, if freedom requires that. But I am one man. If I fall, others surely will carry on; perhaps the memory of me will serve to make them more steadfast."

He stepped forward.

"Oh damnation," Nehru said softly, and followed.

For all his vigor, Gandhi was far from young. Nehru did not need to nod to the marchers close by him; of their own accord, they hurried ahead of the man who had led them for so long, forming with their bodies a barrier between him and the German guns.

He tried to go faster. "Stop! Leave me my place! What are you doing?" he cried, though in his heart he understood only too well.

"This once, they will not listen to you," Nehru said.

"But, they must!" Gandhi peered through eyes dimmed now by tears as well as age. "Where is that stupid handkerchief? We must be almost to it."

■   ■   ■

"For the last time, I warn you to halt!" Model shouted. The Indians still came on. The sound of their feet, sandal-clad or bare, was like a growing murmur on the pavement, very different from the clatter of German boots. "Fools!" the field marshal muttered under his breath. He turned to his men. "Take your aim!"

The advance slowed when the rifles came up; of that Model was certain. For a moment he thought the ultimate threat would be enough to bring the marchers to their senses. But then they advanced again. The Polish cavalry had shown that same reckless bravery, charging with lances and sabers and carbines against the German tanks. Model wondered whether the inhabitants of the Reichsgeneral government of Poland thought the gallantry was worthwhile.

A man stepped on the field marshal's handkerchief. "Fire!" Model said.

A second passed. Two. Nothing happened. Model scowled at his men. Gandhi's deviltry had got into them; sneaky as a Jew, he was turning his appearance of weakness into a strange kind of strength. But then trained discipline paid its dividend. One finger tightened on a Muser trigger. A single shot rang out. As if it were a signal that recalled the other men to their duty, they, too, began to fire. From the armored personnel carriers, the machine guns started there deadly chatter. Model heard screams above the gunfire.

The volley smashed into the front ranks of marchers at close range. Men fell. Others ran, or tried to, only to be held by the power of the stream still advancing behind them. Once begun, the German methodically poured fire into the column of Indians. The march dissolved into a panic-stricken mob.

Gandhi still tried to press forward. A fleeing wounded man smashed into him splashing blood and knocking him to the ground. Nehru and another man immediately lay down on top of him.

"Let me up! Let me up!" he shouted.

"No," Nehru screamed in his ear. "With shooting like this, you are in the safest spot you can be. We need you, and need you alive. Now we have martyrs around whom to rally our cause."

"Now we have dead husbands and wives, fathers and mothers. Who will tend to their loved ones?"

Gandhi had no more time for protest. Nehru and the other man hauled him to his feet and dragged him away. Soon they were among their people, all running now from the German guns. A bullet struck the back of the unknown man who was helping Gandhi escape. Gandhi heard the slap of the impact, felt the man jerk. Then the strong grip on him loosened as the man fell.

He tried to tear free from Nehru. Before he could, another Indian laid hold of him. Even at that horrid moment, he felt the irony of his predicament. All his life he had championed individual liberty, and here his own followers were robbing him of his. In other circumstances, it might have been funny.

"In here," Nehru shouted. Several people had already broken down the door to a shop and, Gandhi saw a moment later, the rear exit as well. Then he was hustled into the alley behind the shop, and through a maze of lanes that reminded him of the old Delhi, which, unlike its British designed sister city, was an Indian town through and through.

At last the nameless man with Gandhi and Nehru knocked on the back door of the tearoom. The woman who opened it gasped to recognize her unexpected guests, then pressed her hands together in front of her and stepped aside to let them in. "You will be safe here," the man said, "at least for a little while. Now I must see to my own family."

"From the bottom of our hearts we thank you," Nehru replied as the fellow hurried away. Gandhi said nothing. He was winded, battered, and filled with anguish at the failure of the march and at the suffering it had brought to so many marchers and to their kinsfolk.

The woman sat the two fugitive leaders at a small table in the kitchen, served them tea and cakes. "I will leave you now, best ones," she said gently, "lest those out front wonder why I neglect them for so long."

Gandhi left the cake on his plate. He sipped the tea. Its warmth began to restore him physically, but the wound in his spirit would never heal. "The Armritsar massacre pales beside this," he said, setting down the empty cup. "There the British panicked and opened fire. This had nothing of panic about it. Model told me what he would do, and he did it." He shook his head, still hardly believing what he had just been through.

"So he did." Nehru had gobbled his cake like a starving wolf, and ate his companion's when he saw Gandhi did not want it. His once immaculate white jacket and pants were torn, filthy, and blood-spattered; his cap sat awry on his head. But his eyes, usually so somber, were lit with a fierce glow. "And by his brutality, he has delivered himself into our hands. No one now can imagine the Germans have anything but their own interests at heart. We will gain followers all over the country. After this, not a wheel will turn in India."

"Yes, I will declare the satyagraha," Gandhi said. "Noncooperation will show how we reject foreign rule, and will cost the Germans dear because they will not be able to exploit us. The combination of nonviolence and determined spirit will surely shame them into granting us our liberty."

"There—you see." Encouraged by his mentor's rally, Nehru rose and came round the table to embrace the older man. "We will triumph yet."

"So we will," Gandhi said, and sighed heavily. He had pursued India's freedom for half his long life, and this change of masters was a setback he had not truly planned for, even after England and Russia fell. The British were finally beginning to listen to him when the Germans swept them aside. Now he had to begin anew. He sighed again. "It will cost our poor people dear, though."

"Cease firing," Model said. Few good targets were left on Qutb road; almost all the Indians in the procession were down or had run from the guns.

Even after the bullets stopped, the street was far from silent. Most of the people the German platoon had shot were alive and shrieking; as if he needed more proof, the Russian campaign had taught the field marshal how hard human beings were to kill outright.

Still, the din distressed him, and evidently Lasch as well. "We ought to put them out of their misery," the major said.

"So we should." Model had a happy inspiration. "And I know just how. Come with me."

The two men turned their backs on the carnage and walked around the row of armored personnel carriers. As they passed the lieutenant commanding the platoon, Model nodded to him and said, "Well done."

The lieutenant saluted. "Thank you, sir." The soldiers in earshot nodded at one another: nothing bucked up the odds of getting promoted like performing under the commander's eye.

The Germans behind the armored vehicles were not so proud of themselves. They were the ones who had let the march get this big and come this far in the first place. Model slapped his boot with his field marshal's baton. "You all deserve courts-martial," he said coldly, glaring at them. "You know the orders concerning native assemblies, yet there you were tagging along, more like sheepdogs than soldiers." He spat in disgust

"But sir—" began one of them—a sergeant major, Model saw. He subsided in a hurry when Model's gaze swung his way.

"Speak," the field marshal urged. "Enlighten me—tell me what possessed you to act in the disgraceful way you did. Was it some evil spirit, perhaps? This country abounds with them, if you listen to the natives—as you all too obviously have been."

The sergeant major flushed under Model's sarcasm, but finally burst out, "Sir, it didn't look to me as if they were up to any harm, that's all. The old man heading them up swore they were peaceful, and he looked too feeble to be anything but, if you take my meaning."

Model's smile had all the warmth of a Moscow December night. "And so in your wisdom you set aside the commands you had received. The results of that wisdom you hear now." The field marshal briefly let himself listen to the cries of the wounded, a sound the war had taught him to screen out. "Now then, come with me—yes you, Sergeant Major, and the rest of your shirkers, too, or those of you who wish to avoid a court."

As he had known they would, they all trooped after him. "There is your handiwork," he said, pointing to the shambles in the street. His voice hardened. "You are responsible for those people lying there—had you acted as you should have, you would have broken up that march long before it ever got so far or so large. Now the least you can do is give those people their release." He set hands on hips, waited.

No one moved. "Sir?" the sergeant major said faintly. He seemed to have become the group's spokesman.

Model made an impatient gesture. "Go on, finish them. A bullet in the back of the head will quiet them once and for all."

"In cold blood, sir?" The sergeant major had not wanted to understand him before. Now he had no choice.

The field marshal was inexorable. "They—and you—disobeyed the Reich's commands. They made themselves liable to capital punishment the moment they gathered. You at least have the chance to atone, by carrying out this just sentence."

"I don't think I can," the sergeant major muttered.

He was probably just talking to himself, but Model gave him no chance to change his mind. He turned to the lieutenant of the platoon that had broken the march. "Place this man under arrest." After the sergeant major had been seized, Model turned his chill, monocled stare at the rest of the reluctant soldiers. "Any others?"

Two more men let themselves be arrested rather than draw their weapons. The field marshal nodded to the others. "Carry out your orders." He had an afterthought. "If you find Gandhi or Nehru out there, bring them to me alive."

The Germans moved out hesitantly. They were no *Eisatzkommandos,* and not used to this kind of work. Some looked away as they administered the first coup de grâce; one missed as a result, and had his bullet ricochet off the pavement and almost hit a comrade. But as the soldiers worked their way up Qutb road, they became quicker. More confident, and more competent. War was like that, Model thought. So soon one became used to what had been unimaginable.

After a while the flat cracks died away, but from lack of targets rather than reluctance. A few at a time, the soldiers returned to Model. "No sign of the two leaders?" he asked. They all shook their heads.

"Very well—dismissed. And obey your orders like good Germans henceforward."

"No further reprisals?" Lasch asked as the relieved troopers hurried away.

"No, let them go. They carried out their part of the bargain, and I will meet mine. I am a fair man, after all, Dieter."

"Very well, sir."

■   ■   ■

Gandhi listened with undisguised dismay as the shopkeeper babbled out his tale of horror. "This is madness!" he cried.

"I doubt Field Marshal Model, for his part, understands the principle of ahimsa," Nehru put in. Neither Gandhi nor he knew exactly where they were: a safe house somewhere not far from the center of Delphi was the best guess he could make. The men who brought the shopkeeper were masked. What one did not know, one could not tell the Germans if captured.

"Neither do you," the older man replied, which was true; Nehru had a more pragmatic nature than Gandhi. Gandhi went on, "Rather more to the point, neither do the British. And Model, to speak to, seemed no different from any high-ranking British military man. His specialty has made him harsh and rigid, but he is not stupid and does not appear unusually cruel."

"Just a simple soldier, doing his job." Nehru's irony was palpable.

"He must have gone insane," Gandhi said; it was the only explanation that made even the slightest sense of the massacre of the wounded. "Undoubtedly he will be censured when the news of this atrocity reaches Berlin, as General Dyer was by the British after Armritsar."

"Such is to be hoped." But again Nehru did not sound hopeful.

"How could it be otherwise, after such an appalling action? What government, what leaders could fail to be filled with humiliation and remorse at it?"

■ ■ ■

Model strode into the mess. The officers stood and raised their glasses in salute. "Sit, sit," the field marshal growled, using gruffness to hide his pleasure.

An Indian servant brought him a fair imitation of roast beef and Yorkshire pudding: better than they were eating in London these days, he thought. The servant was silent and unsmiling, but Model would only have noticed more about him had he been otherwise. Servants were supposed to assume a cloak of invisibility.

When the meal was done, Model took out his cigar case. The *Waffen-SS* officer on his left produced a lighter. Model leaned forward, puffed a cigar to life. "My thanks, *Brigadefuhrer*," the field marshal said. He had little use for SS titles of rank, but brigade commander was at least recognizably close to brigadier.

"Sir, it is my great pleasure," Jurgen Stroop declared. "You could not have handled things better. A lesson for the Indians— less than they deserve, too" (he also took no notice of the servant) "and a good one for your men as well. We train ours harshly, too."

Model nodded. He knew about SS training methods. No one denied that the *Wehrmacht* had better officers.

Stoop drank. "A lesson," he repeated in a pedantic tone that went oddly with the SS's reputation for aggressiveness. "Force is the only thing the racially inferior can understand. Why, when I was in Warsaw—"

That had been four or five years ago, Model suddenly recalled. Stroop had been a *Brigadefuhrer* then, too, if memory served; no wonder he was still one now, even after all the hard fighting since. He was lucky not to be a buck private. Imagine letting a pack of desperate, starving Jews chew up the finest troops in the world.

And imagine, afterward, submitting a seventy-five-page operations report bound in leather and grandiosely called "The Warsaw Ghetto Is No More." And imagine, with all that, having the crust to boast about it afterward. No wonder the man sounded like a pompous ass. He was a pompous ass, and an inept butcher to boot. Model had done enough butchery before today's work— anyone who fought in Russia learned all about butchery—but he had never botched it.

He did not revel in it, either. He wished Stroop would shut up. He thought about telling the *Brigadefuhrer* he would sooner have been listening to Gandhi. The look on the fellow's face, he thought, would be worth it. But no. One could never be sure who was listening. Better safe.

■   ■   ■

The shortwave set crackled to life. It was in a secret cellar. A tiny, dark, hot room lit only by the glow of its dial and by the red end of the cigarette in its owner's mouth. The Germans had made not turning in a radio a capital crime. Of course, Gandhi thought, harboring him was also a capital crime. That weighed on his conscience. But the man knew the risk he was taking.

The fellow, (Gandhi knew him only as Lal), fiddled with the controls. "Usually we listen to the Americans," he said. "There is some hope of the truth from them. But tonight you want to hear Berlin."

"Yes," Gandhi said. "I must learn what action is to be taken against Model."

"If any," Nehru added. He was once again impeccably attired in white, which made him the most easily visible object in the cellar.

"We have argued this before," Gandhi said tiredly. "No government can uphold the author of a cold-blooded slaughter of wounded men and women. The world would cry out in abhorrence."

Lal said, "That government controls too much of the world already." He adjusted the tuning knob again. After a burst of static, the strains of a Strauss waltz filled the room. Lal grunted in satisfaction. "We are a little early yet."

After a few minutes the incongruously sweet music died away. "This is radio Berlin's English-language channel," an announcer declared. "In a moment, the news program." Another German tune rang out: the Horst Wessel song. Gandhi's nostrils flared with distaste.

A new voice came over the air. "Good day. This is William Joyce." The nasal Oxonian accent was that of the archetypal British aristocrat, now vanished from India as well as England. It was the accent that flavored Gandhi's own English, and Nehru's as well. In fact, Gandhi had heard, Joyce was a New York born rabble-rouser of Irish blood who also happened to be a passionately sincere Nazi. The combination struck the Indian as distressing.

"What did the English used to call him?" Nehru murmured. "Lord Haw-Haw?"

Gandhi waved his friends to silence. Joyce was reading the news, or what the Propaganda Ministry in Berlin wanted to present to English-speakers as the news.

Most of it was on the dull side: a trade agreement between Manchukuo, Japanese-dominated China, and Japanese-dominated Siberia; advances by German supported French troops against American supported French troops in a war by proxy in the African jungle. Slightly more interesting was the German warning about American interference in the East Asia Co-prosperity sphere.

One day soon, Gandhi thought, the two mighty powers of the old world would turn on the one great nation that stood between them. He feared the outcome. Thinking herself secure behind ocean barriers, the United States had stayed out of the European war. Now the war was bigger than Europe, and the ocean barriers no longer, but highways for her foes.

Lord Haw-Haw droned on and on. He gloated over the fate of the rebels hunted down in Scotland: they were publicly hanged. Nehru leaned forward. "Now," he guessed. Gandhi nodded.

But the commentator passed on to unlikely sounding boasts about the prosperity of Europe under the New Order. Against his will, Gandhi felt anger rise in him. Were Indians too insignifigant to the Reich even to be mentioned?

More music came from the radio: the first bars of the other German anthem, "Deutschland uber alles." William Joyce said solemnly, "And now, a special announcement from the Ministry for Administration of Aquired Territories. Reichsminister Reinhard Heydrich commends Field Marshal Walther Model's heroic suppression of insurrection in India, and warns that his leniency will not be repeated."

"Leniency!" Nehru and Gandhi burst out together, the latter making it into as much of a curse as he allowed himself.

As if explaining to them, the voice on the radio went on, "Henceforward, hostages will be taken at the slightest sound of disorder, and will be executed forthwith if it continues. Field Marshal Model had also placed a reward of fifty thousand rupees on the capture of the criminal revolutionary Gandhi, and twenty-five thousand on the capture of his henchman, Nehru."

"Deutschland uber alles" rang out again, to signal the end of the announcement. Joyce went on to the next piece of news. "Turn that off," Nehru said after a moment. Lal obeyed, plunging the cellar into complete darkness. Nehru surprised Gandhi by laughing. "I have never before been the henchman of a criminal revolutionary."

The older man might as well not have heard him. "They commended him," he said. "Commended!" Disbelief put the full tally of his years in his voice, which usually sounded much stronger and younger.

"What will you do?" Lal asked quietly. A match flared, dazzling in the dark, as he lit another cigarette.

"They shall not govern India in this fashion," Gandhi snapped. "Not a soul will cooperate with them from now on. We outnumber them a thousand to one; what can they accomplish without us? We shall use that to full advantage."

"I hope the price is not more than the people can pay," Nehru said.

"The British shot us down, too, and we were on our way toward prevailing," Gandhi said stoutly. As he would not have a few days before, though, he added, "So do I."

■   ■   ■

Field Marshal Model scowled and yawned at the same time. The pot of tea that should have been on his desk was nowhere to be found. His stomach growled. A plate of rolls should have been beside the teapot.

"How am I supposed to get anything done without breakfast?" he asked rhetorically, (no one was in the office to hear him complain). Rhetorical comment was not enough to satisfy him. "Lasch!" he shouted.

"Sir?" The aide came rushing in.

Model jerked his chin at the empty space on his desk where the silver tray full of good things should have been. "What's become of what's his name? Naoroji, that's it. If he's home with a hangover, he should have the courtesy to let us know."

"I will inquire with the liaison officer for native personnel, sir, and also have the kitchen staff send you up something to eat." Lasch picked up a telephone, spoke into it. The longer he talked, the less happy he looked. When he turned back to the field marshal, his expression was a good match for the stony one Model often wore. He said, "None of the locals has shown up for work today, sir."

"What? None?" Model's frown made his monocle dig into his cheek. He hesitated. "I will feel better if you tell me some new hideous malady has broken out among them."

Lasch spoke with the liaison officer again. He shook his head. "Nothing like that, sir—or at least," he corrected himself with the caution that made him a good aide, "nothing Captain Wechsler knows about."

Model's phone rang again. It startled him; he jumped. "Bitte?" he growled into the mouthpiece, embarrassed at starting even though only Lasch had seen. He listened. Then he growled again, in good earnest this time. He slammed the phone down. "That was our railway officer. Hardly any natives are coming into the station."

The phone rang again. "Bitte?" This time it was a swearword. Model snarled, cutting off whatever the man on the other end was saying, and hung up. "The damned clerks are staying out, too," he shouted at Lasch, as if it were the major's fault. "I know what's wrong with the bastard locals, by God—an overdose of Gandhi, that's what."

"We should have shot him dead at that riot he led," Lasch said angrily.

"Not for lack of effort that we didn't," Model said. Now that he saw where his trouble was coming from, he began thinking

like a General Staff-trained officer again. That discipline went
deep in him. His voice was cool and musing as he corrected his
aide: "It was no riot, Dieter. That man is a skilled agitator. Armed
with no more than words, he gave the British fits. Remember that
the Fuhrer started out as an agitator, too."

"Ah, but the Fuhrer wasn't above breaking heads to back up
what he said." Lasch smiled reminiscently, and raised a fist. He
was a Munich man, and wore on his sleeve the harsh mark that
showed party membership before 1933.

But the field marshal said, "You think Gandhi doesn't? His way
is to break them from inside out, to make his foes doubt themselves. Those soldiers who took courts rather than obey their commanding officer had their heads broken, wouldn't you say? Think
of him as a Russian tank commander, say, rather than as a political
agitator. He is fighting us every bit as much as the Russians did."

Lasch thought about it. Plainly he did not like it. "A coward's
way of fighting."

"The weak cannot use the weapons of the strong," Model
shrugged. "He does what he can, and skillfully. But I can make
his backers doubt themselves, too: see if I don't."

"Sir?"

"We'll start with the railway workers. They are the most essential to have back on the job, yes? Get a list of names. Cross off
every twentieth one. Send a squad to each of those homes, haul
the slackers out, and shoot them in the street. If the survivors
don't report tomorrow, do it again. Keep at it every day until they
go back or no workers are left."

"Yes, sir." Lasch hesitated. "Are you sure, sir?"

"Have you a better idea, Dieter? We have a dozen divisions
here; Gandhi has the whole subcontinent. I have to convince
them in a hurry that obeying me is a better idea than obeying
him. Obeying is what counts. I don't care a pfennig as to whether
they love me. Oderint, dum metuant."

"Sir?" The major had no Latin.

" 'Let them hate, so long as they fear.' "

"Ah," Lasch said. "Yes, I like that." He fingered his chin as he
thought. "In aid of which, the Muslims hereabouts like the Hin-
dus none too well. I dare say we could use them to help hunt
Gandhi down."

"Now that I like," Model said. "Most of our Indian Legion lads
are Muslims. They will know people, or know people who know

people. And"—the field marshal chuckled cynically—"the reward will do no harm, either. Now get those feelers in motion—and if they pay off, you'll probably have earned yourself a new pip on your shoulder boards."

"Thank you very much, sir!"

"My pleasure. As I say, you'll have earned it. So long as things go as they should, I am a very easy man to get along with. Even Gandhi could, if he wanted to. He will end up having caused a lot of people to be killed because he does not."

"Yes, sir," Lasch agreed. "If only he would see that, since we have won India from the British, we will not turn around and tamely yield it to those who could not claim it for themselves."

"You're turning into a political philosopher now, Dieter?"

"Ha! Not likely." But the major looked pleased as he picked up the phone.

■ ■ ■

"My dear friend, my ally, my teacher, we are losing," Nehru said as the messenger scuttled away from this latest in a series of what where hopefully called safe houses. "Day by day, more people return to their jobs."

Gandhi shook his head, slowly, as if the motion caused him physical pain. "But they must not. Each one who cooperates with the Germans sets back the day of his own freedom."

"Each one who fails to ends up dead," Nehru said dryly. "Most men lack your courage, great-souled one. To them, that carries more weight than the other. Some are willing to resist, but would rather take up arms than the restraint of satyagraha."

"If they take up arms, they will be defeated. The British could not beat the Germans with guns and tanks and planes; how shall we? Besides, if we shoot a German here and there, we give them the excuse they need to strike at us. When one of their lieutenants was waylaid last month, their bombers leveled a village in reprisal. Against those who fight through nonviolence, they have no such justification."

"They do not seem to need one, either," Nehru pointed out.

Before Gandhi could reply to that, a man burst into the hovel where they were hiding. "You must flee!" he cried. "The Germans have found this place! They are coming. Out with me, quick! I have a cart waiting."

Nehru snatched up the canvas bag in which he carried his few belongings. For a man used to being something of a dandy, the

haggard life of a fugitive came hard. Gandhi had never wanted
much. Now that he had nothing, that did not disturb him. He
rose calmly, followed the man who had come to warn them.

"Hurry!" the fellow shouted as they scrambled into his oxcart
while the humpbacked cattle watched indifferently with their liquid brown eyes. When Gandhi and Nehru were lying in the cart,
the man piled blankets and straw mats over them. He scrambled
up to take the reins, saying, "Inshallah, we shall be safely away
from here before the platoon arrives." He flicked a switch over
the backs of the cattle. They lowered indignantly. The cart rattled
away.

Lying in the sweltering semidarkness under the concealment
the man had draped on him, Gandhi peered through the chinks,
trying to figure out where in Delhi he was going next. He had
played the game more than once these past few weeks, though
he knew doctrine said he should not. The less he knew, the less
he could reveal. Unlike most men, though, he was confident he
could not be made to talk against his will.

"We are using the technique the American Poe called the 'pur-
loined letter,' I see," he remarked to Nehru. "We will be close by
the German barracks. They will not think to look for us there."

The younger man frowned. "I did not know we had safe houses
there," he said. Then he relaxed, as well as he could when folded
into too small a space. "Of course, I do not pretend to know
everything there is to know about such matters. It would be dangerous if I did."

"I was thinking much the same myself, though with me as subject of the sentence." Gandhi laughed quietly. "Try as we will, we
always have ourselves at the center of things, don't we?"

He had to raise his voice to finish. An armored personnel carrier came rumbling and rattling toward them, getting louder as
it approached. The silence when the driver suddenly killed the
engine was a startling contrast to the previous racket. Then there
was noise again, as soldiers shouted in German.

"What are they saying?" Nehru asked.

"Hush," Gandhi said absently: not from ill manners, but out
of the concentration he needed to follow German at all. After a
moment he resumed. "They are swearing at a black-bearded man,
asking why he flagged them down."

"Why would anyone flag down German sol—" Nehru began,
then stopped in abrupt dismay. The fellow who burst into their

hiding place wore a bushy black beard. "Now we better get out of—" again Nehru broke off in mid-sentence, this time because the oxcart driver was throwing off the coverings that concealed his two passengers.

Nehru started to get to his feet so he could try to scramble out and run. Too late—a rifle barrel that looked wide as a tunnel was shoved in his face as a German came dashing up to the cart. The big curved magazine said the gun was one of the automatic assault rifles that had wreaked such havoc among the British infantry. A burst would turn a man into a bloody hash. Nehru sank back in despair.

Gandhi, less spry than his friend, had only sat up in the bottom of the cart. "Good day, gentlemen," he said to the Germans peering down at him. His tone took no notice of their weapons.

"Down." The word was in such gutturally accented Hindi that Gandhi hardly understood it, but the accompanying gesture with a rifle was unmistakable.

His face a mask of misery, Nehru got out of the cart. A German helped Gandhi dsecend. "Danke," he said. The soldier nodded gruffly. He pointed the barrel of his rifle—toward the armored personnel carrier.

"My rupees!" the black-bearded man shouted.

Nehru turned on him, so quickly he almost got shot for it. "Your thirty pieces of silver, you mean," he cried.

"Ah, a British education," Gandhi murmured. No one was listening to him.

"My rupees," the man repeated. He did not understand Nehru; so often, Gandhi thought sadly, that was at the root of everything.

"You'll get them," promised the sergeant leading the German squad. Gandhi wondered if he was telling the truth. Probably so, he decided. The British had had centuries to build a network of Indian clients. Here but a matter of months, the Germans would need all they could find.

"In." The soldier with a few words of Hindi nodded to the back of the armored personnel carrier. Up close, the vehicle took on a war-battered individuality its kind had lacked when they were just big, intimidating shapes rumbling down the highway. It was bullet-scarred and patched in a couple of places, with sheets of steel crudely welded on.

Inside, the jagged lips of the bullet holes had been hammered

down so they did not gouge a man's back. The carrier smelled of
leather, sweat, tobacco, smokeless powder, and exhaust fumes. It
was crowded, all the more so with the two Indians added to its
usual contingent. The motor's roar when it started up challenged
even Gandhi's equanimity.

Not, he thought with uncharacteristic bitterness, that equanimity had done him much good.

"They are here, sir," Lasch told Model, then, at the field marshal's blank look, amplified: "Gandhi and Nehru."

Model's eyebrow came down toward his monocle. "I won't
bother with Nehru. Now that we have him, take him out and give
him a noodle"—army slang for a bullet in the back of the neck—
"but don't waste my time over him. Gandhi, now, is interesting.
Fetch him in."

"Yes, sir," the major sighed. Model smiled. Lasch did not find
Gandhi interesting. Lasch would never carry a field marshal's baton, not if he lived to be ninety.

Model waved away the soldiers who escorted Gandhi into his
office. Either of them could have broken the little Indian like a
stick. "Have a care," Gandhi said. "If I am the desperate criminal
bandit you have styled me, I may overpower you and escape."

"If you do, you will have earned it," Model retorted. "Sit, if
you care to."

"Thank you." Gandhi sat. "They took Jawajarlal away. Why
have you summoned me instead?"

"To talk for a while, before you join him." Model saw that
Gandhi knew what he meant, and that the old man remained
unafraid. Not that that would change anything, Model thought,
although he respected his opponent's courage the more for keeping it in the last extremity.

"I will talk, in hope of persuading you to have mercy on my
people. For myself I ask nothing."

Model shrugged. "I was as merciful as the circumstances of war
allowed, until you began your campaign against us. Since then I
have done what I needed to restore order. When it returns, I may
be milder again."

"You seem a decent man," Gandhi said, puzzlement in his
voice. "How can you so callously massacre people who have done
you no harm?"

"I never would have, had you not urged them to folly."

"Seeking freedom is not folly."

"It is when you cannot gain it—and you cannot. Already your people are losing their stomach for—what do you call it? Passive resistance? A silly notion. A passive resister simply ends up dead, with no chance to hit back at his foe."

That hit a nerve, Model thought. Gandhi's voice was less detached as he answered, "Satyagraha strikes the oppressor's soul, not his body. You must be without honor or conscience, to fail to feel your victim's anguish."

Nettled in turn, the field marshal snapped, "I have honor. I follow the oath of obedience I swore with the army to the Fuhrer and through him to the Reich. I need consider nothing past that."

Now Gandhi's calm was gone. "But he is a madman! What has he done to the Jews of Europe?"

"Removed them," Model said matter-of-factly; Einsatzgruppe B had followed Army Group Central to Moscow and beyond. "They were capitalists for bolsheviks, and either way enemies of the Reich. When an enemy falls into a man's hands, what else is there to do but destroy him, lest he revive to turn the tables one day?"

Gandhi had buried his face in his hands. Without looking at Model, he said, "Make him a friend."

"Even the British knew better than that, or they would not have held India as long as they did," the field marshal snorted. "They must have begun to forget, though, or your movement would have got what it deserves long ago. You first made the mistake of confusing us with them long ago, by the way." He touched a fat dossier on his desk.

"When was that?" Gandhi asked indifferently. The man was beaten now, Model thought with a touch of pride: he had succeeded where a generation of degenerate, decadent Englishmen had failed. Of course, the field marshal told himself, he had beaten the British, too.

He opened the dossier, riffled through it. "He we are," he said, nodding in satisfaction. "It was after Kristallnacht, eh, in 1938, when you urged the German Jews to play at the same game of passive resistance you were using here. Had they been fools enough to try it, we would have thanked you, you know: it would have let us bag the enemies of the Reich all the more easily."

"Yes, I made a mistake," Gandhi said. Now he was looking at the field marshal, looking at him with such fierceness that for a moment Model thought he would attack him despite advanced

age and effete philosophy. But Gandhi only continued sorrow-
fully, "I made the mistake of thinking I faced a regime ruled by
conscience, one that could at the very least be shamed into doing
that which is right."

Model refused to be baited. "We do what is right for our Volk,
for our Reich. We are meant to rule, and rule we do—as you
see." The field marshal tapped the dossier again. "You could be
sentenced to death for this earlier meddling in the affairs of the
Fatherland, you know, even without these later acts of insane defiance you have caused."

"History will judge us," Gandhi warned as the field marshal
rose to have him taken away.

Model smiled then. "Winners write history." He watched the
two strapping German guards lead the old man off. "A very good
morning's work," the field marshal told Lasch when Gandhi was
gone. "What's on the menu for lunch?"

"Blood sausage and sauerkraut, I believe."

"Ah, good. Something to look forward to." Model sat down.
He went back to work.